Praise for Harper Fox's
Scrap Metal

"Fox has created a farm in Scotland that will have her fans wishing they were there, while demonstrating that prejudice against gays exists in even remote locales. Readers of M/M romance will enjoy this one."

~ *Library Journal*

"I was captured at page one and couldn't bear to put it down. It was m/m romance writing at its best and I can't recommend it highly enough."

~ *Reviews by Jessewave*

"*Scrap Metal* is a marvelous story of inspiration, hope, and redemption. I highly recommend it to anyone desiring to read something written in the incredible, poetic way which only Harper Fox can deliver, something that they can sink their teeth into and come away feeling fulfilled."

~ *QMO Books*

Look for these titles by
Harper Fox

Now Available:

Driftwood
The Salisbury Key

Scrap Metal

Harper Fox

SAMHAIN™
PUBLISHING

Samhain Publishing, Ltd.
11821 Mason Montgomery Road, 4B
Cincinnati, OH 45249
www.samhainpublishing.com

Editing by Sasha Knight
Cover by Angela Waters

First Samhain Publishing, Ltd. electronic publication: March 2012
First Samhain Publishing, Ltd. print publication: February 2013

Dedication

Dedicated to Jane, who shared my discovery of Arran, and to Arran itself, where the mermaids really do still sing.

Chapter One

They look small enough when you see them in the fields, don't they? The springtime lambs, I mean. Tiny and weightless as clouds.

The first time my grandfather gave one to me to hold, I fell on my backside in the barnyard mud. They're solid. Little lumps of muscle, meat and hoof. Granted, I was five years old when he dumped the first one into my arms, but twenty years later, after a climb up a cliff face in horizontal rain and a three-mile walk, I could still have dropped to my knees beneath the weight.

And wept, if there was any point. There was no one in a hundred wet acres to see. One great advantage of Arran in winter—you could break your heart with dignity. The rain would take your tears, the gale whip them away from you, and beyond the outskirts of the handful of towns and villages that clung to the island coasts, chances were you'd be alone.

A bleak consolation. A sudden gust caught me, flapping the lamb's ears into my face. Even those were not as advertised, their wool abrasive, smelling of sour milk and mud. I stopped to catch my breath and resettle the creature under my arm.

I'd reached the highest point of my grandfather's land. From here on a clear day you could see all the way up to the mountains in the far north, westward to Kintyre peninsula, and even catch a glimpse of the mainland fifteen miles away to the east. Harry's farm occupied the southwestern tip of the island, a grand free sweep of turf bounded only by moorland on three sides, on the fourth by the cliffs that had given the land and the family its name.

Seacliff Farm, a fine inheritance. Or a poison chalice, from another point of view. The island economy was miring down in the recession and looked set to take us with it. These days if a plough or a trailer broke, I couldn't afford to have it fixed, and the wreckage accumulated in our draughty barn. Our second quad bike had just failed, which was why I was out here on foot with my lamb. The farm was riddled with debts and weighted down with the government loans that had been meant to bail us out.

On the verge of failure. The rain made it through my ancient Barbour and sent a cold trickle down my chest. The lamb shivered miserably. Well, if I was getting wet anyway... I gave up, unzipped the coat and bundled her inside. Not her fault, after all, that she and her two hundred relatives would end up under the auctioneer's hammer any day now.

Her hooves scraped my belly through my jumper. Ducking my head into the wind, I set off again, reflecting with bitter satisfaction that at least the place wasn't mine, not yet. Harry had tried to make it over into my name—just in case, he said, he were to drop down dead all of a sudden, though as far as I could see, the chances of that were microscopic, the old sod being just as hale in his mid-seventies as ever I remembered him. I'd refused. I didn't want the burden of it. He wanted to die on the land where he'd been born, and I owed him, so I stayed.

Not forever, though. A long wail rode in on the wind, and I saw, through rain and gathering dusk, the lights of the Calmac ferry. She was heading out. The storm looked set to worsen, but it took a lot to stop her, broad and stately as she was. I simultaneously pitied and envied her passengers. I'd have braved the tempest to be off this bloody island too, heading back to the mainland where I belonged. Where, until more or less this time last year, I'd been happily working towards my doctorate at Edinburgh University, while Harry, my mother and my older brother, Alistair, kept the farm.

These days I didn't speak to anyone about my ma and Al. The reasons for their absence, and my subsequent marooning here, were too bloody stupid. The last time I'd gone through the story, I'd horrified my listener by bursting out laughing. Damn Alistair anyway, with his penchant for cheap package deals. He and Ma always took off for a fortnight in early spring, to gather their strength before the lambing started. Al wouldn't rest until he'd found the best possible bargain. And this last time, his hard-squeezed pennies had bought him...

No. That was best kept to myself, and from myself, from now on. I could live with the silence. The only other soul who cared was Harry, and he wasn't likely to bring it up. The ferry lights vanished off into the dark, and I began my trudge downhill. I didn't miss Al, not as a brother. We'd been too different to be close. He'd been my granddad's darling, though, the natural heir to his farm. My ma's favourite too. I hadn't minded much. His delight in mud, sheep and collies had freed me up to pursue my studies on the mainland.

And now I was home. One light was shining—dully, through the dirty window—in the Seacliff farmhouse. There it lay, hunched down into its hill, stonily indifferent to the wind and rain. In my childhood's memory, it had been bright enough. Always shabby, but full of life, dogs and farmhands everywhere, a smell of baking coming from the kitchen. Now I reckoned you could film a bloody horror movie there. If Harry ever did shuffle off his mortal coil, I might sell the place as a location...

Oh, and there he was. The devil in his own backyard. He must have spotted me from half a mile off. The door to the rear porch was open wide, the old man planted in its frame, blocking the light from behind him. His arms were folded over his sturdy chest, his iron-grey eyebrows lowering worse than the clouds. I wished myself harder than ever onto the mainland boat, or anywhere other than here.

"Nichol, is that you?"

No, it's Princess Leia, come to remind you you're her only hope. I thought about saying it. But you never offered lip to Harold Seacliff, not if you valued your hide. He might be an old curmudgeon, but he was the patriarch, and the only father Alistair and I had ever known. "Aye, Granddad. It's me."

"How come you to be so damned late? I'd have locked the doors on you in half an hour more."

"I don't doubt it." Reluctantly I shoved open the gate and made my way through the neglected kitchen garden to the door. "The other quad bike's on the fritz. I had to walk."

"Where from, to be in such a state?"

"The cliffs. They got through the wire again. Half a dozen ewes followed the ram down the track to the waterfall. It's taken me all afternoon to herd them up again, and..." Here came the hard part. Best I got through it fast, though, because clearly he was going to keep me standing in the rain until he heard the full story. "One of them went over the edge and broke her neck. This is her lamb."

"For the love of God, Nichol."

"I'm sorry."

"That's the third you've lost this week."

I flinched. Insolence was one thing, standing up to his injustice was another. "The third *I've* lost? I can't keep six miles of fence intact on my own. The first two went into the lochan. You told me Kenzie was seeing to that stretch of wire."

"I gave Kenzie his week's notice last Tuesday. He's no' been doing his job right since then."

"But today's Tuesday. You... Oh, Christ. He's gone?"

"Do not take the Lord's name in vain in this house, Nichol Seacliff."

"I'm not in the house." *Besides, a more thoroughgoing old heathen than you never dodged past a minister on Sunday.* "I'm on the bloody doorstep. Kenzie was our last farmhand, Granda."

"It was him or the coal bill."

"Right. So it's just the two of us now."

For a moment his grim face shadowed. I dropped my gaze. If I let myself think about it—and I'd known since I'd opened my eyes that morning, really—it wasn't a year *more or less* since I'd lost my mam and Al. It was a year to the day. I had no idea if Harry had realised the anniversary.

"Give me that lamb." He pushed by me in the doorway and hauled the little creature out from under my coat. "I'll put her to that ewe in the back barn. The one whose twins you let die of cold last week. Gyp! Floss! Vixen! Here with me now, *gallanan.*"

I stepped back and let the tide of Border collies sweep past me. It occurred to me how much time I would have saved if I'd had a dog or two with me today, but there was no chance of that. Vixen, Gyp and Floss were utterly fixated on the old man. I could whistle my way through Handel's *Messiah* and they wouldn't flick an ear in my direction.

I stamped into the kitchen, pulling off my coat and slinging it onto a chair. The cavernous room was almost pitch-black, Harry's miserly candle in the window serving only to throw the space beyond its nimbus into deeper shadow. He wouldn't switch the lights on till the cheap-rate tariff started after six o'clock. Nor would he light the Aga until everyone was home. *No sense in heating empty rooms, laddie.* No chance of a hot bath either, then. Upstairs there was an old immersion heater that would, given an hour or two's notice, do the trick, but there was little point in my trying for that. Harry, who pronounced it *immairgency* heater, would only permit it to be used in an emergency, like when one of his dogs had a chill and needed a soak.

I grabbed some firelighters and a handful of kindling and crouched down before the Aga's vast, intimidating frontage. My ma had known how to call up its fires. It wanted a good clean. I could have done that for myself, but I'd put it off in favour of more pressing daily tasks.

No. More to my neglect than that. The stove had been the heart of the house, and my own heart sank utterly when faced with it. I put a match to the firelighters.

I hadn't let the damn lambs die of cold. I'd put them in a pen with a heater that had given up the ghost in the middle of the night for want of a top-up of fuel because bloody Kenzie had siphoned some off for the chainsaw. We were running on empty, all of us. I wasn't a bad farmer—I'd helped out in the barns and fields here all my life. But I didn't love the work, not the way Alistair used to, and over the last year I'd seen the place fall apart under my hands.

To hell with it. I was soaked to the skin. I pulled off my jumper and the vest underneath and sat shivering in the uncertain light for a minute or so. Then I got up, grabbed a towel from the rail by the sink to dry my hair, and defiantly switched on every light in the room. Harry wouldn't allow a microwave in the house, but we did have a battered kitchen radio via which, when the wind was in the right direction, I could sometimes pick up reminders of modern music and my former life.

I switched it on. A jolt of amusement went through me in spite of the night and the cold. "Traktor", the song was called, its main assurance being that the singer would ride its beat like one, or indeed like a motherfucking train. The profanity was just barely glossed over for the radio edit. The bass with its merciless one-two-three thud jounced into the room, laying hold of my hips like a pair of strong hands. God, I had loved this track, danced away dozens of messy Edinburgh small hours in its grasp. I could see myself by neon in the window's dirty glass. I'd been considered quite an asset to the scene, though no one who saw me in my wellies and woolly hat, up to my ankles in sheep shit, would ever know it now. At least the farming kept me fit. Muscles shifted under my skin as I took one awkward, self-conscious dance step and the next. I wasn't all that tall, and I was too stocky ever to be graceful, but I'd been popular enough.

I closed my eyes. I danced better that way. And I'd always had guidance, some sexy lad or other willing to stand behind me, press up close and sway when I did, and...

I dipped my fingertips just inside the waistband of my jeans. Paul had done that for me, while we bumped and ground in the heaving nightclub crowd, slid his hand down and spread his palm flat on my belly, encouraging, grinning against my ear. Or had it been Ricky? Maybe Jem Purdey from the engineering school, or my postgrad supervisor Mitch... It was all a bit of a blur. I'd played very hard, making up for the years of devoted teenage monogamy on this island. And I was still warm and alive down there, wasn't I, ready to respond to a touch...

The radio signal died. Static hissed, and the beat broke up into shortwave gabble from a shipping channel. I smelled Harry's vile tobacco one crucial instant before the kitchen door banged open.

"What the de'il are you about in here, Nichol? What was that bloody banshee racket?"

I whisked round. I supposed I should be grateful I'd had time to get my hand out of the front of my pants. The old man stood foursquare in the doorway like a bull about to charge. "It was a song called 'Traktor', Granda," I told him meekly. "By a band called Wretch 32."

He observed me in silence for a few seconds. Gyp, Floss and Vixen peered at me around his legs, adding to the scrutiny. "Naked as a babby," he growled, "and the curtains nae drawn." He shook his head. "If it's a tractor ye're interested in, Kenzie's left one broken for you in the barn."

Five hours later I crawled into my bed. I'd fixed the tractor, only to clamber up into her cab, switch her on and have her jerk beneath me like a dying horse and lapse into silence again. Probably I was getting oil stains on the sheets. I couldn't bring myself to care. I'd had to take the one remaining quad bike and make good my temporary fix on the cliff-side fence then slowly prowl the boundary Kenzie had abandoned. The dark little loch, barely more than a pond but apparently bottomless, exerted a dire fascination on the flock. The rain had turned to sleet, and I'd worked by the bike's headlamps, hammering stakes and cutting lengths of wire, my hands turning numb.

I curled up, seeking nonexistent warmth beneath the quilt. My hot-water bottle scalded the bits of me it was touching and left the rest icy. This was where, if I wasn't very careful, I would

15

fall apart. I had weathered the loss of my family, the transformation of my life with a stoicism I knew was dysfunctional. I'd stood dry-eyed through the funerals. But right now I could close my eyes and weep for the loss of my cat.

It was just that she slept on my stomach in winter, keeping off the chill. She had been tiny for a full-grown queen, but her purr would resound through the room like the Calmac revving up for departure. I'd have taken her to uni with me if I could. During the holidays she followed me everywhere, a little shadow with mad golden eyes. Even Harry, whose fondness for farm cats began and ended with their mousing abilities, had bestowed on her the honour of a name—Clover, or *Seamrag* in Gaelic. The luck of the farm.

Well, that one had come back to bite us in the arse. She'd vanished in the night last February, one eerie day before we got the news from Spain. I recalled the old man, standing like a statue in the barnyard a fortnight later, a red-letter bill from the water board in one hand, a broken tractor drive shaft in the other. *Aye, she's gone. And taken with her the luck o' the farm.*

Gloomy old bastard. I balled up tighter, furious with him and with myself. I had maybe three hours before the grim routine of lambing season started all over again. I couldn't waste good sleep time with useless thoughts like this. I couldn't mourn a cat more than I did my brother, and I couldn't...

I couldn't go on.

It hit me with the force of revelation. What the hell was I doing, struggling to hold back the avalanche? I'd have given almost anything to help keep Harry king of his Seacliff acres. I'd ploughed my heart and soul into the struggle for a year. But the game was up. Surely selling now would be better than waiting for the bloody bailiffs.

For about thirty seconds, relief swept through me. I entertained a fantasy of Harry installed in a nice warm bungalow in Whiting Bay, playing darts with his cronies in the pub and revelling in his leisured golden years. Me, I was back in Edinburgh, cranking out my brilliant new linguistic model for my doctorate in between rounds of casual sex down in the Groat Market clubs.

The air castle fell. Harry, cut off from his ancestral soil, fell into a decline and pointed an accusing finger at me from his deathbed. I sat up, anticipatory pangs of guilt going through me. I ran my fingers into my hair. It was no good. No matter what the consequences, we were going to have to let the place go. All that remained for me to work out was how to break it to Harry. Well, I now had two and a half sleepless hours in which to do that.

The gale shook the house. It was a wild winter bitch of a night. Most likely I'd be digging sheep out of snow on my dawn shift. I caressed the patch on the quilt where Clover used to curl. A few black hairs still clung there. Grief and rage burned in my gut, bitter as the storm. Everything was gone.

Glass shattered somewhere off in the dark. I jerked my head up, listening. That was all I needed, for the wind to have broken a barn window. I'd have to get out there and patch it, or we'd lose another set of lambs to the cold.

The sound came again. Exactly the same as the first time— brief, deliberate.

Human agency, then. I threw back the quilt. Prodigal son or not, I didn't really have to guess at the source. I knew every inch of Seacliff Farm. My nerves twitched out into the night, my body responding as if the broken glass had been my bones. Me, my mother, Harry, untold generations of us living and dying on this land... Two panes from the window at the back of the second-largest barn, enough to get a hand inside and undo the catch.

I surged out of bed. Heat blazed through me, a pure and perfect rage. God, it felt wonderful. I had a bloody burglar on my hands. He couldn't have arrived at a worse or better time. I grabbed my dressing gown, shrugged into it over my pyjama bottoms and slammed out of the room.

In the hallway I paused for a second. Alistair's gun cupboard was tucked into a corner of the landing. He'd always kept it conscientiously locked, and a good thing too, since his pride and joy had been a top-end hunting rifle more suitable to big game than the rabbits he'd needed to pick off around the farm. I'd never touched it. Guns, the distancing of predator from prey, had brought on half the horrors of this world. I called myself a pacifist and tried to act like one.

The cupboard was plywood. It yielded to one good kick. There was no chance of waking Harry, who slept like the dead in his bleak mausoleum of a bedroom at the far end of the house. The rifle came easy, sweetly to my hand. I couldn't think why I hadn't gone on an armed rampage before. Tucking it under one arm, I ran downstairs barefoot then paused for a second to push my feet into the mud-caked wellingtons I'd left by the back door.

The storm hit me the instant I left the porch, sideswiping me so hard I dropped to one knee before I could catch my balance. I got up, swearing. I was more likely to shoot my foot off with Al's rifle than anything else. I didn't even know if the catch was on, if it was loaded. Fighting through the wind-lashed sleet, I tried to rekindle my furies. It had felt so nice not to give a damn anymore, and already my workaday brain was trying to spoil that, to furnish me with reasons, with compassion. Who would come all the way out here to break into a barn? Suppose it was Kenzie, disgruntled after his sacking? He'd confessed to me a couple of weeks ago that he'd started using amphetamines to get him through the brutal schedule of lambing and his day job in the village. That must cost. Maybe he'd come back for our one remaining quad bike. God knew there was sod-all else to steal. Poor bastard, he'd offered me a hit of his speed, and I'd been sorely tempted...

Lightning blazed, and the outside security lamp on the farmhouse went out. Ditched into dazzled black, I hesitated then recalled that this beast of a weapon had a torch on it for night stalking. Many a time its beam had scared the life out of me, searching hungrily over the fields. I felt along its barrel till I found what I hoped was the right button.

Cold white light leapt from the sights. A thin, powerful beam, it illuminated one tunnel of sleet-filled air and made a target on the barn wall. I raised the gun until I could see the eastern window. Yes, the top two frames were gone.

Why hadn't I brought the barn keys with me? Why, for that matter, hadn't I stopped to put on a waterproof? My dressing gown was slicked to my skin, woollen deadweight. That made me good and pissed off once again, and I clambered into the barn the same way my intruder had done, grabbing the sill with one hand to haul myself up.

Once inside, I sat poised for a few seconds, playing the rifle's searchlight around the blackness. "Who's in here?"

Something rustled. I jerked the gun muzzle around, but the sound had only been the ewes Harry had put in here to foster our orphan lambs, shifting around in their straw. Their eyes with their eerie wrong-way-round pupils gave back the light of the torch, six green ovoids. Carefully I eased down from the sill.

"I know you're in here," I told the shadows. "I've had a shit day, and if you think I wouldn't use this gun, just come out and try me."

Nothing. All right, that was fine by me. I was in the mood for doing it the hard way. There were only so many places a man could hide in here. The hayloft would be a good start. I laid one hand on the rung of the ladder and froze, listening. A sound from the sheep pen again, but this time... I frowned, trying to work out what the tiny rasp had been.

Like nothing so much as the sounds I made myself on the many, many occasions when Alistair and his mates had set me up for a fright. A giant rubber spider dropping off the top of a door onto my head. Or—another favourite—a string wrapped round the handle of the spooky closet door so it would swing open as I crept down the corridor. Growing up with him had been hard work. I'd been too proud to scream like a girl, and my efforts to stop myself produced a strangled gasp very like the one I'd just heard.

I stalked back to the pen. There were a couple of hay bales

piled up in the corner. The lamb I'd rescued that afternoon, obviously partial to trouble, had managed to squeeze itself in behind them. Its bony little head was down, its tail flicking in frustration. It shifted, and whoever was hiding there made another sound of muffled fright.

"I see my attack sheep have cornered you," I said, tone conversational, hefting the gun. I *had* used it before, hadn't I? Al had tried to teach me how to shoot. The kickback of the stock into my shoulder had knocked me down the first time, but he'd persisted with the lesson. Why had I forgotten? I remembered now. I let my finger curl around the trigger. "Come out and show yourself."

The bales moved. The lamb, undeterred, tried to scramble farther in.

"Christ, why the hell is it trying to...*eat* me?"

I stepped back. Someone was crouched behind the bales. In the harsh blue-white torchlight, I saw a skinny lad about my own age, soaked black hair plastered to his face. He was trying to thrust back the lamb, which was responding to his efforts by catching his fingers into its greedy maw. The scene would have been funny at any other time. It was threatening to crack a smile out of me now, but I resisted. My heart was pounding, adrenaline spiking coldly through my veins. I had every right to shoot an intruder.

"It's not trying to eat you," I said. "It's hungry. It's trying to suckle. Stand up."

"I can't. It weighs a ton."

"Just get hold of it and move it. You won't..." I paused. What would a hardened burglar care if he damaged the livestock? But this one was clearly worried, his hands shaking. "You won't hurt it."

He obeyed. Once he had freed himself and got to his feet, I took him in. He was even less suitably clad for the weather than I was, in jeans, a thin T-shirt and the kind of jacket designer knock-off merchants would flog in the Edinburgh street markets until moved on by the police. He held a rucksack, similarly flashy and cheap, clutched in one hand.

"What's your name?"

He lifted his free hand to shield his eyes. Distantly I noted that they were an odd shade of blue, almost violet in this light, their pupils constricted. He would have been handsome if he didn't look near starved.

His frightened face became defiant. "Sean Connery."

I tried not to roll my eyes. My studies in linguistics had given me a keen ear for accents, and I recognised his. Not Glasgow and not Islands. Something in between, from the long, deprived, desolate stretch of villages and towns along the road from Larkhall. His trashy outfit went well with that. You couldn't reverse the trend, could you? You could force economic migrants off the land and into the cities, but when the cities failed them, they couldn't go back to their farms. The farms were gone. It was a one-way system, and it dumped lads like this into suburbs, concrete-poured hovels like Newhall and Borough Mills, jobless and hopeless. There but for the grace of God...

"Your real name," I said, less harshly. "You owe me that much."

"Cameron." That sounded real. For a second I thought he was going to hand me a second one too, but then he blushed angrily and looked down at his wet, muddy trainers. "Just Cameron, all right?"

"All right. For now."

"Are you going to call the police?"

It hadn't occurred to me. For one thing, I'd left my mobile upstairs by the bed. "In good time. We fix our own problems round here." His eyes widened, and I replayed my words. Yes, I sounded threatening. A nutcase wielding private justice with a gun. Well, if he was frightened, so much the better. "You can start by picking up your feckless bloody lamb and putting it down by that *othaisg* in the corner."

"By the what?"

"The..." I shook my head to clear it of Scotch mist. I was getting really frayed if I was dropping into Gaelic. It was Harry's native tongue, not mine. "The sheep. The ewe. Put the lamb down beside her and give her a prod to make her get up. She's meant to be feeding it."

I watched while he clumsily did as he was told. The ewe lurched to her feet, and the lamb got the idea and went to work, butting her udder, absurd little tail beginning a satisfied swing.

"Doesn't that happen automatically? The feeding thing?"

"It's an orphan. It still smells strange to her. It's a good sign that it's sucking now, but of course it might still die from the cold wind blasting through the windows you broke. Did that occur to you?"

"No. I didn't know there were animals in here. I..."

"It's a farm. You might have hazarded a guess."

"I've never set foot on a farm till tonight. I'm sorry about the windows, okay?"

"That's all right. You're going to fix them. You see those empty sacks over there? Take those and fold them up to fit the frames. There's tacks and a hammer in the toolbox by the door."

"Okay." He glanced around. I saw the nervous twitch of his Adam's apple in his skinny throat. "Have you got any plastic? Sheeting, or a plastic bag?"

"The wind'll tear it to shreds. Use the sacks."

"I meant... Wrap it round the folded-up sacks. That way you insulate and waterproof it."

I stared at him. I wasn't practical, I knew. Born and bred among farmers, I'd learned the basics of my trade, but I'd been like a seal on the rocks—awkward, everything always an effort. Going to uni had been my ocean dive. I'd found my element. And now here I was on the rocks again, missing the obvious. "Okay. Empty that feedbag into the bin. You can tear that up. Pull the hayloft ladder over so you can reach."

He worked well for a displaced townie, doing at least as

good a job as I would have myself. He only banged his thumb with the hammer once, and he took that quietly, exhaling and briefly clenching his fist. I was glad he had his back to me and couldn't see how I'd winced for him. That wouldn't have gone at all with the business of holding him at gunpoint.

"Right," I said when the windows were sealed. "That'll do."

"Are you going to use it, then?"

He was still poised on the ladder, his peculiar blue-violet gaze now calm. It was disconcerting to be at its focus. I said, stupidly, "What?"

"That bloody great Uzi you've got trained on me."

I wanted to tell him it wasn't mine. Nothing to do with me— that beyond the necessities of pest control, I'd never hurt a living thing in my life. I was starting to feel sick in the wake of my adrenaline surge, and very cold. "I don't know."

"I didn't come here to rob you. Just to take shelter."

"You expect me to believe that? Half a dozen farms round here have been ripped off lately."

"What for?"

"Equipment mostly. Tools, chain saws, quad bikes if they can get 'em. Or just scrap metal. The deeper the recession bites, the more that's worth, and..." I shivered, looking off into the dark where the broken hulks of our tractors, ploughs and harvesters lay rusting. "And that's all I've got. Sheep and scrap metal. You broke into the wrong barn."

He shifted uncomfortably. "Ah, come off it. You lot are always pleading poverty, aren't you?"

"Us lot?"

"Farmers. Then the government gives you a great big handout and you're tanking around in your Range Rovers again."

"Right. You think it's okay to rob a farmer because we're all rich."

"I didn't say that. I—"

"Come down off that bloody ladder. I'll show you how rich

this one is."

I marched him out of the barn and back across the yard. When he hesitated in the howling, wet darkness, I gave him a prod in the back with the gun and almost threw up at the savagery of my action. When he moved on, he did so with raised hands. He was thin and defenceless. If he'd knocked on my door for shelter that night, I'd have taken him in. I wouldn't have turned away a dog. But something inside me was breaking, some rope trying to snap. I was seriously afraid I would shoot him. He found the back porch by bumping into it.

"It's not locked," I growled at him. "Open the door."

It was colder inside than out. In summer that had always been such a blessing, I remembered. We'd work all day in a harvest blaze, me and Alistair, come home and step into mushroom-cool shadows, tender on sunburnt skin. It was how the old Arran farms had been built, to keep men, milk and cheese fresh and sweet in summer, and in the winter...

In the winter, if you didn't tend their fires, they died.

"Go straight down the passage. Into the kitchen."

The room stood stark and empty. I flicked a switch, and dusty yellow lights came on, the low-wattage bulbs Harry thought would save him money and wouldn't let me replace.

I stood behind Cameron. I was shivering properly now. "This is where I live."

He looked around. I followed his gaze, seeing the place myself as if I'd been a stranger. Big slate flagstones, old as the foundations. A massive oak table, supported at one end by crates. We'd called the room a kitchen but everything had happened here—meals, disciplinary actions, years of homework. My ma, a farmer's wife at heart, although she'd only had the briefest benefit of a husband, had liked to keep her two front parlours spotless, smelling of polish and disuse. She, Harry, the farmhands, Alistair and me, we'd all piled in and out of here for everything. In the midst of all that chaos, I'd never seen how barren the place was. There was a threadbare rug, a huge cupboard Harry called a *preas* filled with cracked and broken china. The sink—more of a trough, ancient white ceramic—had been installed in the 1880s and not touched since. We still drew water into it from the old lead pump. Cobwebs drifted from the ceiling pan rack, stirring in the draught.

"Why is it so cold?"

"Oil went up fifty percent last year. Coal's the same."

"Are you all on your own here?"

"No. I've got...family upstairs. Brothers. If they'd found you out there, they'd have shot you where you stood."

Cameron took a few steps farther into the room. I didn't try to stop him. He pushed his hands into his pockets and lowered his head. Then he turned round to face me. "But you won't."

Something about the colour of his eyes, the tired patience in them, made it hard for me to think. "I won't what?"

"You won't shoot me. What's your name?"

"Nichol. Nichol Seacliff."

"Nichol...as in Nickelback? Er, like the group, you know—a dollar and your nickel back?"

"No." My aim on him was trembling. The bloody rifle seemed to weigh a ton. My vision kept blurring then returning to painful, bitter clarity. "Nichol with a soft C-H, like *loch*, as in..." I cast around for a strong enough analogy. "As in I'll take you out to ours and drown you if you ever mention that band in this house again."

He smiled. It transformed him. He took two fearless steps forward, laid his hand on the snout of the rifle and gently bore it down. "Aye," he said. "They are pretty shite. You're not going to use this gun on me, Nichol Seacliff."

"No." I stepped back from him until I encountered the edge of the table, then I blindly swung the rifle aside and set it down. I pulled out a chair and sank into it. "I hate the fucking thing." I buried my face in my hands.

I'd been running on three hours' sleep a night since the lambing began. Before that I'd worked through a stinking bout of flu. And before that... I couldn't even remember *before that*,

25

the year that had whirled and crawled and racketed by since I'd got the message from the dean of my college to come and speak to him in his office, and I'd gone down whistling and pulled up short at the sight of the policeman standing by the dean's desk. My brain was ready to shut down at the least excuse. The temporary darkness behind my hands would do. I closed my eyes and drifted.

A familiar scent reached me. There had been familiar noises too, so ordinary that I'd failed to take them in. A rattle of crockery, the kettle's rumble and click. Slowly I lifted my head and straightened. Cameron was standing in front of me, at cautious distance, holding out a steaming mug. "Nichol. Here."

My burglar had made me a cup of tea. I accepted it on reflex. The mug was so warm, and my hands so cold, that it didn't feel as if we belonged in the same universe. "Thanks," I said weakly. "Er... Are you having one yourself?"

"No. I just wanted to give that to you. You looked like you were going to faint or something."

"I'm fine. Just tired."

"I'm sorry I broke into your barn, okay? And sorry for what I said about rich farmers. Look—if you're okay, and you're really not gonna shoot me or turn me in, I'll be on my way."

I tried a mouthful of the tea. I was surprised to find I did take sugar, at one o'clock on a freezing morning anyway. The jolt of it restarted my thinking processes. "Hang on," I said, pushing the rifle a bit farther away from me so he'd know that wasn't part of our dealings anymore. "If you didn't break in to steal anything..."

"I told you. I needed shelter."

"This farm's three miles away from—well, anything at all, in all directions. You could've sheltered in the bus station at Brodick."

He let go a soft breath. His rucksack was over his shoulder once more, one hand clenching anxiously at the strap. They were nice hands, I thought, watching him over the rim of the mug. Finely made but strong. I could see my rescued lamb's attraction to his fingers.

"I lied to you," he said. "I needed somewhere to hide."

Oh, shit. I looked him over again. There was a lively trade in crack along that western route from Glasgow. Occasionally it spilled over onto the island in the form of a runaway junkie with a pissed-off pusher on his tail. My visitor was painfully thin. There were shadows under his eyes.

"Sorry," I said. "You chose the wrong farm for that too. A stranger stands out like a purple cow around here. You wouldn't last five minutes."

"Yeah. It was stupid. I'll let myself out."

"Hang on a second." I pushed stiffly onto my feet. "I'm just going upstairs. Stay here."

He was more or less my size, minus a couple of stone. In my room, I crouched by my linen chest and moved things around until I found a T-shirt and thick woollen jersey, both clean and warm but generic enough not to attract notice. A pair of grey sweatpants as well, and a blanket. That would do.

In the kitchen, he was waiting in the exact spot where I'd left him. He watched me, his face a blank of confusion, while I walked up to him and put the clothes and the blanket into his arms.

"What are you doing?"

"Go back to the barn. You'll probably be warmer there than in this bloody freezer anyway. Get changed before you catch your death. You can keep the clothes."

"But..."

"Leave the blanket somewhere my brothers won't see it if they're up first," I said. "Make sure you're gone long before then." He was still staring at me in astonishment. I turned him round by the shoulders. He didn't resist as I steered him down the corridor towards the door. "And don't come back. There's enough trouble here without you bringing any more down on us."

I unlocked the door and pulled it wide. The expected blast

of cold wind didn't happen. When I looked past Cameron's shoulder, I saw that the rain had stopped. It was the first time it had let up in three days. If I wasn't mistaken, patchy starlight was appearing between the rags of clouds. I drew a breath to point this out, though why I thought a fugitive junkie would have been interested, I had no idea.

It didn't matter. He was gone. I hadn't seen him slip away, and the barnyard, as far as I could see in its shadows, was empty.

A great tide of weariness took me. I stepped back inside and closed the door. The lock was awkward—I gave the keys their usual turn and a half but wasn't sure if it had worked. I couldn't bring myself to worry about it. I'd been worn to the bone before, but this was different. It had a heavy peace in it like honey, and I couldn't fight it back.

I dragged myself upstairs, hanging on tight to the banister at every step. I felt warm for the first time in weeks. Probably I was in end-stage hypothermia. That possibility couldn't shake me either. I got to my room and closed the door behind me. Yes, the skies were clearing. A pale patch of February moonlight lay across my bed. At some point I'd remembered to take my muddy boots off. That was good. That would do.

Surrendering, I crawled beneath the quilt, rolled onto my stomach and slept.

Chapter Two

Three and a half hours later, still half comatose, I cannoned into Harry on the landing. To my surprise, instead of berating me for my clumsiness, he grabbed and held my shoulders, steadying me.

"What ails thee this morning?" he demanded.

"Morning, Granda. Nothing ails me." With my defences down, I ended up talking like him in no time at all. "I'm just tired."

"Aye. Well, if ye will go dancing to yon Wretches and their tractors till all hours, what can you expect?"

"To be tired, Granda." There was no point in telling him I'd put in a night shift and dealt with a burglar since then. "I just need a cuppa."

"You need more sleep. Go back to bed. I'll take the early feeds today."

I blinked, startled. He was sometimes gruffly contrite with me after he'd torn me off a strip, but he'd never actually relieved me of duty. Even the collies, who slept at the foot of his bed and normally greeted me with a snarl, seemed less hostile today. Floss, the pack leader, was sniffing at my hands with great interest. I hoped she wouldn't go too nuts at the foreign scents downstairs, or follow a trail to the barn. I hoped to God Cameron had gone. "Can you manage it all on your own?"

That was a mistake. He let me go. If I'd been ten years younger, he'd have cuffed me round the ear. "Insolent wee *diobhal!* How do ye think I *managed* it while you and your brother were trailing round in your nappies? You think I couldn't still run this whole show with one hand tied up my back?"

"I'm sure you could, Granda." I wondered if he knew he'd mentioned Alistair for the first time in a year. I wondered if he remembered he was dead. Through the window at the end of the corridor, I could see that the sky remained pitch-black. My body, lulled by sleep, yearned to be back in its bed. "Are you serious about...?"

"Aye. Go on with you, while you can still carry those bags under your eyes."

When I woke next it was daylight. Not quite eight o'clock, but a clear day on this sea-lit island brought the dawn in early even at this time of year.

It *was* clear too. I fixed myself a mug of black coffee and carried it out into the sun. There was a bench by the door where my ma had liked to bask in her rare idle moments. I'd been avoiding it, but this morning it felt like no big deal to sit there and lift my face to the warmth. She'd been a royal sun-worshipper, Ma. Not just the holidays to Costa del this and that but Celtic fire festivals out in the fields in the season. By this stage of spring she'd have pissed off the minister already with a dance round the Imbolc fires to celebrate the pregnant ewes and the return of the goddess and her consort king. Maybe that was why we'd had such a long foul winter—maybe Lugh and Brighid missed her as much as...

I grabbed the thought and crushed it. I'd woken up serene. It would be nice to stay that way, at least until the rain began again. I'd had a shower and put on clean clothes, just workaday ones but crisp and fresh from the skin out. I'd let such things slide a bit. She'd have hated that, one of her lads in yesterday's undercrackers. I broke out laughing, scaring a crow off her bird table, also neglected. Maybe later I'd put out a handful of crumbs.

Maybe I'd walk over to the barn. It wasn't often I had leisure for maybes at all, so I finished my coffee first then got up, stretched, and took it slowly. Harry would have seen to the foster ewes and lambs already, so I had no business there, but I wanted to look in on the lamb I'd rescued, which seemed to have inherited more than a normal sheep's share of obtuseness and might well have forgotten again how to feed. I wanted to check the barn was empty.

No. What I really wanted to do was to snuff out the stupid, dull ache in my chest at the thought of that empty barn. What the hell was wrong with me? I eased open the door. Sunlight fell in, illuminating a domestic scene to warm any sheep-farmer's heart—three ewes, each with its assigned orphan lamb curled up next to it. If they were going to reject the infants, they wouldn't let them near. So that was good. I crept past the pen, being careful not to disturb them.

The ladder was resting on the edge of the hayloft again. That was good too. I'd meant to tell Cameron to go there to sleep, where it was dry and he'd at least get the benefit of body warmth from the livestock below, a time-honoured central heating system of ancient Gaelic farms. He'd had the sense to climb up there, and had climbed down too, and heaven only knew where he was now. I wondered if he'd taken the blanket. Not much room in that useless little man bag of his, and he'd be a bit conspicuous hitching a ride with it wrapped round his shoulders. I'd better go up and find it.

I climbed the ladder, looking only at the rungs and my hands. The hayloft was a bonny place on a spring morning, with light shafting in through the rafters, and I didn't want to remember how Al and I had spent more nights up there than in our beds during the summer. Not until I'd reached the very top did I raise my head. And there, stretched out on a bale, lay my night visitor, the blanket tucked round him, still blissfully asleep.

A cat was curled up on his stomach. We had half a dozen black farm cats and finding one here was no miracle—they were parasites for warmth, and would sleep on the backs of the sheep or stabled ponies if they could. Animals seemed to like

Cameron, to judge from Floss's interest and the dubious attentions bestowed on him by the lamb. Carefully I negotiated the ladder's top rung and stood looking down on the sleeping man and the cat. The bale was bathed in light. The repairs on the window below had held up well, but the roof needed attention. Slates were off it, and pale gold sunshine blazed through the gap they'd left.

The cat stirred and yawned, exposing needle teeth and a rose-pink gullet. There was a tiny splash of white fur—I'd called it her milk spot—on her upper lip, just to the side of her nose.

"Clover," I whispered, and she got up, stretched every limb and jumped gracefully down from the bale. I had to be wrong, of course. There had to be more than one little black queen on the island with that mark. She yawned again, fixed me with her look of golden-eyed, loving insanity, and ran casually up my body as if she'd seen me yesterday, piercing my thigh and one nipple en route. "Ouch! You little bastard!"

Cameron shot upright on the bale. "Shit!" he gasped, grabbing at the blanket. "I'm sorry."

"Not you." I could hardly speak. "This... This cat. Where did it...?"

"I don't know. I woke up in the night and it was there. Jesus, what time is it?" He scrambled off the bale. "I went back to sleep."

"It's about eight o'clock. Look..." I could have tried for a reproachful demeanour but doubted I could carry it off with the cat on my shoulder, plucking at the hair over my ear in one of her painful demonstrations of love. "Calm down. The old man's gone out in the fields."

"The old man?" His frightened pallor became tinged with grey, as if the words hurt him. "What old man?"

"My grandfather. It's his farm."

"What about your brothers?"

"There aren't any. I told you that last night in case..." I took gentle hold of Clover's scruff, suddenly ashamed. "In case I hadn't already scared you enough with the gun."

"Okay. I'll go. I'm going." He folded up the blanket and shouldered his rucksack. He looked good in the clothes I'd given him. His frame was lithe and strong. It must have taken a lot of running and privation to strip so much weight from him. "Was your cat missing?"

"For a year. I can't believe she's come back. Cameron..."

He halted in front of me. His eyes were such a potent shade of indigo I thought he was wearing tinted contacts. Anxiety was coming off him in waves.

"I have to go," he whispered. "You're right. I will bring trouble on you."

"What are you hiding from?"

He ducked his head. "Don't make me tell you."

"I won't. Not if you don't want. But I might be able to help you."

"You can't. It's debts, okay? I got in too deep with a loan shark in Glasgow and he's after me. It's not drug money." Before I could protest, he had rolled up the sleeves of the jumper. The insides of his arms were pale, the skin fine and unmarked. "I saw the way you were looking at me last night."

I remembered. If I wasn't careful, I was going to end up like Harry, inveighing against *oigear an-diugh*—young people today—and the decline of society. If it was money trouble, I had no right to pass judgement there. I couldn't see the Brodick sheep-feed dealer coming after me for my unpaid dues, but... "Put your sleeves down. I'm sorry. When did you last eat?"

He had to think about it. "On the ferry yesterday morning. The most expensive sandwich in the world, and then it got rough, and..." He made a face. "Well, I'm not much of a sailor."

"Oh, dear. Listen—my granddad won't be back for a good bit yet. Do you want to come down and have some breakfast?"

"You're kidding. I couldn't possibly."

"Come on. Toast, coffee. I'll fry you an egg." I watched in alarm while a faint sheen of sweat appeared on his brow. He swayed, and I reached out to grab him. "Jesus. You're half starved, aren't you? Come on with me. It won't take long."

I followed him down the ladder. My cat allowed herself to be borne in state as far as the barn door then gave me a parting nip and leapt down. I wanted to seize her by the tail, push her inside my jacket next to my heart and never let her out of my sight again, but she had always been wildly intolerant of all restraint. I watched while she vanished into the shadows of the barn.

The kitchen looked better by daylight. You could see its dereliction more clearly but, like most island living quarters, it faced south to welcome the sun. It seemed that the half-hearted fire I'd started in the Aga last night had taken as well, enough to throw a faint, welcome heat into the room.

I directed Cameron to a chair in the sunlight and went about fixing an emergency breakfast. I'd become quite good at those, shovelling food down Harry and the farmhands before we piled out into the fields. Bread, bacon. The frying pan was soon sizzling nicely on the elderly hob. A couple of eggs—there were more in the basket than I expected, which meant our poor hens, discouraged by the long winter, must have started laying again—and instant coffee spooned into mugs. Neither of us spoke while I worked. He shot me one grateful look as I handed him his plate, then our silence continued until he'd demolished its contents.

I went through mine a little more slowly, watching him in amusement. "A bit hungry, were we?"

"Aye. Sorry." He sat back. "That was bloody gorgeous."

"Can fetch you some more if you like."

"No. You've been too good to me already. I'll help you clear up then I'll..." He stopped. We sat looking at one another. Shadows chased across the room as clouds flickered over the sun. "What?"

"Nothing. So...you came over yesterday. How did you end up out here?" I told myself it wasn't a ploy to delay him. How long was it since I'd spoken to anyone but Kenzie and the old man? All my friends were long gone from Arran, pursuing less-heartbreaking careers. "We're twelve miles from the harbour."

"I know. I tried to find somewhere to crash in Brodick, but I thought I saw one of the guys I knew in Glasgow. So I hitched a ride with a driver taking a night delivery of market veg to Kilpatrick. I paid him in advance for his petrol, but once we're in the middle of nowhere he decides he wants a blow job too." He delivered this casually enough, but he was watching me cautiously, gauging my response. "I'd have given him one—he wasn't bad looking—but he got a bit rough with me. And, you know, I'd already paid."

"Well, fair enough."

"So I ducked out while his back was turned and jumped over the nearest wall. Which happened to be yours. I didn't really think about how badly I was stranding myself."

"No." There were things I was trying not to think about too. How long since I'd heard the words *blow job*, frank and straightforward, from a pair of male lips. How long since I'd had sex. Well, it had to be more than a year, hadn't it? I shivered. I hadn't missed it.

Now was no time to start. In a minute my visitor would be gone. I had no reason to assume he was gay anyway, though the bag and the sharp little jacket hardly screamed straight. Sex could simply be a currency to him. He was beautiful enough to sell his wares...

"Nichol?"

I jolted back to surface. I'd been staring. "What?"

"Are you okay?"

"Yes. Yeah, fine." I made an effort to sound ordinary. "Bit spaced out. We don't get much sleep during lambing."

"Is it just you and your grandfather? What happened to the rest of your family?"

Well, the first part of that story was easy enough. "There never was a dad. Not that I knew, anyway. He stuck around until my brother was two, but my granddad made his life such a misery he shipped out before I was born."

"I'm sorry."

"It's okay. I never knew him, and I don't think my ma missed him all that much."

"You do have one brother, then?"

"I did." God, was I going to tell him? I began almost without realising I'd started, the words tasting of rust in my mouth. "Alistair. He was off with my mother on holiday in Spain last year. He loved a bargain, did Al, and he always got them the cheapest package deal he could score. That time, though... Well, he got a drunken coach driver to go with the day trips and the all-you-can-eat buffet. They were killed in a crash outside the Benidorm funfair."

Once more the ending tripped me over into a painful bout of laughter. I got up and went to refill the kettle before he could react. Maybe I could persuade him to another cup of coffee.

"Nichol."

I turned. Cameron was gazing at me, open-mouthed in shock. His eyes were full of tears. "That's horrific."

"Don't. It was over a year ago."

"But you must have been shattered. Didn't you...? Weren't you close?"

"Not so much to my brother. But my ma—yeah, we were close. And I loved them both a lot, you know?" I switched the kettle on and came to stand behind my chair, absently gripping at the back of it. "It's just...stupid, isn't it? How they died?"

"No. It's sad and horrible."

Was it? Cameron was holding out a hand to me. I took it as naturally as if we'd known each other for years, and I sat back down, my thoughts spiralling. Yes. When he said so, I could clearly see that Al and my mother had met a terrible end. That they were a dreadful loss to me. Deep in my chest, somewhere behind my sternum, something frozen solid tried to stir. Cameron's grip was strong. I gave it strongly back to him. "I haven't really had time to think about it. The farm's a lot of work, and..."

I held still. A new sound had entered the kitchen's morning peace. It was barely a murmur, but it mounted quickly to a thrum and then a roar.

Cameron's hand clamped on mine. "Shit. What's that?"

"My granddad coming back. That's his quad bike. Quick, come over..."

Whatever I'd been about to tell him to do got lost in the squeal of brakes and the clatter of a trailer jouncing to a halt. He let go my hand and shrank back into the shadows just as the back door flew open.

"Nichol!"

Instinctively I ran towards the old man's shout. He seldom hurried himself about his farm business. Something was seriously wrong, for him to have come tearing home like this. There he was in the yard, getting stiffly off the quad bike he normally rode with such debonair grace, looking sick and old.

"What's the matter?"

"The Leodhas ewe's dead. Both lambs too, just about. Get the oven doors open."

I darted to obey him. Thank God I'd lit the Aga last night. Thank God for its inefficiencies too—it might be about the right temperature. Once both lower doors were open, I ran to the back door and took from his arms one of the two lambs he had hauled out of the trailer. I clamped my mouth shut on my instant conviction that we were too late. Years of handling life and death on this farm had taught me the difference. I knew it by touch.

Shit, and we couldn't afford to lose these lambs. We'd shelled out money we didn't have last year for the services of an off-island ram whose offspring yielded beautiful weaver's wool. With our usual luck, only one of the spring births had been a ram—the little tup lying deadweight in my hands now. I knelt by the Aga, pulled out its ancient cast-iron cooking plate, laid the little body on it and carefully tucked it inside. Harry was doing the same thing on his side with the ewe. We sat back on our heels with the same movement. *You're too alike*, my ma had

37

said. *That's why you clash.* That was nonsense of course. I'd been in joyous flight from him and everything he stood for when I'd been shot down.

I stole a glance at him. We did have one thing in common— we were both bloody bad businessmen when it came to losing sheep. Not Alistair. He'd been totally unsentimental, from birth to butcher. He'd shifted the farm from its traditional crofting wool-and-dairy output to meat production. In the past year Harry and I had wordlessly started shifting it back, each of us managing to blame the other for his pitiful softness of heart.

"What happened?"

"Damn ewe had a prolapse. These had already dropped from the cold when I found them."

I stared at the heels of the little tup sticking out of the oven. A faint sound came from behind me, and my focus expanded to include other things that might have died of cold in the night. Oh, God. Cameron.

He hadn't taken his chance to slip out while Harry was occupied. He was planted, in fact, exactly where he'd been standing when the old man arrived. At any other moment I'd have roared with laughter at the look on his face. It was plain as print—*Christ, do these Arran farmers cook their meat live?*

"They were hypothermic," I explained for him, briefly forgetful of Harry or anything else but that wide-eyed blue-violet gaze. "The oven's a last chance. Not for these ones, though."

Harry jerked his head up. For a painful moment I could see him turning over the possibility of ghosts, though Cameron bore no resemblance to Al. Then he hoisted himself stiffly off his knees and into his accustomed fireside armchair. "I suppose you'll tell me in your own good time," he growled, "who the devil this may be."

I must have been turning over answers in my mind since the old man's sudden return. I hoped so, anyway—the lie was ready on my lips, and I didn't like to think I'd come up with it spontaneously. I looked at Cameron. I had no idea what I was doing, no idea if he would pick up the line I was about to throw.

"I forgot to tell you. I got an email off the agricultural college in Dumfries. They wanted to send a student for a bit of work experience—I forgot he was arriving today."

Harry sat back in his chair. He pulled out the Aga drawer and briefly examined the ewe lamb still prostrate inside it then pushed it back in with a grunt that raised a painful lump in my throat. "Work experience?"

"Yeah. We've had students from them before. I thought it would be okay to say yes, but—"

"Student or not, he'll still want paying. Did it slip your mind we turned our last hand off for want of wages yesterday?"

You turned him off, not me. I'd have said it if not for the trace of tears in the old sod's eyes. He'd never wept for his daughter or grandson any more than I had. I was suddenly so bloody sick of him, his farm, the life he'd obliged me to lead, that I didn't care if he bought my story or not. I couldn't even finish it. I'd pack up and leave with Cameron, if...

"Er, no, sir. I don't need to be paid."

Harry and I both jumped. Cameron had taken a cautious step or two towards us and was standing with his hands in his pockets. He looked nervous but resolute. Respectful, too—I wondered who had last accorded Harry a *sir*. I was glad I'd given him the clothes. He could just about pass for a would-be shepherd.

"It's a new scheme," he went on diffidently. "Because of the recession. We work for free if you let us have bed and board. I know you don't know me, so...I'll kip down in the barn if you like."

Harry took him in. I could see the cogs whirring clearly, as if his pragmatic old skull had been made of glass. Inbred suspicion of strangers, and of any innovation I ever suggested, fighting it out against the prospect of free labour... The struggle didn't last long. "Work without pay, will ye?"

Cameron nodded.

"Well, more fool you. Damned if you'll sleep in any barn, though, with this rattling ould hulk of a house and all its bedrooms wasting heat."

That was rich. "You don't heat the bedrooms," I reminded him, and copped a terrible look. I shut up. I'd gained my point, hadn't I? "Sorry, Granda."

"You want to be. Your brother never would have cheeked me in front of a stranger, lad, and I'll tell you now, you're no' fit to hold a—"

"Nichol?"

Harry glanced up angrily at the interruption. I was too busy feeling sick about the way his speech would have ended to react at all, but Cameron had come right up to the Aga and was looking into the open drawer on my side. "You know the... You know the dead lambs?"

"Aye? What about them?"

"Do they...twitch around a bit, then, after they die?"

What was he on about? "No," I said bitterly. "They pretty much stay still, like other dead things."

"Then should you take another look at that one?"

I sprang up. Harry and I were well off our form this morning. Sentiment aside, the beasts were our livelihood, and we'd normally have watched much longer for signs of revival. Cameron was right. The poor Leodhas tup was kicking in his tray, little hooves scrabbling. "Bloody hell!"

I reached to retrieve him, but Harry shouldered me out of the way. "Shift," he commanded, and I gave place to him gladly. Sick of him I might be, but his misery had cut me like a blade, and it was good to see the capable clutch of his big hands around the lamb. He pointed a finger at Cameron. "You, whatever your name is—lad—student—fetch me the Quick Start. Now!"

I stood, blocking Harry's view of him. Cameron was backing up, his face a panicked blank. "White tub in the corner," I mouthed at him, giving him a little shove in the right direction. "Go on. It's marked."

He ran for it. Harry took the tub from his hand. I didn't

need instructions—already I'd fetched one of our sterilised bottles from the pan on the hob, and I held it while Harry poured in a dollop of thick white syrup from the tub. Nothing more Catholic than a convert, and he swore by the stuff now after years of resistance, forgetting, I imagined, that I'd been the one to bring a batch home and drag twin lambs back from the edge of weary death beneath his suspicious gaze.

"Teat," he demanded, gripping the tup between his knees, and I screwed on the rubber nipple and stood clear. Stubborn or not, he was a powerful figure in the life-and-death dramas around here, like the doctor in a mumming play, and he liked to have elbow room and sole charge for his resurrections...

But he looked up and smiled. Not at me—at Cameron, who had backed off as well, pale with the effort of keeping up. "You, lad," he said. "Student. Sit down."

"His name's Cameron, Granda."

"Whatever. I shouldn't have taken my eyes off this tup so soon, and nor should you, Nichol Seacliff. I'm glad somebody was watching on. Here," he said, hoisting the lamb across to poor Cameron, who had sat down obediently in the chair opposite. "You have the first feed of it."

Okay. We were probably sunk. God knew it wasn't rocket science to shove a bottle tip into the mouth of a lamb, but many simple things were mysteries first time round, and this was obviously an absolute first for the bewildered town boy. He tried gallantly to deal with the honour bestowed on him. I tried to help, getting behind Harry's shoulder and offering a mime of how to hold the flailing little beast, how to lift its head to get it to take the teat. But the lamb, having decided to live, was now launched into the next stage of its natural order of business, which was to get itself onto its feet and away with its mother and the flock out of the reach of wolves. It fought and kicked, sending the bottle flying.

"Ach!" Harry exclaimed, after I'd retrieved the bottle and he'd watched another failed attempt, the expensive syrup spraying everywhere. "For a farming student, laddie, you

41

have'nae a clue!"

Cameron looked up. "Sorry, sir." He glanced at me as if for inspiration, though I could only shrug. "Er...we've only done theory of lambs so far, is the thing. The practical's next term."

"What?" Harry frowned, and I was sure the jig was up. He'd be royally pissed off. He didn't like strangers, and he'd never countenance a lie. I got ready to step between them. But after a moment he shook his head. The gesture was familiar to me— sad bewilderment at a world going headlong to the dogs. "Well, I don't know how they think to turn out shepherds that way, boy. You learn by doing. I'll show you when I've got more time. Here—give that to me. I'll get it started in the barn then put it to that ewe that's fostering yours, Nichol."

He stumped away. His sheepdogs were waiting for him by the door. They hadn't barked at Cameron, but they had been distracted, and they followed Harry outside with lowered ears and tight-tucked tails. They took the loss of one of their charges with every sign of human shame.

And we had lost one. I took a last look at the female. She was gone beyond retrieval, though, her little body no more than a shell. Sorrow and laughter fought for room in my chest.

I turned to my visitor, who was still sitting by the fireside, looking as if he might faint. "Cameron, for God's sake—*theory* of lambs?"

"It was all I could think of."

"I can't believe he swallowed it."

"I didn't want to lie to him. I wouldn't do anything to hurt him."

"No, of course not. I didn't mean to chuck you in like that." I frowned, wondering at his intensity. He was watching in the direction Harry had gone, his eyes bleak. "I'm sorry. That story was all *I* could think of."

"An agricultural student?" He returned his attention to me, a tiny smile beginning. "They wouldn't even let me take the school guinea pig home at the weekends. That's how much I know about livestock."

"You know now what to do with hypothermic lambs."

"Yeah. Why'd you do it for me, Nichol?"

"I wanted to give you a chance. You don't have to keep running. Stay here for a bit if you want."

"I thought you said this was a bad place to hide."

"You won't be hiding. You'll be our trainee farmhand from Dumfries. If nobody tailed you out from Brodick, I doubt anyone will find you here. And God knows we could use the help."

"Even from someone like me?"

"Well, you come cheap. And like Harry said—we learn by doing."

I hadn't meant it to sound seductive. I couldn't even work out why it had, except that the sight of him, there by the fireside in his borrowed clothes, splashes of the Quick Start still on his face, made my heart race and my throat tighten. Oh, and he hadn't missed the softened little scrape in my voice.

He got up and came to stand in front of me. "None of my business," he said gently, "but I get the feel I won't be bumping into any of your girlfriends around here."

I held his gaze. It wasn't a challenge, just a question. When I thought about his reasons for wanting to know, a heat began to kindle in my spine. "That's right."

"About it not being my business?"

"About the girlfriends."

He nodded. "Was that difficult, growing up around here?"

"Was it difficult where you come from?"

"Sometimes."

We stood together quietly. Outside, the island day was gathering pace—the first day of spring, it felt like. Harry had left the porch door open. Scents of warming earth made their way in on the air. In a different world—an Eden swept clean of pain, of duty, family ties and loss—I'd have taken this stranger by the hand, walked out with him to the cliff-top meadow where the turf grew springy and rich, and lain down with him. As it was, I had work to do. "Will you stay, then?"

"I want to. I don't know if I can carry it off. I've only got the clothes I arrived in and these ones you gave me, for a start."

Aye. We'd better get you your own or Harry will notice. I tell you what..." Reluctantly I turned away from him and went to the drawer in the huge oak dresser where I kept cash for deliveries and daily expenses. "Go and get yourself kitted out. Don't go back into Brodick—there's a bus on the hour that goes west of here into Blackwaterfoot. They've got a decent farm store."

"All right. You don't need to give me money, though. I've got a few quid left."

"How much?"

"I don't know—a tenner or so, I reckon."

I smiled. "That won't get you far, you townie. You need two sets of overalls, waterproofs, a couple of changes of warm clothes that don't look like they came from Topshop. Boots and gloves I can give you, but you'll need this much at least." I held him out some notes. "Don't worry. It's just a loan."

"Why would you trust me?"

I shrugged. His question had come out hoarsely, and he had flushed up. Maybe I was being stupid, but an old faith was stirring inside me, a willingness to lean on the tides of the universe instead of swimming desperately against them.

I put the money into his hand. "Why would I not?"

Chapter Three

I might have done nothing more than aid the flight of a criminal. I knew that, and about a tenth of me was resigned to never seeing Cameron or my money again.

The rest of me felt wonderful. I couldn't account for the change. All right, I'd had my fill of sleep for once, but that hardly explained the energy surging through me as I set about my daily routine. Occasional glimpses of my cat, darting about among the sheds and outbuildings, kept refreshing my sense of miracle. *The luck of the farm...* I should have told Harry about her return. He was off now at the Campbeltown sheep mart, but the news would cheer his superstitious Gaelic soul when he came back. I wondered how many we'd be sitting down to dinner tonight. We'd stopped sitting down at all over the last weeks, just grabbing what we could on the run. That was bad. I decided to get a casserole going once I'd finished my work outside.

First I had to do the midday round of feeds. Harry had taken our ancient Toyota truck to the mart, leaving me the quad, so that was quickly accomplished, a short exuberant roar around our pastures with bales of fresh hay in the trailer and new blocks for the salt licks. I'd thought we were out of those but a glance into one of the sheds had revealed a last batch of them. Dropping them from our shopping list had been a false economy—the lactating ewes needed the minerals, and the overall health of the flock had deteriorated since we'd stopped putting them out.

Back at the farmhouse, I cleaned out every pen and stall in the barns without pause for breath. The change in the weather had transformed everything. I could shed my layers and stride about the yards in a T-shirt and jeans, sun warming the back of my neck. I felt as if I'd been limping head down through a rainstorm for as long as I could remember.

I was lying underneath the second quad bike, trying to figure out why it had died on us, when I heard the approaching engine. It was too soon for Harry to be home, and we weren't due any deliveries. I stood up, wiping my oily hands on a rag. We very seldom got passing visitors.

Oh, great. There on the track that led down from the main road, jouncing and rolling on its ruts, was the white police 4x4 from Lamlash. The only man privileged to drive that was the last one on the island I wanted to see. I thought about a dive for cover, but it was too late. He'd spotted me and was raising a hand in greeting.

It wasn't that I hated him. In fact it was impossible for me even to dislike him, and I'd got used to thinking of him as PC Archie Drummond, our friendly local bobby, carefully burying memories of the passionate affair we'd carried on until he'd woken up one morning with the urge to join the police. He'd decided the Strathclyde Constabulary would like him better without a gay lover on his bio sheet, and that had been that. I hadn't had a leg to stand on. I'd accepted my offer from Edinburgh uni, so I was leaving too. I just hadn't known that the changes would mean the end of my life's first and only love.

Hadn't seen that one coming at all. I cringed inwardly when I recalled my shock, my protests. Jesus, I'd made a fool of myself. Of course it all felt faint and far away to me now, but still I found it hard to play it cool around Archie. I'd been living like a hermit for the past twelve months and had scarcely seen him. It might have been nice if he'd arrived when I was striding through the meadows with the wind in my freshly washed hair instead of here in the yard, daubed from head to foot in motor oil and manure. You know how it is with ex-lovers—you like to look as if you're doing okay. Just ordinary pride, not at all a desire to shove down their throats what they're missing...

Archie stopped just beyond the gate. He got out of the Rover, being careful to avoid the mud. I'd once accused him of wanting to join up just for the sake of the uniform, and he did make it look good, the smart black setting off his rangy build and the hair we'd agreed long ago was a nice shade of auburn, not ginger. He was in his dress jacket, every silver button neatly done. He looked so prim and proper. I knew better.

I ran across the yard and climbed up to lean over the top of the gate. "Morning, Sergeant Howie! Are there no' any missing bairns on Summer Isle for you this morning?"

He slammed the Rover's door. The once-over he gave me had something of its old appreciation in it. Come to think of it, Archie had never minded me dirty. "Oh, a *Wicker Man* crack," he said, nodding and smiling patiently. "How original. No, no bairns—just a couple of stones gone from the top of your roadside wall. Everything been all right here?"

"Yeah, fine." I got off the gate and swung it open for him. "Haven't got time to keep the fences right, let alone the drystone. How are you?"

"Oh, grand. On my way to some secret policeman's ball or other on the mainland. Thought I'd just run down and see you were shipshape... Och, Nicky." He came to a halt in the gateway, squinting up at the barn's eastern wall. "Have you had a break-in?"

I winced. He was always too sharp-eyed for my own good. And *Nicky* was for lazy, long-gone days at our camp on Kildonan beach, rolling around in the seagrass. "No. Just the wind last night. I patched the windows up."

"What—the wind cleverly broke just those two little panes? Have you checked to see nothing's missing?"

"Like what? A sheep? A bale of hay?"

He rolled his eyes. "How about an ATV or the contents of your oil tank? You need to sharpen up, you know. People are getting desperate around here. Eamon at Corriegills had six hundred gallons of boiler juice siphoned out just last Friday. Come on. Let's have a look around."

He set off for the barn door and I followed him, not having a lot of choice. I was grateful to be feeling more cheerful this morning. A visit from him yesterday might have put me on my knees in tears at his feet. We'd been friends since junior school, our sudden mid-teen transformation into lovers a blazing surprise to us both. We'd dealt with it shoulder to shoulder, breath to breath, just as we always had everything else in our lives.

"How's it all going, then?" I asked, casual as I could. The barn was warm and peaceful now, dreaming in hay-scented sun. "Cleaning up the mean streets of Torbeg and Ballymichael living up to expectations?"

He was glancing between the broken window and the ladder to the hayloft. "Aye, it pays the bills. And they're not... They're a lot less particular than I thought they'd be, about hiring... Well. I had to sit through three or four lectures on equal opportunities and respect for gay officers. Talk about preaching to the converted."

"And are you?"

"What?"

"Reconverted?"

I hadn't meant to be sarcastic or harsh. There it was, my old Gaelic sandpaper, the accent the well-spoken Edinburgh boys teased me for and tried to get me fired up on a subject to hear. Precise, abrasive, quiet because it never needed to be loud. Recon-*vair*-ted.

Archie turned round and looked at me in surprise. "Well," he said uncertainly, "what if I am? They're a lot more liberal these days. What if I made a mistake?"

I couldn't believe what he was asking me. I'd paid off a bit of my sleep debt, but there were still weeks of exhaustion piled up in my brain, sand in the works. *Did you just walk in here five years after dumping me cold and try to pick me up again?*

No. That would be outrageous, insane even by Archie's standards, though he'd never been lacking in nerve. The last year had made me so painfully serious, every little thing a life-

or-death drama. I let the mad idea go, a butterfly out of my unclenched hand. There were plenty of others, way more likely, to replace it.

"Did you just walk in here," I enquired, hooking my thumbs into the back pockets of my jeans, "because you're bored and you fancy a quickie?"

"Och, Nicky—"

"Don't you *och, Nicky* me. Look at the colour of you—bright bloody scarlet underneath that ginger, like the idea would never occur to you." I paused, a prickle of excitement beginning in my spine. "Anyway, am I saying no?"

His mouth fell open. Well, why not? I'd had a long and lonely year. Perversely, now I had my old lover in front of me, a hard-on beginning to disfigure the cut of his uniform trousers, I was thinking of someone else entirely. Of indigo eyes dilating with horror at my dumb, tragic family history. A bony hand reaching fearlessly for mine...

For the first time in months, impulse won out over weariness. Why the hell not? I shifted, letting him see how little harm a year of hard physical graft had done me. "Cat got your tongue, copper?"

"No. No, but..."

"Come on, then. I haven't got all day." Not turning or taking my eyes off him, I began to back towards the door.

"Where are you going?"

"Outside."

"What's wrong with in here?"

I grinned. Archie had got wary, as we grew older, of alfresco sex. I hadn't argued his caution. We'd heard of the teacher sacked from his job in Ardrossan, of two lads beaten half to death for a kiss outside a pub. Today, though, he was on my turf. My terms. "You know I never do it in front of the sheep."

"Oh, like they're going to tell..."

"No, but they talk amongst themselves. And the collies understand them, and Harry understands the dogs."

"You're nuts, you know." He was smiling helplessly back at me.

"Ah, well," I said, unfastening the barn door. "Catch as catch can."

I gave him a run for his money. Out in the sunshine it felt good to stretch my limbs, and I pelted headlong through the yards and outbuildings, picking the muddiest route I could. *Police chase on remote Arran farm*, I thought, half choking with laughter. Archie's training hadn't hurt him any either—he was close on my heels all the way, his breathing hard but controlled.

I darted round the back of the shearing sheds and let him corner me. "All right. It's a fair cop."

"Oh, Nichol..."

I didn't want him kissing me. The feel of that, on my mouth anyway, brought back too many memories, threatened my control. A stand-up quickie, this was, two busy men with something to work off on one another. I thrust him back, diving to tongue his ear and neck the way he liked.

He banged me up against the shed wall and we tussled. "Where's your granddad today?"

"Off with his sheepdogs at the Campbeltown mart. Nobody's gonna see us."

"I don't care."

Yeah, you do. Already he was turning me so his back would be to the wall, not mine, and he could keep a lookout. His hands were on my shoulders, pressing down. He liked our blow jobs that way round as well.

"Oh, no." I chuckled, resisting. I whipped the smart black-brimmed cap off his head and set it jauntily on my own. "Where's your heart, PC Silverbuttons? You owe me that much."

"Now, Nicky, don't you go getting sheep shit on that." He made a grab for the hat, which I evaded. Then, as if acknowledging his debts, he sank to his knees.

It should have been great. God knew I shuddered and writhed as he unzipped my jeans, thumped my palms against the woodwork in front of me and cried out when he took me into his mouth. I snatched great breaths of the bright air to stop myself from coming on the spot. I lasted barely thirty seconds anyway. Archie wasn't playing me for time, tonguing me hard, grabbing my backside to encourage my thrusts. It should have been great and it was, but given my year-long abstinence, unrelieved except by occasional half-asleep sessions with my own right hand, given how I'd missed him, it wasn't the mind-blowing state occasion it ought to have been. I came, and I never lost awareness of the moment. Didn't miss a trick of how he was hurrying me along. Not about to wait and let me see to him afterward either—through post-orgasmic tears I watched him frantically jerking off, shooting into his tight-clenched hand.

He knelt panting, resting his brow on my thigh. When full strength returned to my legs—and they'd never been in danger of giving way entirely—I took my hands off the shed wall. Carefully I helped him to his feet. I placed his cap back on his head then did my best to brush off some of the mud and hay strands that had attached themselves to his uniform. I fastened my jeans. His hands trembled as he dealt with his own zip and buttons.

"All right," I said hoarsely, wiping away a glimmer of semen from his lower lip with my thumb. "That was grand, Archie. But...we should leave it at that. Yeah?"

His relief was palpable. I could see him trying to hide it. "Yeah. Look, I'm sorry. I didn't mean to screw you around. I don't really know what I was doing, coming here and..."

"You were horny. Me too. Don't look so devastated."

"Yeah, but..."

"Shut up. Come in and have a cup of tea."

I moved around the kitchen quietly, letting him compose himself. I was getting a hell of a lot of traffic through here today. I superimposed Cameron's thin, untidy image over Archie's, where that solid policeman was sitting now in the same chair, and I wondered if I'd ever see my night visitor again. I couldn't sense him eastward back towards the mainland. Maybe he'd kept going west, hitched a ride on a trawler and was headed off to Kintyre. My heart ached out after him. I'd known him for five minutes. I didn't understand.

Archie looked up as I handed him his tea. He'd regained a little colour. "Ta," he said. "Seriously, Nicky—thank you for not freaking out."

"No reason to." I didn't take the chair opposite, as I had with Cameron. I hitched myself up to sit on the work surface, not too close, not too coldly far away. "We don't have to talk about it any more now."

"Okay. Well, leaving all that aside... I didn't come here just to mess with you, believe it or not. I think someone did come over your wall, and I'm pretty sure you had a break-in. Seriously, are you and your granddad all right? I worry about the pair of you, all the way out here. Especially now you're on your own."

I watched him thoughtfully. He'd always been leery as hell about letting anyone know we were lovers, and ultimately that had finished us, but that had been his sole cowardice. He was a good man. His concerns for me and the old man were genuine.

"We're managing. The last few months have been tough, but once we get through lambing we'll be fine."

"Are you sure? I heard in town you had to turn off Joe McKenzie."

I made a face. "Good news travels fast. Just tightening our belts a bit, that's all."

"Mind you don't run out of buckle holes. Er...did you hear about Shona Clyde, by the way?"

I frowned. A twinge of anxiety touched me. Shona was our neighbour, or the nearest thing we had to one, the owner of the wealthy dairy farm inland across the hill. She was a lovely woman, a real West Isles flower, who like many a one before her had allied herself to a mutton-headed brute of a husband whose idea of fun was to get himself leathered in the Brodick pubs on Saturday, drive home and knock her about. "No. Jimmy hasn't hurt her, has he?"

"Not at all. He's done her a great big favour and dropped down dead of a stroke."

"No way. You're kidding me."

"Serious. Happened last week while he was on the rampage in town. Shona gets everything—the farm, the house, the livestock. You want to think about her, Nicky, once her natural grief has subsided a wee bit. She's a wealthy widow. And the land adjoins your own."

I swallowed my reflexive shout of laughter. In fact I managed to school my expression to an earnest mask, a mirror of Archie's, as if I were giving the proposal thought. "Well, I will," I said at length. "Only—I don't want to shock you, mate. It's just that I think I might be gay."

"Oh, funny." Archie picked up a Biro from the table and flicked it accurately in my direction. "All right. If you won't marry money, will you take a loan off me? Just to tide you over, let you hire a replacement for Kenzie till the lambing's finished?"

I pushed down off my perch by the sink. My throat was hot and sore. I couldn't keep up with the melting of my permafrosted world, the places where the tundra was breaking into flowers and streams. Archie got up before I could reach him, his expression apprehensive, but he caught me as I walked into his arms. I did kiss him then, just once on the cheek, like the brother he was trying to be to me.

I held him tight. "Don't be soft," I whispered. "I don't want your hard-earned police pennies."

"I mean it. What are you living on? You can't run this place by yourself."

I eased him back. I wasn't much of a strategist, and I knew the chances were I'd never see Cameron again, but this seemed like an opportunity. "I won't be. I forgot to say—one of the farming colleges is sending me a student out. A free one, believe it or not."

"Really?"

"Yeah. I'm expecting him any time, unless he's thought better of it. So we'll be okay, especially now spring's coming. Now, aren't you late for somewhere?"

"What?" He glanced at his watch. "Oh, bloody hellfire. The ferry. I'm going to miss the two-fifteen."

"Not if you run for it now. Put your blue light and the siren on. Go."

He returned my kiss, swift and sincere, a warm press to the corner of my mouth. "All right. I love you, Nichol. We won't be strangers, eh?"

"No. We'll stay in touch. Now go."

I followed him out. I stood in the yard and watched while he scrambled back into the Rover, and gave him a wave as he drove off. The sound of his engine gradually died, and there was only the song of the offshore breeze, one note for the cliff-top turf and another for its passage through the leafless hawthorns and gorse that lined the track up to the road. The sky, though still brilliant, felt empty and vast overhead, a kind of ringing vacancy. The sheep had fallen silent, and there was no sign of the barnyard cats, my own in particular. Maybe luck, like Archie Drummond, had only made a flying return visit to the farm.

I shivered in the wind, folding my arms over my chest. Often as I wished Harry at the devil, the place was bleak without him. If he didn't return—if, as seemed likely, Cameron was gone...

I pulled myself together. At least such fancies around here didn't have to be idle ones. Taking time off for afternoon sex had bulldozed my workload into an intimidating heap. I was cold and depressed in the wake of my endorphin rush, that was all. I'd find my jumper, wherever the hell I'd left that, and get on with things.

Shadows flickered in the yard behind me. I spun round, almost sure I'd seen someone. But the sunny space was empty, the only movement the dance of the coltsfoots that lined the grassy verges round the barn. They must have sprung up overnight, or maybe in the last five minutes, or maybe I'd only been too busy to notice them before. My ma had loved them. She'd taught Al and me to watch out for them as the first signs of spring—that and blackthorn blossom, which now I came to look was also lacing the hedgerows. She'd taught me the fascination of flowers that came before leaves, appearing out of nothing on the earth and on bare twigs. In autumn she made gin from the blackthorns, which by then were called sloes and yielded dark berries with a velvety blue-grey bloom.

My jumper was folded on the arm of the bench by the door. My jacket too, and I could have sworn I'd left that crumpled somewhere in one of the sheep pens. My head spun a little. She'd never been what you'd call a fussy parent, my ma, and if we shed our clothes around the place, she wouldn't pursue us with them. She would, though, pick them up if she came across them on her own trips round the sheds and barns, and return them to that bench so we could find them.

I must have caught the habit without realising. I wasn't alone in being influenced. As far as Harry had been concerned, wildflowers had no place in his barnyards, and he and Ma had fought like tigers over his weedkiller spray. He hadn't touched them last year or this. He hadn't laid a hand on any of her favoured herbs or blossoms, not even the patch of nettles she liked to keep for the red admiral butterflies.

Something shifted in my chest. It felt too big and awkward to be grief. Damn Archie anyway, coming here and stirring me up with his lousy effort at a pass and his kindness. Damn Cameron too, while I was at it, for cracking my ice enough to let Archie in.

I went and picked up the jumper. I felt its sun-warmed fabric for a moment. It smelled of home, of my ma, but that wasn't wonderful—Harry and I were still working through the mountain of washing powder she'd scored off a wholesaler in Glasgow. In her way she'd loved a bargain as much as Alistair.

There were no miracles going on here, no messages. Just my own sleep deprivation, a too-bright sunlight and a wind full of voices from the sea. I'd be hearing mermaids next.

I shrugged into the jumper and my jacket and went back to work.

Chapter Four

The time for the last eastbound bus came and went. I didn't notice. I thought I heard the distant roar of its engine, but I couldn't look up—a ewe I hadn't even been sure was pregnant had decided to deliver triplets more or less on my feet when I went down to the south paddock with the evening feed. She managed it without complications, though she looked as surprised as I felt. I watched in relief as each bloodstained little bundle appeared, dropped to the turf and showed signs of vigorous life. Thank God for that. When it came to sheep obstetrics, I could deal with the basics, but that was all. There was no mobile signal down here to summon the vet and little chance that I could pay him anyway. Like most triplets, the lambs were tiny, and I hoisted them and their startled dam into the trailer to take them to the shelter of the barns overnight.

I drove carefully. The trip back to the farm took ten minutes, about the same length of time as the walk from the bus stop on the main road. Harry's Toyota was parked on the drive. I forced myself not to hurry the task of settling the ewe and her sudden family into the pens, despite the horrible visions I was having of Cameron pinned down under one of Harry's efforts to be friendly. These, with someone new, took the form of half an hour's intense interrogation. *Which village did ye say ye came from? Do you know the Maguires? The Fitzherberts? The McAndrews? What does your father farm—dairy? Beef? Sheep?* I shivered in apprehension and quickly checked the gender of the new arrivals, knowing it was the first thing he would ask me. I'd better get inside.

I needn't have worried. The old man was sitting in solitary

state by the Aga, one collie to each side of him and one across his feet. He looked like some ancient god of the forest and hearth, wreathed in his lung-clutching pipe smoke, accompanied by his totem beasts.

I entered cautiously, trying to stay out of his miasma. "All right, Granda?"

"Aye."

I went to turn the oven up. At some point between mucking out the pens and getting a blow job off Archie Drummond, I'd put together and set a casserole to heat. It had been ticking over all day. The kitchen smelled good for once, less desolate. I'd made more than enough for three. "How was Campbeltown? Did you meet Will McLeish?"

"Aye."

I rolled my eyes. The monosyllabic answers didn't mean things had gone badly for him at the mart. Probably the opposite—he just wanted me to come over, sit within his fallout zone and give my full attention to his news. He wouldn't have been indulging himself with the pipe or the fireside idleness on a bad day.

I washed my hands clear of mud and afterbirth and took the hot seat opposite him. From there I could see down the hall to the open back-porch door and into the yard, though I was losing hope. I set aside the stupid, dull ache in my chest. "What did McLeish have to say, then?"

"The Leodhas agent's making deals with all the Arran farmers for next season's wool. He's no' dealt with a Seacliff before. We came to terms."

I could imagine. The family talent for business had skipped past me, but Harry drove a bargain like he rode his quad bike.

"That's good," I ventured. I wondered if he'd forgotten we only had one Leodhas ram, and that newborn tup would need a year's growth before he got interested in providing us with more. That his lambs in turn would need a season or more to come into their fleece. I didn't want to throw cold water, though. Harry's satisfactions over the last year had been few. My instinct was to add to them if I could. "That last ewe in the south pasture—one of the ones we thought was barren—dropped triplets this afternoon. Two tups and a female, all healthy."

"Two males? What number ewe was it?"

"Seventeen." I'd sprayed it in matching purple on her lambs before leaving the pen.

"Seventeen? Nichol, you idiot, that was the last one we put to the Leodhas stud. That's three males we've got now."

I tried to smile. When he was this pleased, being called an idiot was almost a caress. And it was a good thing—three rams could start us off a flock with this desirable weaver's wool. We would still have to wait at least two years for it. I tried to imagine two more years struggling here. Two more winters.

I looked out into the empty yard then back at the old man. Life had felt brighter to me for a few hours today, but who was I trying to kid? If Harry was building air castles, we were in a bad way.

"Granda," I began, lowering my head into my hands. "I'm not sure we can—"

"Hello?"

I sat up. Gyp, Floss and Vixen sprang to attention too. Before I could move to stop them they were running, a black-and-white torrent, in the direction of that uncertain greeting. I darted after them. They weren't vicious dogs, but they could overreact in defence of their lord and master, and the sight of them bearing down in a pack would scare the daylights out of a stranger...

Out of Cameron. He was standing by the gate, one hand still on its latch. In the other he held several carrier bags from the Blackwater farm-supply store. His face was a picture. The dogs had surrounded him and dropped to the ground, muzzles low, haunches tensed to spring.

"Hi," he said with fragile calm when he saw me. "Any thoughts or advice?"

"Yes. Just keep still."

"Is this normal?"

"No, actually. I can't think what they're playing at." I glanced behind me. Harry had appeared in the doorway. His shoulders were quivering oddly. God, I hoped I hadn't upset him. "Granda, do you want to call off your hounds?"

"Aye, in a minute."

"Now would be better, if you could. What the hell are they doing?"

"They're..." He lapsed to wheezing silence. I swung to face him. Slowly it dawned on me that the old sod was shaking with laughter. "They're after rounding yon lad up."

I had another look. He was right. This was what the dogs did when a sheep had detached itself from the flock. Apparently it was the funniest thing Harry had seen in some time. I couldn't remember when he'd last laughed like this. It was quiet, and he was almost expressionless, but tears were beginning to run down his cheeks.

"Well," I said, as repressively as I could, "there's no need. He'll come quietly. Won't you, Cameron?"

"Given the chance, I'd be happy to."

Harry pulled himself together. He uttered one of his weird, coded whistles, the ones I could imitate but never make work for me, and the collies leapt up as if pulled by invisible strings and loped back to his side. He jerked his head curtly at Cameron. "Where's yon lad been?"

He seemed to be having trouble with the name. I knew that was how some forms of senility started. Then, he also just sounded like his curmudgeonly self.

"*Cameron*," I said patiently, "has been to Blackwaterfoot to get some things he needed. Is that all right with you?"

"Aye, today. Work shifts start tomorrow, though. Bring him in to dinner, Nichol. He'll want some meat glued on those runt-pup bones if he means to survive around here."

He turned and trudged into the house. I was alone in the

sunshine, the coppery westering light, with Cameron. I didn't quite know what to do. Left to impulse only, I'd have gone up and hugged him.

"I'm sorry," I said, sublimating the urge into an awkward folding of my arms. "He's so blisteringly bloody rude."

"I think I quite like him."

"You came back."

"Yes. I'd have been here sooner, but I got off at the wrong stop. Had to walk a mile or so down the road."

"Oh." I overcame my paralysis enough to go and take some of the bags out of his hands. "The driver would've told you where to get off if you'd asked."

"I didn't want to look like a stranger."

We set off together across the yard. We were shoulder to shoulder. I didn't know why that seemed to take the edge off the twilight wind and drive to far distance my conviction that I couldn't live on or work this land anymore. "Did you get kitted up, then?"

"I think so. I bought the things you said. Can I pull this off, though? He's already seen I don't know one end of a sheep from the other."

"So he won't have high expectations. And remember, you're free, so he'll get what he's paying for."

Cameron chuckled. "Aye. He'll certainly get that much."

"And I'll be around. I'll keep you straight."

He gave me a sidelong look. The wind was blowing his black hair across his eyes. I wanted to brush it back, to get a better view of the burnished lights the sunset was calling from their violet.

"Thanks," he said softly. "But I think *straight* is the last thing you'll be..." He winced and came to a halt. "Ouch."

"What's the matter?"

"Think I burst a blister."

I looked at his feet. He'd dispensed with his trainers and was wearing a pair of new green wellingtons.

"Did you walk down from the bus in those?"

"Yeah. Like I said, I didn't want to stand out. So I took off my city-boy shoes, and I put on these. I thought they'd be comfortable."

"So they are, with two layers of thick socks."

"Oh. No, I'm barefoot."

I hissed in sympathy. "You'll be cut to shreds. Come on in. We'll get some plasters on you and some antiseptic, and—"

"Nichol, no. At least...not while your granddad's around."

"He's all right. He won't eat you."

"Okay, but I just don't want to look like an arse in front of him. Any worse of an arse, anyway. I'll patch myself up later."

I nodded. I let go the steadying grasp I hadn't realised I'd fastened on his arm, and he hobbled on, visibly swallowing the pain to make a decent stride of it. I didn't quite get his anxiety about the old man, though Harry was enough to make anyone nervous. Then I could only think about the sight of him from behind, skinny but head held high, nice firm backside making the borrowed sweatpants look good.

I ran to get the door for him. "Well, you know two agricultural secrets now," I said, ushering him in. "Where to find the Quick Start for the lambs, and not to go commando in your wellies."

He gave me a luminous smile, and I thought about adding a third—that Harry's sheepdogs only cornered a beast like that if they wanted to bring it safe home—then decided not to push my luck.

We had a peaceful meal. Harry confined himself to extracting a short genealogy from Cameron, who responded with what I thought might be mostly the truth—that he was town born and bred, and a Beale of the Larkhall Beales, who'd never distinguished themselves in any way he knew of. To my surprise, the old man at that point gave him a look of something near approval—I barely recognised it—and told him he could be the first, if he carried on his studies and settled himself on a farm. *Something better for your own bairns, laddie.* I bit back a groan, but Cameron didn't seem fazed by him. We sat around the rickety table even after the casserole was eaten and the remains of it wiped up with bread. I couldn't remember the last time we'd hung around for one second longer than we had to.

Cameron thanked me nicely for the food, and I shot him a smiling glance. He'd certainly done a quietly passionate justice to it. Already he looked a bit more solid.

"Can I get you any more?"

"Better not. I'm meant to work for my keep, remember?"

"Yes, but—"

"The lad's right. Take him out on your late rounds, Nichol. If you set off now, you can check the cliff-top fences before dark."

I looked up. Harry was scanning both of us with a kind of grim satisfaction, probably at the idea of packing me out into the cold night. Something more to it than that, though. I tried to read it. His eyes were glittering oddly. Maybe it was even more fun to have a weary, underweight town boy to kick around.

My temper stirred. "Is it all right with you," I said, "if I show him to where he'll be sleeping first?"

"*B'e sin a'chuirt, mas e gura bi fàg mise 'am aonar.*"

I care not, as long as thou art gone. I raised my eyebrows. Almost impossible to translate the old language into bright modern English, particularly when it came to Harry's thunderous pronouncements.

"*Fior mhath,*" I responded involuntarily. *Very well. As it pleases you.*

I got up, Cameron rising with me. Suddenly we were an ancient tribal clan, receiving orders from our chief in the ancestral shieling. I gestured Cameron ahead of me towards the door. One day there'd have to be a reckoning, if the old man kept playing it *Highlander* like this. All right, he'd lost his beloved heir, but I wasn't one of his sheepdogs to be ordered about, and I wouldn't have him snarling—even in a foreign language—at a guest...

"Wait a bit."

I stopped dead. That was the trouble. He was my lifetime's voice of authority. I'd developed habits of obedience long before my free adult will had kicked in.

"Which room will you give to yon lad?"

"Granda. His name is Cameron. Not *student* or *boy* or *yon*—"

"In fact it's just Cam."

We both looked round. He'd spoken gently, as if shy of breaking our confrontation, which I supposed from the outside did sound as if it might get settled with claymores. "At least...that's what everyone calls me. So..."

An awkward silence fell. Harry chewed on the stem of his pipe, glaring at us from under his eyebrows. Then he sat up and set the pipe aside. "Give yon lad the room opposite yours."

"What? That room's—"

"I know damn well which room it is. The rest are barely furnished. Do as you're bidden, *leanabh*. Go now."

The weird light was still in his eyes, a kind of blank sheen. I couldn't figure it out. Perhaps he'd taken to lycanthropy in his old age. I wouldn't put it past him, and the moon was almost full... Quickly I scooped up Cameron's shopping bags and half pushed him out of the room. I really didn't want to know.

Out in the hallway, Cameron glanced at me uneasily, taking a couple of the bags from my hand. "I didn't mean to cause a fight."

"You didn't. At least—there's not much that doesn't cause us to fight, so don't worry about it. Go on up those stairs." I followed him, this time keeping my eyes to myself. I'd been a pretty naïve arrival on the Edinburgh scene, but I'd taught myself to tell a boy I fancied him by looking him in the face, not the arse. "We fight over sheep feed, politics, heating bills and every other thing we talk about."

"Was he all right? He looked a bit... I don't know. Not well, maybe."

"Oh, he's fine." A flicker of concern crossed my mind, but I dismissed it. Harry was always fine. I'd never known him ail a day in my life. "Mind, it's not like him to use the Gaelic without checking you could speak it too. He'd normally think that very rude."

"And is it?"

"Traditionally, yes. The islanders had a rule—they'd never speak it when an Englishman was by. So as not to make him feel left out. And of course more and more Englishmen came, so..."

"You wiped yourselves out with your courtesy."

We'd come to a halt on the turn of the stairs. It took me a moment to notice. It was one of the darkest, most melancholy places in the old house, but for once it didn't oppress me—not the mean, chilly draught stealing in through the cobwebbed windowpanes, not the dead bulb dangling uselessly overhead because only Alistair had dared scramble the full height of the stairwell on our wobbly stepladder to fix it. If Cameron—*Cam,* he'd said, and it suited him better, pure and direct—wanted to stop here and talk, that was fine by me. "Yes, almost."

"I'm not an Englishman."

"No." *No, you're a flower of the west Glasgow wasteland, a proof I'd almost forgotten that nature is everywhere, astonishing and bountiful.* "I'm guessing they didn't teach it to you in school, though."

"They barely taught me English."

"Well, no more did they teach it to me, for all there was meant to be a revival. It's a dying language. Best they let it go."

"Where did you learn it, then?"

"I didn't. At least, Harry tried to drum some into me while I was growing up, but I never really took it in. And neither of us should have been speaking it in front of a stranger, so I'm sorry."

"Maybe I don't count."

He was smiling faintly. I considered his tone. It could just mean that the old man had felt easy enough in his company to forget his manners, a compliment of sorts. It could also mean *perhaps I don't exist.*

"Oh, you count," I told him, not really thinking what I was saying, "or he'd never have offered you Alistair's room."

"Alistair? Oh, my God. Not your brother's."

"Yeah. You could've knocked me down. He hardly mentions Al. I don't think either of us has even been in there since..."

"Nichol, I can't possibly."

"I know. It's weird that he offered. But in a way I don't see why not, and he's right—it's probably more fit for human habitation than anywhere else in this barrack. Come on, let's go and have a look at it at least."

The door wasn't locked. Cam watched me warily while I pushed it open. He thought me strange, I imagined, for doing so with such a steady hand. My own calm puzzled me. Unconsciously I'd avoided the place for a year, not so much as glancing at it as I went past, and now I simply couldn't work up any sense of the occasion. After all, it was just Alistair's room. If we'd stripped it and cleared it I might have felt more, but as things stood—untouched, unchanged—this could have been any one of the hundreds of times when I'd walked in, welcomed as a kid, in our teenage years as often as not shouted at for failing to knock. *Nicky, you wee tick! In the unlikely event of you ever finding a girlfriend, I'm gonna do this to you!*

I smiled. I had been a classically annoying little brother, hadn't I—always in the wrong place at the wrong time. There were Al's football trophies, his collection of posters from rock festivals. He'd had this room all his life, and there were his unsuccessfully hidden traces of childhood—a box of soft toys shoved halfway into the wardrobe, the painted-over Doctor Who wall panels showing themselves in bas-relief, the ghost of a TARDIS travelled on forever now. There was his unmade bed.

I turned away. Cam was planted in the doorway, white as a sheet. "Look," he whispered. "It's a grand room. And I'm the last man in the world who should be choosy, but..."

"But you'd rather sleep in the barn. Aye. Me too." I hustled him gently back out into the corridor and closed the door behind me, turning the latch round tight. "There's a room just round the corner here. Use that one."

"I don't want to offend him. Your granda, that is."

I didn't think you meant Al. "You won't. He sleeps off by himself at the other end of the house. Just...duck into Al's room if you see him coming, and he'll never be any the wiser."

I showed him into the bleak little cell round the turn in the corridor, which had nothing worse to face in it than a bare divan bed and perishing cold. "Jesus, it's freezing. I'll get you some bed linen and a load of blankets."

"Later. It's okay. This is fine."

He'd laid a warm hand to my shoulder, as if I needed calming. I didn't. I was abysmally cold, inside as well as out. It was just that if I didn't do something for someone, make this room more habitable, provide food, see to the sheep, I was going to leap out of my crawling skin. "I'll get them. They're just in the airing cupboard down the hall. I'll find you a couple of hot-water bottles too, and... Oh, wait. I forgot about your feet."

"My what?"

"Your blisters. Come on. The bathroom's just down here."

"Oh. No, it's okay. They're fine now. It was just walking down from the—"

"Cam, let me see to them, all right? We've got work to do on foot tonight, and you'll be screwed if you get them infected."

He followed me obediently, though I'd seen the puzzled shadow in his eyes. I didn't know what the tremor in my voice had been about either. Great—probably he thought I was some kind of foot fetishist. To dispel this impression, I turned my back on him while he sat on the edge of our tomb-like bath. "Take your wellies off. First-aid kit's in here somewhere. Looks like it last saw action at the Somme, but Ma keeps it well stocked up. Yeah, here we go."

"Sorry. These bloody things seem stuck."

"They're always tricky at first. Here, let me."

He hesitated then extended one foot to me. Not looking at him, I grasped the boot behind the heel and drew it off. There was a knack to it. Al had showed me, helping me into and out of my first pair. "Okay. Other."

"Ta. I haven't had wellies since I was about six."

"Floral ones, were they?"

"They might have been."

I went to work with the TCP and plasters. No wonder the poor sod had been limping—he had blisters the size of bottle tops on both heels and under his anklebones. I tried to keep my touch impersonal, but it was hard. His feet were clammy cold. I wanted to rub them, clasp the toes between my palms...

I glanced up. He was clutching the edge of the bath. "Sorry," I muttered. "Can't think why I didn't let you do that for yourself. Didn't mean to freak you out."

"You haven't. It's just..." He withdrew his foot from my grasp, not hurriedly. "I haven't had a proper wash in days. God knows what state they're in."

I smiled in relief. "They're fine."

"It was nice of you to do that. I don't get looked after so often I'm going to chuck it back in anyone's face."

"Och, it was nothing." A warmth was stealing up the back of my neck. It would be a blush if I wasn't careful. I concentrated on packing the first-aid things away, trying to lose the echo of his cool, silky skin on my palms. "I wish I could help you with the wash, as well, but there's virtually no hot... Although wait. Hang on."

I got up. For a second I stood still and listened, but all was quiet from downstairs. I pushed the bathroom door open and followed a well-worn track down the corridor, the one that wouldn't call any telltale creaks from the boards. Reaching into the airing cupboard, I found the switch for the water heater and threw it, careful not to let it clunk. The old man could pick that sound up from half a field away.

Mission accomplished, I crept back to the bathroom. "I've put the emergency heater on."

"The what?"

Immairgency. Oh, God—I *was* turning into Harry. "Sorry. The immersion. It takes about an hour to do anything, but by the time we get back there might be enough for a bath. Me and Al used to share one—I mean, we'd share the water, take turns, if one of us wasn't too filthy, fight over who got in first..."

"Nichol. Breathe."

I had been breathing, hadn't I? Now he mentioned it, though, my lungs were in a knot up under my throat. I'd been on the edge of nervous babble. "Sorry. Just didn't want you with an image of me and my big hairy brother—"

He broke into laughter, and the weird tension building around us dissolved. "Okay. Why is it a covert op to switch your water heater on, then?"

"Old man won't have it. He thinks it's too expensive. And he's right, but you'd not think once a week was pushing the boat out too far."

"What about that great big lamb incubator you've got downstairs?"

"The Aga? Yeah, that should give us water. But the only one who really knows how to deal with it is Ma, and..."

"That's the second time."

I was tucking the first-aid box, with its rust flecks and red cross big enough to be seen from passing Spitfires, back into the cabinet. I was distracted. "Second time what?"

"That you've said *is* instead of *was* about your ma. Did you realise?"

Such a gentle, ordinary question. We'd used to be better, in the Highlands and Islands, at dealing with the dead. Infant mortality, outbreaks of typhus, hard winters—we'd lived with our departed closely, often outnumbered, talking to them easily in poetry and songs. Now we had inherited—I had—a modern-day mainland silence. I hadn't opened my mouth about Ma, and no one, not even Archie, had dared ask. I wished we had a loo in here so that I could sink down on the seat. But that was off down the corridor, something she really had insisted on, in a household of three men and a shifting population of farmhands. There was only the edge of the bath, if I wanted to sit down.

Cam was making room for me. I went to join him, a little stiffly, not touching. "I didn't realise, no." I didn't realise I'd left the Aga in its state of neglect because that was her job, hers— she kept the fires in my home as surely as she kindled them at Beltane and Samhain in the fields.

"Does it feel like sometimes she's still here?"

I started. He hadn't asked it like a counsellor, a well-meaning comforter trying to get me to talk. He was watching the bathroom's shadows intently, as if...

The door creaked and swung open. This time we both jumped. It took me a moment to look down far enough to match cause to the effect. Keen-edged relief swept me. A tiny dark shape, insinuating itself into the room by main force. "Oh, is it you, Miss Buttinsky? Don't you knock?" Yes, my cat—with a huge moustache. "Oh, God."

The rat was the size of a small squirrel. She was having trouble carrying it, not that she'd admit it, but I could tell by the set of her shoulders. There must have been a battle royal to bring it down. The weight of it was making her waddle slightly. As I watched, she came to stand in front of me, looking me over consideringly. Then she turned and dropped her prize onto Cam's naked foot.

To his credit he stayed still. "Nichol, that's a..."

"Bloody great barnyard rat, aye." I bit my lip. You didn't laugh at such offerings. "I'm so sorry."

"Any particular...reason for this?"

"Yes. It means that, out of the two of us, you're the one she thinks needs feeding up."

"All right. Grand. And what's the etiquette, please?"

"Well, to really make her happy you'd pretend to eat it, but you're doing pretty well not to scream and run away."

"Not really. I'm just paralysed with horror. You do know it's still warm?"

That did it for me. I creased up. Thankfully Clover had finished her business and was leaving, stalking away with her tail in a satisfied interrogative. She was heading towards my room, as if she'd never broken her habit of spending her nights there.

"Oh, Cam, I'm sorry. That's gross even by my standards. Are you all right?"

"Fine. Can I move my foot now?"

I sobbed and choked on laughter. I snatched a breath to stop it. It hurt, like gravel shifting inside me, made my chest feel like it was full of sunshine and blood. "Aye. Come on—we'd best do these late rounds. Get into some of your new things, especially thick socks, and I'll meet you downstairs." I bent down and gingerly picked up the rat by its long pink tail. "Shall I dispose of this? Or will you be wanting him for later?"

"Och, *Nichol.*"

It was almost dark by the time we set off, the only light left in the sky a serpent of rose gold across the sea. Our famed Arran sunsets had been wiped out by rain for so long that I was reluctant to spoil it, but I flicked the quad bike's beams to full as we left the track and struck out over the fields.

I took it easy in deference to my passenger. It was a long time since Archie had deigned to hell around on a bike with me, but I knew it was a rough ride. The quads were single-seaters technically, one and a half at a stretch—or a crush, more like it. The pillion either hung on to the back of the saddle, or...

I hit a tussock and bounced the bike hard. Cameron gave a startled yelp then burst into wild laughter, I pulled up, grinning too. God, what a sound—unfettered, like a kid's. "Sorry. You okay?"

"Aye. Nearly went crack over nips into yon bloody bush, but I'm fine."

"Crack over nips, eh? What a nice Larkhall lad." I let the engine idle. "I know we've barely met and all, but if you hang on to me, you'll be safer."

"You don't mind?"

"Course not."

He put his arms around me tentatively. I gave his hand an encouraging pat—it was only a business arrangement after all, never sparking the slightest frisson in me when Kenzie was hitching a ride—and he closed his grip.

That was better. We had a lot of ground to cover, and now I could give it some welly. After the first good bump or two, he got the idea and hung on properly. I picked up speed and felt him duck his head against my shoulder to shelter from the wind. "All right back there?"

"Yes. Go faster if you like."

I chuckled. "Fun, is it?"

"Hell, yeah."

I closed my fist on the throttle and took off. His grip was powerful. Whatever the reasons for his loss of weight, they hadn't yet impinged on the essential inner force of him. I could take a lot of his skinny warmth at my back, I decided, gunning the quad up to the last crest before the long slope towards the cliff's edge and the sea. From there I'd get an idea of the task ahead, how far the flock had scattered, if any looked like they had new lambs at foot. Fill up the bale feeders, see to any casualties, begin the endless round of fence checks...

"God almighty. Stop."

I braked so hard he nearly went over my shoulder. "What? Did I hit something?"

"No. I just want to see... It's so beautiful."

"Jesus." I snapped off the engine. "You scared me."

"Sorry. But look at it."

I was looking. I looked at this landscape every day, through sea frets, rain, or just the mists of my exhaustion. I didn't need him to tell me it was lovely, on those rare days when it cracked open its casket of jewels.

Or did I? That serpent band of light had found its reflection, its shimmering twin, in the sea. The air between them was on fire, casting the cliffs in bronze, throwing a weird burnished radiance right into the zenith. Ailsa Craig island burned on the horizon, its sugarloaf turned into a pyramid, as if Giza had set sail from its sands and paused here on some unimaginable journey, to Atlantis maybe. Yes, I'd been looking. But I hadn't seen it in months.

Cam dismounted from the bike and came to stand beside me. "Incredible place," he said softly. "What's it called?"

"Just Seacliff, as far as I know—like the family. Seacliff Farm."

"Seriously? That's wild. Crazy romantic."

I stole a glance at him. The transfiguring light had caught him too. If anything deserved to be on the cover of a book...

"Not really," I said, gruff in proportion with my desire to tell him so. To undo my grip on the quad's handlebars and reach for him. I did let go with one hand, but only to point at the glittering water then the towering faces of rock that lined the shore. "It's pretty basic really. Sea. Cliff." I turned in the saddle and gestured back the way we'd come, where Harry's windows had taken the sunset, almost as if he'd put on all the lights and kindled a comfortable fire. "Farm."

"Nichol, did you ever see...?" Cam paused, and I frowned at the unsteady hitch in his voice. I couldn't have upset him, could I? "Did you ever see a film called *Young Frankenstein*?"

"Yeah, of course. It's one of my favourites."

"Do you remember when Igor's driving Professor

Frankenstein home to the castle, and they hear something howling, and the girl says, 'Werewolf'? And Frankenstein says, 'Werewolf?', and..."

"And Igor starts pointing and says, 'There, wolf. There, castle.' Okay, okay, I get it." I shook my head, helplessly mirroring his smile. "Fair enough. I don't know how I got so blind to it all. Or so grumpy about it, for that matter."

"Are you kidding me? You must have been through hell."

His voice had changed completely. Now its huskiness was something else—a sympathy that passed like a blade through my hard-won defences. God, and I wasn't going to have to reach for him—he had put out a hand to me, careful but unafraid. I held very still while he brushed his fingertips across my fringe.

"Were you very lonely?"

Desolate. I hadn't known till now. I didn't bloody want to know. If I let that come to surface, he would see it. He was a stranger, a runaway. A criminal, to take the view that Archie Drummond would, an unknown who had broken into my life and would like as not be gone in the morning.

"Sometimes," I managed. I couldn't say more. If I opened my mouth again, he would see how badly I wanted him to kiss it.

Oh, God. He saw anyway. A sweet concentration gathered in his eyes. He leaned a little towards me. I heard the wind in the gorse, the whisper of the sea far below us then nothing but the pulse of my own blood.

"Cameron..."

He twitched as if I'd woken him. He scanned my face anxiously, a pallor shadowing his own. "Sorry," he said, stepping back. "This isn't getting the sheep sheared, is it? Hadn't we better get on?"

I wondered what he'd seen to put him off. I was suddenly cold, despite the milder wind and my layered-up clothes. I told myself I was relieved—what the hell had I been thinking?

"Feeding them and checking their fences will do for

tonight," I said. The serpent in the sky was almost gone, a vast world's-edge dark coming down. "It's a big enough job, though. Come on."

Chapter Five

Next morning I left Cam to sleep while I tackled my early work. He'd done well the night before, watching attentively while I patched a length of fence then offering to fix the next himself, bumping round uncomplainingly with me to round up the stragglers. I passed his door quietly. There'd be plenty for him to do later—and, perversely, after months of solitude, I needed some time to myself. What would have happened if he hadn't backed off? That was easy. Either he'd have woken up in my bed or I'd have surfaced in a cramped-up tangle with him in his single. I'd have slept with him, blind with hunger, no questions asked.

And that was insane. I needed to look at my own motivations. Would I have flung myself at any willing stranger who'd crossed my path? Well, there had been Archie. He felt like a distant memory though, pale as the light appearing in the east as I hauled bales out of the trailer. I tried to substitute his image for Cam's in my head. I tried the same with a whole range of my Edinburgh boyfriends then a couple of idealised gay wet dreams from films and TV. No, not a flicker. It was as if a current had switched itself on when I'd laid eyes on Cam and a whole lot of others had switched off.

I didn't understand. I was at once relieved that he'd put the brakes on and mortified. I'd started to feel quite confident of my pulling power in Edinburgh. Those had all been quickies though, nothing that had to stand up under scrutiny in daylight. A quickie was all Archie had come back for yesterday. He'd found me perfectly resistible five years ago, when I'd been begging him not to break us. Maybe a one-off was all I was good for, my obvious enthusiasm the only qualification required.

I slammed the bale feeder gate shut without looking and jammed my hand in the steel bar. Yanking it free, I doubled up until the pain subsided. If I let go, howled and swore, I'd scare the contentedly munching ewes who'd turned up for their breakfast. What the hell was wrong with me? I'd pushed Archie's rejection aside and moved on. I knew how to work the bale gates. Teenage insecurities were for mainlanders, not farmers. I squinted at the hole the catch had torn in my knuckle. Quite deep, but my tetanus shots were up to date. I sucked it, wiped it on the back of my jeans and got back on the quad bike.

On my way up the lane to the farm I paused for a second, listening. I could hear the roar of the other quad. That was weird—I'd told Harry it was broken past redemption. It would be just my luck if he'd come down this morning, turned the key and had it spring back to life. But when I came into the barnyard he was standing beside it, hands on his hips, his face an odd mix of suspicion and wonder. Cameron was flat on his back on the cobbles, wedging a panel into place, closely watched by Vixen, Gyp and Floss.

I pulled up beside this interesting group. Cameron started guiltily, as if caught red-handed. "Morning, gentlemen," I said. "Everything all right?"

Harry looked at me. "Yon lad's fixed the bike."

"I can see that, Granda."

"You're a bonny lad, Nichol. But you couldnae fix a bent straw."

I nodded. I was nobody's mechanic. And I hadn't been Harry's bonny lad for as long as I could remember, which took the sting out of the observation. "What did he do to it?"

"Devil's work, it looked like."

Cameron sat up. His face was streaked with engine oil. "The ignition was gone," he said. "That's why it wouldn't start. But you can, er...bypass the ignition." Flora poked her face over his shoulder, as if to inspect his work, and he gave her a nervous pat. "It won't work from the key anymore, but if you gaffer-tape these wires together, then pull them apart when you want it to stop..." He demonstrated, making the engine snarl into life and fall silent. "I can put a switch or a button on it if you like, if I can get the part. But for now at least it works."

"Aye, it does that." Harry got onto the bike. Reaching down, he gave Cam a clap on the shoulder I knew from experience would leave a mark, probably the only thanks he'd ever get. "There's *min-choirce* on the stove, Nichol, if yon lad wants his breakfast." He revved the engine, and the dogs leapt up onto the bike behind them, perching with unlikely balance. "Or lunch, I should call it at this hour."

Well, it was almost seven o'clock. I watched him roar out of the yard. Then I put a hand down and helped hoist Cam onto his feet. He had put on his new overalls but still somehow looked more ready for a catwalk than a day on the farm. I steadied him. "Did you just hot-wire my grandfather's bike?"

"I came down and he was struggling with it. I thought I'd have a go."

That's a Glasgow carjacker's trick. I thought about saying it, but he looked apprehensive enough already. And he'd never tried to kid me he'd been training for the priesthood there. I decided someone in my family ought to be gracious. "Nice job. Thanks very much."

"It's nothing. I'm quite good at that kind of thing. I'll have a bash at anything else you've got that needs fixing up."

"In that case you'd best come and fortify yourself with some of Harry's *min-choirce*, if you can stomach it."

"What's *min-choirce*?"

"Porridge, with a dash of pepper to stop you catching cold. It's actually quite good if you can keep it down."

"Sounds fine to me. I'm pretty hungry." He gave me a shamefaced smile. "Again."

"That's all right. The one thing Harry never kept us short on is food. Fuel for his machines, and you'll burn it off, believe me. Did you sleep well?"

"Like the dead. And..." He glanced at his wrist. I could see a mark where a watch had been, but it was gone now. I didn't like to think of the circumstances that had forced him to part with it. "Apparently too long. Do you always get up this early?"

"During lambing, yes."

"Well, tomorrow wake me up too. I want to earn my keep, Nichol, if you and your granddad are letting me stay here. I want to work."

I took him up on it. Harry did too, returning from his rounds with a list of errands and odd jobs he'd apparently gone off on purpose to compose. Cameron set to, creosoting planks for a new pen, clambering about with me on the barn roof to assess the need for new tiles, native wit and an unembarrassed willingness to ask questions serving where his experience failed. Only when we got a delivery of fencing staves from Brodick did Cameron vanish into the house, and I wondered if between us the old man and I had slaved him into the need for a nap. Then I was too busy dealing with shouting delivery lads and armfuls of wood to give it thought.

Half an hour after the boys had gone, I leaned with Harry on the drystone wall that looked out over the south paddock. He had been silent for some time, and I wasn't about to start the conversation. I was too lost in wonder. Cameron was riding the newly fixed quad bike back and forth across the field. That wasn't amazing—he'd said he'd wanted to put it through its paces and to get the hang of riding one. He was also now a startling blond.

I hadn't thought to question the chemical tang I'd noticed when I'd gone in earlier to fetch cash for the wood delivery. What with sheep dip and fertilisers, the house was often less than fragrant. Harry stood beside me, his weathered face creased in a mask of concentration. Eventually he made the smallest gesture in Cameron's direction and said, "Have you managed to find another damn fool to work for free on this farm, then?"

"No, Granda. That's the same one we had before. I...think he's dyed his hair."

Harry straightened. He gave me a very serious look, and I braced. "Nichol," he began. "It's the devil of a slander to speak of a Christian, but you don't suppose yon lad's the least bit of a *gille-toine*, do you?"

I choked. There was no word for *queer* in Gaelic, as if the concept had never occurred, or hadn't been different enough to attract its own label. There was *co-sheòrsach*, a careful modern rendering of homosexual. *Gille-toine* was the closest the old language got, and it was pretty crude. *Arse-lad*, literally. Maybe *shirt-lifter* was nearer, or even Ali G's *batty-boy...*

I shook myself. This wasn't a linguistic game, though I'd forgotten how much fun those were. "Will that be a problem for you? If he is?"

He lapsed back into thoughtful silence. "No," he said after a moment. "If he puts his hours in, what business is it of mine?"

Now, for Harry, this was a bit cosmopolitan. I watched Cameron absently. The sun was catching his new blond crop, and he was starting to make the quad bike steer like a young knight's charger beneath him. Lovely, I thought. And I had always put my hours in around this place as well, hadn't I? I'd never come out to the old man—it just wasn't what you did—but perhaps this was an opportunity. *Would it be a problem if I was too?* I drew a breath. "Granda..."

"Mind, I don't want this whole island thinking the same about you. Is it no' time you found yourself a girlfriend?"

My heart sank. One thing for a farmhand, quite another when it came to his sole surviving heir. "Och, like you give me time."

"Make time then, laddie! I worked twice as hard as you at your age, and still I found the time to court your granny, and just as well for you, or Caitlin and you and your brother wouldn't be here."

Caitlin. A cold shock went through me. The last time I'd

heard him say my mother's name, he'd been on the phone to the embassy, arranging for the return of the bodies to the UK. *Seacliff, Caitlin Elizabeth. Alistair James.* And as for those of us who were still here... Was he forgetting? I glanced across at him. No, he remembered. His fists were locked together on the wall, his face bitter. God, if he'd been offered a choice out of the three of us, picked the one he most wanted to live...

The quad bike's engine howled, and I looked up in time to see Cam hit a ditch and go flying. He landed on his outstretched hands, ducked his head and turned his crash into a roll. It was still pretty undignified. He measured his length on the turf, then after a moment in which I could neither breathe nor think, leapt back onto his feet and went chasing after the bike.

The power of speech returned to me. "Bloody hell."

Harry didn't comment. Then, soft and wicked as the February wind off the sea, I heard that dreadful barrel-organ wheeze of his begin again.

"Granda," I said, as reprovingly as I could. The worst thing about that laugh was its power of infection. Twice in forty-eight hours I'd heard it now—both times at someone else's misfortune, granted, but better than the desolate silence. "He might've broken his neck."

"Aye." Apparently that hazard just added zest to the fun. I rested on my elbows, lowered my head. He heard the snort I couldn't repress and gave me a shove on the arm. "Aye, it's *consairned* you are about him!"

"I am. I'm not laughing, just..." I was, though. My throat convulsed. "For God's sake. Stop it."

Neither of us could, for the best part of a minute. Afterwards I stood fighting for breath, knocking away tears with the heel of my hand. Beside me, Harry calmed down enough to pick up his train of thought. "You know, I heard in Campbeltown that Jimmy Clyde took a stroke and dropped dead."

"I heard that too. I'm not sorry, not for Shona's sake

81

anyway."

"No, she's a bonny lass. And she's free now, Nichol. You could do worse."

I suppressed a groan. I couldn't believe I was getting this from the old man too. And, come to think of it, whether I announced my sexuality to him or not, how the hell had he managed to miss me and Archie chasing each other round his barns and paddocks all these years? Wilful blindness, I supposed, although while Al had been alive he hadn't had to worry about the Seacliff succession. Probably there were a couple of little grey-eyed beauties flourishing in the villages already.

Then, did I care what he thought? I was doing my best for him now. I didn't have to swear away my future for him too. The sun was blazing down. Off in the field, Cameron looked up and flashed me a smile whose brilliance could warm me across any distance.

"I tell you what, Granda," I said. "You're still a fine figure of a man. Why don't you set your own cap at Shona? You'd probably have better luck than me."

I intercepted Cam on his way back into the yard. He had parked the bike and was making his way on foot, his movements stiff. That had been a spectacular dive.

"Hi there, Billy Idol."

"Oh, God." He came to a halt in front of me. "It hasn't worked, has it?"

I stepped close to take a better look. There were still streaks of black amongst the pale chemical gold, I could see now. Daringly, I reached to take a lock between my fingers and thumb. "Well, you're very dark. My ma used to put some kind of bleach on hers before she tried to go blond. Why'd you do it?"

"I wasn't sure I was going to. I bought it when I went to get my farm gear—the last thing I got with my own money. When all those delivery lads turned up from Brodick, I thought maybe one of them might know Bren McGarva, might recognise me, so..."

"Oh, it's a disguise, is it?"

"Protective coloration, maybe."

I chuckled. "Jesus. It's anything but that." The breeze stirred the sable and gold. He looked like an ermine caught short on a bright summer's day. "It's...kind of conspicuous, Cam. Actually it looks bloody gorgeous."

Our eyes met. And there we were on that brink again—the same place we'd found ourselves the night before. My mouth went dry. "Sorry. I don't mean to... Er, Bren McGarva—is he your guy in Glasgow, your loan shark?"

"Yeah. Don't ask me about him, Nichol. Please."

"All right. But—it might not be as bad as you think. I mean you might not have to be this scared. If this bastard's after you... One of my mates is a policeman. Maybe he could help."

"No. No police."

"He's not a scary one. Just an island bobby."

"No." Cameron swallowed. I heard the painful little sound. Then, as if realising how his refusal might come across, he put out a hand to catch mine, lightly entangling our fingers. "Look, I haven't done... I'd never do anything to hurt you or your grandfather, okay? But the police would make it worse."

I shrugged. I didn't want him to see how deeply his most casual touch could move me. "Fair enough. We'll just have to rely on your brilliant camouflage, then."

"Oh, God. Maybe I should try and dye it back."

"I wouldn't—not yet anyway. It might just fall out." I should let go of his hand. His fingers were so warm in mine, though—a clever, tensile waiting strength, as if there were all kinds of things his hands might be capable of. "Try not to worry, eh? We really are on the far shore of creation here. And I can lend you a woolly hat, like the Edge off U2. You'll be okay."

"Okay. Jesus, what did you do to your knuckle?"

"Caught it on the gate. It's nothing."

"I think I can see bone." His grip tightened. I couldn't resist him. When he set off for the house I followed him. "Come on, big tough farmer boy. My turn to patch you up."

Chapter Six

The weather held, not just over the next few days but into the following fortnight. No one came to track down and wreak vengeance on Cameron, and I did not blunder again through his barricades. Brightening mornings came and went, each sunrise a little sooner than the last. Cam launched himself out of bed at the same time as Harry and me, and although at the breakfast table he sometimes looked like a half-fledged bleached sparrow chucked out of its nest too soon, a cup of instant and a fry-up sent him staunchly to work by my side.

Winter gave way to a rare island spring. We got them like this once every decade or so—primroses on the turf outside the back door, ravens pairing off to take a punt on an early breeding season, rolling and tumbling on the air above the roadside trees. I'd been starting to think my memory of the last fine transition from February to March had been a childhood dream, but here it was, swelling the ash buds, painting the birch twigs purple.

One morning Shona Clyde appeared, looking like Persephone and clearly thriving in her widowhood. Too much of a lady to notice Harry's dreadful winks and efforts to leave us alone together, she offered us the use of her three strapping farmhands to get us through the lambing. She was refitting her house and all her outbuildings, she told us, and the lads were just under her feet. At her expense, of course, and she wouldn't take no for an answer. I'd tried to say no anyway—stupid West Isles pride—but at that moment she'd spotted Clover in a patch of sunlight by the barn door, nursing three fat kittens. One of those wee rat-catchers would do as payment, Shona said, when it was weaned.

The luck of the farm returned in triplicate. Now when I tried to sleep I had four contestants for the quilt, the offspring mewling and farting and wrestling while their mother looked on in serene and perfect pride. I didn't care. My days were suddenly so much easier I felt lightheaded, almost sick with relief. We still had vicious frosts and sudden stillbirths, but with Cameron and Shona's boys to help, my shifts came down from eighteen hours to a perfectly reasonable twelve, and I began to look about me.

The house was a mess. Some of it was inevitable, but there was no need for the rest of it—no need for us to live like we were camping out, shivering through the March nights. One morning I thought I heard my mother singing in the kitchen. This seemed so ordinary that I went down unquestioning, to find Cam there with the radio on, crouched thoughtfully by the stove. And after all it was an easy enough job to fix. We didn't talk much. I hadn't told him the roots of my reluctance to tackle it, and I wondered if he guessed, kneeling beside me on the sooty hearth. The flue was blocked, and a couple of plates were off their hinges.

I was pricklingly aware of him, the way he smelled when the metal fought him back and he joined grim battle with it, reaching up to the armpits in the Aga's guts, his T-shirt sticking to him. He was starting to fill out a bit, packing his weight on in compact muscle. I could see tough cords appearing in his forearms from all the work. In a way I hardly understood why we were fixing the damn stove, not stretched out in front of it in each other's arms. A fine spring morning, the house to ourselves, both of us young and conveniently gay, and I was powerfully attracted to him even if...

That was the problem. I had no idea how he felt about me at all. In that regard, anyway—his daily companionship was sweet to me, and he sought me out even when our labours didn't demand we work together. I hadn't known him long enough to call him a friend, but it was getting on that way. He was funny, smart, an attentive listener. And I caught him looking at me, but those indigo eyes hid as many truths as they revealed—the glow I took for yearning could simply be concern, the unobtrusive care he seemed to have decided to take of me. A touch to my shoulder and a gesture upstairs when midnight had passed and I was yawning over paperwork, my frequent cuts and scrapes attended. He'd never followed me beyond my bedroom door, though once or twice I knew I'd made it pretty clear he'd have met a warm reception.

That night when Harry got home the house was singing. The thrumming chant was so well known to both of us that at first he didn't notice, just as I hadn't really taken it in late that afternoon when the fire I'd set got big and hot enough to send the water around. Victorian radiators creaked, their connecting pipework shuddering to life. Until the system settled, the whole house would rattle and vibrate like a trawler revving up for open seas.

Harry stood with his hands in his pockets, looking at the bright Aga frontage. I went to take my place beside him. There was every chance that he'd object. I hadn't asked him. Fuel was scarce, and he'd never shared my views on hot baths and bedrooms where you couldn't see your breath on the air. Cam was getting the pans out, ready to put on some dinner. He had a gift for fading into the background when family business arose, though by now I reckoned the old man would have included him. His affectation of forgetting Cam's name was just that—a trick to annoy me, and I'd heard him bellowing the full-length version loud and clear enough across the yards when he wanted help with something. In unguarded moments I'd heard him call him *son*.

"We can't afford to run this, Nichol."

Thanks for fixing it. Well done. My usual reflex of hurt and irritation didn't fire. I'd met Cam's eyes when we'd finally managed to wrestle the plates back onto their hinge, and the satisfaction I'd seen there would do for me.

"Well, when you turned Kenzie off, you said it was him or

the coal bill. I reckoned we should use the coal." There. Highland logic to match his own. Waste not, want not, use everything and squeeze the last penny. "I know we can't keep it going all the time. But it won't hurt the house to heat it through from time to time, keep off the damp."

He looked as if he was about to argue. Then his face cleared oddly of expression and he sat down, the dogs running promptly to their places round his chair. "Aye. Your mother would have said the same."

I shifted awkwardly. He had leaned forward to rest his elbows on his knees, as if seeking relief from inner pain. I'd have touched any other man, asked him what was wrong. How was it that I couldn't reach a hand to my last living relative? "Granda? Is something the matter?"

He jerked upright. "Aye! It's half six at night, and I haven't had a crumb to eat since breakfast. What use are you anyway, if you cannae have dinner on the table when a man gets home?"

I nodded, relieved. "Hardly any use at all, Granda. It won't be long."

Backing off, I joined Cam by the sink. "Do you mind," he asked me in an undertone, "when he talks to you like a downtrodden 1960s housewife?"

I grabbed the peeler he passed me and started work on the potatoes. "Not so much as when he treats me like a serious young farmer and the heir to all his acres. That's when I'm really in trouble."

"You don't fancy it, then—your predestined lot? Ruler of all you survey?"

"God, no." I shivered. "That was meant to be Alistair's job. Give me back my study and my student digs. I like—oh, I don't know. Cities. Bright lights. Raunchy hip-grinding music in clubs."

"Yeah? Well, we can manage the music for you." He switched on the radio. "This picks up Radio 1 between bursts of Sheep Shit FM, doesn't it?"

I shot a furtive glance across the room. Harry was still

seated in state by the fire. His back was to us, but I could see the top of his head, the listening tips of his ears. "Better not. His lordship doesn't care for it." I raised my voice slightly. "And he only pretends to be deaf."

But I didn't switch the music off. Cameron had it down low, and I couldn't resist the soft beat reaching out to me from London, through all those miles of static and sunset sky. I struggled to identify the track. Long time ago—late '90s. I'd only been a kid, but...

Cameron's hip brushed mine. No—a tiny bump, just on the off beat. "A Blur song, isn't it?" he whispered.

"Oh, yeah." The dark, insinuating intro rippled over my skin. The pulsing beat came again, and Cam, en route between fridge and cooker, took another dance step, jouncing my hip once more. I chuckled. "That's right. What are you up to?"

"Blur, 'Trimm Trabb'. I saw them play it a couple of years ago, at T in the Park."

Another bump, soft and sly, dead on time. The track got down to its good, scratchy, dirty-rock business, and on Cam's next pass I intercepted him, stepping round his back, giving him a push with my arse. "T in the Park—what, back in 2009? I was there for that. Maybe we walked past each other in the crowd."

"No."

"Why not?"

"Because I wouldn't have walked past you."

My heart turned over. I couldn't look at him. Grinning, I let him take me by the hand and tug me in a short, sharp diagonal across the flagstones. I was dancing to Blur with a beautiful guy in my own kitchen—maybe island life had something to be said for it after all. *I wouldn't have walked past.* Still I couldn't meet his eyes, though I sensed that his were fixed on me. Suddenly the signal cleared and bass and soaring electric guitar blasted out into the room.

I choked with laughter. "God, Cam—turn it down."

"No."

I spun round. That was Harry, gruff as the bark of a dog. He hadn't stirred in his chair, but I saw to my amazement that one of his gnarled old hands was flapping, beating time.

"What?"

"Let yon lad have his music. I've heard worse. He's got better taste than you, Nichol, with your foulmouthed songs about tractors."

So we proceeded to have supper—me, my grandfather, Cam and Shona's three farmhands—while the Zane Low show played in the background. I was too astonished to mind the old man's sudden relenting, even if since my earliest teen years he'd forbidden me the radio, my CD player, even an iPod with headphones on if he thought it was taking my mind off my work.

We were a peaceful group round the table, the lads chatting enough to let me entertain my thoughts in silence. It didn't take me long to build a little world where Harry, who clearly was already half-charmed, became so fond of Cameron he didn't bat an eyelid on finding out for sure he was not only *gille-toine* but in love with his *gille-toine* grandson. So fond that Alistair's shadow vanished from my life, because Harry had a replacement, someone he could care for just as much, and I could drop back into my old accustomed place—second-best, tolerated, never make a farmer of me but that didn't matter...

"Nichol?"

I blinked and came back to surface. Cameron was watching me, smiling and frowning. "You all right?"

"Yes. Sorry. Woolgathering."

"Well, you're in the right place for it."

I sat up, stretching, stifling a yawn. Shona's boys were saying good night and gathering their things. I responded politely, told them to come and get their breakfast the next day. If Shona wouldn't let me pay them, I could at least keep them fed. I saw them out and came back to the kitchen, ready to tackle the washing up. Cameron was clearing the table. Harry was struggling to open the window, whether in reaction to the still-lovely evening outside or a protest against the Aga's new warmth, I wasn't sure. I went to help him, and together we pushed up the cobwebbed old sash. Cool, sweet air swept in, rich with sea salt and gorse and the heady-scented thyme that was beginning to spread its cushions on the cliff-top turf.

Harry leaned his elbows on the sill. He said, slowly, as if to himself, "*Bidh am beithe deagh-bholtrach, urail, dosrach nan càrn.*"

I picked up a tea towel. If Cam was washing up, I would dry and vice versa, a quiet routine we'd wordlessly established from his first day here. The old man's words sang in my head. My memory reached out for their sequel, though surely I'd forgotten it. Twenty years or more since Harry had stood me between his knees and read mac Mhaighstir's poetry to me.

But something remained. It was as deep in me as the urge to join in with Cameron's dance. It was something to do with red-gold light from the west, the promise it held of longer days, island waters brightening from grey to teal and seal-blue—yes, of *an t-samhraidh*, Gaelic summer, distilled and held safe in a poem like a song.

I smiled, took the glass Cam handed me and said, "*Ri maoth-bhlàs driùchd Cèitein.*"

"Wow. What's that?"

"A poem of Alasdair mac Mhaighstir Alasdair's. *Òran an t-Samhraidh*, the 'Song of Summer'. He lived on the mainland northwest of here, up at Ardnamurchan. I didn't know I remembered."

Harry turned a little in the window. "You do, though, don't you? *Mar ri caoin-dheàrrsadh grèine...*"

"*Brùchdadh barraich roi gheugaibh.*"

"Aye." Nodding, Harry limped over to a seldom-touched bookshelf in the corner. He took down a slim blue volume, its cover worn with age and use. As usual when I'd pleased him he was acting like I wasn't there, gesturing with the book towards Cam. "He sucked it up like a wee sponge, laddie—that and any other *Gàidhlig* I taught to him. Not like his fidgety brother. Nothing stuck in that lad's head unless it had wheels or wool. Nichol, now—he spoke it better than English by the time he was seven."

Well, this beat being the focus of burning scrutiny for my sins. To Cam I was still visible, anyway—he was watching me intently. "Could you?"

"Yes, I think so. But I've lost it all since."

Harry banged the book down onto the table. "If ye have, it's for want of practice. And running away to stuff your head full of every language but your own, as if there's any call for one man to know so many tongues."

As if there's any call for bloody Gaelic. I bit it back—didn't want to lob that hand grenade—but other protests rose, resentments I'd thought I'd set aside. "Granda, I'd had a job offer from the UN as an interpreter."

He stared at me. I'd never spelled out for him—never intended to—the price I'd paid for leaving Edinburgh. What was the point? There'd been no choice. A silence fell, the more dreadful for the sounds of spring twilight drifting through the open window. In a calm frame of mind, I'd have done anything rather than wound him, because to my plunging dismay he did look hurt, his weather-beaten all-year tan washing to an unhealthy grey. I didn't know how to back down.

Cameron slid the dish he'd been rinsing into the rack. He dried his hands on a tea towel, calm and casual, as if the air in the room hadn't been about to catch fire. He came to lean on the sink unit beside me. "Really? Which languages?"

I shrugged. I'd heard my ability called a gift, but I'd never been able to see it that way. To me it seemed strange that other people lacked it. "Oh, you name it. The usual stuff—French, Spanish, Italian. I can manage a couple of Eastern Europeans at a push. And Greek. Russian."

"Bloody hell."

"It's not a big deal. I...I wouldn't have taken that UN job anyway. I was studying linguistics—why languages develop, how they fit together. That's what interests me."

"I'm not surprised you lost some of your Gaelic."

But I haven't. That was what I wanted to say to Harry. *I remember every word you taught me, in here with the book and out on the moors and the shore where you pointed to* dobhar, *the otter,* iasg-dearg, *the salmon, the eagle* iolair *whose name you pronounced like the upward yearning of wings*—oh-lia, oh-lia.

I couldn't get my mouth open. Instead I went to the table and sat down. I kept a couple of chairs between me and Harry, and I let the streaming sunlight block him out too, a dazzling curtain through my eyelashes. I picked up the book, fingertips easily finding the place for the *Òran*.

"It's probably more mislaid than lost," I said—to Cam, not to Harry. Retraction and forgiveness weren't how we dealt with one another. We snarled like wolves then returned stolidly to our pack life. "I couldn't forget these poems—not when I was taught them so young."

"Can I have a look?"

"Yeah, of course."

He came and sat next to me, close enough that I could feel his warmth but leaving a safe inch clear for Harry's sake. "Which part did you just say?"

"These lines here. It's hard to do justice to them in English, but it's something like the fragrant birch tree is branching over the cairn, damp with soft dew, warm in the sunshine, the fresh young buds on its boughs."

Cam ran a finger down the page. I wondered if there was something in his blood, as there had been in mine, which let him find in the strange words the shapes of familiar things. Animals, sunlight, trees, sea and sky. A language born when there had been little but these things to describe, and tightly bound up with them still.

"Will you read it again?" Cam asked softly.

"Yes, sure." There was a feather drifting on the table's surface—Clover's work, no doubt, and at some point I'd find the rest of the poor bird. I picked it up and trailed the tip of it along the lines as I read, so he could see where I was. Finishing, I drew the feather back lightly, as if by accident—over the roots of his nails. "There. Better in the original, isn't it?"

"Lovely. You do realise, though—there's not a single letter in all that you pronounced the way it's written."

I smiled. Yes, that was Gaelic for you—wrapping you in mists right from the start, from the motorway signs on the border that said *failte—welcome*—and were meant to come out of your mouth as *fawl-cha*. "Yes, I know. That's part of the beauty of it somehow, part of how it keeps its music. It's not as hard to pick up as you'd think, once you know the sounds."

Beauty. Music. I still couldn't look at Harry, but from the corner of my eye I saw that his grip on the chair had relaxed. I couldn't forget the poems, not when I was taught them so young. *Did you hear me, old man? It's the nearest I can come to saying sorry.* I turned the page. The summer poem was long, a great cadenced paean to life such as only a man who'd lived through West Isles winters could sing. Softly I began the next verse. Harry stood listening for a few moments longer then quietly walked out of the kitchen, pulling the door shut behind him.

I stopped reading. Reverently I closed the book, and I drew a deep breath. "It's you that wants to be working for the bloody UN, not me."

"What?"

"You stopped us from having a fight."

"Oh." Cameron made a wry face. He rested his elbow against mine, closing up that safe inch. "Sorry. I meant to be subtle."

"Oh, you were. I didn't even realise what you were doing until it worked. Anyway, why are you apologising?"

"You might need to fight him."

"I do. But I don't need to hurt him, not over..." I stroked the book's faded cover. "Not over stuff like this."

"So you are, in fact, fluent in Gaelic as well as half a dozen other languages."

"I'm afraid so, yes."

"God almighty. Why are you hiding all that under your bushel?"

"It's not that much use to me here. And I couldn't afford to go back, even if—even if things were different." I smiled, trying to shake off my regrets. "It was a nice intervention. Thanks."

"You're welcome."

We sat quietly in the gathering dusk. I kept turning the pages of the mac Mhaighstir book, but I wasn't seeing them anymore. My thoughts drifted. Far off across the moors, a curlew gave the first three notes of a flight song that would soon grow to crescendo and cascade down through the island skies all summer. Cam was pressing his shoulder to mine. *I wouldn't have walked past you,* he'd said. Any second now, if I turned to face him, he would kiss me. There was no possible reason why not...

"Come on, then. We'd best get started on the late rounds."

I bumped back to earth. His shoulder had just been companionable. While I'd been thinking how his mouth would feel on mine, he—the monster Harry and I had created—had been worrying about feeding schedules. I got up quickly. Dignity was better than nothing. "God, yes. I hadn't realised how late it was."

And yet, in the deep part of the night, I thought he'd changed his mind. I wasn't sure what had woken me. I lay flat on my back, watching the shift of ash-twig shadows on the ceiling, cast there by a slender new moon. Clover and her brood were absent on a hunting trip, so for once I had the bed to myself. I was warm and clean, having spent about an hour up to my armpits in Aga-heated bathwater, carefully washing every chilly, neglected inch of myself. There'd been plenty for Cameron after me, and probably the tank would have stretched to a third, though Harry hadn't shown himself again after supper and had more than likely washed in the burn to remind us what a pair of poofs we were.

I smiled in the darkness, tucking my hands behind my head and stretching. If Harry and I weren't careful, life might become something other than a hellish crawl from one day to the next, and what would we do then?

A board creaked in the corridor outside my room. I sat up. I'd left my door off the catch so the cat could push it open if she wished. "Clover, *cagaran?*"

"No. Just me. I'm sorry."

"Cam." The door inched open a little way. "It's all right. Come in. What's the matter?"

"I..." Gingerly Cam let himself into the room. He closed the door behind him and stood in the moonlight, his back pressed to the wall. "Okay. This is really fucking stupid. I heard a noise."

Instantly my mind was full of Glasgow villains come to drag him off. Well, they'd have to go through me. I'd locked Al's gun away, but I knew where to find it. I swung my legs out of the bed. "What kind of noise? Where from?"

He held out a hand. It wasn't quite steady, I noted, and he was terribly pale. "Nothing bad. At least...nothing human, far as I could make out. Nic, is this place haunted?"

The first time he'd shortened my name. An odd time for it, but it was sweet to me, sweet as my short-lived first thoughts on hearing his voice. "Well, if anywhere ought to be, I suppose this is it," I said, tucking my feet back in. I remembered my folded-up jacket on the bench, the sound of Caitlin's voice in the kitchen. "But not as far as I know. Why? What did you hear?"

"Hard to describe. Maybe I dreamed it. It was like some lost soul howling, like..." His eyes went wide. "Christ, like that."

It took me a second to work out what was bothering him. I was so used to the cry rising softly from beyond the windows— pitching up into a scream then dying back into mournful, musical silence—that I barely heard it anymore. Like breeding owls and the night-time mutter of ewes over their lambs, it had always been part of my childhood song of spring. I broke into laughter. "Cam, you pussy. That's a great northern diver out on the Sound."

"A what?"

"A bird. The Americans call them loons."

"You're kidding me. No way is that a fucking bird."

"Honest."

"What's...?" The call came again, echoing up from the sea. To me it was exquisite, opening the space between water and heaven, bearing the sense of that huge vacancy down to me in my safe human world. "What's wrong with it?"

"Nothing. That's its love song. Pretty sexy stuff as far as Mrs. Loon's concerned... Honestly, Cam, look at the state of you. Come here."

He let go his backed-up stance against the wall and came to me uncertainly. He had on a pair of my pyjama bottoms but was naked from the waist up, gooseflesh crawling. When I reached to take his hand, he was ice cold, and I realised the temperature had plummeted, stealing hard-won heat from the house through its ancient rafters.

"Want to come in for a minute? Get warmed up?"

He hesitated then nodded, and I gave his hand a little tug.

"Come on, then. It's okay."

He closed his eyes as if about to take a plunge. Well, I was unknown waters. Shifting over for him, I tried to show him they were safe. Shallow, if he wanted. Just a warm body in a bed. I put out an arm, and he stretched out awkwardly beside me. I couldn't fathom the sound he made as he laid his head on my shoulder. There was relief in it—frustration and fear too. I was at once glad and sorry I was wearing a T-shirt, that I couldn't feel the brush of his lips on my bare skin.

"What's up?" I whispered, gently ruffling his hair.

"I feel stupid now."

"Don't. *I'll* never remind you you were scared out of bed by a waterfowl."

He chuckled painfully. "Great."

"More to it than a bird, though, isn't there? Why are you so frightened?"

"I have bad dreams."

As if on cue, the diver raised its lonely cry again. Cameron shivered and hid his face.

"It's okay," I told him, pulling him close. "I tell you what we'll do. Tomorrow we'll go for a walk and find one of the damn things. Once you've heard it by daylight it won't bother you anymore."

"We don't have time for walks, do we?"

"We'll make time. Okay?"

He nodded. His hair had survived its chemical assault and moved softly against my cheek. It smelled of the Ivory soap my ma had also bought in bulk and stored in heaped-up boxes in the cupboard. I probably smelled of the same, but on him I could detect it, catalysed by his body chemistry into something exotic and new. Shyly he slipped an arm around my waist.

I turned a little to face him, to welcome him. Mercifully the sheets and quilt had bunched up between us at hip level. I hated myself for getting an erection when he'd only come to me for comfort, but the more I thought about it the worse it became, so I tried for deep breaths and conversation. "What do you dream about?"

"I never remember."

That was a lie. I didn't know why I was so certain, except that I was fairly sure that since his arrival, he'd told me as much of the truth as he could, and this sounded different. I stroked his ribs. They were still too prominent, but he was getting there. I didn't want him to be starved, or cold, or afraid.

Forgetting myself, I kissed the top of his head. "I wish I could help you."

"You do help me. So much more than I could ever have

expected, you and your grandfather both. I could never..."

He faded off. I felt him twitch in my embrace, tensions building. I wondered if he was having the same problem I was, and briefly prayed it was so—I could lift the tangled bedclothes away then, entwine our limbs, end our dance in flaring heat and fireworks. "What is it?"

"Harry. What time does he get up?"

"Not for a couple of hours yet. And he doesn't do a bed check, so..."

"You wouldn't want him finding out, though."

"There's nothing to find." *Not so far, anyway.* "Don't stress about him. Why does he worry you so much?"

"He doesn't. Just... Are you even out to him?"

"No. I never found anyone it was worth having the row with him about." *Oh, not so far anyway. Not until now.* I wanted to say it. No matter how he felt about me, no matter how painfully I might strand myself. Somebody had to make the first move. "Listen. If I'd met you in the crowd at T in the Park, I wouldn't have walked past you either. I..."

"I should go."

I drew a breath to protest. Already he was easing back from me, though, detaching himself. "Cam, don't let the old man bother you. I will talk to him, if you—"

"No. It's nothing to do with him." He rolled away from me and got up. For a second I thought he was going to walk straight off, but then he turned and looked down at me unhappily, arms folded tight over his chest. "You probably think I'm a cocktease. I can't explain."

"A... God, no. No such thing. Don't run off."

"I can't stay. I can't explain."

I lay propped on one elbow, looking at the door he'd silently drawn shut behind him. I thought about going after him. I was afraid he'd throw his things into his rucksack and disappear as swiftly as he had arrived, and I wasn't sure what lengths I'd now go to prevent that. He wasn't a cocktease, no. But he was bloody beautiful, and I was starting to fall for him.

There were no creaks on the stairs, no rattle of the outside lock. He was still here. So was I—alone in my room, wide awake now, with a hard-on so vigorous there was only one way out. Damn, I hadn't meant to. Even here by myself it felt like a betrayal, a broken promise, because I'd really meant to offer him nothing but warmth and my bed, and now my mind was quickly recreating him, sketching him back into place, short, vivid strokes. I pulled back the bedclothes that had sealed us off from one another and plunged down into the place where he had been, grabbing my cock, already starting to come. I groaned out his name to the space between the pillows. Muscles in my backside and thighs bunched powerfully, and I thrust and thrust and climaxed much harder than ever I had on my own, sobbing with the force of it.

I lay facedown, lungs heaving, aftermath twitches running through me. My solitary endeavours often left me depressed, but not this time. This time a weird joy was pulsing in my veins—that I could still fly that high, feel so much. And that had been only for the fantasy of Cam, the idea of him. The reality would be... I couldn't imagine. Maybe I wouldn't always have to—I was beginning to think we might get there, that his problems weren't with me. No, this time I was just going to fall asleep, my hand still wedged beneath me. I couldn't even move out of my wet patch.

My last coherent thought was that at least these days only I ever had to wash the sheets. I buried my face in the crook of my elbow and dropped into smiling oblivion.

Chapter Seven

Harry looked at me in astonishment when, the next day, I told him I wanted a few hours off. Not for a shopping run to Brodick or any of my permitted off-site activities, but to go for a walk with Cameron.

"A walk?" he echoed, as if I'd asked him in Dutch. I understood his confusion. Men who worked the land seldom felt the need to stride about it in their leisure hours, just as it sometimes took an outsider to remind us that our moorlands and sunsets were beautiful.

I could tell he was bewildered by my choice of companion too. After my conversation with Cam the night before, I was reluctant to hide. I considered coming clean. *Actually, Granda, I'd like to go for a walk with a lad I really fancy. The thing is, I'm gay, and so is he, and I think if we had some time together and he could chill out a bit, the pair of us might stand a chance. It would be really great if we could have your blessing because, for some unknowable reason, he seems to think the world of you.*

I said, shoving my hands into my pockets and looking at the ground, "It's a nice day, that's all. Everything's done around here. We'll, er, go down past the forestry plantation and check the fences while we're there."

Even that had been tough enough. I went to find Cam, who was struggling with a baling machine in the yard. He looked up as I approached. There were shadows under his eyes, as delicate as the sea-violet colours in them. "You all right, Nichol?"

"Yeah, fine. Come on. We're going for a walk."

"Harry wanted me to try and fix this."

"Fix it later. Come on, while it's still sunny." I set off down the track. At first I thought he wouldn't follow, then I heard him running to catch up.

He fell into step beside me. "I think I like it when you take charge."

"Sorry. Didn't mean to sweep you off. But I said we were going to have a walk, and we're having one."

"Won't Harry mind? Not about you, I mean. But I'm the hired help."

"Even farmhands get holidays. And you look tired. Did you sleep last night, after...?"

"After I got the creeps and came jumping into your bed?"

"Yeah. You know, there really was no need for you to jump back out."

"I know. No, I didn't get much sleep after that. My bed was cold, and those bloody birds of yours kept it up until dawn."

"Next time stay."

We followed the track uphill to the place where it met the road. I reminded him, townie that he was, to walk on the right. There was scarcely any traffic, but the long straight stretch tempted men in white vans to drive at stupid speeds, and it was best to see them coming. Deep culverts lined the road, their banks now bright with primroses. Beyond a touch to his arm from time to time to keep him from slipping, I kept careful distance.

We walked in a silence broken only by lark song and the curious electrical chirring of lapwings. After half a mile or so the seaward view to our left became obscured by pine trees, a straggle of saplings in protective tubes at first then great dark ranks of them, blocking out the sun. Ahead of us was the sign for the Board of Forestry's Claigeann plantation. We crossed the road and entered the shadows, the sound of the wind and the lapwings fading away. Cameron fell back a little. When I turned, he was looking up into the sunless canopy.

"What is it?"

"Why can't I hear the birds anymore?"

"The pines shade out everything underneath them. Other trees and undergrowth don't stand a chance. There's a few types of bird that can live on the needles and cones, but not many."

"It's a bit eerie, isn't it? Oppressive."

I smiled. "No pleasing you, is there? Last night you didn't like the birds. Don't worry, we're not going to walk through here." I guided him past the information kiosks and maps for the trails the Board had put in to try and make the place tourist friendly. A narrow rocky path led sharply up out of the car park. "Claigeann means a rock like a skull. That's all this was when Al and I were kids, just bare rock. We used to come climbing. Then the Board planted it up, but you can still get through and out this way. Come on."

We were breathless by the time we broached the ridge. I let Cam walk ahead of me so he would get the first, best surprise of the view, and I tried not to think of all the places up ahead and all the ways I could try to persuade him there would be no harm in loving me. I'd tell him he was safe, that no one could hurt him now. That, if he wanted, there need not be strings, or chains, or whatever else he feared—though I questioned my own honesty on that last point. I couldn't imagine letting him go as things were now. How would I feel once I'd found out how his come tasted, once I'd opened up my flesh to let him in?

Sternly I restrained my thoughts. The idea was not to pressure him, to let him find his way to me. If there was a sheltered half circle of soft mossy turf on the edge of the cliffs, warm enough after a springtime like this to have honeysuckle tumbling over the rocks, that was just too bad. We were out for a walk. I was going to find and show him a great northern diver, and that was all.

He took off his jacket and slung it over his arm. He was getting into better shape, but this climb was challenging him—I could hear him breathing, fast and deep. I now had such a riveting view of his backside that I forgot about the vista ahead, the one I'd brought him here to see, and when he stopped I crashed into him, instinctively grabbing hold of him to keep from knocking him down.

He didn't seem to mind that. My arms went round his waist, and he seized my wrists, laughing, as if he wanted to keep them there. "What's wrong with you, you great ned?"

"Sorry. Miles away. I nearly sent you off the bloody cliff."

"Yeah." He was still hanging on. "Way to go, though. What a view."

"Pretty good, isn't it?" From here, the northward side of the Skull rock, Machrie Bay opened out in a great green crescent, fringed by gleaming sand. Only a few white crofts interrupted its salt-marsh wildness. The water of Kilbrannan Sound, crystalline jade by the shore, soon plunged to black, sprinkled all over with wind-driven wave crests. I could feel the press of Cam's backside against the top of my thighs. I was just a little taller than he was, and more broadly built—he fitted there sweetly, as if we'd been designed in two long-separated parts and were finally clicking together.

The breeze shifted. The scent of the sea rode up on its warmth. Salt, thyme and a strange coconut honey from the gorse just starting to come into serious flower on the cliffs...

Tears suddenly stung my eyes. Making sure Cam was steady, I let him go.

"Nichol? You okay?"

"Yes. Yeah, of course." Was I? I couldn't think of any reason to be otherwise—beautiful afternoon like this, the world spread out at my feet. My stomach had gone tight, though. Something to do with that particular scent in the air. I'd never encountered it anywhere else, not in just that plangent combination of flowers and water and earth. "You know, I haven't been here in years."

"Why? It's so beautiful."

"I think the last time was with Al." I didn't think. I knew. The last time was with Al because I used to come here all the time with him, even when we were older and not getting on well anymore. We'd come out here and find our truce, a temporary peace, in the clean sea air. It was Al's favourite place. We'd even managed a day out here, a scramble around on the rocks, during my last holiday from university, when he'd spent the entire evening before carping at me about what an effete academic I'd become, afraid to get my hands dirty now around the farm. By the time we'd got home we'd been friends.

There was a fence on the far side of the track. It was a beautiful sturdy forestry one, far better than Harry and I could afford. Well, I'd told him I'd take a look. I went and leaned both hands on it. Yes, solid—far more so than anything else in this spinning, badly made world. I wondered if I'd eaten something wrong at lunchtime. If, for the first time in my life, I was going to faint.

Last year's birch leaves rustled, the golden trail of them that lined the edge of the track. I tensed. Desperately as I'd craved Cam's touch, just now I couldn't have borne for anyone to lay a finger on me. He seemed to sense that and took up a place by my side, leaning his back on the fence and looking out towards Kintyre. I lowered my head until my brow was resting on the wood of the top bar. I clenched one hand round the back of my skull, which felt as if it wanted to blow apart.

"How the fuck can he be dead?" My voice sounded strange to me, hoarse and raw. "You saw his room. Everything's the same. How can he not be...here?"

"I don't know."

Of course he didn't. What a stupid fucking thing to ask him. Me, I'd have come out with some nervous platitude or other, probably—*you'll get used to it* or *yeah, it's a funny old world*. By contrast, *I don't know* seemed sensible. Almost a relief.

"And my ma. Harry's got her room locked up but that's a shrine too. Her clothes. Her hairbrush. How can she not need them anymore? How can she be...?" *In bits on a back road in Spain*, that was going to end, but I couldn't speak. My field of vision was fringed with black, red glitter starting to cover the rest.

"Did you see the bodies?"

I flinched in shock. The question's blunt force swept my eyes clear, let me get a breath into my lungs. "No. There wasn't enough left."

"Then you'll probably never get your head round it. I don't know what's best—to believe it completely or not."

I never cried. Whether it had been growing up with a tough and sarcastic big brother or a grandfather who looked with astounded contempt upon all signs of weakness, I didn't know, but I'd lost my capacity for tears. If I'd been on my own here, without the weird safety valves Cam's words provided, I might have thrown up or passed out or lost the back of my skull in some mystical biochemical explosion and left Harry to clear up the remnants of his last kinsman.

My lungs heaved dryly. Hard silent waves of tension went through me, spasms that squeezed shut my eyes and tore at the muscles of my gut. The ordeal continued for a time I couldn't measure until Cam began stroking my back—the lightest touch, just up and down between my shoulder blades—restoring pattern, rhythm, something to follow.

Involuntarily I began to breathe in time, one harsh gasp and then another. I let go my death grip on the fence. "I...didn't even like him all that much."

"He was your brother. I'm so sorry, Nic. About your ma too."

I straightened. Sky and trees spun round me for a second then settled down, put in their place by the warmth of his arm round my waist.

"Thanks. I'm all right now." I wondered who he had lost, to know so much about seeing bodies or not. A grandfather, I decided. Only a man with that sort of gap inside him would put up with Harry as he did. "Come on. I was meant to be taking you on this amazing walk."

"So you can, when you don't look like you've been hit with a bag of wet sand. It looks nice down there. Let's just go and sit for a while."

Down there. Yes, that was where I'd wanted to take him—the cliff's-edge patch of turf, shining in the sunshine ahead of us. I'd been right about the honeysuckle. It was pouring over the rocks in a crazy profusion, as if the island had been putting out flags for a royal visitor. I'd had such plans for him, in that sheltered half circle, with only the gulls and the coal-eyed fulmars to watch. I'd have found and stilled all his fears. I knew what I was doing, after my apprenticeship in Edinburgh, after all those boyfriends. I'd have pleased him from the top of his bleached head to the soles of his healed-up feet.

And now I could barely walk. He had to help me the few yards down the track. My bones ached dryly, the way they had during my last bout of flu. The worst of it was that I would have to explain myself. He was too kind a lad to let an outburst like that go untended. He'd want me to talk about it, pull more thorns out of me, and I knew that would be for the best. *Talk to me about it,* the college counsellor had said to me. *You've just lost your family. React.* I'd sat in silence, my head and heart vacant. Walked out, packed my rucksack, caught the ferry home.

Cameron aided me over a tumble of stones and steered me to the foot of the very rock where I always sat when I'd come here alone over the years, to read and watch the birds and see how many languages I could argue with myself in. Apart from my tasks around the farm, I'd been very free.

Cam unfastened his jacket from around his waist and laid it on the turf. "There. Sit down."

I wanted to argue—the coat was the nice lightweight fleece he'd bought from the farm store, and I didn't want it damp—but I didn't trust my voice. I was afraid that raw-throated monster might come back. Still, in a minute I would try and talk to him. If he was determined to help me, I would make an effort to be helped. I sank down gratefully, leaning my back against the sun-warmed stone. He came and sat on a low rock beside me, and I braced for questions.

"So...that forestry land we just walked through. Does that adjoin your grandfather's?"

I glanced up at him. He had tenderly settled me down, and his hand was on my shoulder, but his attention was fixed on the slope above us, his deep blue gaze assessing. I found I could speak after all. "Yes. In fact I think it still belongs to him."

"It does? What's so funny?"

"Nothing. The land's only leased to the Board. We're still responsible for the boundaries, so remind me to look at the fences on the way back."

"Okay. Do you get anything back for the timber they produce?"

"I don't think so. Alistair set the deal up. He always handled that kind of thing."

He'd made me look towards the plantation too. My head tipped back. The pounding pressure in it eased as my skull came to rest against his thigh. His fingers brushed through my hair, just once, brow to crown, and I relaxed.

"You look tired, Nic."

"I'm fine. Gimme a minute and we'll go on. There's a cliff walk down to the caves then three miles of beach, and I'll take you for tea at a nice pub in Auchagallon if you're up for it."

"Or you could just close your eyes. It's all right. I'm here."

"That's just it. I meant to make the most of you."

I felt the ripple of his amusement, a twitch in the muscle where my cheek rested. "Some other time, eh, Romeo?"

"If you knew how often we were gonna get time off together round here, you wouldn't..." I caught my breath. Up from beyond one of the great stark ribs of rock that reached from the beach out to sea, a cry arose. Three notes, the first two a musical sob and the third a wild reach heavenwards, a call to wake up God. Cam's hand went still on my head. I pointed down towards the glittering waters. "There's your night monster, love."

I hadn't meant to call him that. It had fallen from me so

naturally that maybe he wouldn't notice. The Celtic language groups had a range of endearments that passed easily from man to man, and still influenced English speakers within their old domains, like a Dubliner's *darlin'* to his best mate, perfectly acceptable. *That's right, Nichol. You explain that to him.*

"More like a mermaid than a monster now."

He didn't sound perturbed. His fingers had resumed their movement through my hair.

"It's odd you should say that," I said, a little dryly. "You know the town Lamlash, just down the road from here? It's named after Arran's local saint—in a way, anyway. He was called Molaise, and his island was Eilean Molaise, which nobody could pronounce, and over the years it got boiled down to Elmolaise, Limolas, Lamlash... Anyway, he wasn't a bad sort as far as Christian saints go—didn't chop down the groves or turn the merry dancing girls into circles of stone—but he couldn't abide all the mermaids."

"The mermaids, eh? Were there a lot of them back then?"

"Oh, yes. Ten a penny, singing their hearts out on the rocks, with all their bonny bosoms on display. So he turned them into birds, and the only thing left of them was their song."

"It seems a shame."

"Yeah. My ma says they were only fooling him, though. Just humouring poor old Molaise so he wouldn't be bothered by thoughts of their attractions in his lonely cell at night. She told me she once saw one turn back."

"She must have been quite something."

"She was. She..."

If I began telling Cam what had been extraordinary about my mother, the cramping pain would start again. I could feel it trying now—coiling in my guts, clenching an iron grip round my lungs. I couldn't do it again.

He leaned close over me, drawing my fringe back from my brow. "Tell me all about her later. Sleep for a little bit now."

"I don't need to sleep." The dance of the sun on the water

was hypnotic, though, a million flakes of gold continually shifting form. As I watched, a dark shape emerged from behind the spar of rock. He was sleek, majestic, the light flashing off his white breast. "There's the diver. See? That one's a male."

"Yes, I see him. Beautiful."

"And there's the female after him."

The lights were blurring. I leaned my head into Cameron's lap. He rubbed at the back of my neck, scratching lightly, and I shuddered, falling safely, letting go.

"There," he whispered, his mouth a moth brush over my ear. "The love song must've worked."

Chapter Eight

"Nicky Seacliff! You wee fucker!"

Not the most traditional Highland greeting. I came to a halt, shopping bags swinging in my hands. I recognised the voice. We were just outside the Hamilton, Kenzie's favourite pub in Brodick. Slowly I turned around. Oh, great—there he was on the pavement, his fists bunched by his sides. Pissed as a fart, his accent thickened by booze to a hairy, barely penetrable blanket. That was good going, I had to admit, for eleven o'clock on a Saturday morning.

"Hello, Kenzie," I tried. "You all right, then?"

"No, I am nae all right, you mockitt little queer."

I took a deep breath. You could score worse things than cheap Scotch in the Hamilton Arms. I set down my shopping bags. It was coming up to the middle of the busiest day in Arran's one busy town, and the street was full of passersby, neighbours, friends and tourists. I had to keep this low-key if I could. The worst of it was that I'd brought Cameron with me. He hadn't wanted to come, but I'd been feeling so much better that the thought of a day off the farm, a bit of shopping and a nice lunch out, had made me almost lightheaded. And I loved his company. I wanted to share my pleasures with him. It had been long enough now that he didn't have to worry about thugs from Glasgow spotting him, I was sure of that. I'd persuaded him. We'd jumped into Harry's old battered Toyota and torn off.

"Nichol, who is this guy?"

"Don't worry about him. Leave him to me."

"Has he no' told you about me, blondie? Has he no' said he turned me out of my living tae install your wee pansy arse?"

I flinched. An unwanted heat stirred inside me. He could sling mud at me if he wanted—not at Cam. "It's none of your business Kenzie, but he's a student, I'm not paying him. Anyway, in case it slipped your memory, my granda turned you off, not me."

"Och, a Seacliff's a Seacliff—all the damn same."

Were we? I hadn't thought we were that redoubtable a clan, especially now we were reduced to two. "I was sorry when Harry told me what he'd done, okay? I know you've got family."

That had been the wrong tack. Kenzie's eyes blazed, a sickly chemical light. Yeah, he was high—I could see the throb of his carotid from here. "The fuck you care about my family!"

The fuck you *care about them, if you're down here spending your benefit on crack.* "Do you want to come back and work for us for free?" I asked him roughly. "Because that's all we can afford."

"And you think that's all right, do ye? To turn off decent men if you can get the job done free?"

No, I didn't. I sighed and leaned down to pick up my shopping bags. I didn't think it was all right to farm out call-centre work to India, or all right to give Indian workers shit pay to do it. I didn't think *we can get it cheaper somewhere else* was ever fair, or in the long term sustainable. But I didn't have any answers.

"You've got a good right to be angry," I told him. "If times change and we can take you back, we will. I don't know what else to say to you. Come on, Cam."

I turned to walk away. People were losing interest, thank God, starting to go about their business. Public opinion had never meant much to me, but I hadn't meant to drag Cam here to get called names in the street.

"Jesus," I said, when he fell into step at my side. "Sorry about that."

"It wasn't your fault. Don't worry about my wee pansy arse. That guy—Kenzie—is he all right? He looked like he was off his face to me."

"Yeah, he's had a skinful, God knows what of. It is my fault in a way—I should've argued with Harry when he decided to—"

"Nichol, look out!"

His warning gave me time to whip round. Part way, anyway—Kenzie hit me on a diagonal, a flat-run rugby tackle that sent us both crashing to the kerb. I landed hard on my back. The air left my lungs in a harsh bark, and my bags of fresh salt block and sheep vitamins went flying. At least we hadn't made it to the supermarket yet and it wasn't Harry's meagre quart-a-month indulgence of Johnnie Walker getting smashed in the street. That would have pissed me off.

I was pissed off anyway. I lurched onto my hands and knees, coughing, shaking my head clear of stars. Kenzie had overdone it, shot over me and landed in the gutter.

"Kenzie, you twat!" I rasped. "Leave it alone!"

"Aye, you'd like that, wouldn't you, fairy boy?" He was scrambling upright. "Aye, I bloody know what you are! Yer granda may be blind, but I didn't knock around that farm for years and years and not see you screw the living daylights out of Archie bloody—"

Oh, no. I got there just in time, my backhand whack across his mouth, clumsy but a decent silencer. Half the people in this street knew Archie Drummond, and Archie had given up everything—myself included—for his secret. That gave me a peculiar right to keep it. Kenzie staggered back from me, snarling.

"Button it," I warned. "You're no holy angel yourself."

"Better a junkie than a fudgepacker."

"A *what?*" To laugh at him was a mistake. He wasn't in the mood. But for God's sake, here we were, two grown men brawling in the street in daylight, the Victorian majesty of Brodick Castle rising up behind us. Tinny bagpipe music drifting from the woollen-mill store across the road. "Kenzie, for God's sake. I haven't heard that one since high school."

"I'm gonna kill you, you piece of shit!"

He meant it. Whether it was him or the speed buzzing round in his system I didn't know, but this time when he went for me he hit me like a truck. I deflected his haymaker so that it only grazed my jaw. The impact carried, though, knocking me back against the wall of Malcolm's fish shop—brickwork not glass, thank God, or I'd have been laid out among the herring. He grabbed me by the shirtfront, ripping buttons, damn him. I'd dressed up a bit for today. When I shoved him off me, some of the fabric went with him. His next punch landed square in my gut.

He shoved his face into mine, his lips curling bestially. "You fucking faggot. Fight!"

I did my best with him. We weren't too badly matched in terms of strength. But I was sober, and I really didn't want this. I'd never been much with the punching and wrestling round my schoolmates had engaged in, and when you grew up with a brother like Al, you either took a gun to him or learned negotiation skills.

Peripherally I saw Cameron, backed flat against the wall. His face was white as bone. He looked sick, scared shitless. That was good, I told myself, ducking a roundhouse from Kenzie and landing a blow for myself. I didn't want him involved. Not his problem.

Kenzie flailed out and caught me on the bridge of the nose. Fat blue sparks exploded on my retina, blotting out the mundane Brodick street. God, maybe he *was* about to kill me. Who would stop him? Al was dead. Archie had left me. I was alone.

Kenzie got the drop on me, tackled me off the kerb and right out into the road.

Tyres screeched. Something shot past me. Just a blur, but Kenzie's weight vanished off my chest. Reflexively I rolled aside, got my arms and legs under me and sprang upright. A car was stopped two feet away from me, the driver's face behind the wheel a pale astonished oval. In the middle of the street—yes, bang on the white line, between one set of cat's-eyes and the next—Cameron was crouched over Kenzie's supine form.

I ran to him. I grabbed his fist between one savage punch and the next, hauled him up and back. Kenzie had his arms crossed in front of his face, as if he were warding off a demon.

"Cam! Stop it!"

But he twisted in my grasp like a wet wildcat, tore away from me and pounced again. This time when I grabbed him I couldn't pull him off. He got a blow past Kenzie's defences that made him yelp. Desperately I glanced around for some burly lad to help me out. I'd used to have friends in this damn town...

Ah, no—better still, a good Arran-bred woman. Belatedly I recognised the car, the huge beast of a Subaru Shona Clyde had acquired for herself after Jimmy's death. Shona scrambled out, her eyes wide. "Jesus, Nichol! I nearly ran you down."

"It's all right. Give us a hand here, will you?"

She looked delicate, but that was as far it went. She'd spent her adult life herding cows and giving her bastard of a husband as good as she got. She nodded curtly and waded in with me. I seized one of Cam's shoulders, and she took the other. Between us we hauled him bodily up and away from Kenzie, who after a moment flipped onto his front, scrambled upright and took off as fast as his legs would carry him. He threw us one terrified backward glance then disappeared, weaving into the crowd.

"Nichol, what the hell happened?"

I glanced at Shona. She still had a good firm lock on Cam, as did I. His face was quite expressionless, his eyes filled with wild sapphire lights. He looked scarcely human.

"Oh, Kenzie had a go at me," I told her. "Harry had to turn him off a few weeks ago."

"Aye. I heard he'd been running his mouth in the pubs. Are you okay? You're bleeding."

"Fine. He just popped me on the nose."

Cameron jerked in my arms and I tightened my grip. "Cam, for God's sake. It's okay. He's gone. This one went off like a firecracker, Sho."

"Well, he obviously..." She shut up and turned her clench of Cam's shoulder into more of an embrace. "Hey, you. What's his name? Cameron? Cameron, love, it's all right. Nicky's okay now. Nicky's okay."

I stared at her. She never called me Nicky. And Cam didn't need to be baby talked, did he—a man big and lairy enough to send a hopped-up thug like Kenzie running for his life. But he had stopped straining against my grip.

He blinked and wiped a hand across his eyes, visibly coming back. "I saw blood," he said, turning to Shona. "I just saw his blood."

"I know. It's a nosebleed, that's all. Isn't it, Nichol?"

"Er...yes," I agreed distractedly. She gave him a little push towards me, as if handing him over. I put an arm around him. "That's right. Come away now, sunshine."

"I'd best go, unless you lads want a lift anywhere. I'm stopping traffic."

"No, we're okay. Thanks for helping. And..." I glanced back at her car, still at an angle in the road. "And for braking in time."

"My pleasure." She stopped on her way into the driver's seat. She gave me a once-over and a bright grin, and I realised my shirt was hanging open. "You want to be careful, Nichol Seacliff. Next time someone tells me that I ought to marry you, I might just listen."

I guided Cam away. He came with me passively. On the kerb, I stopped to pick up our scattered shopping, and he helped me. As he tucked the boxes back into the bag I was holding, I saw the tremor of his hands. He was breathing too fast. He wouldn't look at me.

I took him gently by the wrist. "Come with me for a second. Come on."

An alleyway ran down between Castle Street and the seafront road. A few yards into its shadows, when I could hear the seagulls and get a glimpse of the mill-pond blue of the bay, I stopped. Cam leaned against the wall. He was definitely shivering now, probably in the backlash of whatever adrenaline surge had turned him from terrified bystander into my unsuspected secret weapon. What had he said to Shona? *I saw his blood.*

I turned to him. "Cameron, you nutcase."

I'd have taken him into my arms. As soon as he read my intention, he grabbed me by the shoulders, holding me back. Finally his eyes met mine. They were frightened, dark with a plea I couldn't interpret. "I'm sorry."

"I was handling him, okay?" As soon as the lie was out, I reviewed it. "Well, no. He was beating the crap out of me. But you can't... You can't flip out like that, not over a stupid street fight. I thought you were going to kill him."

"Don't." He let go one of my shoulders and briefly pressed cold fingers to my mouth. He was focussing now, beginning to see me. Releasing his grip on me, he tugged lightly at the torn-open fastenings of my shirt then suddenly ran his fingertips down my chest, making me shudder. "Are you all right?"

"Fine," I said hoarsely. I was meant to be giving him a telling-off—couldn't have him wreaking chaos in the streets of Brodick every time something upset him—but all my words had melted away. He had leaned his brow against mine. All I wanted was to hold him, crush his skinny frame against my own strength until whatever fears plagued him were gone. Why couldn't I? The barriers were still there, intangible and barbed, higher than ever now. Worse, I was a hypocrite. I loved that he'd dashed to my rescue, bloody loved it. Right or wrong, I bloody loved that he'd been ready to beat Kenzie to death for me.

I kissed him through the barricade, just once on the brow. "Listen," I whispered. "Thank you. You can't do it again, but...thank you." We stood together in the gull song and the iridescent air, full of subtle sea lights even in this alley. Arran was always like that, I remembered. I remembered, for the first time in years, that I loved it. "Shall we just go home?"

He'd found a handkerchief in one of his pockets. Absently, as if tending a child, he licked one corner of it and began to ply it over the blood on my shirt and my face. "We haven't done our groceries yet, have we?"

"No, but they can wait. I'm a mess, and you..."

"I'm okay now." He glanced up from his work. The fear, the odd pleading, was gone from his eyes. Had I somehow answered it? He was even managing a faint half-smile. "No, let's stay. If we just fasten up your jacket to cover all this, and smooth down your hair... There. You're decent."

"You sure you don't want to call it a day? You're very pale."

"Am I interesting too?"

"Bloody fascinating. I think it would take a lab and a team of psychologists to figure you out. What happened to you, Cam?"

"Shh. Please let's not talk about it. I want to go shopping like a normal person, get your granda some of his Reynolds tobacco."

"Okay. It's Black Ox he smokes, though."

"Just because it's cheaper. He likes the Reynolds for a treat."

Did he? I'd had no idea. Yes, I thought—this tender little homicide now watching me anxiously again was definitely lacking a grandparent. It seemed to me tragic that he'd stumbled over Harry as a substitute, but I supposed that couldn't be helped. "I never knew that. Did he tell you?"

"Yes, when we were cooped up fixing the baler last week. Do you mind?"

I grinned. "God, no. Of course not. Anything to keep the old sod sweet. Come on, then—we'll go down the Co-op and you can get Harry his present. I owe him a bottle of Johnnie myself."

For as long back as I could remember, the front-street supermarket had played out the same tape of 1980s classics to help part the Arran shoppers from their money. "Tears of a Clown", "Baker Street". Incongruously in the midst of this, an unedited cut of "Relax". Cam and I arrived in time for this, and I steered the shopping trolley, watching him.

He rode out the first couple of minutes, gravely selecting for us the best deals on tinned goods and cereals while Frankie urged him to hold back from the brink of orgasm—didn't let the grunty climax distract him from courteously handing an old lady's dropped purse back to her. Only when the final explicit squirt resounded through the aisles did he set down a bottle of ketchup and start to smile. "That sell a lot of fizzy pop, does it?"

"Must do. Radio 1 banned it, Mike Read went into a moral decline over it, but the Brodick Co-op serenely plays on. I used to think it was something to do with cleaning fluid."

"I can almost beat that. I used to think he was singing *when you want a car.* I was fixated on die-casts at the time, so I reckoned he was telling me not to blow all my pocket money at once."

I broke into laughter. I was developing various aches and pains now, and the bridge of my nose was throbbing something fierce, but I also felt stupidly lighthearted. If one type of barrier remained locked in place between me and Cam, others seemed to have dissolved. He'd walked close by my side all the way down from Castle Street, steadied me when I forgot the newly installed automatic door and tried to push it open.

Next up was "Solsbury Hill". Leaning past him to grab a bag of pasta, I gave him the sly hip bump that was now our invitation to the dance. Even if I never got to kiss that sweet expressive mouth, I'd settle for feeling this close to him.

He chuckled and snaked an arm round my waist. "Are you okay?" he asked, pulling me clear of a pyramid of bean tins. "You're getting a shiner, you know."

"I'm fine. Kenzie's all gob and no kilt."

"Yeah, he's a pussycat. I didn't really take his job from him, though, did I?"

"Not a bit of it. That was all over before you arrived."

119

"Who was he shouting about back there?"

"What? Oh, when he was calling me a wee mockitt faggot and suchlike?" I hesitated. The trolley was parked across the freezer aisle, but we otherwise had it to ourselves. He'd dropped his hands to my hips. Our movements to the beat of "Solsbury Hill" were tiny, barely perceptible, but in beautiful synch. Suddenly I wanted to tell him about my first love, the pain and the price of it. "I had a boyfriend at school. We were just friends for years and years, but when we grew up, all that changed. I don't think either of us even thought about it, we just...loved each other. Screwed the living daylights out of one another too, as Kenzie kindly put it. His name was—"

"Nicky?"

I swung round. There by the checkout, unloading special-offer six-packs of cola onto the conveyor belt, was Archie Drummond. He'd always been a caffeine freak. He was in his civvies, looking very tall and fresh, and thoroughly interested in my companion—not that he was looking Cam in the face. His gaze was fixed on the place where I'd forgotten to let go of his hips.

I released him, not in any hurry. Why should I care if my ex saw this? In fact a faint tingle of satisfaction had begun under my gut. I recalled the first time I'd met him in the street with his new girlfriend, how coolly he'd introduced her. It wouldn't do him any harm at all to find me dancing in the aisles with the bonniest lad on Arran.

"Archie," I said. "You all right?"

"I should be asking you. Did you run into the barn door again?"

"I ran into Joe McKenzie. His fist, to be accurate."

"Oh, shit. He's been coming off the rails for weeks. Did this just happen?"

"Aye, up outside Malcolm's fish shop. I'm surprised no one rang for you."

"I just came off shift." Archie's unattended six-packs began to logjam the conveyor belt, but he ignored the cashier's impatient grunt. "I'll go and find the stupid bastard now."

"I wouldn't bother. Tell you what, though—Jen McKenzie's gone back to live with her mother at Invercloy. You might want to nip up there and check he's no' taking it out on them."

"All right. So, er..." He leaned forward as if trying to glance past my shoulder. His smile had a trace of unease in it, and once more I felt faintly gratified. "This must be the new farmhand I've been hearing so much about."

I wasn't sure how he'd heard anything at all. Cameron had barely left Seacliff since his arrival. Still, he'd been out and about in the fields on the quad bike, and I supposed on a place like Arran I wasn't likely to have kept such treasure to myself for long.

"Yeah," I said. "Sorry, Cam. This is Archie Drummond, an old friend of mine. Archie, this is Cameron. Just so we're clear that I didn't sack Kenzie for him, he's a student doing work experience. A volunteer."

"Well, they say one of those is worth ten pressed men." Archie stepped forward, his hand outstretched. I hadn't glanced at Cam during the introduction, and I was surprised to see the look on his face now. He'd shifted so that he was almost concealed behind me. He moved to meet Archie as if he'd been shoved in the back, and he kept his gaze somewhere between the Co-op's scuffed lino and the far wall as he held out his hand.

I was surprised. His manners, even when caught so desperately short as on the night of his arrival, had always been open and sweet. Now he was colourless, almost sullen. I scarcely heard his greeting to Archie—a bare syllable—and then he fell back, as if seeking shelter.

"Cam? You all right?"

"Yeah. Bit tired maybe."

"Well, you've got a good right." I floundered, trying to find some way through this encounter suddenly turned awkward and chilly around me. "Cam waded in when Kenzie was getting the better of me. Pretty much saved my neck."

"Did he? That's good." Archie had folded his arms. There was now a small queue at the checkout, and the cashier had moved on to sighs and drumming fingers, but Archie's attention was fixed upon Cameron. I knew that look. What had started as anxious, far-from-unwelcome jealousy had focussed to something else. I hadn't seen much of him in action as a copper, but I'd been out with him once when he'd come across a small-time crack dealer plying his trade in the pub. "Where did you say you were studying, Cameron?"

I cut across Cam's reply. "He didn't. It's a college in Dumfries. Archie, do you have to sound like a great big plod?"

Archie shrugged. He kept his eyes fixed coldly on Cam. "Occupational hazard. What's the matter, Cam—didn't he tell you I was the village bobby?"

Cam didn't react. Then he said, faintly, "Is it okay if I wait for you in the truck, Nichol?"

You don't have to go. I nearly said it. If anyone should go it was Archie, preferably with my boot up his backside. Then it struck me that maybe I was being stupid. I'd told the agricultural-student story so many times now I'd started to believe it myself, conveniently forgetting the little I knew of the real one. Maybe Archie recognised him.

"Yeah, of course," I said, pulling the keys out of my pocket. "Go on. I'll not be a minute."

I watched him retreat. He didn't hurry, but I wondered if that was because he wasn't quite steady on his feet. He looked thin and defeated.

Deciding that the best defence was a good strong offence, I rounded on Archie. "Oh, that was nice, PC Drummond. Why didn't you just slam him down over the ice-cream fridge and frisk him?"

Archie was watching him too, his brow rucked up into a frown. Then he turned back to me, spreading his hands. "I'm sorry. I thought I recognised his face." He sounded genuinely contrite. "Seriously, Nic—I didn't mean any harm."

"Then why scare the shit out of him?"

"Well, he's no reason to be scared of me, if—"

"*Did* you recognise him?"

"I'm not sure. For a minute... No."

"Leave it alone, then. He's a good lad. He's been no end of help with the lambing, and he's even got Harry eating out of his hand." That reminded me. We'd been going to pick up the tobacco at the checkout—Reynolds, not Black Ox. "I've got to go. Of course I'll have to wait at the end of this great big queue that you've caused."

"No, no. Put your stuff through with mine."

I shook my head. "Police corruption. Bloody disgraceful." But I wanted to get back to Cam, and I helped Archie hoist the rest of his boxes and bags out of the trolley, adding mine to the heap at the end. "It's not like you to be such a pain in the arse. Is anything wrong?"

"No. Why should it be? Just... How much do you know about him? I never knew Harry to take on anyone sight unseen before."

"He never knew anyone who'd work for nothing but a bed and a bowl of *min-choirce.*"

"Harry's porridge? Your lad can keep that down?" Archie blew out his cheeks, whistled softly. "The right farm boy finally came along. Look, I really am sorry. Tell him so for me, will you?" He gave the enraged checkout girl what he probably thought was a winning smile and handed over his card. "Er, he does seem nice, actually, Nic. A wee bit dishy, I could say. Are the pair of you—?"

"*Archie.*" I didn't care what the likes of Cashier Morag thought of me and mine, but Archie used to mind intensely. I didn't know what it meant that he was forgetting himself in public like this, but I was sure he'd regret it. "No, as a matter of fact. But keep your voice down."

"Oh, good."

Now what the hell did that mean? I didn't have time to wonder. Archie had taken his card back and was slinging groceries vigorously into his trolley at the far end of the desk. His grin was bright and unreadable. "You know it's Reggie Fletcher's birthday next week?" he said, backing away. "He's meeting me and a few of the lads for drinks in the Barley on Tuesday night. You should come, Nicky. We hardly see you anymore."

The weather had changed. A fine rain was drifting in veils across the hillside beyond the Co-op car park. A few birch leaves, gold coins from last autumn, were clinging to the roof of the red Toyota truck. The air carried a deep fresh tang after the stuffy grocery aisles—moss and resin, and a trace of diesel from the incoming ferry. I could hear her distant thrum.

Cam was curled up in the passenger seat. He'd propped his feet against the dash. I was beginning to work out that it was typical of him to have taken his shoes off before he did so, even in Harry's ancient farm runabout. His head was tipped back, his eyes closed. The springtime had arrived with him—I'd grown used to seeing him in sunlight. But it didn't shine on anybody all the time. Just now he was pale as the rainy sky, a fragile shape behind glass.

I opened the driver's door carefully, afraid he'd fallen asleep, but he unfolded and flashed me an uncertain smile. I lifted the shopping bags over into the backseat and climbed in beside him. "Here," I said, holding out the packet of Reynolds. "I picked up this for you."

"Ta. Here, I—I'll give you the money."

"No. Just give it to him. He'll be pleased." We fell silent. The misty rain drew patterns on the windshield. After a moment I sighed and reached out a hand to his wrist. "I'm so glad you came with me to Brodick and met my nice friends."

He snorted faintly. "Yeah, it was fun. I...I nearly kept walking."

"I'm glad you didn't."

"Maybe you shouldn't be. Did your friend recognise me?"

"No." I tightened my grip, rubbing my thumb over the delicate bone. "He was just being an arse. In fact he told me to say he was sorry."

"Nichol, why do you let me stay? You've only got my word that I haven't done something..." He trailed off, voice scraping dryly. "Something terrible."

"Your word's all I need." I realised as I said it that it was true. I couldn't rationalise it—could only see, in flashing replay, the moment when he'd shot past me to wrestle Joe McKenzie to the ground. I trusted him. "Forget Archie, okay? Let me take you to lunch. Preferably where nobody knows me, though on this island that's a tall order."

"I think I want to go home."

The ferry had almost reached dock. Her song had slowly risen, making the Toyota's elderly windows shiver in their frames. She was always bigger than I remembered, a moving wall of red and black in my rearview, engines vibrating as her pilot manoeuvred her parallel to the wharf.

The sight of her met my conviction—pretty deep, I could now admit to myself—that no good man would want to stay with me for long. Of course Cam would want to go home, now that the heat that had chased him out here had died down. He'd had a life over there on the mainland, even if he never breathed a word of it to me. Family, a boyfriend. Maybe the equivalent of the old man whose tobacco he had set reverentially down on the dashboard, even if his duties there were only visits to a grave.

Then I understood. My heart gave a great painful lurch of relief. He wasn't looking at the ferry. I was glad I hadn't voiced my warning that he'd have to wait while they refuelled her and restocked her cafe with crisps and extortionately priced sarnies. The fact was that recently I'd started to think of the farm as *home* again too.

I gave his wrist a squeeze and let it go, took off the handbrake and put the truck into first for the gear start she now required to get her off her marks. "Come on," I said, trying not to smile. "We're still on a day off, at home or not. I'll fix us something when we get back—a picnic, if the rain stops."

I steered the truck up out of Brodick, past the fancy Victorian villas in their rhododendron seclusion and out onto the moor. I loved this road, and once beyond the speed-restriction boundary I put my foot down, aiming for the distant shape of Holy Isle. It was a nice straight run as far as the curves down into Lamlash bay, and the Toyota knew the way, even if I had to help her out a bit with the pattern of new potholes that appeared on every trip. I swung her around one neatly then spoiled it by hitting the next couple hard. "Ouch. Sorry."

"Not as sorry as I am. Can you slow up, Lewis Hamilton?"

I glanced at my passenger. His hands were clamped together on his lap and his jaw was set.

"You all right?" I asked, easing off the gas. "You're the colour of last week's cod."

"Thanks. I'm okay. Just...not sure I'm on for a picnic lunch."

"You feel sick?" Alarm seized me. I hadn't really seen the first part of his fight with Kenzie. "Did you get a bang on the head earlier? Are you hurt?"

"No. Maybe it's just your Christ-awful driving."

"You loved it on the way down. You kept asking me to go faster."

"I know. There's no pleasing some folks, is there?" He swallowed dryly. "Now I need you to stop."

"Oh. Oh, okay." I patted the white-knuckled knot of his hands. "Can you hang on five seconds? I can get right off the road just here."

"Wherever. Just stop."

I pulled into a layby on the next curve. It was a viewpoint stop for Holy Isle, but poor Cam wasn't interested in the landscape. He undid his seat belt and half fell out of the truck. I stayed where I was to give him some privacy, then when the sounds he was making became distressed, I got out too, grabbing a box of tissues from the back. He'd made it as far as the verge and was crouched there shivering, his head down. It was raining pretty hard.

I pulled off my jacket and wrapped it round him. "Cam?"

"Go back to the car. I'm a mess. I..."

"Hush up." He was surrounded by nettles. I grasped a few and tore them out of his way then offered him a handful of tissues. "What's the matter? Was it that business with Archie in the shop?"

"Dunno. No, not that—just a flu bug, or something I had for breakfast. Oh, God."

I held his shoulders. Breakfast had been put paid to as far as I could see, but he was still struggling, his efforts painful. I stroked his back. This was my fault, whatever was causing it— I'd really twisted his arm to come, and then I'd subjected him to Doreen's caff—where they stopped short of frying Mars bars but only just—a punch-up in the street and an impromptu police interrogation. "Do you want me to run you back into town, love, find a doctor for you?"

"No. I'm okay." He sat back on his heels, coughing and making unsteady use of the tissues. "I just want..."

"What?" If he told me, I'd organise it. Rip it down from heaven or fish it up from hell.

"I wish I could be somewhere quiet for a bit, away from people, and not think, or feel, or..."

"Okay." I could do that for him—part of it anyway. My ma's living room was peaceful. I could field Harry and the farmhands and the dogs. Get myself out of his way too, because I assumed *people* included me, and I didn't blame him one bit. "Are you up for driving home? I'll take it easy."

"Yeah." He blew his nose. "You shouldn't call me *love*."

"You don't like it?"

"You hardly know me. I'm not lovable, particularly..." He let me help him to his feet and wiped gingerly at the front of his shirt. "Particularly not right now. And I do like it—too bloody much."

I couldn't figure him out. I gave up trying, for the moment anyway. His deathly pallor had given way to a flush, and I felt heat radiating off him as I aided his scramble back into the truck. Maybe he *was* coming down with something. "Don't worry about it. Don't worry about anything just now, okay?"

I set off at a much more sedate pace along the coastal road. The rain continued steadily, and the squeak of the truck's rusty wipers set a rhythm to the silence, kept it from awkwardness. I'd found we could be quiet with one another anyway, though just now the air between us was too fraught for that kind of peace. We were halfway through Whiting Bay before Cam spoke again. "Shona really likes you, Nic."

"I like her too," I said cautiously. "She's always been a good friend."

"No. Not like that. And your mate Archie—that's who Kenzie was yelling about in the street, wasn't it? Your first boyfriend."

"Long time ago. Lot of water under the bridge." I stopped for a file of school kids at the zebra crossing. "Archie's a ladies' man now."

"Could've fooled me. You're a popular lad, Nichol Seacliff."

I blushed. "Oh, yeah. Golden boy of Brodick, that's me. I especially felt that when Kenzie was banging my skull off the fish-shop wall." Why did it matter to him anyway? It wasn't as if he'd arrived too late and found me taken, sharing a police house with PC Drummond or ruling supreme over next door's farm with Shona's babies tumbling round my feet. I was embarrassingly free. I thought about pointing that out to him. But when I glanced across, his eyes were closed. He was shivering finely, his beautiful profile unreadable. The last of the kids scattered off the crossing, rear guarded by a lollipop lady who glared at me as if I'd been revving and honking my horn. I put the truck back into gear and focussed on getting us home.

Chapter Nine

A pile of post was jamming the door. For a farm on the edge of ruin, we didn't half attract a lot of credit-card offers and glossy junk mail. I pushed a handful into my pocket and guided Cam ahead of me into the hall. "Come on through. There's nobody around."

"It's all right. I'm better now."

"Yeah, you look it. Just come and sit down here for a bit."

My ma's front parlour wasn't the sealed-off shrine the upstairs rooms had become. It didn't get much use, but we'd take the occasional veterinary health inspector in there, and Harry would sit in state there for an hour on Sunday mornings, the *Farming Times* spread on the polished table where a Bible might once have been, as if in distant memory of Sabbath idleness. It was very quiet. The deep, cool peace of it stilled Cam's protests as I gestured him in. Time had faded what once must have been some fairly eye-popping chintz wallpaper to the ghosts of roses, and the light fell gently through the tall windows.

"Sit down," I said, gesturing to the big armchair by the fire, and watched in concern while he obeyed me. The vigour was gone from his movements. He curled up in the chair—shoes off again—and wrapped his arms round his chest.

"Are you cold?"

"A little bit. But I'm fine, Nichol, really. I can work."

"No, thanks. Don't want you passing out in the sheep dip." I knelt by the hearth and put a match to the kindling, which blazed up cooperatively. There was a blanket folded up on the sideboard. My ma had been working on embroidering it, and her mother and grandma before her, but none of the female Seacliffs inclined to the feminine arts, to judge from the sepia photos I'd once seen of those formidable elders out in the fields, looking more at home with scythes in their hands. The pattern had never been finished. There was still a needle attached. I couldn't see how to undo it without breaking the thread, and I hesitated. Then the air around me seemed to stir, and the thread untangled in my hands.

"Nichol?"

I brought the blanket over to Cam. He was wide eyed, watching a place by the sideboard. "What's the matter?"

"Maybe I'm not fine. I saw..."

"Someone standing near me." I shook out the blanket and wrapped it round his shoulders while he was too distracted to object. "A woman."

"Yes."

"Don't worry about it. I don't, not anymore." I smiled, turning a caress of his hair into a diagnostic touch to his brow. "And you are a bit warm, so you can put her down to fever if you like. Now, could you face anything to eat?"

He made a face and shuddered. "Sorry. No."

"Cup of tea and some aspirin?"

"Sounds good. But I can get it myself. Seriously, I didn't mean to go all Marlene Dietrich on you. There's no need to—"

"Listen." I crouched beside the chair and took his hand. He could make of that what he wanted. If he needed a loving friend without complications, that was what he could have. "If you've got some kind of bug, you'll shake it off faster if you rest for a bit. And I know my so-called mate scared you half to death back in the shop. If you ever want to tell me why, I'll listen. And if not, that's fine too."

Reluctantly I let go of his hand and went to make him his tea. I encountered Harry in the hall. He looked at me as if it were midnight and I'd fallen through the doorway reeking of booze. "Ah," he grunted, patting Floss proudly as she snarled at me. "Back, are you, after your morning of idleness?"

"That's right, Granda. The dissipations of Brodick proved too many for us."

"Good. I'm away out this afternoon, and the baler wants fixing again. Yon lad can do it."

Irritation stung me. Harry was getting to me much less badly these days, but I twitched at the threat of exploitation to Cam. And as for this bloody affectation of not being able to remember his name... "No, he can't. I think he's getting flu or something. He's not well."

"What?"

My God, was that concern on his face? I wasn't sure, never having had an example to work from. I dug in my pocket for the baccy I'd brought in from the truck. "Here. He bought you this. You could've told me you preferred this one, you know. I'm sure we could've stretched to it."

"Where is he?"

"In Mam's parlour. He's having a rest, so don't you bother him or let the dogs through. I just came to make him a cup of tea. Have we got any aspirin down here?"

"Aye, somewhere in the *preas*."

I turned away to search for it. I could sense him behind me like an old volcano on the boil, brow dark with thunderclouds, searching for words.

"This is what comes of racketing about *am baile*," he began. *In those damn towns*, as if Cam and I had spent a morning with whores in Bangkok. I ignored him. "He'd no' have caught flu out here in the clean air."

"Granda, we went shopping." I had my head deep in the cupboard and paid no attention to the angry thump of china on wood, the rattle of the fridge door. "Toilet rolls, sheep pills. We weren't exactly..."

"That'll be how you got the black eye, then—buying toilet roll?"

"No. Ran into the barn door." I doubted he'd avenge me for

131

my own sake, but God knew what he'd do to Kenzie if he felt there'd been an insult to the clan. I found the aspirin, straightened up. "Oh. Are you making Cameron's tea, then?"

"Doesn't it look that way? Och, Nichol, you're a clumsy lad for a Seacliff, aren't you? It's as well that God looks after bairns and idiots. Your ma used to say the *sidhe* had swapped you for a fairy child."

"Well, play your cards right and they might bring the real one back some day." I watched while he spooned enough black tea into the pot to give poor Cam hallucinations. "Er...that looks a little bit strong."

"It'll do him good." Fiercely he stirred the cauldron, then when he was satisfied, poured a dark stream into the mug he'd set out. "Will he take some of Driscoll's elixir, do ye think?"

I repressed a shudder. Driscoll's—a kind of paste that tasted of horse liniment—had haunted my youth. It was Harry's favourite cure-all, and worked damn well since nine times out of ten it scared everyone out of being sick in the first place. "Best not. His stomach's a bit off too."

"Aye, aye. You took him to that Borgia queen Doreen's, didn't you, instead of having your *min-choirce* here... There. Take him that."

"Why don't you take it yourself? He likes you, for reasons best known to himself. And I think he might be missing his own granda."

To my astonishment he turned away, as if he would actually break the habit of a lifetime and indulge the tender feelings I knew sometimes stirred in his flinty old bosom. But he stopped in the doorway. "I never once brought you *your* tea."

This was true. I shrugged, smiling. "I can overlook it, if you're being good to him."

"You're no' a jealous boy, I'll give you that. All those years I had to favour your brother, since I knew I'd never make a farmer out of you..." He glared at me suspiciously. "What's so special about yon lad in the parlour, then?"

"You tell me. You're the one taking him his tea."

"Ach, no." He thrust the mug at me, so hard the top inch of its contents went overboard. "It softens the young, to have their elders wait on them."

"I don't think once would have ruined him. Where are you off to this afternoon, then, all dressed up?"

"None of your business. Make sure the pasture troughs are sound, to make the most of this rain. And you can have a try at fixing the baler yourself." With that he stalked away. He *was* rather dapper for a Saturday afternoon, his Barbour exchanged for an ancient but respectable tweed. The wild thought struck me that he might be heading for Shona's, and I shook my head, imagining myself with little—what would they be?—uncles and aunts, I supposed, provided Shona hadn't fled the island screaming...

I eased the parlour door open. Cam was curled up where I'd left him, but the room was filled with a low, rich purr, and when I looked more closely I saw that my fickle cat had settled herself on his lap, nothing but her ears protruding from the blanket. "You have company."

"Yeah. She brought a couple of kittens in too, so mind where you stand."

"I will. I gave the old man your present."

"He was properly touched, I hope."

"I'll say. He made your tea. He nearly brought it to you himself before he remembered his dignity." I handed Cam the mug and a foil strip of aspirin. "I've got a million things to do, so..." Absently I began sorting through the mail in my jacket pocket. "If you're okay, I'll leave Clover in charge of you, and... Oh, shit."

"What's the matter?"

I sank down in the chair opposite him. The logo on one of the envelopes was familiar to me. I'd first encountered it around this time last year—a bank in Edinburgh, one of several with whom Alistair had taken out loans to get us through what was meant to have been a brief rough patch. Last year they'd only wanted a percentage and their interest. I'd scrawled them a

cheque and forgotten about it. Now the whole lot had fallen due,
I ran a hand into my hair. "Shit. Fuck. Shit.

"Is this sudden-onset Tourette's, or is it something I can
help you with?"

I looked up. My first reflex was to hide the letter—a bill this
size really would break the farm, and I was ashamed. I knew I'd
let things slide. My mouth was dry. "It's nothing."

"Let's have a look."

He was holding out his hand. Slowly I extended the letter to
him. His expression was so kind that I could hardly help it,
though I was mortified by the way the paper shook in my grip.

"Sorry," I said. "No reason I should be inflicting my
financial disasters on you."

He scanned the letter. After a moment he gave a low
whistle. "Okay. That's a bit of a bugger, isn't it?"

"Yeah. I—I just forgot about it."

"And these guys, the Midlothian—their interest rates are
something fierce. Would nobody else make you the loan?"

"Alistair took loans out everywhere. He was great at that
kind of thing. We'd have gone belly-up ages ago if he hadn't
kept finding ways to squeeze us through." I swallowed. "He'd
never have let this happen. Shit, Cam. I'm such a screwup."

I felt a gentle pressure on my ankle. When I looked, Cam
had extended a sock-clad foot to rest against me. A kitten
promptly shot out from under the chair to pounce on him, and
he picked it up gently, detaching the wicked little claws. "Ouch,
you wee sod," he said without rancour. "Nichol, if I tell you a bit
about my desperate past—Bren McGarva and all that—will you
try and hold off on calling the police?"

I frowned. I couldn't see the relevance. On the other hand,
anything he was willing to share with me from that time, I
wanted to hear, and right now I'd welcome the distraction. "Go
on."

"It's not just that I owe him money. I was kind
of...employed by him. I was broke, and I did a job or two for

him, and I saw that the bunch of thugs he ran with could barely count to ten. I'm not good for much, but I do have a decent head for figures."

"How ever did you get involved with him?" I was weirdly relieved. *Employed* had given me an instant vision of Cam on a street corner, waiting for custom while some big Glaswegian pimp lurked in the shadows.

"I was at art college, if you'd believe that. I'd been working two day jobs to put myself through, and they both bloody folded. A lad I knew from my bar work put me in touch with McGarva. I knew he was shady, but..."

"I'm not gonna judge you, Cam."

"Well. What with one thing and another I ended up doing quite a lot for him, and a lot of his cash went through my hands. I suppose I became a bit of an informal accountant to him. That got me in deeper than I'd ever meant to go, and I—I was arrested a couple of times. That's why I was scared your copper friend might recognise me."

"Wow. You were an underworld money man." I tried not to sound too impressed. McGarva's cash could have been for anything. Drug money, trafficking... But I found it impossible to connect such badness with the man in front of me now, wrapped in a blanket, his tired face sweet with concern about my trivial problems. "You don't have to worry about Archie," I said. "He really is the village bobby. He didn't know you at all."

"You're missing the point. If I could run a Glasgow gang lord's finances, I might be able to help you a bit with yours. Are you serious about not letting me work outside today?"

"Deadly."

"All right. Then let me make myself useful in here. If you bring me your accounts, I'll take a look at them, see if I can't find a way of squeezing out a payment for Midlothian."

I wasn't optimistic. I really hadn't glanced at the paperwork I'd signed last year, lost in mists of grief and—I knew it now—sheer fury at Al for leaving me alone to deal with this. The bank wanted six grand, and soon. But I appreciated Cam's offer, and

I went through to the chilly little study next door where Al had kept the paperwork, and selected what I hoped was the most relevant here. I'd made occasional efforts to add to it, all the while feeling that it was pointless, that Harry and I and the farm were circling the financial drain at increasing speed. I brought the box back and set it down in Cam's lap, careful not to dislodge Clover.

"Okay. But where are your accounts?"

"Er... Here. These are them."

"Nope, handsome. This is a collection of receipts and invoices. I can see you've used some paperclips, and that's laudable, but your accounts are the books where you write all these transactions down. Does Harry keep those?"

"No. Alistair did it all. God, I feel really stupid now."

"Mmm. That'll be why the UN offered you a job—because you're so bloody thick."

"Great. I can tell you how broke I am in seven different languages."

Cam snorted. He ruffled my hair, and I remembered how it had felt to fall asleep with my head in his lap in the sunlight. I wished I could do it again.

"Look, it'll be all right," he said. "You must have had some sort of records last year from when you did your tax returns. Can you find me those?"

"I... I'm not sure we did. Someone came out, an inspector. He was a local guy, and he knew about Ma and Alistair. I think he just cobbled something together and took pity on us."

"Okay. Good, I'm glad he did. I hate to say this to you, but...you do know it's April again, don't you? I'm not sure they'll be lenient with you twice."

"Oh, fuck. Shit. Fuck."

"All right. Don't panic. I can cobble too. Have you got a laptop with a spreadsheet package?"

"I had one. When I had to drop my thesis last year I lost all my funding. I had to pay some of it back too, so..."

"You sold it." Once more his hand brushed over my hair. "Things really did hit rock bottom, didn't they?"

"They did. And little sign of upward progress since. I really don't know how the hell we're still here."

"Well, let me see if I can find out. Have you got an A4 notebook and a ruler?"

"Probably. No calculator, though."

"Don't worry. I could use the mental exercise. Find me those, and then you go and do agricultural stuff for a bit. And try not to worry too much, okay? These things aren't usually as bad as they seem."

I shook my head. I was afraid that once he got started, he'd find out they were considerably worse, but I was too grateful to argue, and the sensation of someone giving a damn about me was once more threatening my self-control. Fresh air and hard outdoor graft were the best answers for me, and the truth was that I had to get away from him for a while. The more I went through with him—fistfights, tending him in sickness, sharing with him my stupid domestic griefs—the more I ached to touch him, storm his barricades.

I got up, my head spinning slightly. "Okay. It's really good of you." In the doorway I paused, struck by something he'd said. "You were at art college?"

"Briefly, yeah."

"Was it painting, or..."

"Sculpture, kind of. Drawing up designs and making them out of spare parts of cars, fences, scrap metal—anything I could get a hold of, really."

"Wow. I'm sorry you couldn't go on with it."

"It's not much loss. I wasn't setting the Clyde on fire." He smiled and bestowed on me a look whose yearning I could have sworn equalled my own. What the hell was holding us apart? "Get me my things. Then go work the fields, bonny farm boy, and I'll see you later."

It was almost dark by the time I got done. Harry hadn't
returned from his mysterious jaunt, and now the lambing was
over I'd had to send Shona's lads back home. I hadn't realised
quite how much work Cam had been taking off me in his quiet
way. Wearily pulling off my coat and boots in the porch, I
resolved to talk to Harry about finding some way to pay him,
Kenzie or no Kenzie—he was definitely worth more than just his
bed and board.

I went through into the kitchen. There was no sign that
he'd fixed himself any supper in my absence. Lamplight was
shining from the half-open parlour door.

"Cam?" I said, pushing it wide. "I'm back. You okay?"

He was sitting at the polished table, his shirtsleeves rolled
to his elbow. All around him were neat stacks of paperwork,
and in front of him several sheets of calculations and the open
A4 book, which I could see from here now contained column
after nicely ruled column of figures. He looked utterly
exhausted, but when he saw me he seemed to light up from the
inside, and I felt as if I did too.

"You smell like a cool summer night."

I came and straddled a chair next to him. "Is that a good
thing?"

"It's very good."

"You've been pretty busy."

"I wish I had better news from it all for you. Still, I can—"

"Ah, Cam," I interrupted him. I was tired and sore, and all
the muscle-wrenching labour in the world wouldn't serve to
banish my desire for him, or my conviction that I'd never be
good enough—for him or for anything else. I couldn't even keep
my granda's farm. "You can't make a silk purse out of the sow's
ear I've made of things here. I've run the place into the ground."

He laced his fingers together for a moment. Then he
reached for the book and flipped back through a few pages.
"Nic, I know you loved your brother."

"What has that to do with—?"

"I'm sure he did his best with all of this, okay? But it's not you who's been running it down."

"What do you mean?"

"Going through this stuff, I'd say Alistair was great at shifting debts around. But he was just staving off disaster. He took out loans with some real sharks then borrowed off bigger ones to try and pay them off. I reckon...best will in the world, the farm would've crashed in a year or so anyway."

I sat back. I felt very strange. Weights were lifting from me, but I wasn't sure I was ready to let them go. Al did practical things well and I did them badly. That was enshrined in Seacliff family legend. The failure of our business here had been my fault for so long that the guilt had become a kind of scaffold to me, a prop. "I don't understand. He was always so sure of himself."

"It might have been bravado. He was in trouble."

"God almighty. Can I do anything to put it right?"

"You don't want to sell the place up, do you?"

"I couldn't. Harry was born here."

"But what do you want? You were born here too."

We sat looking at one another. He kept wrong-footing me by putting me first. I'd grown up in a family with a patriarch and a domineering older brother. Even my ma, loving though she'd been, had eclipsed me. I hadn't minded—I'd never known different, and they were good people, a wolf pack tolerant of its omega when they noticed it was there. *What do you want?* A question in violet eyes now fixed on mine.

"Me? I don't know."

"Yeah, you do."

"All winter all I could think about was selling it. I was on the brink of trying to tell Harry the night you arrived. Now I'm not so sure."

"What about your studies? You gave up everything to come back here."

"I'd love to finish. I'd love to..." I paused, long-neglected dreams reaching surface, "...to pack up the Toyota, get on the ferry—not the Calmac, the Brittany one—and drive down through France. I'd like to rent a medieval tower in the Southern Pyrenees in some sizzling-hot valley where it never rains, stay there all summer and figure out the origins of Basque."

"See? You did know."

I began to laugh. That had been pretty specific. "Looks like. What can I do, though? The farm's Harry's, not mine. I couldn't sell it even if I wanted, and these guys from the Midlothian will come and break our kneecaps if we don't pay up."

"No, they won't. I phoned them this afternoon. I hope you don't mind."

"You... Wow." For me that was the equivalent of walking into the dragon's cave and calmly requesting a chat. "No, I don't mind. But...didn't they ask you security questions and stuff?"

"The ones your brother wrote in red Biro on the back of their first letter?" He picked the paper up and showed me. "Sometimes it's easier to call and say you can't do it—put the ball in their court, see how they'll react."

"Don't they just call the bailiffs? Foreclose?"

"Expensive exercise for them. And if you go bankrupt, chances are they'll get next to nothing from your assets. I suggested a year's extension, twelve instalment payments."

"Won't they kill us with the interest?"

"I told them to freeze it where it stands, or we wouldn't be able to do anything for them at all."

"They never accepted that."

"The agreement's in the post. It's tough times—everyone's just trying to grab what they can."

I drew a deep breath. I seemed to have extra space in my lungs for it now. "Bloody hell. Look at the big pair of Wall Street balls on you!"

"That's all right with you, then?"

"Christ, yes. Thank you. Even with that sorted, though—can we make it? What about the tax return?"

"Well, now that I've made you some books, I reckon I can fix them up."

"What—cook them, like for your criminal taskmasters?"

"No, you idiot. But there's things you can claim—allowances, grants, low-income supplements—that you haven't been doing. Legally. And these loans your brother took out, I can consolidate those. The reputable Scottish banks don't want to see farms like this shut down. They go for a song then get turned into caravan parks. I bet I could find you a good deal. And, looking at all this lot..." He pushed the papers around thoughtfully. "I'm not sure you've even earned enough this year to go over the threshold. You might not need to make a return at all."

I got up. I wasn't sure what I was going to do. He looked so lovely sitting there, weary in the lamplight. He wasn't ill, I decided—he'd been shaken so badly by his encounter with Archie that it had made him sick, and the marks of his fright were still on him. I vowed I'd never let him be so scared again, whatever had happened in Glasgow. I didn't care what he'd done.

I put out a hand to him. "Come here."

"Don't get too excited, Nic." He let himself be drawn to his feet. "I'll do the research, fill in the forms if you'll let me, but it might not work."

"I don't care. I mean, I do, but it's the fact that you've spent all day even trying to sort this stuff out for me. *Beannachd do t'anam is buaidh.*"

"What's that mean?"

"Blessings on your soul and your future. It sounds horrible in English."

His hand tightened on mine. "No, it doesn't. Please don't take it back. You've no idea how much I need a blessing."

"And you've worn yourself out. Come here with me and sit

down."

The fire I'd lit for him earlier had settled to a glow, a little sunset to match the vast one casting its last lights into the room. I led him by the hand to the sofa that faced the hearth. It wasn't a large one, and when we sat down, our shoulders touched. Thighs too, and there were our joined hands. I wasn't much given to admiring myself, but I loved how my arm looked curved over his. Like Harry, I had year-round weather tan. His skin was paler, ivory in the firelight. His upcoming musculature matched mine. I turned my head and found him already looking at me, lips parted, eyes fathomless.

"Nichol..."

"Yes?"

"If this place is Harry's, why doesn't he help you out with the finances?"

"Harry? Um..." I grabbed a cushion and flipped it as casually as I could across my lap. "Harry doesn't do money. Not since it was beads and barter, anyway."

"Well—I adore your granda, but I think he should at least try and get his head round it, to make life a bit easier for you."

"Oh, right. Will you be telling him that, then?"

"I might have a go."

"Cam, love—do you really want to talk about Harry just now?"

"No. And you can move that cushion."

I leaned towards him. My hand was still locked in his, getting crushed against the back of the sofa. Now I was so close to him—now I could feel his assent, like a sparking cloud of fireflies around me—I hardly knew what to do with myself. Blindly I reached and grasped the fabric of his shirt with my free hand, crushing it. He took hold of my face, guiding me in, and I closed my eyes, helplessly opening my mouth as it brushed over his. Hot tears stung between my lashes. I was afraid my ragged breathing would break into sobs, but he pulled me home, silenced me in a clumsy, bruising kiss.

A sweetness I'd forgotten life could hold burst inside me. I moaned, and his tongue edged past my lips, the movement rough and shy. Finally he let go of my hand, seized my shoulders and drew me down on top of him, as far as the stupid little sofa would allow. His kiss was sending waves of seismic gold through my whole body, bearing me somehow past the danger zone of coming like a horny teenager inside my jeans. I could hang on. As long as he wanted, even if my skin was burning, my cock trapped and straining for erection in our tight press of hip to thigh. God, I'd roll him off the couch, hit the rug and tussle with him, love him into such an ecstasy that he wouldn't be able to tell where he stopped and I started...

"Oh, Nic! Nichol, I can't."

I tore back. I braced up on my arms and stared at him. His hands were down the back of my boxers, clutching my arse. I could feel his shaft against my belly. Which part of that meant *can't?*

But he wasn't there with me in the moment anymore. I felt our severance, a door slamming shut, a guillotine blade slicing down. We lay unmoving for a second. Then he twisted out from under me and crashed to his knees on the floor.

I knelt beside him. He'd balled up with his back to the sofa, his brow pressed tight to his knees. Now it was his turn for a fit of Tourette's—he was cursing a blue streak, the words indistinct but his fury and frustration clear. When I put out a hand, he flinched from me.

"Cameron. Jesus, what is it?"

He jerked his head up. He was almost unrecognisable with bitterness. "Don't," he rasped. "I've done it to you again. I'll get out of here, okay? I'll go."

"What—if I can't fuck you, you can't stay in my house anymore?" Maybe he hadn't expected me to be so blunt. Whatever it had been, he caught a breath. I tried the reach to his shoulder again, and this time he didn't move. "You haven't done anything to me—nothing I won't get over. I'm not an unexploded bomb." The fact that I felt like one was my own

143

problem. Had to be. He was still rock hard and so was I. It wasn't bloody fair. "But you have got to talk to me. Right now."

"I can't."

"Is it a health thing? Because I haven't been an angel either. Archie was my first boyfriend, not my only one. We'll use—"

"Nichol, stop."

"Did McGarva hurt you? Pimp you out?"

"No! He had boys for that. Girls too. He wasn't gonna use the accountant."

"What, then?"

He uncoiled. For an instant I was scared. This was maybe the face Joe McKenzie had seen just before Cam had tried to put his lights out. "Don't you get it? I'm not good enough for you—never could be, never will. I'm dirty. I'm fucked up. I've done things, seen things you couldn't even imagine. And you— you've never even had a bad thought in your life. You're not fucking capable."

I looked into the space between our two bodies. "I'm having bad thoughts right now."

"Oh, I know about those ones. I know you've had your boyfriends. I can tell by the light in your eyes, the way you dance and move that lovely arse of yours. But you grew up here, Nichol. Your heart's as clean as seawater. You're—"

"Don't you dare say *innocent*. I'm twenty-five years old. I've survived the death of my family out here, and..." I ran out of qualifications. "And even if I am, if there's some kind of...*corruption* going on around here, which I don't believe for a second—don't I get to choose?"

"You don't get to choose it from me. No." He rolled away and got to his feet. I watched helplessly while he went to the table and began packing up his books and paperwork.

"Cam, whatever it is—I can stand it, really I can."

"No." He put the lid on the box. "I'll get started on this lot tomorrow, if you want me to. Unless I've screwed with your head and your cock too much, in which case I'll be gone by the morning."

"Don't make me answer that. I've made enough of a fool of myself tonight here anyway."

He stopped on his way to the door. "Oh, no. You're not a fool. You're..." He put out a hand as if he would touch my face, as if he could see something there no one else could. "Beautiful Nichol. You've got no idea, have you? No idea at all."

Chapter Ten

The next morning I got up a little earlier than usual, and I brought him tea and toast on a tray. I wanted to show him there were no hard feelings, that my head and my cock could cope with him just fine. I also wanted to make certain he was still there, and my heart was beating fast against my ribs as I padded upstairs and tapped the edge of the tray against the door.

There he was—sitting up with a confusion of dreams dissolving from around him, focussing and giving me a surprised and lovely smile. I'd brought my own breakfast too, and a couple of the newspapers we'd picked up in Brodick the day before. I sat on the end of the bed, handed him a paper and unfolded one of my own. Our silence, at first tense, became easier, aided by the chacking of the jackdaws who'd colonised the chimney above his room and were building their nests on the principle of dropping twigs down it until enough of them stuck.

When we did start to talk, it was ordinary—tasks for the day, how best to distribute the sheep pills. I was ordinary too, I was sure. I'd omitted to brush my hair, and I had on a particularly ancient jumper. I was fairly certain I was nobody's beautiful anything.

Harry inadvertently helped us back onto an even keel. He was waiting in the barnyard when we went down, and over the next few days loaded onto us such a regime of extra work that the idea of sex became no more than that—an idea, a ghost, a nice warm thought between falling into bed and dropping into worn-out sleep. He'd developed an anxiety to fix up all the barns and outbuildings, finish roofing work and the construction of the new pens, before the winter. It had just turned May—I saw my ma out in the lanes, gathering armfuls of hawthorn blossom, and had time to smile at her before the light changed and took her away—and I tried to convince Harry we had all summer for the work, but he growled and called me so many variants on *shiftless*, Gaelic having plenty of them, that it was easier simply to run and lift rocks when he told me.

On Tuesday afternoon I found a message on the phone from Archie, reminding me about the get-together for Reggie Fletcher in Brodick. I thought I was too tired, but that evening, stripping out of one set of sweat-damped clothes, it struck me that it might be nice not to haul into another pair of overalls ready for the late shift. I reconsidered Archie's invitation. I'd been dancing to Harry's unrelenting tune all day, and I was well ahead of schedule. It wasn't beyond the bounds of possibility that I could take a night off.

In the back of my wardrobe were some clothes I hadn't touched since I'd folded them into a rucksack and left behind the lights of the Edinburgh scene. I reached in and extracted a pair of charcoal-grey designer jeans. The name was stamped in gold across the butt and might as well have read *queer*. Man, I'd loved those jeans. They fit me as if they'd been made for me and had drawn the late-night talent down like flies. I threw them on the bed and regarded them thoughtfully, hands on my hips. I had a shirt that went with them, delicately patterned in grey and white. That was a good fit too, following the lines of my shoulders and waist. Nothing squeezing, nothing spare. A black leather belt with a heavy but plain silver buckle. I checked that there was no one about to question my manoeuvres, had a shower and washed the plaster dust out of my hair.

When I came to put the shirt on, I found things had changed a bit—I had to leave the top two buttons open to accommodate a new inch or so across my shoulders, but I didn't dislike the effect of that, in the fly-specked square of mirror which was all I had for the display of my vanities. The jeans still clung to me lovingly.

In my top drawer I found a bottle of cologne bestowed on me by my last Edinburgh lover. I didn't dare put any on—Harry would detect it from miles away—so I sprayed a little in the air and walked through it, a trick taught me by a female dorm mate, and apparently the classy way to wear scent. Well, I was sure I could still dredge up a bit of class.

I went slowly down the stairs. I hadn't yet made my mind up to go anywhere, and I was idly turning back the cuffs of my shirt when I noticed the kitchen door standing open, light spilling out into the hall. Harry was sitting at the far end of the table. He looked subtly different, and it took me a second to work out why—he was wearing his reading glasses, the ones he'd rejected in disgust because he'd been prescribed bifocals, something only required by old men. The cardboard box containing our financial paperwork was open on the table, and Cameron was gingerly tendering to him the book of accounts. I noted with amusement that although Cam had seated himself reasonably close, he was just out of cuffing range. I stopped on the stairs to look at the pair of them, so serious in the lamplight. Quite a tableau. Harry's brow was knitted, but he took the book, and when Cam pointed out the income column on the left—a tactful place to start—he planted one thick forefinger on it and began to read.

I'd made no noise, but Cam looked up. He stared for a moment as if he didn't recognise me, and then—first time in my life I'd ever produced such an effect—his mouth fell open. Silently he pushed back from the table and came to intercept me at the foot of the stairs.

"Hiya. You two all right in there?"

"Yeah. I've told him I'm scheming to cheat the taxman, try to get him onside that way. Bloody *hell*, Nic. You look good enough to eat."

Eat me, then. It was on the very tip of my tongue. There he was, taking me in from crown to boots with every appearance of pure hunger, and there was I, fancying the pants off him so bad

I'd have leaned over the banister for him right now, provided we'd locked Harry up in the kitchen. This was bloody ridiculous.

"Ta," I said lamely. "I was thinking of maybe going out."

"To meet Archie?"

I nodded. Oh, he didn't like that. It was nothing to do with his shady past, either—lights came into his eyes I hadn't seen before, a little touch of hot green to set off the violet. I considered telling him it was a whole bunch of mates I was meeting, not just my ex. Then I decided there was nothing wrong with worrying him a bit on that account. "Just for a few hours. Everything's done here, more or less. Can you manage?"

"Yeah, sure. Have a good time."

Cue for me to go. My wallet was on the hall table, the keys to the Toyota hanging by the door. Not the most elegant vehicle for a night on the lash, but it was that or the quad bike.

I didn't want to move. I loved the way he was looking at me. And he was planted right in front of me, not visibly inclined to let me past.

"I think I'll just sneak out," I said faintly. "Harry'll call me ten types of fairy if he sees this outfit. Will you cover for me?"

"I'll tell him the urge came upon you to drystone the pasture by moonlight or something. Leave him to me." He leaned on the newel post. His fingers traced the enigmatic patterns in its ancient black oak. I waited, allowing him time to come up with his delaying tactic—my destination tonight was by no means certain, and all these bonny clothes could come off just as easily as they had gone on. It was chilly in his bare little bedroom, but well soundproofed, and we would soon warm up. "I was thinking..."

"Yes?"

"Ways we could rustle up a bit of cash. You know the broken tractors in the barn? I've tried everything I know to fix them, but I think they've gone the journey."

I struggled to focus. "Yes. Yeah, I know them."

"They're just rusting in there. Looks like you've accumulated a whole load of other scrap over the years as well. I was thinking we could sell it off for parts or meltdown. Metal prices are still at a premium, so..."

"Oh, right. Archie said one of our neighbours got ripped off for a whole lot of it." I didn't mind Cam's tiny flinch at the sound of his name. *Yes, Archie.* "Still, though, how would we sell it? I've often thought it'd be easier to let it be nicked."

He looked at me from under his eyelashes. I had an uncomfortable sensation that he was reading my mind. "Well, there's this thing," he said softly, one corner of his mouth quirking up. "It's new, and I'm not sure it'll come to anything. But it's called the *internet*, and there's this giant mart on it called eBay, and—"

"Shut up," I told him, grinning. "Surely we could never eBay that lot."

"I already took the liberty of trying. I listed it as a job lot in the net café at Lamlash. For pick up only, obviously, but I bet the dealers will be down like locusts."

"Okay. That was a great idea." Then a better one occurred to me, and I forgot my urge to tease him. "Oh, you know what? You go through it and see if there's anything that sparks your creative drives. I wouldn't mind seeing some of these scrap-metal sculptures of yours going on."

"No need for that. Let's just sell the lot."

"Seriously. What else would you need? Alistair had a phase of trying to patch stuff together—I think there's gauntlets out there somewhere, a mask, cutters. And what do you call those welding guns?"

"Oxyacetylene torches."

"That's it. He had one of those. Why not?"

"Because we're trying to make you a profit, not set me up as George Rickey in your barn. Still, though, if anything's left over..."

"You'll think about it? Good." I wasn't sure why I was filled with such sudden enthusiasm for this project, except that I liked to see people doing what they loved from time to time, and not just what they had to. Maybe I was projecting my own painful desire to lose myself in the joys of Chomsky's universal grammar once more. No. I wanted what was good for Cam. And suddenly I was deeply ashamed of myself for trying to rattle his cage. "Listen, this thing tonight isn't just with—"

A thump from the kitchen. I knew it well. My granddad's fist meeting the surface of the table, the opening note of a symphony of rage and disbelief—at the conduct of his grandsons, the prices of feed, any other provocations from an intransigent world. "Cameron!"

Cam glanced over his shoulder. "Oh, shit. I'd better go."

"Cameron, laddie, are you there? You are no' telling me we've spent five hundred pounds on feed supplements this blasted quarter. Nichol!"

"You don't have to deal with this," I whispered. "I can stay and sort him out if you like."

He grabbed my hand, gave it a brief warm squeeze. "No. Run for it while the going's good. Quick, before he smells your nice cologne."

Archie was nowhere to be seen in the Harvest when I got there. Tuesday nights tended to be slow, and Mac the bartender soon spotted me scanning the tables, affecting not to notice the disgusted looks I was copping from the grizzled old fishermen having their pint by the fire. I was late, Mac informed me. Archie had gone on to the Catfish. Mac had a sarcastic air about him. I thanked him and left, tugging out my shirt at the back to hide the worst of my labels. Perhaps Brodick wasn't yet ready for my big-city style.

But my alarm bells were starting to sound. The Catfish seafood bistro was one of the only places on Arran you could eat without the accompaniment of electronic bagpipe music. It was quiet, candlelit, nicely situated right on the waterfront. For many years it had been the place Archie and I repaired to on a date. I jogged down the alley. I was more than half minded to go straight back to the truck, but I just had to check that Reggie and the rest of them weren't gathered round a table in there, enjoying birthday drinks and waiting for me, unlikely scene though that was.

No. Just Archie. He was seated in our favourite spot, the table for two in the half-moon window that looked out over the bay. When I pushed open the door, he glanced up guiltily, lowering the menu he'd been studying. I came to a halt. Donald Croft, who owned and ran the place, greeted me casually, as if it had been an ordinary night. To all intents and purposes it was—Archie and Nichol meeting for dinner, as if the last five years had never happened. I'd walked into the lobster pot.

And, now I came to think of it, Reggie Fletcher's birthday had never been in May. I knew that. Had some part of me consented to this trap?

Archie, with a look of a man as well hung for a sheep as for a lamb, offered me a cautious wolf-whistle. "Wow, Nicky. You dressed up for me."

I swept up to the table. I wasn't about to cause a scene, even though there was only a handful of other diners to entertain. I pulled out a chair and sat down opposite him. "No," I said softly. "I dressed up for a night on the town with the lads. Where are they, Archie?"

"Oh, you know how it is—a few of them dropped out, and..."

"Bollocks. You set me up. Why?"

"Well..." He gestured at Donald, who appeared at the table so fast with a bottle of wine he must have had advance instruction. The wine was Chenin Blanc, my favourite for a nice fish supper. "I never get to see you anymore, do I? Thanks, Don, I'll pour it myself."

I waited, staring blindly across the waterfront, till Donald was out of earshot. "Why didn't you just ask me?"

"Would you have come?"

"Of course not."

He sighed. I didn't look at him while he poured out the drinks. It was a pretty summer evening, and there was plenty for me to watch on the beach—innocent dog walkers, old ladies enjoying their stroll, young couples of the type who could fling their arms around each other and snog in full sight of God and Brodick Castle.

"All right," he said after a long, tense silence. "I'm sorry. Why don't you just go?"

"I've driven all the way down from Seacliff for this. I've been up since five o'clock. I think I'll have my dinner while I'm here."

"Yes. Good." Another small gesture, and there was Donald again, pencil poised, as though he had no custom on earth but our own. "I'll have the scampi, please. And the mackerel for Nichol, with horseradish, and can you remember to crisp up his chips?"

"*Archie!*" That did turn a few heads. With an effort I restrained myself. I sorely needed a drink, I realised, and I grabbed the glass of cold Chenin and knocked half of it back without noticing. "For God's sake. I haven't been pickled in formaldehyde since we last—"

"Och, no. I'm sorry," Donald interrupted smoothly, as if it had been his fault. "Would you prefer something else, Nichol?"

I wouldn't. The mackerel was the best thing on the Catfish menu, and I did love my chips well crisped. I thought about demanding Dover sole to make a point, but I was here now, wasn't I? Lunch had been a sandwich, and I was bloody hungry. "No. No, that's fine, thanks."

He was gone, taking the menus with him. Archie leaned his elbows on the table. He'd dressed up too, in a smart white shirt and a little waistcoat I'd bought him on one of our day trips to Glasgow. He said, nervously, "You still like some of the same things, then?"

"Yes, I do." The wine was extremely good, for example—I polished off my glass and didn't protest when he instantly poured me another. "Just don't bloody *order* for me."

"Sorry. I thought if I got everything to the table for you fast enough, you might at least stay long enough to eat."

"I don't get it, Archie. Why would you even want me to? You stopped us coming here because you didn't want to look too gay." *And three weeks later, you dumped me.* I swallowed the bitterness of that, but a wicked humour stirred in me. "Oh, hang on. Is it an outreach programme? Helping the minorities to trust the police?"

"That's harsh, Nicky. I'm not saying I don't deserve it, after everything I did to you, but...it's harsh."

I turned the wineglass in my hands. Two thoughts were forming in my head—first, that although I'd done my share of excess student drinking in the city, I was well out of practice now, and secondly, that although Archie had sat and justified himself to me for the better part of three hours on the night of our breakup, he'd never then or since admitted *doing* anything to me at all. We were adults, he'd said. People changed. I should learn to accept it.

The wine met painful memory and I said, not even meaning to, "You broke my heart."

"Oh, God. Don't."

"Why not? You brought me here for this nice tête-à-tête. What did you think we'd end up talking about—your brilliant career?" I caught my breath. I'd had no idea I was still so angry. When I finally looked up and met his eyes, he'd gone pale as only a redhead could, proper parchment white, the freckles standing out across his nose. I shook my head. What the hell was the point of making him miserable now? I topped off his glass and my own. "How's the brilliant career, Archie?"

"Truth? I can't believe I gave you up for it."

The anger died. I wasn't much good at holding on to a grudge. Maybe all I'd ever wanted was to hear he regretted it, that I hadn't been easy to bargain away. "Is it...not working out for you, then?"

"Oh, Nicky, I'm bored stupid. The highlight of my week was a callout to Shiskine Golf Club. Someone's buggy had gone missing. And it hadn't even been nicked—just parked in the wrong bloody shed. I found it. Case closed. PC Drummond triumphs again."

He could make me laugh. I'd forgotten that. I considered pointing out that he'd marred the compliment of his regrets a bit, but he looked so woeful. And nothing could come of this anyway—whatever he thought might be the results of his ambush, we were just two old mates meeting up for a meal.

Don brought the scampi out, and the fragrant mackerel, and another bottle of wine. "I'm sorry it's not turned out to be gunfights and car chases," I offered, and saw him relax a bit. "Sorry I snapped at you too. Look, let's not spoil dinner. What else is going on with you? How's your sister and your mam?"

That was the trouble. We could just drop from hot debate like that into ordinary *craic*. We had all our history and our childhoods to fall back on, all our routines. It was very routine of us to come to the Catfish for dinner, talk about family and friends, have a few drinks and go back to Archie's flat. He didn't even have to ask me. At the end of our meal, we peaceably split the bill, got up and left.

There was the familiar street, his prosaic top-floor perch above the bank. Arran didn't run to police accommodation, and maybe it was reassuring to the Scottish Royal to have a copper living up there. He'd left the lights on. There was the set of mossy steps you had to negotiate to get to his back door. There inside me was that rippling, floating sense that if I wasn't exactly drunk, I certainly couldn't drive home, and on such occasions I always stayed the night.

Stayed, and once Archie had checked the doors and closed each set of curtains carefully tight, we'd go to his bed and screw one another blind. He'd become quite good at it, I recalled, especially considering he'd started with me from scratch and quite uninstructed. He could put me on my knees on the mattress, find his way into my body and do what was needful until I came, though he'd made me so scared of the neighbours that I never lost my sense of the moment, of having to hang on to the bedhead and bite my lips to keep from yelling out. My own prowess had been satisfactory too. We'd been young. We'd had no one else to take all this out upon, and God knew we'd loved one another.

He let me in, and I stood in the living room, remembering. It was very routine of him to come up and kiss me, then to take my hand.

He led me to the bedroom. Nothing had changed there either. It was the plain, functional space it had always been. Even the duvet cover was the same, though a few shades paler with sunlight and laundering. Brown and blue stripes, with curtains to match, a relic of the eighties donated to him by his mum.

I cast around me for something unfamiliar, anything to mark time's passage and remind me that I had moved on and so had he. To bring it home to me that I was about to climb into his bed out of habit. God, those bloody awful curtains, and I knew the inside of them so well... Yes, there they were, tightly shut.

Still, once he'd sealed us off from the world, he liked me to be naked. I could see his reflection in the mirror by the wardrobe. He was watching, waiting. I would strip down, then so would he, and we'd get under the duvet and rather decorously kiss and roll around until we were ready, as if following directions in a textbook. All right. Nothing wrong with that. There'd be no strings—he wouldn't dare try to attach one, not after the way he'd left me—and I'd be a better, saner friend to Cam with some of my steam blown off. Actually, I wished I felt a bit steamier. Something about Archie's beige nylon carpet, as I bent to take off my socks, was quelling my erection. The food and drink weren't helping, and neither was my sleep debt. Glancing down to unfasten my shirt, I stifled a yawn.

"Nichol!" He grabbed me fiercely by the shoulders, spun me round to face him.

That woke me up. "Archie? You all right?"

"No. I need you. I've got to have you, right now."

Well, this was new. I snatched a couple of breaths as he backed me up towards the bed, then lost them as he landed on top of me.

"God's sake," I managed, chuckling. "What's got into you?"

"I was so stupid to let you go. I'm not gonna get my damn promotion, gay or straight. I'm never gonna get off this fucking island."

But it would've been a fair deal otherwise? I knew I should ask. I shouldn't be letting him rip his way into my last designer shirt, sending buttons flying, though that hardly mattered since I'd most probably never get off the fucking island either. Nothing mattered. My ma and my brother were dead. I was trapped on a rock in the ocean with an old man who clearly wished—one day he would come out and tell me to my face—that I'd died in Alistair's place. And the light that had shone into this, the sunshine and the springtime beauty, was meaningless because no matter how completely I had fallen in love, Cameron couldn't return it, would be gone one day between sunset and a shift in the wind...

Cam. Archie got me properly pinned down and planted a kiss on me, a big one right on the mouth. There was nothing wrong with Archie's kiss. Nothing, except every detail of it— taste, heat, pressure—threw me back to the Saturday night, when I'd wanted Cameron so much I'd wept, and he'd pressed his mouth to mine and silenced me. *Cam.*

I pushed Archie off me and rolled away. My head spun with the force of revelation and I sat up. "No. Sorry, Archie. No."

"You're kidding." I felt the mattress shift as he came to kneel behind me. "Come on. You were getting undressed for me."

"I know."

"Is it because I didn't give you time? I'm sorry. I'll do whatever you want, Nicky. You know I can make you enjoy it. I'll open the curtains."

I laughed painfully. "Don't be daft. I don't want to flash our goings-on across half Brodick—I never did. Just didn't want you to be ashamed."

"I was, I know." His hands landed hard on my shoulders, kneading, trying to pull me back. "Forgive me."

"Already have. It isn't that."

"What, then? Oh, God—*not* that wee rag tail of a—"

"Shush, Archie. Don't call him any names." Honesty was boiling up in me. I couldn't keep this raw flower of truth from unfolding, not to spare Archie or Cam or myself. "It is about him. Yes."

"Oh, *shit*, Nichol." Archie dropped me. He subsided onto his backside. "Are the pair of you...?"

"No. I'm not sure we ever will."

"Then..."

"I want to wait for him. I don't care how long."

A silence fell. It ought to have been dreadful, but I wasn't really attending. My senses were stretched out between this little box of a room and the miles of dark moorland that divided me from Seacliff. A curlew silence, lapped round by waves, and on the far side of it another room, another box. It was late. Cameron kept farmers' hours by now—he'd be in bed. I wished to hell I hadn't drunk so much I couldn't drive home.

"Archie, are you over the limit? Could you take me back?"

"You've got a fucking nerve."

I turned to look at him. He'd drawn his knees up to his chest and was glaring at me over them.

"What?"

"You turn me down for some—bloody little bird you imagine you've got in the bush, then you ask for a lift home. Is this it, Nicky—did you work out a way to get revenge on me?"

"Jesus, no. Of course not."

"*Of course not.*"

God, was he mocking me? My outrage at being suspected of an unworthy thought... Given back to me like that, I sounded like Harry, whose stiff Highland notions of honour had always struck me as antiquated and naïve. Maybe I had a few of my own.

"Oh, no," he went on, rocking himself, clutching his bony knees. "You'd never stoop so low."

"I don't know what I'd do. I haven't really been tested. But I didn't set out to take some Machiavellian bloody revenge on you tonight. I'm sorry, okay? I didn't know myself how I felt until you started—"

"Oh, *please* spare me the details." He unfolded from the bed. "I am over the limit. Probably just as well for you, because there's every chance I'd drive us both off a bloody cliff. Here." He tugged open the wardrobe door. "Pillows. Blanket. You know where the sofa is."

I stood, clutching the blanket. The corridor was dark, the bedroom door firmly closed. I was disoriented, and I wanted so badly to be home that I gave thought to trying to walk. I hadn't meant to screw Archie over, any more than—I could see this now—he had meant to abandon me. But there was no point of comparison, no connection between the way I felt for him and whatever the hell it was now rising inside me, unstoppable as the sun. I'd been a kid when I'd fallen for Archie. And now I was grown up.

Not that I felt too mature, marooned out here with my bedlinen. I was about to head for the living room—maybe call and price up a taxi ride—when the bedroom door swung wide.

"Give me those," Archie said, taking my burden out of my arms. The light was behind him, but I could just see the traces of tears on his face. "You have the bloody bed. I'll take the sofa. I'll tell you for free, Nicky, there's no one called Cameron registered at any of the Dumfries farming schools I know."

"You checked?"

"Yeah. You might not have known how you felt, but I saw it the second I laid eyes on you in the shop the other day."

"Then why did you...?"

"Ambush you? Try to sabotage it? Ah, come on. Not

everyone in this world's as fucking saintly as you. Don't you remember that 'Big Yellow Taxi' song you made me listen to all summer a few years back?"

"What? Look—please let Cameron alone. Maybe he hasn't told me everything, but he hasn't done anything your lot need to come after him for. He's a good lad."

"He'd damn well better be." He pushed past me and disappeared into the living room.

I lay down in the familiar, alien sheets. I didn't think I'd sleep, but it took a lot of emotional trauma to disarray a farmer's sleep pattern, and soon I was drifting. I remembered the song, of course, especially the harsh reminder in it that people seldom knew their blessings until they lost them. Not me. I knew what I had, even if to all intents and purposes I didn't have it at all. I closed my eyes and joined my ma in the night-drenched garden at Seacliff Farm, and together we kept the watch.

This would be a walk of shame I hadn't had to do for a while—an early-morning dash beneath Harry's radar from the truck to my room to get changed. He was nowhere to be seen when I bumped the Toyota cautiously into the yard. Thanking God for small mercies, I slithered out and quietly closed the door. I didn't even have a jacket to throw over the crumpled shame of my torn shirt. I'd left Archie's flat as soon as I'd woken up sober, and taking one of his seemed a bit of a nerve after the night before.

The hall was cool and dim. Good. Maybe I'd got back at just the right time, after breakfast but before the early feeds. Maybe I hadn't even been missed.

I was jogging silently up the stairs, and Cam was jogging silently down them, and our near collision on the landing sent both of us springing apart like scared cats. He was dressed ready for work. He grabbed the banister to steady himself. "Jesus, Nic."

"Hi. Yes. Sorry. Er, good morning."

"To you too." He took me in, base to apex, and I was ready for anything to appear in his eyes but a look of pure, unguarded pain. "Are you all right? You didn't come home."

"I'm fine. Things got a bit...complicated. Where's Gruffalo Bill?"

"Off in the barns somewhere. You'd better go get out of your glad rags before he comes back."

I watched him run down the rest of the stairs and out into the grey dawn. Why didn't I go after him? Just the brief sight of him in his coveralls had taken my breath, made me want to snatch him into my arms and tell him that whatever he was thinking, it was pretty sure to be wrong. But what then? The last frail shield I had against him would be gone. If I told him why I hadn't slept with Archie, knowing me I'd tell him why, in words of one syllable, fatal and beyond retraction. Grab his hand and take that running jump with him off the cliff, ready or not...

Shit. I was chilly, exhausted and disproportionately hungover. If Harry hadn't been waiting behind the door with a rolling pin for me, that meant I'd got away with the night, but I still had one of his uniquely painful days ahead of me. Love, life and probably even death would have to wait on the old man's schedule. I picked up a telltale button that had dropped onto the carpet, took a deep breath and ran.

Chapter Eleven

I didn't catch up with Cam again until lunchtime. It was a beautiful blue-gold May day, and sunshine and labour had burned off the worst of my headache. I washed my hands under the outside tap then followed unfamiliar sounds of clattering to the main barn. It was empty now, the sheep all out to pasture and too soon for the autumn's hay harvest.

On my way over I glanced up at the windowpanes I'd never got round to fixing from that fateful night in February. Cam's repairs with the plastic and sacking had held good, and I had a superstitious fear of replacing the glass. The night of his arrival had gathered a kind of magical resonance in my mind, recalling the legends of the mer-bride my ma had told me. The mermaid was happy to stay amongst the human people of her husband's clan, but when he became jealous of her wandering along the strand—for she'd split her tail into two legs just to please him—and he locked her in the cellar, why, a mermaid she became once more, and she swam out through a drainpipe and was never seen again. I didn't want to seal up Cam's gateway into my life, as if I took it for granted that he would stay.

There was little of the mermaid in the man hoisting great chunks of rusting metal from one side of the barn to the other. His hair was very blond today, though, catching pale fire in the light that fell from the high windows. I leaned in the doorway. When I said his name, he almost dropped the wheel arch he was carrying. Then he steadied himself, as if determined to finish his task, and let it gently down into the heap of engine parts and bodywork. He gave me a smile too bright for the shadowed unease in his eyes.

"Oh, there you are." He straightened up, brushing orange flecks from his hands. "Your scrap sold off nicely, by the way."

"Really? That was fast."

"I told you it'd be popular. I got the bus to Whiting Bay last night after you'd gone, watched the end of the sale in the caff. It all got quite fierce. We can pay half the Midlothian bill and still have change to spare."

"Half..." I lost a breath. That red four-digit figure was still burned into my retina. "You got three grand for that lot? No *way*."

"Way," he said wryly, reminding me it hardly became a good adult Scotsman to turn into Mike Myers when astonished. "The guy's coming tomorrow with a truck to pick it up, tractors and all. And I heard back from a couple of the banks. They'll do a consolidation loan for the rest of what you owe, get the repayments down to something manageable. Also, as a small West Highland agricultural business, you qualify for tax relief and couple of nice handy grants."

Just yesterday I'd have gone over and hugged him. The impulse died painfully, making me clench my fists in the pockets of my coat. "That's amazing. I don't know how to..."

But I did know how to thank him, a little bit anyway. I was standing right beside the tool chest where Alistair had kept his welding gear. The lid creaked as I raised it, sending dust and spiders flying. "Cam, come and have a look at this lot."

"Found something else to sell?"

"No. For you, if you want it." Just yesterday he'd have crouched beside me and rested his shoulder on mine while he looked. Now he was keeping his distance. "Are these things any good?"

"They look great."

He became interested despite himself and leaned in to pick up the mask and the blowtorch. I caught his body heat and a trace of peroxide. I said softly, "You got your roots this time."

"Yeah. I'm a bit more expert now. Is it stupid of me?"

"No, I don't think so. The world's getting used to me having a gorgeous blond student enslaved on my farm." There were gauntlets down at the bottom of the box as well. To get them I had to shift my brother's childhood cricket bat, which had somehow ended up in here, initials lovingly carved into its handle. "So did you put aside a few pieces of the scrap to work with, like I told you?"

"Yeah, I did. Just a few bits that wouldn't sell."

"Good. You could've taken more, though."

"The point of the sculptures was kind of that they used up things no one else wanted. Burst tyres, rusty wire. I used to go scavenging around the landfill sites."

"Well, Harry would be only too happy if you'd scavenge off the rubbish from around this farm. Where is he, by the way?"

"He went off in the truck about half an hour ago. He said..." Cam paused, and for the first time that day I heard the quiver of amusement in his tone. "He said it smelled like a tart's boudoir."

I snorted. "Great. Where was he off to? Did he have on his good tweed coat?"

"He just said he had business elsewhere. And yeah, he was quite dressed up."

"My God—I'm starting to think the old sod's got a girlfriend." I stood up, gently closing the lid of the chest. "You know, if he's not around, we could get away with lunch. I mean stopping for it. It's not that I don't love gnawing on a loaf while I herd sheep, but..."

"I shouldn't really. I've got a lot to do."

"Come on. It's lovely out there. We'll grab an hour and a picnic on the cliffs. And..." I swallowed dryly, with a sound he must have heard. "And I'd like to talk to you, Cam."

Lunch was quick to prepare—a couple of slabs of fruitcake lifted from what Harry thought was his secret supply, and a pack of Cheddar cheese. These unlikely partners went well together and had always been the picnic of choice for me and Al, high energy, low maintenance and easily shoved into a pocket. I was glad it didn't take long because Cam wouldn't even come into the kitchen with me, and when I went back outside, he was perched uneasily on the top bar of the gate, looking ready for flight.

I led the way down the path towards Kildonan beach. I hadn't been there since my return to the island, not on account of painful family memories but because the ruins of the abandoned runrig farms struck painfully on my imagination. A few hundred years, I'd thought, and Seacliff would be no more than a tumble of stones in the turf.

I saw Cam looking at the parallel lines that marked the moor as far as the cliff's edge. "They're cultivation strips," I said, slowing up so he'd hear me over the fresh breeze. "The soil's so poor, the people who lived here back in the 1800s had to heap it into ridges for drainage and fertilise it with seaweed. You can grow quite a bit that way—enough to scrape by, anyhow."

"What happened to them?"

"No matter how hard they worked, they were always in debt to their landlord. So when he had the chance to lease the land to a wealthy single tenant, he called in his arrears and evicted them. A lot of landowners thought that was a great idea at the time."

"The Clearances."

"Yeah. It's a lonely place. Haunted."

"Beautiful too."

I looked again. Yes, it was. A minister had come to the rescue of the homeless, starving villagers here, paid them steerage class to Canada on the next ship. I'd often thought half-wistfully of their sorrowful escape, the island disappearing into their dreams and their memories as the horizon receded. But there was new life on this land now. The runrigs lay peaceful in the sun, clothed in green. Down on the beach, on the bars of black volcanic rock that ran into the breakers, I could see groups of seals hauling out to enjoy the midday warmth.

I touched Cam's arm, just lightly but enough to make him start. "Come on. The tide's turning—we might see otters if we're lucky."

We didn't talk for the rest of our way down the rock-strewn climb to the sands. Once on the beach and not struggling to find our footing, the silence became electric, and I knew I had to speak, though my heart was beating harder than the wings of the raven I could see fighting the wind to regain his cliff-face perch.

"Listen," I began, roughly, as if I were about to tell him off. "When I went to Brodick last night—"

"Nichol, don't."

I stopped. Cam had halted a few feet behind me and was watching me miserably.

"I want to explain," I said, but he held a hand out to me.

"No. You don't have to struggle to tell me things I already know. Let me talk."

"Okay, but..."

"Hush up. You got back together with Archie last night. I'm glad about that, because somebody like you should never have to be lonely. All I want to say is—I'm sorry I didn't find you sooner in my life. I'm sorry I didn't know you while there might have been a chance."

I took a breath. For a moment I studied the ripples in the sand at my feet. The air was rich with the tang of seaweed. No wonder my ancestors had lugged it up to the cliff tops to revive their land—it smelled of life, of brine and blood. For me from now on it would always mean happiness, the dawning of a joy so great I wasn't sure I could contain it.

"Let me tell you about last night with Archie," I said, not looking up. "It was meant to be drinks with a whole bunch of my friends. But when I got there it was just him, and—yeah, I got drunk, and I went home with him and I got into his bed. It was what we always did. Then I started thinking about you, and I got straight out again." Cam's mouth had fallen open slightly. I thought I'd better clarify. "I couldn't let him touch me. I don't think I could let anyone but you touch me now, and I don't care how long I have to wait for that."

What had I been expecting? For him to jump into my arms or make me a little speech in return? As it was, he walked straight past me and carried on towards the sea. The sun was in my eyes and I couldn't make out his expression. I followed, stumbling over the long strands of kelp. "Cam? Are you all right?"

"I'm fine."

His stride was powerful, elastic. He was moving like a man with huge weights lifted from his shoulders, and I didn't dare imagine that what I'd told him had produced this effect—just jogged to keep up with him. He was wearing the jumper I'd given him on the night of his arrival. It almost fit him now, and a moment later I saw why. Without breaking stride he pulled it over his head, exposing a torso still pale but warm as new milk in the sun, skin smooth over compact muscle. Helplessly I thought of the seal bride again, how she'd cast off her human skins and returned to the ocean. Her people were there to greet her today, heads and tails held high as they basked, making the shapes of smiles or crescent moons.

"What are you doing?" I enquired.

"It's a beautiful day." His words came to me in tatters on the sharp sea wind.

"Not that beautiful. You'll catch your death."

"No, I won't. Not now." He tied the jumper round his hips and suddenly took off at a flat run.

The seals, safe here for centuries now, gazed placidly as he made for the water's edge and pelted along the shore, sending spray flying. I wished I shared their insight. There was a child in me who wanted to strip off too and dash around on the sand, but I'd had to move so far away from boyhood pleasures that I couldn't close the gap. Cam reached the deep inlet that bounded this stretch of the beach and circled back to me, still at top speed. I'd had no idea how strong and fit he'd become. He was beautiful in motion, his feet barely touching the sand.

Automatically I put out a hand to catch the one he was extending to me, and he grabbed me as he passed, pulling me after him. I gasped and burst into laughter, letting myself be hauled round in a huge half circle. "What are you *doing*, you bloody nutcase?"

"Running." He reeled me in, and I went willingly, a fish jumping out of the water to be caught. "The sun's so bright. I just want to run, or..." He threw his arms around my neck. "Or dance. Dancing would do. What'll we dance to, Nichol?"

"Absolutely anything you like." I was grinning helplessly. The beach was deserted, but no amount of spectators could have made me let go of him. He was already swaying to his own inner beat, drawing me with him. I hooked my thumbs into the belt holes of his jeans. "The Killers are nice in the open air."

"Yes. Oh, yeah—'Human' would be good." He held me tighter, his hips creating for both of us the song's exuberant four-time. He began to sing me snatches of the lyric, laughter shaken, endearingly off-key, bloody thrilling in warm breath against my ear, the enigmatic query about whether we were human or...

"Dancer," I responded, clasping him. At this moment most definitely dancer, an armful of sunlight and energy, ready to burn up and disappear. I kissed his cheek, wanting to make him human again, human enough to stay with me, and he turned his head hungrily. His mouth met mine.

Our movements slowed and stopped. He laced his fingers in the hair at the back of my head and kissed me with such solemn passion that my fears changed and I thought I'd be the one to burn or melt into sunlit seawater and vanish into the sand.

I shuddered, the world falling away from around me, and I cried out in protest as he ended the kiss, pushing me a little way back. "Cam..."

"I want you."

"Oh, thank God." I rested my brow against his. "Yes."

"I know right here might not be practical..."

"Right here if you want."

"I'm probably hallucinating, but...I can see rainbows over the top of that cliff. What's there?"

Reluctantly I loosened my grasp enough to turn and look. "It's spray from the Cliaradh waterfall." I hadn't been there for years. Not for the joy of it, anyway—it was a favourite place for Harry's sheep to escape to when they broke through the fence, and I'd spent several hard winter nights with a torch between my teeth, extricating their sodden woolly bodies from the crevasse. As with most other beauties of the island, I'd lost the sense of its magic. And now, with Cam in my arms, I remembered.

The waterfall cascaded from the cliff top in three huge drops, each of them broken by a horizontal outcrop of black rock. Towards its base, about twenty feet from ground level, the curtain broke up into countless smaller down-rushing fans, each of them throwing off a rainbow halo of spray. To see it in full glory you had to get close. It was tucked back into its own ravine, the notch it was still carving into the lip of the cliff. The first intimation of its presence was its voice, a growing subsonic roar from behind dark walls of gorse and thorn.

Cam pulled ahead of me—we'd walked up from the salt-marsh plain hand in hand—and I let him go, the better to enjoy the sight of his first sight of it. He was still naked to the waist. As I watched, he began to run again, unsteadily this time, blindly grasping at the branches of ash saplings. The track became a muddy ribbon here, treacherous underfoot. Around the foot of the falls was a tumble of ferns and fallen rocks.

He drew closer and closer, reaching out to catch the spray, and then when he came to the edge of the night-black pool where the cataract plunged to meet the stream, he did as I had once done—came to a swaying halt, steadied himself, and lifted his hands high in an instinct of greeting, worship, exultation, something I'd never been able to define for myself but saw clearly in his face as he turned back towards me. His smile was wide and dazzling, his eyes their most limes melting indigo.

"Come here," he called to me across the mud and the vast music of the falls. "Nichol, love, come here."

I didn't know which of us knocked the other to his backside in the mud. We collided hard. I grabbed him in time to stop him cracking his head on a rock, but then we were down, fighting, oblivious to hurt. He pulled my coat off my shoulders and aided my scramble out of it, dragged me with him onto the stones. My jumper went next, and the T-shirt underneath, both of us moaning in frustration at the time it took.

"God, Nichol. Any more layers?"

"That's what you get when you undress a farmer."

"It's like peeling an onion. What am I gonna find in here?"

His hands were on my belt buckle. I lay back to let him find out, gasping at the chill of spray-soaked rocks on my spine. He undid my belt and my zip then gave a sob of laughter at the thermal long johns underneath. "Oh, these should be passion killers."

"Are they?"

For answer he dragged them down, the jeans on top of them and my boxer shorts beneath. My naked backside scraped on stone, but I could hardly feel it, or somehow the cold shot answering fires into the root of my cock, and he gasped as he exposed me. "Oh, Nic."

"All right for you?"

"Bloody lovely. So big."

"I've been waiting for you. Let me see you too." Together we got his trousers and briefs down round his thighs. His shaft sprang up hard and ready as soon as it was released. "You can't have had any complaints," I whispered, painful shudders of excitement running through me.

He was a beautiful dark Gael under all his disguises, his cock arching out of a rich black pelt, deep rose red and striated

170

with veins. We reached for one another on the same half-starved impulse. I grabbed his backside and pulled him tight against me. The hot press of him was almost too much and I cried out, a prayer to the sundrenched sky that I not come right now, that I hold on at least for...

What? I didn't know. We thrust and struggled in the mud, grazing knuckles and buttocks, mouths locking together then tearing apart when the need to breathe or yell became too great. It was enough—more than. I would give it all up any second, catapult my soul to join the ravens wheeling over the cliff. He was there too, bruising me with his grip.

"Cam..."

"Yeah, sweetheart?"

"Want you to fuck me."

"Ah, no. Till the cows come home—when we've got the equipment, but not..."

I jolted up to kiss him. "Now. I trust you."

"Then *don't*, stupid. Why? Why would you trust me?"

"Because you wouldn't do it to me if you weren't clean. And you *are* gonna do it."

"Nichol, I am damn well..." he stiffened in my arms, and I thought I was going to lose him, but he caught his breath and rode the crest out, "...not. Oh, Jesus. I had one lover in Glasgow. Not that I loved him. I hated him."

"Bren McGarva."

"I never let him near me without a condom."

"I lost count of my boyfriends in Edinburgh. I was wild, though, not stupid. I'm clean too."

"This is still bloody madness."

But he reached behind me and dragged my coat across a flat slab of rock almost under a wing of the falls. I choked on laughter as we struggled up onto it. We were going to get soaked. Already stray droplets were bouncing off his back and shoulders. I should have been freezing my arse off, but he was making me burn.

He laid me down, pushed an arm under my head, cradling me. "Ah, Nichol, you daft sod, it's not just condoms we're lacking."

"Can manage without if you go easy. Have done before."

"Me too. It hurt like fuck."

"You won't hurt." Reluctantly I pulled out of his embrace. I needed to lose the restriction of my clothes, the jeans and underwear tangled round my thighs. I knelt up for long enough to deal with those, and then I was naked under the waterfall, lungs shallow and tight with the wild joy of it. "Anyway, I can improvise."

"You look like a sea god. What are you on about?"

"Make you slippy. A bit more than water and sweat, anyway..."

I pushed his knees apart and leaned over his cock. His shout bounced off the cliff face as I sucked him into my mouth. Partway there anyway—I'd need a bit of practice before I could tackle such a lovely length as that in its entirety, and I briefly wondered how I thought it was going to fit in my backside. That would be up to him, though. I almost lost track of my intentions in the pleasures of tonguing him, learning his shape, starting to taste pre-ejaculate...

"Stop." His hips lurched, and he clenched a hand in my hair, stilling us both. "If you want me to do this. Stop now."

He was hauling deep breaths, his face flushed and starred with spray. So beautiful. I sat up and moved to straddle him, but he uncoiled with a wildcat's grace and seized me by the shoulders. Bore me back until I was flat out on the rock, staring at him and the rainbow zenith. "You want this?"

"Yes. Yes."

He knelt between my thighs. He slipped his hands beneath my buttocks and I lifted for him, moaning when he shifted his grip behind my knees. And I was wrong—it hurt like hell, when at last the head of his cock found my entrance and pushed in, so bad at first that I couldn't cope, and grief and frustration rushed in on me like thunderclouds. "God! I can't..."

"Hang on a second." He leaned right over me, letting go of my legs and embracing me. The only hope for me seemed to be clutching him back, clinging for dear bloody life. Arms weren't enough—I raised my thighs to clasp his hips, and the angle changed, and he slipped inside all the way.

I lay sobbing. He held me tight, keeping my shoulders off the rock. I let my head arch back, and his first thrust tore from me the howl I'd been trying to contain, a cry for all the lonely pain of the year just gone, all the hunger, the cold endless nights. Again, his shaft jolting hard into the core of me, and I howled for my ma, for the brother who had been flesh of my flesh. Again, and his stroke found my prostate and I came roaring back into the moment, ghosts flashing off in the sun. Just me and Cam. Me and this perfect lover, fucking me hard beneath the waterfall. I writhed and bucked to meet him, matching his pace. He was rigid, muscles bunching under my hands.

"Come on," I grated out for him, tight against his ear. "Come on. Harder. Yes!"

Liquid fire burst inside my spine. I took fire like an oil spill, all over myself—felt my coming blaze up in my balls, my elbows, the arches of my feet where they were flailing in the air. My toes curled and convulsed with it. My arsehole clamped and gaped, and my muscles locked, squeezing frantically up and down the length of his cock. My scream shot skyward once and then I couldn't make a sound, my mouth contorted in silent wailing as I spurted against his belly, a fierce endless spending that turned the sun blood red in my vision and almost stopped my heart.

"You," I choked out, when I next got a breath, when he was still riding me down the far edge of the explosion, thrusting at me carefully, his shaft still massive in my arse. "You. Let go."

He buried his face against my neck. I wrapped a hand around his nape, squeezing his wet hair. He thrust twice more and went desperately still. "Nichol!"

"What is it?"

"I can't..."

"Oh, you can." I organised such muscles as I had at my command down there, the ones not numbed out in cold fire, to give him a great hard squeeze. My balls were still straining, aftershocks of climax still surging through me. "Come on, *ionmhainn.* I love you. Give it up."

He groaned as if the pain of death was on him. I clung to him, seeing him through it, and yelled out as one of the aftershocks burst up into something else, a joyful wrench of my whole being. His wet heat shot into me. He burst into racking tears.

"I'm sorry," he rasped, powering up one more time into my body, holding us both briefly high in the zenith, up with the clouds and the ravens, safe in the hands of God. "I'm sorry. I love you. I love you too."

We'd pushed it too hard. I wouldn't have undone a second of it, but I knew, helping Cam struggle to his feet, that we'd driven our first time to its far extreme. I wasn't sure I could walk, and he was shaking so deeply all I could do once I'd got him upright was hold him, bracing him against the tremor. He was bedraggled, soaked through. I was no better, but I felt my greater strength and solidity, my capacity to keep warm with his skinny frame—less strapping now than I'd thought, his wild flare of energy spent—pressed against me.

I kicked at the coat with one foot. No good. It had saved me from scouring my back raw on the rock, but it was waterlogged, useless for shielding him. "Come away," I said. "Let's find your clothes."

"Give me a minute."

I stroked his back, rocking him. I'd stay here all day if he liked, naked as I was. Longer—I'd known what it was to have him hit climax inside me, and just now I had no more ambitions. I'd stay until the waterfall turned our flesh to mineral, and there we'd be, a sign for future lovers who found their way here...

Voices echoed up from the track. I caught my breath and listened, and Cam raised his head from my shoulder. No, not lovers, not unless someone had brought a coachload of them here. It was May, the opening of the tourist season, though I'd thought we'd be safe for a week or so longer on this far-flung strand. Walkers. A lot of them from the sound of it, and I recognised one voice among the chatter—Craig from Whiting Bay, whose many summer jobs included guiding wildlife treks. *If you'll just make your way up here, folks, and mind how you go... These are the* Cliaradh *waterfalls.* Cliaradh *means "singing" in Gaelic, and if you listen close you'll hear...*

"Shit!" I let Cam go. He scrambled with me to collect our sodden things. My jumper, his too. He was still in his jeans, just about, but mine were on flagrant display, hanging from the gorse bush where they'd landed when I'd chucked them aside. My boots, one wedged in the rocks, the other underwater. Stifling horrified laughter, we grabbed everything up, and I shepherded him urgently through a gap in the bushes. "Up there. Quick."

A tiny sheep-track led into a tumble of boulders. Praying that only someone who had had to track sheep there would know of its existence, I bundled Cam ahead of me into the sheltering rocks. He tripped and went down on one knee, but we'd come far enough, I hoped—Craig and his walkers were ten yards away from us, well within earshot if we scrambled round anymore.

Catching Cam by the armpits, I drew him into a niche and sat him down. My T-shirt was quite dry. My jumper too, somehow. I shoved them at him, and when he hesitated, pushed them over his head by main force, tugging the sleeves the right way out. I clamped a hand across his mouth, and we stared at one another, frozen. He was decent—covered, anyway—but I was bollock naked.

"Well, I don't know about singing," a cut-glass English voice declared, "but I don't hear those strange noises anymore. What do you think those were, Craig—badgers?"

"Don't be ridiculous, Geoffrey." That was Mrs. Geoffrey, I assumed, just as Sassenach and penetrating. "Everyone knows there aren't any badgers on Arran."

"Maybe it was foxes, then. The vixens make terrible sounds when they're in heat."

I crushed my palm harder to Cam's mouth. Mercifully he shot out a hand to cover mine, and I squeezed my eyes shut, silently convulsing. Poor Craig—he'd told me maybe one in ten of the tourists he brought out here actually noticed the falls. The rest complained about the mud or all the wildlife they hadn't seen.

"Maybe it was wildcats. Or seals," he offered dubiously, and I lowered my face to Cam's shoulder and kept it there until—finally, *finally*—the group finished its inspection and began to filter away down the track.

I jerked my head up. It was that or suffocate. My lungs filled, with a kind of sucking bark not at all unlike that of a seal, and I fell into Cam's arms, howling with laughter.

Cam said, in a perfect Counties falsetto, "Poor Geoffrey," then dissolved himself, clutching at me, sobbing for breath.

When finally we calmed—and it took a long time, far more than reaction to our close call pouring out of us—he was still shivering, his hands on my shoulders still cold.

"Here," I managed, reaching for the other sweater. "Put this on too."

"Nic, I'm wearing all your clothes already."

"I'm okay. Warm again now."

"How can you be?"

I pressed a hand to my own chest then reached out to his. "Tough island bastard. City boy."

His tear-streaked face shadowed. "I'm not a city boy. Not anymore."

Instantly I was sorry. He'd invested a lot—everything he had—into this island life of mine. "No, you're not," I agreed, stroking his hair, which was starting to dry into pale flaxen spikes in the sun. "This is where you live now, here on this freezing rock with me. Just give yourself awhile to acclimatise. Tell you what..." I shook out the coat, which was still clammy wet but had a detachable lining. Undoing a few poppers, I extracted the lining and wrapped it round both of us. I pulled him close to me. "There. Now you need to eat."

The cheese and fruitcake were squashed but still good. He pulled a face when he saw the combination, but I tore off a little of the cake and pushed it into his mouth before he could protest, following my advantage rapidly with a piece of the rich salty cheddar.

"*Nichol,*" he said in disgust, but that was at me, not the taste, and after a moment he grinned. "Yeah. Really lovely. More, please."

We ate in companionable silence, huddled together on our rock. I knew I should make some moves towards getting dressed, but now I was warm again I loved the feel of my just-fucked skin tingling from the waterfall, sore enough in my deep core to remind me how thoroughly he'd had me.

As if he'd read the thought, he glanced up at me. "Are you okay, then?"

"Oh, you know. I can feel where you've been."

"Ah, Nichol—if I've hurt you..."

"No, you daft git. You were so good with me." I rubbed my brow against his, shivering into solemnity. "I've never felt anything like that. I never want to lose the feel of you inside me."

"Well, next time—lubricant. A mattress. I'll show you how good I can be with you then."

I shuddered. *Next time.* And—oh, that husky, half-smiling promise...

"We don't need lube for everything," I whispered, unable to believe that my cock was twitching again. I kissed away salt crystals from the corner of his mouth, tasting allspice and cinnamon. "Are you still cold, love?"

"Yes. Make me warm. Lay me down."

It was simpler this time. It wasn't as slow as I'd have liked, not as much proof for him that I could take it gentle, make it last, because the moment I'd rolled with him down into the moss, stones and seagrass I was lost, but that didn't matter. He was ready too, urgent and electric, pushing up his hips to seek mine. It was where we should have started—just a roll around, cock to straining cock—but God, it was sweet now, climax seizing both of us before a minute was up, together this time, wringing gasps and muffled cries from us, and then—after an exchange of weary kisses, barely formed endearments—bearing us both off resistless into sleep.

The sun was still high when I woke. At this turn of May—the astrological Beltane, Ma had told me, the sun reaching fifteen degrees of Taurus, the ancient cross-quarter—the bright afternoons would stretch out almost to infinity. Cam was sitting up, watching the glittering shore. He must have woken before me. He'd taken off both of the sweaters I'd forced on him and tucked one behind my head, spread the other over my belly.

"I'm not much better at wildlife than poor Geoffrey," he said, "but I think I can see an otter."

I could barely move. The marrow of my bones felt filled with honey. I pushed up, yawning. Yes, there he was—a big *beist-dubh*, a sea otter, tawny spine turning silver as he dived around in the kelp. "Oh, yeah. He's a beauty, all right." I slipped an arm around Cam's shoulders. "I think... Yes, look. He's got something."

We watched in silence while he dragged a fish almost as long as himself out onto the rocks. The sounds of his crunching carried clearly up from the shore, and when he'd finished his meal he settled to wash, licking his spiked coat into order, either unaware of us or untroubled by our presence.

Cam folded his arms on his knees and rested his chin, his expression wistful. "I wish I really did belong here," he said after a few moments. "I wish the place was...written into my name, the way it is in yours."

"What—Seacliff? Don't you like being a Beale, then?" I squeezed his shoulders. "It's a good old clan name."

"Yeah, but it's not mine. I told your granda that because it's really common around Larkhall. I...I do really come from there."

I took this in. "Are you really Cameron?"

"Yes." He turned to look at me. "Yes," he said again, with a deep, soft emphasis. "Always your Cameron. But I never knew my dad any more than you did yours, and his last name's meaningless to me. I feel like I don't have one."

"Well—you know, Seacliff's not my dad's name either. My ma took her maiden name back after he left." I smiled, remembering. "She said she should never have been fool enough to give it away. And she called her sons Seacliff too, legally changed it on our birth certificates. Part of our matriarchal heritage, she told us." I hesitated. I laid a hand gently to the side of Cam's face. I didn't think I'd ever see my mother's ghost again after today, and I couldn't have said why, except that I had a sense she had been waiting around to see me made happy.

"If she'd lived, she'd have seen you as one of her sons. I'm certain of that. So..." A piece of golden seagrass was swaying in the sunlight, softly back and forth as if it wanted to catch my attention. I reached to pick it, and I twisted it round in a circlet and knotted it, and I took his hand. The little loop I'd made fitted closely round his third finger, not at all a bad guess. I twisted the long ends around and around, and made another knot, and kissed his palm to comfort him as one hot tear and then another rolled down his face. "So there you are, *ionmhainn bhan*." *My fair-haired beloved.* "Cameron Seacliff."

Chapter Twelve

His heart was still full of secrets. I knew that. Even after we'd redistributed enough of our clothes to make a civilised journey home and were slowly walking back up the beach, shoulder touching shoulder, he ducked his head and evaded my questions about Bren McGarva. I was happy to let them go. I was full of a dazed joy that seemed to renew itself every few seconds, like surf on the incoming tide, obliterating everything that had gone before, and no matter what his past, Cam was here with me now. I'd make him forget, now he'd let me close enough to try. I'd start the world again for both of us from scratch.

It felt as if the universe approved my plans and was trying to wave me on through. From the moment we got back to the farmhouse and found Harry by some miracle still out on his day trip, I concluded fate was on our side—we could walk in unmolested in our sandy, dripping clothes. We could have a hot bath and stay in it until it went cold, discovering that it would accommodate a bruised, loving, near-exhausted fuck, and after that we'd stumbled out to catch up on our afternoon's work. I'd been rehearsing in my head some kind of story about rescuing a sheep from the waterfall, but knew I couldn't have got through it. The smile hovering over my heart would have turned into a grin, and I'd have told the whole helpless truth.

Which I wanted to, but not yet. I knew all the things Harry would say, and I wanted for a little while to keep this new happiness, this bright sacred flame, just between Cam and me. If Cam had asked me to acknowledge him, I'd have stood up to the old man straightaway, but predictably he shuddered at the suggestion, so I buttoned my lip and left all of us in peace.

Harry inadvertently cleared our path by coming down with some kind of cold and taking to his bed for a few days. It was nothing serious, he testily insisted, and he wouldn't have taken a blind bit of notice of my suggestions that he rest and go easy, but Cam could influence him where I failed. I stayed out of that exchange, drying dishes, letting the two of them get on with it. *There's never been a day when I haven't worked this farm with my own hands,* gugairneach comhachag! A barn-owl chick, that was, presumably a reference to the spiking blond hair.

I pressed the tea towel to my mouth to stop a laugh.

Aye, but if you don't rest now, you might end up more poorly still, and then who will hound the life out of Nichol all day? You know how he is. He'll be up till all hours, playing his records too loud. And the laugh I'd heard, rumbling and reluctant, had been Harry's, not my own.

He wouldn't have a doctor, so between us we took such care of him as he would allow, and his absence from around the barns and paddocks gave us a sweet wild freedom for our first days as lovers. If we finished our rounds early, I could climb with him into the truck and drive out to places I'd loved since childhood and hadn't dared go near in my bitter adult grief. You mostly travelled Arran on the road that followed the shore, but there was one route called the String which led directly across the island's belly, through rolling hills now turning green and gold in the May sun.

I parked the Toyota in a layby—no tourists this time, and the landscape around so spectacularly open we'd have plenty of time to see any coming—and we followed an ancient drover's track over the crest of Beinn Ordha and into the sheltered valley beyond. I'd meant us to stop in the copse of birches I'd always thought would do for mac Mhaighstir's Summer poem, but we never got that far—were stumbling to a halt, tugging at one another's clothes, as soon as we were well out of sight of the road.

Still, I could see them. "The fragrant birch tree is branching over the cairn," I whispered, and Cam laughed and told me to say it in Gaelic, and I got as far as the *bidh am beith* before we crashed down onto the blanket I'd tossed onto the heather. *"Brùchdadh barraich,"* I managed, rolling him onto his belly— *the fresh young buds*—and then was silent, concentrating everything I had into fucking him with such gentle ardour that he would never look back, never think again of Bren McGarva, the last person to plough and possess the shuddery inner recesses of his flesh. I could keep him safe, keep him my Cameron Seacliff forever.

He'd hung the blade of seagrass from a nail in his room, still in its circle. It was the first thing he saw in the morning, the last before he closed his eyes at night. Everything would be fine. He groaned out my name, surged passionately up onto his hands and knees and clutched at the blanket while he came, and I kept my pace—deep, fast, riding easy on the lube and his frantic willingness to let me in—until he was quite done, only then throwing my head back and shouting my own completion to the echoing hills.

I took him to the Machrie stone-circle site, where poor mainlanders who thought one mysterious ring was a wonder came to be astounded speechless at the twelve or more scattered like raindrops on a pond across the vast moor. Like most island men I had mixed feelings about tourists, but I'd always enjoyed meeting them en route down from Machrie, their eyes wide and dazed, guidebooks crumpled in their hands because no description could hope to come close to the reality.

I'd intended my trip there with Cam only to be a walk, a chance to show him one of the wonders of his new home. But as well as the circles there were monoliths, great silent towers commanding attention from miles around, and we walked for miles to stand before the tallest of all, gazing up at its great red sandstone shaft and rounded head, until Cam swallowed in a way I recognised as a desperate attempt to hold back laughter, and I said in hushed tones, as if conveying a deep archaeological secret, "Some people say it looks like a great giant cock," and watched in pleasure as he doubled up. And somehow—power of suggestion, power of the stones, which out here continued their silent injunction to the children of their builders that they dance, weave the strands of life and death into circles, connect themselves with earth and sky through the blood-hot medium of one another's bodies—we ended up entwined in its shadow.

We ended up at last in my bed. It was a chance we shouldn't have taken, but Harry was back on his feet again and had gone off grumbling with his dogs to see what kind of a mess we had been making of the farm while he was ill. He wouldn't have much to complain about, I reckoned.

I'd been up in my room getting into a fresh set of coveralls when Cam tapped on my door. I'd ruined the first set showing him the delicate art of the sheep dip, and was about to spend the afternoon teaching him how to shear. We were eight hours into what would probably be a sixteen-hour day. The barns were clean, the livestock all where they should be, the fences in good repair. I called to him to come in, and he entered diffidently, as if we hadn't kissed each other breathless in the porch five minutes before. He'd only been in my room once before, on the night the birds had scared him, though I wandered freely in and out of his. It was as though he regarded mine as some kind of sanctum.

"You okay?" I asked, hitching up my coveralls. I hadn't yet shrugged into the top half. It was too warm a day for a vest underneath and I paused, letting a slow smile start. I loved the way he looked when something about me had caught his attention. Intent and focussed, as if nothing else mattered to him and I was the only serious business in his world. "Aren't you going to get changed? It's not that the smell of Econo-Dip isn't a huge turn-on, but..."

"I stopped to look at the post."

"Oh, God." I was facing up to bank statements these days instead of shoving into a drawer, but a business envelope still could make me shudder. "Something bad?"

"No. No, actually—not bad at all. The farming grant I applied for came through, but..."

"Did it? Wow." I took the sheaf of papers he was holding out to me. "That's amazing. And we don't have to pay this one back?"

"No. They want to keep you in business, not pull you under. That's why you only get to spend it on agri products from the other businesses they sponsor. But that's not what I wanted to show you." He came a few steps farther into the room then stopped, as if he wasn't sure of his welcome. As if I wouldn't happily have made my bed his for as long as he cared to stay in it. "You remember when you told me Harry still owned the land at the Board of Forestry plantation?"

"Yes." I did vaguely remember, though most of that day was a blur of sleep in my head. "What about it?"

"I just thought it couldn't be right, that the Board was growing timber there and paying nothing to their landlord other than the rent for the ground. I mean, they make a huge profit, and the land's never the same afterwards. It'd cost a fortune to convert it back for grazing or whatever. So I made some enquiries, and—yes, the landlord gets ten percent of all timber-yield proceeds. It's written into the lease."

It was hard for me to work up indignation. I didn't yet know ten percent of what, and I was so pleased with my agri grant that I felt quite well off. Still, Cam had been to a lot of trouble, and I had a duty to protect my granddad's interests if I could. "What, so...they're in breach? They just haven't been paying it?"

"That's just it. The guy I spoke to at the Board was quite offended. Your brother opened a separate deposit account just for that payment, and it's been going in all the time."

"I don't get this. I wasn't paying much attention when the whole probate thing went through, but Alistair didn't leave a will. Wouldn't any accounts of his have been made over to Harry?"

"It's not Alistair's account. He opened it in your name."

"In mine?"

"Yeah. I don't know—maybe he was more worried about the farm going under than he let on, and he thought he could keep the fund from bankruptcy proceedings that way. Or..." Cam paused. I could almost see the cogs of his benign cunning whirring around. "Much more likely, I bet he was trying to provide you with a bit of a cushion if the worst came to the worst. Anyway, here's a letter from them. They didn't mind dealing with me to a certain extent as your, er, financial manager, but they said they'd send the details of the account and what's in it straight to you."

I sat down on the bed. Cam handed me the envelope, and I began absently to rip it open. *A bit of a cushion...* The only likely thing around here was Cam's attempt to sell me that version of events. I thought about Al, cheerfully materialistic, shunting debts around like engines on his old train-set tracks. He'd told me, when I'd decided to stay on at Edinburgh uni for my doctorate, not to expect any support from him or the farm. There'd been no malice in it, just a complete incomprehension. I hadn't asked for help, so we'd parted peacefully enough, and during term times I'd waited tables at the local TGI Friday's and taken on odd interpreting jobs to pay my rent. He wasn't the cushioning type. I could certainly buy that he'd set me up as a tax dodge, though. He'd once hidden stolen cartridges for Harry's air rifle in my pushchair, my ma had told me, so he could load up and have a go when her back was turned. Smiling over the memory, I read the couple of paragraphs the Board had written to me.

I looked up at Cam. Whatever linguistic gifts I had seemed to have been extracted from my ability to deal with numbers. I really did struggle, even with simple things like ten-percent amounts, and anyway I couldn't believe what I was seeing. "Cam, these guys made a hundred and twenty grand off the timber last year. That means..."

"That means there's twelve grand in the account," he prompted me kindly. "They're set to make about the same this year, and they pay out every six months, so in June..."

"Another six grand. That's... That's eighteen."

"That's right, Stephen Hawking."

I fell back on the bed. I stared up unseeing at the ceiling. "My God. I can pay off the Midlothian completely. I can pay a whole lot of our debts, or... No, wait. I can offer Kenzie his job back."

"Kenzie?"

"Yeah, yeah. I know he was an arsehole, but he's all right as long as he's working, and we didn't act fair by him, turning him off the way we did." I waved the unbelievable letter at Cam, instantly reading the shadows that had filled his eyes. "And I can start paying my overworked, brilliant, gorgeous volunteer." I held out my arms, and he came shyly to kneel over me, his sweet grin starting. "What?" I demanded, pulling him down into a kiss. "You think I only need *one* farmhand around this place? How about an advance right now?"

"I'd love one." My cock was lifting. He put down a hand to me, his breath catching softly in his throat. "We can't, though. Not here."

"Why not? There's no law says we can't do it with a roof over our heads."

"Not this one. Not your bedroom."

"What? It's just a room."

"It's yours."

I held his face between my hands. I was trying to work out his objections, but there were depths in those eyes that would never be open to me. I told myself I accepted this. I had so much of him it didn't matter. "I'm not some kind of...hallowed ground, you know," I whispered. "Not something special, or sacred, or—"

"You are to me. Oh, God, Nichol, you are to me."

I stripped him carefully. I kissed each part of him as it appeared, indulging in a little worship of my own. Maybe he was right—maybe there was some kind of sanctity in the air of this ordinary room where I'd spent so many nights of my life I couldn't remember the start of them. If so, it came from both of us. It was *because* of both of us. It sprang up from the places where our bodies touched, where our minds lit up with desire. He was part of it, part of whatever it was he revered. I couldn't find the words to tell him. I skinned out of my coveralls, and I drew him down with me onto our sacred bed.

I'd never seen him stark naked by daylight. I left the duvet folded back, the better to enjoy the lovely shock of it. He no longer ate like a starving wolf cub, and his weight gain had levelled off at that delicious stage where he looked strong and fine but I could still see every detail of his framework, of how he was made. To touch these details with my fingers wasn't enough. I leaned over him and brushed my open mouth across his collarbones, pressed my tongue into the notch between. His ribs were still clearly marked—I kissed them too, each one, until he was moaning and arching up for more. I dwelt for a teasing while on his nipples, giving each my thoughtful attention, catching the taut nubs between my teeth for a delicate bite. His hand was on the back of my head, the gentleness of his caress not hiding its urgency. A less polite young man would have been pushing me south.

Chuckling, I set off of my own accord, licking and kissing my way down his median line, where silky hair the shade of bitter chocolate made me think of a time when he wouldn't have to peroxide away his identity in our chilly bathroom. Maybe sooner than he thought, if all these grants and wonderful payments meant I could get the farm back on its feet. It would be my castle then, and I'd show all hostile comers how an island chieftain defended his realm...

"Nichol, please," he ground out, recalling me to my present duties. I cradled his balls against my palm, lifted, pressed them against his body until I could feel the waiting throb of life in them, a vibration like a powerful car being revved on its handbrake. Then, when he was sobbing and tenderly calling me every kind of bastard under the sun, I took him into my mouth.

It was easy. I'd remembered how, and I was much more relaxed without the possibility of Craig and his trail of ~~sightseers breaking my stride~~. Oh, yes—I shifted to kneel between Cam's thighs, opened my throat and sucked him down. His cock head filled my airway, but I didn't panic—tucked my hands under his arse to restrain the panicked recoil he was trying to make on my behalf, and breathed through my nose, not fighting my gag reflex but letting it roll up and crush him.

He held out through ten seconds of this then came in a great stormy rush, half drowning me, thighs convulsing as he thrust up into my throat. "Jesus, Nichol! Jesus!"

I released him, coughing. He was sitting up for me already, holding out his arms. I collapsed into his embrace, grinding my hips against his until he was thoroughly done. "It's okay," I croaked. "I'm fine. I'm fine."

"Me too, you great soft..." Words and breath failed him and he hung on to me, chest heaving. Then he got hold of my jaw and guided me in for a kiss, swollen mouth, fresh come and all. He was robust about body fluids, I'd discovered, and we'd enjoyed a few sublimely messy exchanges. "That was fantastic. But be careful, will you? It's not an audition for the bloody circus."

I snorted with laughter. "Thanks. Seriously. I'm grand."

"Good. Glad to hear it. Now get yourself lubed up and fuck me."

"What? Are you sure you want me, so soon after..."

"Yes. Completely. I can feel you properly then, concentrate on you. It doesn't even feel like sex, just like being *with* you in the best way I..." He rolled away from me, tugging open the bedside drawer. "I can't explain. Please just do it."

I curled up around his back. His hair was in a damp tangle—I buried my mouth in it, tasting his salt. He was reaching around blindly in the drawer. I knew where the KY was, and I snaked an arm past him to grab it. "Okay. Nothing I want better, sweetheart. But I hope it feels a *little* bit like sex."

He shook with silent laughter. I uncapped the tube and spread so much on both of us I almost slithered off him. Too much felt like almost enough. I could handle a rough dry fuck myself but nothing would have made me go at Cam that way. Early afternoon light was spilling in through the window. Archie would have closed the curtains, even though there was nothing out there to see us but the ravens.

Cam rested his cheek in the crook of my arm and groaned as I entered him, the sun turning his fine skin translucent. He was flushed, his eyelashes sticking together with tears. He grabbed my hand and drew it to his mouth, sucking on my fingers while I found the hot depths of him. He curled over onto his belly, encouraging me, opening up. A seismic rush of love for him went through me, welded tight to orgasm. From ten miles out I could hear my own shattered cries, but I couldn't stop them, couldn't do anything but hang on to him and spill and spend myself into his flesh...

Didn't stand a chance of hearing Harry's footsteps on the stairs. Beneath me Cam jerked and tried to push up. The door creaked but I couldn't make it mean anything. My head was full of lights and stars.

Cam grabbed my hip. "Nichol," he rasped, his voice faint with horror, and the stars cleared.

My grandfather was standing by the bed. His black shape blocked the sun. I snatched one breath and rolled off Cam, reflexively grabbing the duvet and bundling it over him to shield him. Did it make it better or worse that the old man had his damn dogs with him? Vixen's ears were on high-pricked, astonished alert, but the other two had sat down as if making themselves comfy at the theatre.

I struggled off the bed. My crumpled coveralls were within reach—I snatched them, grimly reflecting that just now they were covering too little too late. "Granda!"

His face was like a granite block. His brows had drawn down so far I couldn't see his eyes. "What in Satan's name is going on in here, Nichol Seacliff?"

189

It was bad news when Harry evoked the devil. He hardly needed to—the sunlight behind him was giving him horns. His mud-covered boots looked ready to split and reveal his cloven hooves. I could almost smell brimstone drowning out the sweet tang of Cam's sweat. I shifted a little to the right in a hopeless effort to hide him. "Nothing you had to see. Why did you come in?"

"I heard thy banshee wailing from the yard. A man run through by a pitchfork might make such a sound."

"What—in my bedroom?" My voice wavered, and a warm hand landed on my spine. Oh, God—that was Cam, scrambling off the bed to stand beside me. Blindly I tried to push him back. "Don't you knock?"

"Knock, you unmannerly whelp? In my own house?"

"Aye, in the part of it where you kindly let me lay my head!" I hadn't meant to shout, but there was no other answer to the old man's roar. It was that or surrender, and I loathed the infantile fear worming into my guts. "It's your own lookout what you see, if you blaze in here like a prize bloody bull—"

"Be silent!"

My voice died in my throat. He'd never had to tell us twice when we were children, and he'd never had to raise a hand to us. That barked-out command was enough. It still was.

"You grew up without a father, lad. I thought it my duty to supply that lack." If Harry was aware of Cam at my side, one arm tight—bless him and damn him—round my waist, he gave no sign. He was glaring directly at me, beginning to turn me to stone. I knew what was coming. I'd always known. "I fed you, housed you, clothed you. If I heard you cry, I came to you, and you didnae bid me *knock* when I pulled you off the blades of the plough you and your brother were messing with. I could see all along I had only one grandson worth rearing, but I never stinted you on that account." He paused, and a dreadful grey bitterness gathered on his face. "Much reward I had for it. I never was a man of faith. I'm glad of it—I've never had to question God for taking your fine brother and leaving me with you. With a wee freak of nature who'll never leave so much good in this world as a son of his own to carry on his name, and maybe wipe out the shame his father brought on it."

He was done with me. At last his attention shifted to Cam. I couldn't speak, but I put out a hand in a gesture of warning, of hopeless warding-off. *Don't. Not him.* Useless, of course. "And as for this bleach-polled *gille-toine* that I've fed and sheltered too, at least he's shown me what you are. I'm grateful to him—I don't have time left in my life to waste on finding out."

He turned and walked out. He would have slammed the door if Vixen's tail hadn't still been in the way. I listened, breathing shallowly, to the fading thump of his feet down the stairs.

Cam padded over to the door—closed it quietly then came back to stand in front of me. He took hold of my wrists. His eyes were bleak, all his beautiful colours washed out. "Nichol," he said. "Oh, Nic. Don't let this break you."

It should have. I had a crack running through me, a fracture line, and Harry had just delivered to it what should have been a mortal blow. But the truth was that I'd been cringing from the chance of that blow, dodging its ghost, since Alistair's death. Maybe even for years before, as I stumbled through my adolescence, unresentful but always aware of Harry's pride in my brother.

It was over, the thunderbolt spent. I was still alive—and, God knew, I'd just been spared the long-dreaded task of telling him I was gay. The only thing I cared about was the man in front of me now, naked as day, clutching my wrists.

On whose behalf I was fucking furious. "Stay here."

"Where are you going?"

"After him. He always did this to me—dropped his bomb and walked. Not today."

"Nichol, go easy. He's an old man."

"He's an old bully." I extricated myself from his grasp and began to pull on my clothes. Suddenly pain bladed into me, sharper than anything Harry had been able to inflict. "Yeah, he's an old man. But did you hear what he *said* to me?"

"I did. You'd be within your rights to kill him. Only...don't."

I found a pair of shoes. I gathered up the papers Cam had brought to me from the morning's post. One of them had got into the bed with us and was beyond redemption, but the rest were fine. I paused in the doorway. Stupidly, childishly, I had wanted him to be wholly on my side. But he'd taken to Harry from the start, hadn't he? And the old man, for a wonder, had returned his goodwill. They'd formed a kind of bond, which Cam had just seen shattered.

"Stay here," I repeated more gently. "I'm not going to kill him. But I do have to stand up to him—for both of us—or he's going to eat us alive."

I left him sitting on the edge of the bed, looking too old for his years. Looking already consumed, as if anything I might do to fend off Harry's wrath would come too late for him. That took some of the wind from my sails, but I still had a fair breeze in there on my own account, and it blew me into the kitchen, where the old man was waiting.

No, not waiting. He was opening tins for the sheepdogs' lunch, his back to the door. He didn't expect me to follow him, and why should he? After my boyhood tongue-lashings, I'd taken myself off to hide in the far reaches of the barn until the heat died down. Or until my mother interceded for me... Well, she was gone, even the bright echo of her I'd been seeing since Cam arrived.

No. Something stirred in my chest. I pulled out a chair by the table and sat down. I felt as if someone had put a soothing hand onto my heart, and done it from the inside. She wasn't gone at all.

"Granda," I said, and it wasn't the bark I'd intended. "*Ag éisteachd.*" *Listen to me now.*

He didn't turn. He continued to clatter around with the collies' bowls. Well, that was all right. I could tell from the set of his shoulders that I had his entire, bitter attention.

"You're right. You were the only father me and Alistair had. I'll never be anything but grateful for that, but..." I rested my elbows on the table, spread my hands. I almost wanted to laugh. "You had to be our dad because you'd scared the original right off the island and back to God knows where. He can't have been worth much—not if he caved in to you—but we never got the chance to find out. You bullied him away. That's why things are as they are."

He put the dishes down and came to a halt. I wished he would look at me, but I couldn't make him. "It's okay," I went on. "You were good to me. I never even minded that you loved Al best. That's why—when we lost him and Ma, when they died, you never had to ask me to come home. You took it for granted that I would. Took for granted I'd give up my education and come back here to herd sheep. But...I couldn't leave behind everything I was in Edinburgh, Granda, not even for you. I should've told you I was gay, but there's been nobody who mattered enough until now." I picked up the papers, organised them into a heap. "Speaking of which. Your bleach-polled *gilletoine* upstairs cares more for this place, for you, than maybe Alistair ever did. You don't have to speak to me, or..." my voice scraped dryly and I swallowed, bracing up, "...or distress yourself by ever laying eyes on me again, but come and see these papers. Please."

He was a nosy old sod, and curiosity got the better of him. God knew what he thought I was going to show him. He slammed down into a chair as far away from me as he could, and I slid the papers over. "He's really good with money. He's found all kinds of grants for us, and that forestry land of yours yields a dividend on timber. Alistair..." I hesitated. Something vengeful in me would have liked to say, *Al hid it from you.* "Alistair put it into an account I didn't know about. But it's all there, twelve grand of it, and more to come. Cameron found all that out. He's paid off the worst of our debts. Just bear that in mind the next time you see him. He's saved us."

Harry took his glasses out of an inner pocket and set them on his nose. The gesture, his need for them—the furrow of his brow as he squinted for focus all served to soften my anger, I struggled to remember how much I hated him. He studied the papers for a long time, and then he got up wordlessly and went to the dresser. He pulled an envelope from the drawer and dropped it on the table in front of me. "I have papers for you too."

"What's this?"

"I didnae open it. But I didn't give it to you either, and what you think of that I do not care."

The envelope was addressed to me. I tore it open, bewildered. Since when had he taken to withholding my mail? I glanced at the contents. It was just a prospectus from Edinburgh, advertising their new course in linguistics. "I don't understand. This is nothing. Why did you hide it?"

"It's from yon mainland university, isn't it? No doubt summoning you back."

"No. Not at all. It's just a circular, an advert for one of their correspondence courses. Nothing I could afford to do even if I wanted."

His frown deepened. "Damnation," he growled. "Why must they send their junk here?"

"Why would it be a problem for you?"

No response. He sat down again and began turning over the forestry papers as if the discussion was over.

I couldn't absorb the idea that he had tried to hang on to me. "It wouldn't be a problem now, would it?" I asked. "If I were to go. If you were to see the back of me."

"The back of you? I've just seen considerably more of you than that, you…" He met my eyes and actually thought better of whatever he'd been about to call me. "Ach, God, look at you anyway. Aren't you the spit of your mother? She might as well be sitting there instead of you. I never thought to see her put in the ground before me—not her or your brother either. She was my bairn, Nichol. With you gone, I'd have nothing left."

My mouth went dry. "Well...I don't mean to go anywhere. Not unless you chuck me off your land for being a—"

"Quiet. I don't want to hear it." He was up again, this time heading for the door. He stopped by my chair for a moment, prodding a finger down onto the Edinburgh brochure. "This nonsense they've sent you—is this what you'd want?"

"I don't know. I haven't looked at it. Yeah, probably, but it's not an option. Listen—before you banish Cam as well... If it's the *gille-toine* thing that upsets you, that's not really him." I had to try. I didn't know why Cam thought so much of the miserable old bastard, but that was the one thing I could save. I braced up for a big lie. "It was me. I pressured him, okay? He only did it because he felt obliged to me for—"

A swift rush of footsteps down the stairs. Only half of them, I thought, and yes, there was poor Cam, stumbling into the room with the air of a man who'd been sitting halfway up them, listening unhappily to make sure no blood was spilled. "No, Nicky," he said, striding over to me. He stretched out a hand and I automatically took it. "Don't you say that. Mr. Seacliff, I love this place. And I...I'm grateful to you for everything you've done for me, and I'll leave if you want me to. But I loved your Nichol the moment I saw him. I always will."

Joy hit me, a compact high-speed truck. It knocked out the ghosts from me, sent my second-best childhood flying. I wasn't alive by grace of some administrative error on the part of God, who'd chosen to call home the wrong brother. As usual, elation sparked in me unholy laughter. Forcing it back, I stood up and wrapped an arm around Cam's waist.

"You know," I said, "if it's having no heir that worries you, there's always bonny Shona from over the hill. Maybe she'd let us have a surrogate with her. Then the kid can inherit her acres as well as yours, *and* keep the bloodline intact." I was joking, but beside me I saw Cam give a short, loyal nod, as if the prospect of a baby with a man he'd known for less than four months was no big deal to him.

Way too much for the old man. He gazed at us for a

Harper Fox

moment as if we'd been a pair of ladyboys dressed up for a drag version of the Folies Bergère, and then he turned his back and slowly walked away, forgetting even to summon his dogs. Cam and I stared after him, hand in tight-clenched hand.

Chapter Thirteen

Seacliff Farm was quiet after that. The peace had an aftermath quality to it, as if some natural disaster had struck and left us all alive but shaken. Cam and I moved around the old man cautiously, in a state of eggshell truce he seemed for his part to return. We kept our exchanges—even a touch of hand to hand, anything stronger than a warm glance—well out of his way. Cam kept his distance altogether. He was courteous with Harry as ever, but the shy friendliness he'd offered before, the daring approaches he'd made to a joke with him, were gone. If Harry missed them, he gave no sign. We worked, ate together round the kitchen table, keeping conversation to the weather and the livestock, and let the dust settle.

On the fourth day, another letter came for me from the Edinburgh distance-learning centre. I was first to the post that morning and I took it outside, planning to glance at it and recycle before the logo on the envelope could cause any aftershocks. I sat on my ma's bench by the porch, nursing a mug of coffee. I would have to ask them to stop sending me brochures, I supposed.

It wasn't a brochure. It was a letter thanking me for payment and enclosing full details of the PhD course in linguistics on which I'd been enrolled. My first batch of coursework had been dispatched and an introductory phone appointment with my tutor scheduled. Cam appeared in the doorway, and receiving no response to his greeting, sat down cautiously beside me.

"Is this your doing?"

"No. Not a bit of it."

"Have you seen Harry since breakfast?"

"Yes. He was heading down to the south barn to carry on the re-roofing."

I folded up the letter and tucked it back into its envelope. I put the envelope into a deep pocket of my coveralls, where it wouldn't get muddy or torn, and I could take it out at my leisure and think about its promised delights. Phonetics, dialectics, morphology and syntax... My mind was reaching out like a light-starved ivy stretching tendrils to grab at a fence.

I turned to look at Cam, who was beaming broadly. "Wow," he said.

"I know. I can't believe it. I'd better go and find him."

Harry was dangerously perched at the very top of a ladder on the south barn roof. I'd given up telling him we didn't need to worry about fixing it till later in the year.

"Hoi," I said quietly, not wanting to startle him. "I've had some mysterious mail."

"Oh, have ye now?" He continued fixing slates into their place in the new wooden framework. "What interest do you imagine that could hold for me?"

"None, I should think. But I'll have to cancel it, you know. We can't afford this."

"Don't you be telling me what I can and can't afford on my own farm." The ladder wobbled precipitously. I made a steadying grab for it. "Yon lad has showed me his accounts. I have my money for the timber, and..." He picked up a mallet, waved it at me threateningly. "And whatever I have besides is no business of yours."

"You've got it all stashed in your mattress, haven't you? I always knew."

He took a handful of nails, stuck five of them into his mouth and hammered the sixth into a beam. I had to wait until he'd disposed of them all before he spoke again, and when he did he sounded altered, unlike himself. "Yon lad is at odds with me, isn't he?"

I sighed. "Why don't you try calling him Cameron? I'm not saying that'll fix things, but it might help." I braced the ladder while he lurched for a new set of nails. "He's not at odds with you, no. He's just...upset."

"Very well, then. Yon lad—Cameron—is upset with me."

"Are you honestly surprised?"

"No. I have said a thing to him I now regret."

Personally I thought it had been more than one. I considered asking him how he felt about the things he'd said to me, but I knew there was no need. His feelings, his regrets about those—his apology—were here in my pocket. "Why don't you tell him you're sorry?"

More hammering then a reverberant silence. "It is no' becoming for an elder to lower his head to the young."

"It is no' becoming for him to call the young a bleach-polled *gille-toine* in the first place."

"I suppose he has foolish pleasures like your own, Nichol. I suppose he'll wish to occupy himself with something while you fill your brain with outlandish languages no honest man could ever wish to learn."

It took me a moment to interpret the outlandish code being spoken to me now. "Yes," I said, catching on. "He likes to make sculptures out of spare parts and scrap metal. I found Al's soldering kit in the barn. He doesn't need much more than that—just somewhere to work, and a bit of time."

"Fòir le tròcair orm." Mercifully save me—a plea to heaven to let him understand, or bear at least, the vagaries of the young.

"He expects nothing of the sort, of course. You could just say you're sorry."

"Did all the sheep die in the night, *leanabh*?"

I rested my brow on the ladder's silky wood. I hadn't thought to be called his child again, not in that caressing old word. It shouldn't have mattered to me. And things *had* changed—I didn't rely on it, could live without it if he chose to withhold that or anything else from me again. Still, it was good to hear. "I don't believe so."

"Then you have work to do. Elsewhere."

The storage shed nearest the house was echoing empty. I only discovered this when I went in to collect a sack of feed. I knew where everything was and hadn't bothered to switch on the light, and I stopped, frowning, when my hands passed through the space the sacks had occupied.

A faint blue twilight was falling through the shed's single window. Cam was sitting on an upturned crate, one knee drawn up to his chest. I might not have noticed him, but his blond flag gave him away. Dust motes floated around him, catching a sapphire gleam. He looked up at me, expression unfathomable. "You didn't do this, did you?"

I walked into the middle of the vacant space and glanced around me. My eyes were adjusting. Only that morning the shed had been full of feed, cartons and other detritus that had no home elsewhere. A long workbench had appeared from somewhere, new electric extension cables curled on it like orange snakes. In one corner, all the tractor parts and other scrap Cam had set aside had been neatly piled up.

"No," I said. "Not me. I'm not sure how he did it either."

"I saw Dave and Eddie from Shona's farm about the place this morning. I didn't think anything of it."

"Did he give you...? Are Al's tools in here somewhere?"

"Yes. In that beautiful wooden chest over there, along with new gauntlets and half a dozen canisters of propane for the torch."

I went to stand beside him. "Budge up," I said, and made room for myself on the packing crate. I put an arm around him, and held him close when he leaned into me. "It's okay. It's okay."

"What am I going to do? How do I thank him for this?" He rubbed his brow against my shoulder, and I felt the heat of his conflicting thoughts. "I'm not even sure I should, after the other day. The things he said to you."

"He lost his daughter and his grandson. He's never, ever talked about it. Those things he said—that was him grieving for them. He'll probably never mention them again."

"He might as well have stabbed you. How could you bear it? How could you bear coming second with him all your life?"

"I came first with my mam." Kissing the top of his head, I considered this. "No. Just differently. I come first with you."

A fervent nod, a silky brush against my cheek. "Always. Forever, if I get any choice in the matter."

I closed my eyes. This was how it would feel, then, to want a whole future with someone. To see it unspooling in front of me, a wide Highland track, swept with sun and infinite possibilities. I hadn't thought to find out this soon in my life. Forever. *A-chaoidh*, in Gaelic. A beautiful, dangerous, mesmerising word. "Yes. Me too."

"Good." He shifted a little, pressing his mouth to the pulse in my throat, to the sensitive angle of my jaw. "But what do I do about this? I'm still so pissed off with him. And I kind of want to go and throw myself at his feet."

"I know. He has that effect. Look, we're not a family who talks. We never have been. He's never going to say to us, *sorry, lads, I was wrong, I'm proud of my gay grandson and his partner.* And he'd die if you went in and tried to thank him for setting this place up." I took his hand, undid it from its tight clench on my shirt and kissed its palm. I'd do better than a seagrass ring for him shortly, I decided. There was a Celtic silversmith away up in the north whose work was almost fine enough to do justice to such a hand. "Just...be the way you were with him, if you can. He loved that—having someone around who respected him but wasn't afraid to tell him what was what, have a bit craic with him. And come in here and use this stuff, just like I'm going to open up the pile of papers and books that arrived this morning from the uni and use those."

Harry and I circled the new structure in the shed. We moved warily, slowly, neither of us wanting to be first to speak. His idea of art was the print of horses in moonlit waves that had graced every respectable household wall in the '50s, and my realm was words. Neither of us was qualified to judge. Normally that wouldn't have stopped the old man, but a dynamic had shifted between us and he trod carefully around me now where Cam was concerned.

Finally he stopped, put his head on one side and took in the skeletal, gaunt arrangement of warped metal plates from top to bottom. "Is this what you young ones call art these days, Nichol?"

I wasn't sure. I'd have liked to ask the artist, but he had made himself scarce, slipping out into the yard as Harry and I came in. For me, the picture had been Cam himself, at work on this strange construction. He'd looked more like a docker than a sculptor, a welder riveting bulkheads in a shipyard on the Clyde. For all Harry had eased off on his schedule—mine too, giving us both time for new projects—Cam seldom got in here before dusk, and he liked to work by the light of the torch. In its ice-blue glare he was ready for the Olympian forge, I thought, a young Hephaestus restored to straight-limbed health. The rhythmic clang as he hammered out sheets of metal called me from my books and into his domain, and I would sit quiet and watch. There was nothing subtle or tranquil about his approach. He went at it with the same focussed effort he brought to his tasks around the farm. It was a beautiful struggle, and soon he would be daubed in rust stains and soot, red-black on sweat-damped, straining muscle. I always meant to leave him be. But when he noticed me—when he flipped up the plate of his visor and grinned at me, the gun still burning in his hand—I was lost.

I tried to pay attention to the product. He'd let it be known it was finished, casually throwing out over our morning coffee and the newspaper that he was done. There'd been no signs of any grand opening, so Harry and I had made our awkward way there after hours, embarrassed to have arrived at the same time. I wanted to be able to say something intelligent about the sculpture when next I saw Cam. I could see that it was powerful, as tensely packed as he was with hidden significance. But whereas I'd picked my way past a good few of his locks now, I couldn't quite grasp this. It seemed oddly chaotic, for all the intent that had gone into its creation. The shadows fell strangely on it.

I realised the overhead bulb was on. Harry had automatically pulled the cord when we came in, and a dusty yellow glare lay over everything. There was still plenty of light in the western sky, so I switched the overhead off and came to look at the sculpture again, from the window side this time.

I broke into laughter. It was just so bloody perfect. "Granda," I said. "Come over here for a second."

He saw it immediately. No one who lived around here or loved this part of the island coast could miss it. In this light, from this angle, the random sheets and links became a down-rushing flow. I could almost see the rainbows.

"*Damnar mi,*" Harry declared under his breath, a phrase as near to *well, I'll be buggered* as Gaelic got. "It's the *Cliaradh* waterfall, as sure as you're standing there. You know—the place where you lost all those sheep."

I now had so many better associations with the place that I barely registered the gibe. "Yes, I know. It's fantastic."

"Aye. You can fairly hear the mermaids."

I glanced at him, puzzled. If he'd even been aware of any mermaid tales around here, he'd never given any sign of it. He wasn't a man to hear them or to see them combing their hair on the rocks. To me, if anything, he was the rocks himself—crusted with barnacles, unchanging, same now as he had been when he put me on his shoulders and bore me down to see the seals on Kildonan strand.

Movement in the doorway distracted me. There was Cam, leaning one shoulder on the far wall, hands in his pockets. The step I'd taken to see him had thrown his sculpture back into dynamic chaos, beautiful still, demanding interpretation. Our eyes met. "So," I said to the old man, who was still absorbed in his study of the piece. "What do you think?"

"If you'd told me so sorry looking a lad had such a thing in him, I'd have laughed. Why doesn't he make more and put them for sale?"

"Don't be mercenary. He's only just started."

"If he wants to starve, he can do it in a garret, not my farm. We could stick a few up by the roadside. Tourists will buy anything."

Cam's head went down. His shoulders quivered. I decided to push it. "Is that all you have to say, you old Philistine?"

"What do ye want? I'm glad I cleared the shed for him." He was silent for a moment. There was better to come, I could tell— Harry Seacliff face-to-face with modern art. "He's no' such a waste of space as I'd thought."

That finished the poor artist off. He buried his face in his hands.

"Well, maybe he's like his sculptures," I said, loud enough for him to hear. "You have to see him by a certain light."

In the weeks that followed, there were things I forgot. Summer blossomed over Arran, and I forgot the black winter cold. Forgot the sting of hail on my nape, the world of freezing mud and incipient frostbite. Cam and I worked hard as ever, but we took our leisure out into the gilded, heat-hazy hills, and there—watching their slopes and crests over his shoulder, clinging to him while he loved the living daylights out of me—I forgot about pain.

I felt I had it all. My mind had shaken off the rust of a year's disuse, and I'd made a fresh start on my thesis. Having that reconciled me to the dumb-muscle labour of the farm, which transformed into valuable thinking time for me, and then, as the season went on, something more—a work I'd undertake willingly, for the sake of seeing this patch of land I'd grown up on thrive and flourish under my hand. The old man seemed to sense the change and started to work with me instead of frogmarching me from behind.

The three Leodhas wool tups grew up big and healthy. With the money from the grants we were able to bring in more help for the planting season. Kenzie had vanished off the island, but his missus and his eldest kid were just as good at fencing and herding as he had ever been and came up from Brodick part-time, evidently more relieved than anything else at his departure. Archie ceased to press on my conscience—the next time Cam and I ran into him, the circumstances were even less promising than our performance in the grocery-store aisle, but if he'd noticed the swift ravenous kiss we'd stolen in the front of the Toyota before putting on our best behaviour for our shopping run, he gave no sign, and greeted Cam civilly, talked to him about the weather.

The days began to pass in a sunlit dance, and I forgot.

Chapter Fourteen

"How's it coming on, then?"

I surfaced from an ocean of linguistic abstracts. A mug of coffee—my fifth that afternoon—had appeared at my elbow. I had an assignment due the next day, and Cam, in between taking over all my work around the farm, was keeping me supplied.

"Not bad." I scrolled back up a few pages on my laptop screen. "If kids from non-base-positive linguistic groups can easily learn base-positive languages, there must be an inherent link to bridge the two."

"Really? That's fantastic." He stood behind me, took the knots out of my shoulders with a few deft, delicious strokes then planted a kiss on the side of my neck. "If only somebody other than you on the whole planet cared."

I grinned. "Cheeky bastard." Other people did care, as I'd discovered since our newfound financial stability had allowed me to get broadband installed. I had a lively network of other far-flung rural academics who divided their time between their dissertations and hard manual graft. My sense of isolation, both at home and globally, was gone. "There's a guy in Reykjavik who thinks I'm the new Noam Chomsky."

"There's a guy in your kitchen who might mind that if he knew what it meant."

I stretched my arms up, drew him down to me. "Don't worry. He's ninety years old, and he's got a beard you could lose a sheep in. And it just means I'm incredibly clever."

"Oh, I see."

He brushed his lips over my ear, and the screen blurred in

front of me. He ran his hands down my chest, and his fingers probed under the waistband of my jeans, finding the target an inch below my navel where I'd touched myself the night of his arrival, dancing in the kitchen on my own. I didn't know what lay under there—an energy centre, my ma would have said, a chakra—but he could make me hard with the lightest pressure on the spot, a clockwise circling.

"How's things in the shed?" I managed, sounding only a little strangled.

"Not bad. I've started something new. Not sure if I'll dare finish, though."

I didn't push. He was gruffly enigmatic about his art, and I would see the results when they were done, not before. "Are you getting time, what with Harry being out of action and doing all this stuff for me?"

"Harry's better today. He did the light feeds. And Jen and Kenzie junior are great."

"Okay. Good. Then have we got time for a quickie?"

His chuckle broke against my neck, making the hairs rise. "I have, yeah. Not so sure about you."

"I want you, Cam. Want to taste you, swallow you down."

"Och, God. Is there anything hotter than a well-brought-up island lad talking dirty?"

"I don't know. You can tell me when I'm sucking the come out of you."

"*Nichol...* Laundry room do for you?"

"Oh, yeah."

I hustled him into the concrete five-by-five space where we kept the ancient washing machine and luxurious new dryer. It was well ventilated, the windows high and small. Harry had to put up with the occasional casual kiss these days, the sight of his grandson on the sofa with his arm around another boy, but there we drew the line for him.

I pushed Cam up against the dryer, blindly slammed the door behind us and dropped to my knees. He was so wound up and ready that I barely got him into my mouth before he cried out, buried his hands in my hair and let go, and I was little better. We'd managed a good few slow dances now, keeping it quiet in my room, the door firmly locked, but mostly we still jumped one another like randy tigers, the sights and sounds of climax in the one driving the other half crazy with need.

"Cam," I choked out as soon as he withdrew. "Please..."

"Yes. On my way for you, lover." He knocked me down with gentle force onto the concrete floor. He stretched out on top of me, pushing a knee between my thighs, reaching to cradle my skull. He drove his free hand into the gap between our bodies, clasping me so tight and hard it didn't matter that the explosion tore me apart—he brought me home again, brought me down safe. In one piece somehow, locked in his embrace. He was the heart of my world, my gravity, my sun. My life before him was a dream from which I'd joyously awoken. He turned this dusty cell into a prince's chamber, hung it with satin and silks. I loved him.

He helped me onto my feet. We brushed one another down, fastened zips and shirts. He put my hair back into some kind of order, wiped away traces of semen from around my mouth. Then he steered me back through into the kitchen, pulled out a chair and sat me down in front of my computer again. "There. Now work."

"You're kidding."

"Nope. That's due in the morning, and I want to proofread it tonight. Here—your coffee didn't even have time to go cold."

He was gone. I drank my coffee and tried to collect my thoughts from their scattered orbit. The afternoon sunlight was delicious. Just for a while I drifted, resting my chin on my hand. Philology was fascinating, but so was the view from the kitchen window. I'd watched it through all seasons, through all the years of my life. It was perfect now, dreaming in the heat. A flock of lapwings had settled on the sweep of moor nearest the house and were involved in some mysterious parliament, emitting their curious cries, more akin to a computer game than birdsong. My lover, tanned in his white T-shirt, was making his way back to the west pasture where he was fixing a stretch of wall. Harry had showed him how to drystone, and he'd picked it up straightaway, as I never had in all the old man's years of trying to get through to me how block fitted to block in the courses. They'd worked together wordlessly, both of them content. Scents of thyme reached me.

Thyme, crushed grass, a tang of petrol. I listened, and a familiar thrum began to rise on the breeze. Soon it was a roar, and I smiled as Harry broached the horizon on our one remaining tractor. He'd been off-colour for the past few days, but he'd sworn he wasn't about to miss a ploughing season. His father had done it with horses, and his father before him, and so on back into the mists of Seacliff time. There'd probably been some proto-Seacliff here in the Paleolithic, stamping along behind his team of oxen.

The tractor was more or less held together by its rust. The plough blade was new, though, a grant acquisition of which Harry was savagely proud. There he was, a splendid charioteer in woolly hat. He must still be feeling the cold, and I wondered if he'd got out of his bed today just so he could try his new toy. I watched him manoeuvre the tractor into position, the southwest corner of the field he was going to plough to set our next crops of oats and barley. The engine's snarl became a steady beat. Back and forth he would go, in a pattern that looked simple but took years to perfect. A straight furrow, a neat turn. Back and forth.

I turned my mind to my work. Words and ideas came to me, disciplined somehow by the rise and fade of the tractor's motor. I typed rapidly for a while then stopped to check a reference in a book.

The lapwings were taking off. There were a good few hundred of them, and they cast a shadow like a lazy seal in water. I wondered what had startled them, though it only took one bird to send a ripple through the flock's weird composite awareness. Their combined wing-beat made something flutter inside my own head, a hypnotic effect of their shimmer. Unease touched me. Probably it was only Clover or one of her grown-up, predatory brood, stalking rabbits in the long grass.

No, not Clover. She'd been asleep for hours in her customary spot while I worked, on a cushion I set out for her to keep her off my laptop board and have her within companionable arm's reach. She was sitting up now, without any of her customary stretching and gargoyle yawns. She stared out into the warm day, and seemed to come to a grave, still attention, which transfixed mine.

I stood up. At the far end of his furrow, Harry executed a perfect turn. The field sloped downward to the north, and as I watched he picked up speed. Beyond the northern boundary lay the deep little lochan that never dried up in the warmest of summers. It was the one place on the farm I didn't like, the water brackish and opaque, silent on its secrets. An awkward piece of land, the field above it difficult to plough, but we had to make the best of every acre. I realised I was waiting for Harry to slow down. He should be pulling up right now, getting position for his next change.

I watched. This was stupid. Why wasn't the old bastard putting on the brakes? A flash of white caught my vision. That was Cam, pelting frantically for the quad bike parked by the gate. I didn't see him get there, though I heard the bike roar. All I saw was Harry and the tractor hit the barbed-wire fence and sail on through.

I ran out barefoot. That was something Arran farm boys learned not to do, not unless they wanted lockjaw off the first rusty nail. I didn't notice till the thistles were catching round my ankles, pebbles bruising my soles. By then it was too late. I'd vaulted one five-bar out of the yard and was blazing onward to the next. I couldn't have done it if I'd been asked politely, but they felt like nothing to me now. Like toys, bits of matchwood. I took the gate into the paddock with one careless hand on the top rail and landed running. I couldn't see over the hillcrest from here. The most direct route would be across the plough, but it was fresh, the brown earth damp and fragrant, just starting to call down the seagulls. Too rutted underfoot for speed. Instead I turned and belted up the margin of the field, where summer's first poppies were glowing, spots of scarlet that burst on my retina and blended with blood haze.

The tractor had torn the fence to shreds. Three posts were out of the ground, the wire between them snapped and tangled. I crashed to a halt at the gap, breath heaving in my chest. I couldn't tear my eyes off the ground, off the tyre marks. They ran straight out from the end of the last furrow and continued, two deep channels, into the turf beyond. From here—from the crest above the loch—there was only one place left to go. I knew that. I didn't have to look. I wouldn't look. I'd fallen asleep in my sunny postcoital daze, perhaps—I was asleep at the kitchen table, one elbow ready to slip off the edge and jolt me out of this dream. It didn't fit. I couldn't fit it into the pattern of my universe, that a minute ago I'd been there and now I was here.

But that was how disaster came. I took hold of one fence post, not flinching when a barb drove into my palm. Alistair and my mother, sitting on a bus at a junction outside a Spanish theme park. Most likely it had been sunny there too, light streaming in through the windows. That was how endings began. I raised my head. There was the quad bike, slewed to a halt on the shore. No sign of the tractor, the old man or Cam.

I'd kept my silence until now. I'd needed all my breath to run. As I raced down from the crest, the names formed themselves in my throat and began to tear out of me, cry after cry. "Granda! Cameron! Cam!"

Only the lapwings replied to me, skirring in the empty hollow sky. I didn't understand how the surface of the water was so calm—not to have swallowed so much so fast and leave no sign. Harry had told me and Al that it was bottomless, but I'd thought that a story to scare us away. It had worked. We'd never swum here.

The shore didn't admit a headlong dive. Too shallow for the first few strides, the mud sucking viciously—I waded in clumsily, scanning the murky water. Nothing. Then, when I was hip-deep, the bank angled sharply out from under my feet. I didn't bother to fight. I welcomed the drop, kicking off at my last instant of purchase, plunging down.

Five thousand years of slow-layered peat had turned the water sable. Sunlight only penetrated the top few inches. Beyond that all was black. I'd snatched one shallow breath before going under, and it didn't last me long, no more than twenty seconds of blind reaching in the dark. Not good enough. I mastered myself with a terrible effort and went up for air. With it came adrenaline, a great rush that wiped away my fear. I was a good swimmer. I was strong. Since Cam's arrival I'd eaten and slept well, recovered from the winter. Everything I loved was just beneath me in this water—I would bring it home.

I gathered myself and dived. The water seemed to welcome me. I didn't have to fight my own buoyancy the way I would in the sea. The freshwater cold gripped my limbs. I struck out downwards, shirt and jeans weighting me. Long pale shapes drifted near me, catching the last of the light, but when I grabbed at them they dissolved into reeds, the pondweeds that were the only things that could live in the peat-acid depths. Three more strokes and I was blind, hunting in the pitch-black. I tried for method. I should quarter my search area, not fumble over the same spot again and again. I was strong. I was, as I'd told Cam not twenty minutes before, very bright.

I was lost. My breath ran out and for a heart-stopped instant I didn't know which way to go to get more. Up looked like down in here, just sterile blackness above and below. Fireworks silently burst in my brain, and then there was the faintest gleam of gold—oh, God, Cam's hair, I prayed, his absurd bloody attempt at a disguise that would let me save him now... I lurched for it, thrusting out a hand, and it turned into sunlight. The surface burst open around me, delivering me into the air. I sucked it in gratefully—once, twice, three times, till the red blossoms faded—but I didn't belong here anymore, not in this bright upper world. It was utterly vacant for me. I dived again.

Again and again. The fourth time I saw the tractor, a blue gleam as clouds came and went in Arran skies I thought I'd seen for the last time. The cab was at a sixty-degree forward pitch, and when I grasped its frame and reached inside it was empty. I convulsed and breathed water. An unwanted urge to survive propelled me back up—for the last time, I knew. The flooding of my lungs was horrible, was triggering expulsive reflexes, but beneath the seizures—already beginning to be a little less bad, less of a terror than I'd imagined—there was a waiting peace.

Shapes in the water beside me. Not reeds this time—something solid, real and struggling. I broke into the light one more, and Cam surfaced beside me, the old man clutched tight in his arms.

I found purchase in the mud. Not much, just a foothold, but it would do, and I swung round and seized Harry's shoulder. Cam had the other one still, though his shallow sobs for air sounded desperate, a breath off dying. Between us we got the old man into some kind of a tow hold. He'd lost his hat. His head lolled back and I tried to support it, unable to bear its limp abandonment, but then I needed my free hand to clutch at the turf and help Cam haul him, inch by scrambling awkward inch, up onto the bank.

I found some solid ground beneath my feet and took over. "I've got him," I rasped, taking him by the armpits, and Cam dropped to his knees, letting go.

I dragged the old man a couple of yards higher up onto the shore. He was deadweight, tearing muscles in my back and shoulders, but I couldn't register the pain. Once he was clear of the water, I ran back for Cam, who had collapsed facedown into the shallows and looked set to drown in the last inch.

"No. Sweetheart, come on." I grabbed him under the ribs and lifted, gasping with relief when he reanimated and began to struggle like an outraged cat. "Up here a bit. I've got you. Breathe."

I dumped him on the turf beside Harry. Yes, I had both of them. One was choking and retching up the water from his lungs, so I turned my attentions to the other—to my grandfather, supine in the sunlight in his oldest anorak, the one he used for heavy-duty days, and his much-patched corduroy trousers. He'd lost one wellington too. His foot stuck up, big and bony, in its wet sock. He would be so pissed off about the other boot.

"I'll get you a new pair," I said, as if he'd complained, and I dredged up my memories of a high school first-aid class and tipped his head back to check his mouth for obstructions. Nothing, but he was full of water. I had to do something about that. I remembered a line from *The Odyssey*—Odysseus crawling up onto the sands, more dead than alive after a shipwreck. *The sea had soaked his heart right through.* I liked it better in the Greek. Such beautiful mournful sounds. Harry's sea-soaked heart lay, a lead weight, in his breast, and I felt my own turn to lead and cried out, a weird harsh sound like none I'd ever made before. "Granda, no!"

Cold hands closed on mine. I looked up and Cam was there, his hair plastered down on his brow, his eyes hollow. "Let me help you."

"No. I have to do it." I had to breathe for Harry, if there was anywhere inside him for the air to go. I didn't bother feeling for the flicker of life in his throat. If it was there he still needed air, and if it wasn't he needed air anyway. Air was something I could give.

We'd never been much of a family for touching. *Go and kiss your granda* was for little boys whose grandfathers did not resemble a granite outcrop. To place my mouth on his twisted my guts with weirdness and repulsion, and I angrily curbed the response—I'd have done this without batting an eyelid for a stranger. I breathed out, remembered I was meant to close his nose off and did it again. I couldn't remember how many times I was meant to repeat this before I pushed on his chest. I sat up, shuddering. "Shit. I don't know how."

"Let me try."

"No, just tell me... How many times do I breathe?"

"Twice. Twice, I think, then about thirty compressions."

By the time I got to fifteen my head was spinning. There was a boiling pain in my throat I couldn't allow to be grief, and my lungs wouldn't fill between my exhalations. My arms were trying to fold. When Cam pushed me aside, I didn't have the strength to fight him off, and I subsided onto the turf and stared at him numbly. He was doing everything right, I was sure. Even half drowned he looked competent, his face as intent as if he were working on a sculpture. That same focussed passion. Breath after breath after breath, and then stiff-armed compressions, his palms flat to Harry's chest. Yes, all that was good. I couldn't understand why he stopped after the fifth or sixth round and sank down beside him. I couldn't understand why he was crying.

The one thing neither of us had done was check for a pulse. It seemed like a solution, and I lurched forward, grabbing Harry's wrist. Nothing, but I knew it was difficult to find there sometimes. Better to feel the carotid.

Okay. Nothing was working here. I had to find the next step, get past this stupid impasse where my grandfather, my last living relative, lay dead on the shore of a loch. It was still the same beautifully sunny day it had been when I went into the water. Solutions had to lie all around me. What the fuck did people do?

They called for help, of course. We lived in our own little world on Seacliff Farm, dealt with our triumphs and catastrophes ourselves. That was ridiculous—what did I carry a mobile phone about with me for? It was still in the pocket of my jeans, though God knew how, except Cam had said I wore them tight to drive him crazy. I knew there was no signal down here. Clambering onto my feet, I shook my head clear of stars, and then I ran.

The slope up from the loch was steep, my clothes heavy on me. And something had happened to my muscles, which felt rigid and rubbery at the same time. The climb seemed to take me forever, but when I staggered out onto the moor near the road, I reckoned I had almost made it. The signal was good just along this stretch—I used to sneak out here to call Archie. I prised the phone from my pocket and stared at its blank, waterlogged screen.

I woke up. I returned with a shudder to the surface of my mind. I knew Harry was gone, but still I had to get help out here in case there was a ghost of a chance. I looked down the road for a car to flag down, but the black tarmac ribbon was empty and could stay that way for hours. The nearest place to make the call was from the house. I couldn't leave Harry alone, though—couldn't leave Cam alone with him. Best I send Cam and keep vigil myself. All right, that was something to do. Swallowing hard, I tore back down through the nettles and the bulrushes.

Cam was balled up by Harry's body, his hands locked round the back of his skull. I dropped to my knees beside him and tried to take him in my arms, but he flinched from me, shaking with sobs.

"Cam. Cam, love, I need you to go back to the house." He didn't respond. I put a hand on his shoulder. "My phone's dead. Please, go back to the house and call an ambulance."

The wind stirred the reeds, sent a spectral pattern dancing over the water. Abruptly I ran out of everything—the shock that had kept me moving, breathing into a dead man's lungs, and the brief commonsense that had tried to come to my rescue afterwards. I was sick and cold.

"Cam," I tried one last time. "Help me. I need your help."

He uncurled and lurched to his feet. His breath was coming in great ragged gasps. He took a step backward, fell on his backside and scrambled up. Tears were streaming down his face. He met my eyes, and a desolation passed between us, a hollow despair I would never forget.

"I'm sorry," he choked out, turning away, beginning to run. "I can't. I can't."

Chapter Fifteen

I sat in an office at the War Memorial Hospital in Lamlash. At last the afternoon had clouded over, as if belatedly catching up with events. I watched the rain beginning to fleck the window. I'd taken time to wash and comb back my hair, and I had on clean clothes. I was dry-eyed, composed. My hands were folded in my lap. The window looked out over Holy Island, where the Buddhist monks tended their goats.

"Nichol?"

I blinked and returned polite attention to the grey-haired man sitting opposite me. His name was Dr. Ferguson, and he was part of the background of my island life. Mumps, measles, childhood jabs. Broken bones, holiday inoculations. A kindly family doctor. If it was hard for me to focus on him now, it was just that he was so familiar. This office too, with its plants and blue-tacked art contributions from the children's ward. If you'd asked me, I'd have said that placing a terrible one-off event on a mundane background would have highlighted the tragedy, not blurred its edges, not made it into a horror you read about in the papers in a country an ocean away.

"Nichol, is there somebody at home who can look after you? You've had a dreadful shock."

Somebody at home. I gave this thought. It was a chance for me to piece together the time between the loch shore and this quiet room, and I welcomed it. I wanted to make sense. I'd ended up making the 999 call myself. I'd dragged Harry a couple more yards up the bank so his feet wouldn't get any wetter than they were. I'd thought about covering his face, but unless I took off my shirt—and that had seemed all wrong—I hadn't had anything to do it with. As a last idea, I'd turned him on his side. The recovery position, that was called. I'd heard stories of miracle revivals. Then I'd run back to the house. The call itself had been easy. Everyone knew everyone on Arran. I hadn't had to give a postcode or directions. As soon as I'd said *Seacliff* the operator knew, and then it was all out of my hands.

The house had been silent. I'd hung up and stood listening, looking through the kitchen doorway. There was my laptop on the table, the mug of coffee Cam had brought me. A small-scale Marie Celeste, that scene, a tableau in a museum. From upstairs had come a clicking sound, shocking me with flashing, unwanted images. The turn of a key in a bedroom door had come to mean sex to me, the quiet exclusion of Harry, his dogs and the world, the prelude to scenes of unimaginable pleasure. I'd gone upstairs and stood outside Cam's room, resting my hands on the doorframe. He hadn't responded to any of my questions, my pleas to tell me at least he was all right, until I'd threatened to kick in the door.

I'm all right. Leave me.

I'd gone back down. I'd heard a siren, for a second as faint and sweet as the beginning of the great northern diver's song, then just an oncoming wail. I'd stumbled up the track to the road and waited. There'd been police—not Archie, who was off at a conference in Glasgow, thank God—as well as an ambulance. Later, when the paramedics were struggling with the stretcher and the angle of the slope, a fire crew had arrived. Nobody had let me help. I knew most of them—the bobbies, the medics, the firemen—but they had had their grim business masks on, and they had set me aside. I'd stood clutching a gatepost and listening to the fire crew's plans for retrieving the tractor until one of the ambulance lads had told me it would be a few minutes, that I had time to go and get changed.

"Nichol. Are you with me, son?"

I blinked. Doc Ferguson was watching me in concern. He'd actually had to wave a hand in front of my face. "Yes. Yes, sir. I'm sorry."

"Is there someone at home? Because I heard... Well, I don't want to pry, laddie, but I heard you had a friend living up there with you now. A bit more than a farmhand."

I floundered for something to say. *Yes, he's my lover,* didn't seem right, to the nice old man who'd looked at my six-year-old tonsils, weighed me and told me I was a fine wee lad. I wanted to say something about Cam, something good to silence in myself the rising howl of loneliness. Just yesterday—Christ, a couple of hours ago—I'd have sworn my life away that he'd have been here by my side.

"He helped me," I blurted out, clenching my hands in my lap. "He tried to save Harry too."

"All right. And he's at home?"

"Yes."

"Good." Dr. Ferguson got up. He went to a trolley in the far corner of the room, and I sat watching passively until he turned back to me, a syringe in his hand. "Roll up your sleeve for me, son."

"What's that? I don't need..." I quickly reviewed my words and actions since I'd arrived at the hospital in the backseat of the police Rover. I thought I'd done pretty well. "I don't need sedating or anything."

"No, I know you don't. It's a broad-spectrum antibiotic, that's all. Some of those deep lochans have bacteria in them, legionella. It's not like pulling someone out of the sea."

"Then Cameron..."

"Your friend? Yes, he'll need something too. I'll give you a prescription to take back for him. They're tough on the guts— that's why I'm giving you yours as an injection—so make sure he has something to eat with them, and a glass of milk to help keep them down."

"Okay."

He swabbed my arm and popped the needle home. I tried to feel the sting of it, but it happened to someone else, some other tidy, pale-faced zombie sitting in a neon-lit office. Somebody else could still taste loch water, and deep under that—a warm faint trace from another world—the salt of his lover's come.

Ferguson put his kit away and sat down opposite me. One of the papers on his desk was a police report. "I see you told Sergeant Maguire that Harry just...took his tractor through the fence and into the field."

"Yes. He was ploughing." I wasn't a bad hand with the furrows myself. I could still see in my mind's eye the moment when he ought to have turned. I could feel the dragging weight of the blade, the resistance of the soil. "He ended a furrow and just carried on."

Ferguson sighed. "I bitterly regret the necessity of carrying out an autopsy on your grandfather. He'd have detested it. In fact, given the circumstances and what I've seen of him lately, I'm going to recommend strongly to the coroner that we give it a skip."

"Right," I said automatically. I couldn't begin to link the concept of Harry and autopsy in my head, so I was spared the horror of it. His death was unexplained, though, and Doc Ferguson was trying to do me a favour. My ma had taught me always to be grateful when there was cause. "Thank you." I rubbed my brow, trying to think. "Er... Have you seen my granda recently?"

"Ah. He didn't tell you. He said he'd give it thought, but...I'm not surprised he didn't."

"I'm sorry. My brains are full of water. Tell me what?"

"He wasn't well. Och, I've seen it a hundred times with men like him around here—great husky farmers, so strong in themselves that by the time they do start to fail and come for help, it's too late. He had a heart problem, a bad one. I had a few appointments with him, gave him medication, but really it was only a matter of time."

"Christ... No, he never told me. Couldn't it be treated?"

"No, not by then. It was nothing congenital, so we don't need worry about you, except...if I know you, lad, you'll have just about killed yourself trying to get him out of that loch."

"Cam too." It was very important to me that everyone knew Cam was good. "Cameron tried."

"Yes. You should both know that Harry was probably dead before he hit the water. Most likely he had a massive heart attack at the wheel of his tractor. An autopsy would confirm it, but as I say, we want to avoid that if we can."

I leaned forward and rested my elbows on my knees. I pressed my fingers to my lips for a moment, then I looked up. "The appointments you had with him, the times when you saw him... Was he very dressed up?"

"Oh, you know Harry. He was one of the old school—treated doctors like they were someone special. Yes, he was always very smart when he came here—always in his good tweed coat."

Rain, wind and ghosts. That was what we had up at Seacliff Farm. When the yards were empty and the house doors closed, those were our harvests.

Everything was just the same. Sergeant Maguire dropped me off at the top of the track, and I walked down through the greening corridor of elder and honeysuckle, early summer foliage whispering around me. My arm ached now from Ferguson's jab, and I was beginning to feel the strained muscles in my back. I took it slowly. Each view and perspective on the house opened up to me just as it had always done. The gate answered my push with its usual creak. Harry's Toyota was parked by the barn where he'd left it. His dogs were sitting by it in a row. They regarded me implacably as I approached. Pity like broken glass moved in my heart—I should do something for them, feed them or take them indoors. I held out a hand to Vixen, who growled at me, and then all three turned and crawled under the truck's chassis, ears lowered, tails tucked tight between their legs.

I couldn't comfort them. There was sod all they could do for me. If there had been a moment for me to break down and cry,

221

that was it, but the cold bitter pain in my chest pitched and passed. I let myself into the house and stood in the hallway.

I would have given anything for Cam to have been waiting for me on the stairs. He'd been terrified, gutted by his ordeal. He'd loved Harry just as much as I did, pouring out on him the affection I was now sure he'd once given his own grandfather. I could imagine the kind of life he might have had. An absentee father, maybe, and a mother too busy working to pay him much attention, or taken away from him by something else, maybe by drink or drugs. Grandparents often stepped in for kids like that, came to mean more to them than their mams and dads. I didn't blame Cam for bailing on me, not at all. But he'd had time to calm down a bit now. I'd thought he would be there.

I climbed the stairs stiffly. I could tell without trying the door that his room was still locked.

"Cam," I whispered. But that was no good, and with a surge of painful love that burned me as it rose, I steadied my voice and said, loud enough for him to hear, "Cameron Seacliff."

Silence. Maybe he was asleep. Then a fear took me, so vast and terrible it wiped out all the previous horrors of my day in one knife-blade sweep. I banged my fists on the door. "Cam, do you remember how I said I'd knock your door in if you didn't tell me you were all right?" I left it ten seconds, counting off the beats of my heart. "You've no' told me you're all right."

The old doors were tough. So was I. Harry's build and bull-like strength were waiting in me. I could dance around and dress it up in little designer shirts as much as I liked, but I was bone of his bone, with my mother's bright blood coursing hot through my veins. I took two steps back, got my balance and drove my foot against the lock.

He was curled up in the shabby old armchair by the window. He flinched when the door flew wide, so I knew he was alive, and for a second that was enough for me. His face was hidden. I stood looking down on him, breath catching in my throat. "Cam. Why didn't you answer?"

He was still in his wet clothes from earlier. They had dried on him a bit in places but otherwise were as soaked as when he'd crawled out of the loch. He must have sat like this since I left. His mute rigidity was an effort not to shake with fever. As I watched, the desperate self-discipline broke and he curled up tighter, moaning.

"Jesus!" I darted to his side. He tried to cringe from me, but I unceremoniously pulled his head up—unless he could find a truck to crawl under, he would just have to put up with me—and felt his brow. "You bloody idiot. You're burning."

"Leave me alone."

His voice was raw, as if he'd wept for hours. I'd never cried over any stage of my family's extermination. There'd always been something more urgent to do. There certainly was something now.

"Get up," I ordered him. When he didn't respond, I leaned over him and half lifted, half dragged him out of the chair. "Come on, love. Got to get you out of these clothes." I waited until his feet were under him then tried to let him go, but he suddenly animated and seized me in a bruising grip, as if he'd just recognised me.

"Nichol. My Nicky."

"That's right. Now, for God's sake, let me get you undressed." I pulled up his T-shirt and dragged it over his head, completing his dishevelment. If I looked too hard at his heat-flushed face, his tousled hair, I would shatter with pity or desire. In the circumstances, I couldn't understand at all the latter, except I knew that young soldiers had turned to one another in the trenches. And I wasn't alone—as I undid his jeans, he reached for me, trying for a kiss.

"Not now, hot stuff. Just take those off—these nice wet undercrackers too, the whole lot. Okay..." I snaked out an arm and grabbed his dressing gown from its hook. I was still having to fend him off, and I couldn't blame him—the last time I'd been in this room, parting him from his clothes, the scene had been wildly different, ending five minutes later in a short, spectacular throw down over the dressing table. "That's a boy. Put this on.

Right, now bed for you." I looked critically at his narrow divan. "My room, not here. I can make you more comfortable there."

"I don't need bed. I'm fine, I just..." He grated to a halt and stopped trying to unfasten my shirt. He rested his brow on my shoulder. "Oh, God. My head's killing me."

"I know. What else hurts?"

"Throat's sore. And I'm too hot... Don't bundle me up in this bloody dressing gown."

I bundled him tighter. I put a hand into the hair at his nape and stood holding him, rocking him lightly. God, I'd been in and out of the sea and the lochs around this place all my life. I was achy, but that was from my exertions, and I knew I wouldn't take any further harm from my dip. The city lad from Glasgow, though... "You've got a fever. What Harry would call a *teasach*, a chill to your kidneys. We've got to keep you warm, and the doc at the hospital gave me some pills in case you've picked up anything worse."

"Harry... Ah, Nichol, let me go!" He tried to head off, back to his chair or maybe out the window, from the anguish on his face.

I blocked him. "All right. The hard way, then."

I could probably have slung the lad who had arrived here five months ago across my shoulder. He was a more difficult prospect now, but my room was just along the corridor. He grunted in astonishment as I picked him up. I had his surprise to thank for his lack of objection—like Clover, on the rare occasions I affronted her by daring to scoop her off the ground—and I made the most of it, hefting him into my arms and moving fast. I carried him up the couple of steps that divided the two levels of the landing, shouldered open my bedroom door. "There you go." He'd fastened a reflexive hold on me and I undid it reluctantly, setting him down on the bed. "Hang on there a second while I turn the quilt down."

"No. Stop it. I don't—"

"Be quiet." I didn't want to hear it. There was no guilt, no sense of undeserving, I wasn't feeling too. His grief pressed on mine like stones on a bruise. I was bewildered—I'd thought we would be such a comfort to one another. What if it had only been Harry he'd loved? Sick with that thought, I spoke roughly. "You're not well. I've got to get you sorted out. I can't cope with much more today, so...please, just get into bed."

He did as he was told, his movements stiff. He curled up on his side as if his stomach hurt, and I pulled the quilt up over him then added two blankets from the trunk for good measure. "Just stay there."

I ran downstairs. We had an array of hot-water bottles, relics of various winters, and I chose the three newest and put the kettle on. While it boiled I phoned the hospital, getting through to Dr. Ferguson on the number he'd given me. He sounded grim. I told him Cam's symptoms, and he listened with concern but advised me to get the tablets into him and keep him where he was if I could cope, two coaches having smashed into one another head-on just outside Brodick, throwing the tiny hospital to the limit of its resources. I thanked him and hung up.

Already my local disaster was receding, taking its place in the weave, which my ma had warned me could be dark as Black Watch tartan, hard to understand, and like any other happy little kid I hadn't listened. I put the water bottles and a glass of milk onto a big tray. I remembered what the doc had said about food and added a rudimentary sandwich, placing a dash of pickle on the cheese the way my patient liked, and I carefully balanced the whole lot upstairs.

I was sorry for my morbid reaction. If Cam was shattered by this, it was for me to be strong. I knew nothing of the roots of his pain, and the poor bastard had nearly drowned himself trying to save Harry.

"Here," I said, setting the tray down on the bedside table. "Can you sit up for a second? Got some really massive horse pills for you, and you have to take them with some food." He emerged from under the quilt and pushed himself up wearily. I reached for the hot-water bottles. "And I know these are the last things you want, but we need to burn this out of you here if we can. There's been a crash in Brodick, and the hospital's in chaos."

"No doctors."

"We'd be lucky to get you one at the moment anyway, but—
"

"No doctors. No police."

I tucked the bottles under the quilt, frowning. He was pretty out of it. If the antibiotics didn't make a difference—and if he'd just caught his traditional Highland death from being wet and cold, they wouldn't—he'd get medical help if I had to airlift him to Glasgow.

"Well, I can't pretend you flaking out on me like this isn't a nuisance, but..." I stroked his hair. "It's not against the law."

"No police, Nichol."

"All right. Take your pills like a good lad and I won't have to call them."

It was the wrong thing to say and the right one—he shivered as if he had taken me seriously but knocked back the tablets unprotesting. He even managed a bite of the sandwich when I put the plate into his hands then choked faintly and pushed it away. "Sorry. Can't."

"Okay. Just try and keep those down, though." I stood over him until he'd finished most of the milk, then I eased him down onto the pillows.

He soon fell into a light, restive sleep. I sat on the edge of the bed and watched him. Looking after him had given me something to do, a shield against thought. His eyelashes flickered, casting pain-filled shadows. What happened next? When I'd come home for Alistair and Ma, it had all been sorted out. Harry had arranged the funerals, keeping me at ferocious arm's length. We'd just had to wait for the bodies to be flown in from Spain. What did I do for the old man now? The stupid thing was that he was the only person I wanted to ask—him or Cam, now locked away from me in grief and fever dreams. I'd forgotten how it felt to be alone.

A shift in the wind brought sounds of restless bleating up from the south pasture. Another thing I'd forgotten—sheep needed tending, no matter who died. The realisation came as a relief. Jen and Kenzie junior weren't scheduled to work today, and the whole farm with its daily round of demands was waiting for me, held in stasis since that sunny afternoon moment when I'd looked up from my computer screen and everything had changed.

I brushed strands of damp hair back from Cam's brow. He didn't stir. I waited for a while, until his breathing had settled. I'd started keeping a notebook by my bed again, for those mornings when I woke up with brilliant ideas about syntax and semantics dancing round in my head. At least now it served to write him a note. I kissed the hollow of his temple and left.

I was gone for a couple of hours. It was another phase of shock, I knew, but everything felt very numb and normal. I didn't have to think at all while I went about my tasks, and by the time I finished, an incandescent summer twilight was just beginning, the sun dipping westerly under the rainclouds and blazing them gold and pale green. It was a normal time to knock off work and come home. The dogs wouldn't come out from under the truck for me, but when I opened up the shed Harry had used for their kennel and took them out some dinner, one by one they crept from their hiding place and loped inside. I dealt with that, even though checking the shed to see they had water and locking the place up meant I found two of Harry's jackets and a selection of his pipes. This was where he'd come and talk to them in Gaelic when the world was proving difficult for him. They would sit before him in a triangle and listen.

I shouldn't have left Cam alone. When I went up, I found him much worse. I ran to his side. His breathing was harsh, his eyes open and fixed on some distance way beyond me. As I leaned over him, he grabbed my shoulders and gasped out, "Don't tell Nichol!"

"Jesus." I clapped a hand to his brow. He was radiating dry heat. The luminous twilight had got into his eyes and turned into flickering blue-violet fire. "All right, sweetheart. Going to get help for you."

His grip clamped savagely tight. "No police! Don't... Don't tell Nichol..."

I lifted him into my arms. "Okay," I whispered, pressing kisses to his ear. "I won't. I'm going for a doctor, not the police."

"I killed him. I killed the old man."

Oh, God. That was what this was about. "No. You nearly died trying to save the old man." I detached his bruising hold on me and pushed him down flat on the bed. More urgent still than getting him medical help was conveying to him this understanding. "You did everything you could. I know you're sick, love, but try to listen to me—I saw Harry's doctor today. The old man had a heart condition. He probably died at the wheel of his tractor and crashed into the loch after that. There was nothing you could have done."

"I killed him. Please don't tell Nichol."

"You must have loved him very much—your own granddad, I mean."

He looked at me blankly.

"Right. Here's the deal, sunbeam. You stay here, and I'll go fetch someone who can take away your fever. Then you'll see you didn't—"

He flipped away from me and struggled out of the bed. Before I could even reach a hand to him, he'd darted across the room. My door had its ancient, seldom-used key too—I heard with disbelief the click of the lock. "Oh, that's good. Funny. Give me the key, Cam."

"I can't."

He edged along the wall. I got up and began a move to intercept him, but gently. There was nowhere for him to go, and anyway, he looked ready to drop.

"Don't be soft. Give me the key and come back to bed."

Somehow I'd forgotten the window. The day had been so warm I hadn't noticed the inch at the bottom of the sash. It was the work of an instant for Cam to grab it, push the frame high and fling the key out into the air in a gesture so passionate he nearly followed it. I grabbed him round the waist before he could.

"You fucking idiot!"

He collapsed into my arms. I considered asking him if he was bloody happy now, but the fresh tears flooding his face gave me my answer. I hauled him off the windowsill, dumped him back into bed and covered him up in the quilt and blankets once more—make him sorry he'd locked himself in with me—before going to assess the damage.

All right. No way was I going to kick this door down any time soon. My room was in the ancient part of the house, its timbers five inches thick, the lock the kind you'd fit if you had a dangerous nutcase to contain. I gave the handle a last diagnostic shake then turned away.

The window was twenty feet up. I could jump that, and as a last resort I would. A broken ankle was likely but wouldn't stop me crawling to the phone. If I landed wrong and knocked myself out, that would leave Cam alone and sick upstairs, so a last resort it had to be.

I leaned out and examined the rotting trellis where my ma had grown the bright rugosa roses that thrived on our salt sea winds. I'd climbed that before—upwards, when late home from a clandestine meet with Archie, and at the age of seventeen. That wasn't a great option, nearly ten years and three stone later. Bizarrely, I could see the damn key, gleaming in the last of the sunlight, right in the middle of the rooftop of Harry's Toyota. I straightened up and turned back into the room. Nothing about this was funny, but I almost wanted to say to Cam, *Bet you couldn't do that again...*

He was sitting bolt upright, the duvet clutched in his fists. I didn't know what hell he was staring into, but his pupils were massive, all his amethyst and blue sucked into the black. He said, very clearly, "His name was Stu Duggan. He owed Bren McGarva money. He lived in a flat up in the Easterhouse estate, and one night we went there, me and Bren and four other lads. He answered the door. I didn't know he'd be so old."

I sat down heavily on the bed. I unclenched one of his hands and got it into mine. I wasn't sure what good that would do, but maybe it would hold him here with me in my world. In the world I'd reconstructed around him. "Cam, don't."

"I begged him to give McGarva something, anything at all. But he said he didn't have it, and Bren said we were going to make an example of him, so anybody else who borrowed money off him around Easterhouse would know better than to fuck him around. He had white hair. He was a big strong old man but he fell down straightaway." He paused, his throat convulsing. "We hit him, kicked him. He shouted and cried but we kept on, and then he was quiet. He had a dirty brown carpet. You could hardly see the blood on it. There wasn't any money anywhere, so Bren grabbed his telly and his wristwatch."

I stroked his fingers. There was still some warmth in mine, though it was fading. "Then what happened?"

"I ran. I ran and ran, and Bren sent his lads after me to shut me up. I got to Ardrossan and there was nowhere left to go, so I got on the ferry to Arran. And when I was there—when it was quiet, and I could breathe, and there were the mountains and the sea and everything—I couldn't fucking stand it anymore, what I'd done. So I turned round to go back to the mainland and turn myself in. But it was late, and I got caught in a storm. I hid in a barn."

I had to get help for him. I told myself that was why I was letting him go, releasing his cold fingers from mine. "You stupid bastard," I said hollowly. "Why'd you throw the key out the window?"

"I met Nichol. There was another old man. I thought I could make it up, make it right."

I swallowed what felt like a mouthful of gravel. "Listen, I...I'm gonna have to take a jump for it. You need a doctor."

"No. No doctors. No police."

I could see now his terror of them. I could see why having Archie look twice at him had frightened him sick. I backed away towards the window, a story coming together in my head, a world falling apart. Stu Duggan's squalid Easterhouse flat sprang up around me. I heard the thud of boots, heard his winded cries. I didn't know very many old men, not well enough to flesh out a reconstruction, so inside my head it was Harry who doubled up on the brown carpet, begging his assailants—begging Cam—to stop.

It didn't work. I could put Harry in the victim's role, and I saw Bren McGarva and his three hired thugs, no problem at all. Cameron there with his boot in, though—no. It was like expecting a mountain wildcat to come down from its fastnesses and brawl and piss with alley cats. And yet, God help both of us, his words had rung with absolute truth. He'd told me he loved me with just that same feverish ardour, close and hot against my ear while he fucked me.

I bit back a moan. I had other things to do than drop to pieces here. As for the police—no, that wasn't my job. Harry's retributive sense of Highland justice might have spoken differently, but he was gone now, and I was on my own with the privilege of choice. Poor Duggan was long dead. I could deliver Cam to the law and not raise anyone back to life. No point. His secret was safe with me, if he could keep it himself. I'd have to tell the doctor he'd been raving. I pushed the window sash up a bit higher and began to climb out.

"Nichol?"

I froze. That was such a different voice—newly woken, sane. When I turned to glance back, he was looking at me, not through me. He was the man I knew. "Nic, what am I doing in your bed? Are you...? Why are you climbing out the window?"

I swung my legs back in. He was still flushed but lucidity had returned to his gaze. I sat on the windowsill. "What do you remember?"

"Was I supposed to...? Did I forget something? I was

231

putting the next course on the drystone. I heard Harry's tractor go by. It didn't sound right so I looked up and..." He fell silent. He cupped his hands in his lap and stared down into them, as if he could see unfolding in their palms all the ensuing horrors. "He's dead," he whispered at last. "Harry's dead."

I went to him. He grabbed me as soon as I was within arm's reach, and I didn't resist him. His desolate sobbing should have been my own, and I tried to let it go through me, tried to be reached and to react. His fever pitched again, and I was ice, shielding him, impenetrable. The next time he pleaded with me not to tell Nichol, it didn't feel odd. I didn't know where the hell that naïve farm boy had taken himself off to, but he wasn't here, holding the murderer he loved.

A couple of times when Cam seemed ready to tear apart with fevered shudders, when his breath rasped and became shallow, I made an effort to pull away, but he wouldn't let me go, not without hurting him, and at last the long day ended, and a heavy soft rain began to come down with the night, its whispering song filling the room. My eyelids and limbs grew heavy. Cam's fists twisted in my shirt then fell open, and he put his arms round my neck like a kid. "Oh, Nicky. Don't leave me."

The sound of a car engine jerked me out of the pit. I sat up, dazed. Beside me, Cam was sleeping with the abandon of utter exhaustion. His breathing was easy, his skin cool.

I stumbled to the window. By the time I got there, I'd remembered everything, or pretty much all of it—the last few details sailed in and hit me like stones as I leaned on the sill and looked out. Shona's cobalt Subaru was pulling into the yard. It stopped, and she got out, looking fair and fresh as a harebell in the morning sun. She opened the back door, reached in and took out a huge armful of lilies, roses and chrysanthemums. She glanced about her, listening for signs of life.

I cleared my throat gently. "Hi, Shona."

She jumped and looked up. "Oh, Nichol. You're up there." She frowned. "Sorry. Pointing out the bloody obvious... People never know what to say, do they?"

"No. It's difficult."

"I can't believe it about Harry. I can't believe he's gone."

"I know."

"Er...I brought you these. Did I wake you up?"

I had no idea what time it was. "No. No, it's fine. What beautiful flowers, Shona."

"Can I...? Can I come in?"

"Yes, sure." I gave it thought. "Before you do—I know it sounds a wee bit odd, but there's a key just on the roof of Harry's Toyota there. Would you bring it in? The door's open."

"Yes, of course." She didn't look fazed. Maybe this was how she thought grieving men behaved. She'd put up with enough peculiarities in her own domestic life, perhaps, not to be concerned by mine.

"And would you mind very much coming upstairs and unlocking this bedroom door?"

She came to a halt. She'd already calmly collected the key. Now she looked at it, and back up at me, her lovely face a picture over her armful of flowers. "Good God, Nichol."

"Whatever you're thinking, you're nowhere near the truth."

"Right. Er, okay. I'll be right up."

Thirty seconds later, the key turned in the ancient lock. Shona didn't say anything, and I for my own part couldn't think of a way to open a conversation. We exchanged a silence, then I heard her padding discreetly off down the stairs. Cam was still out cold. I rested a palm on his brow and tucked back one limp, out-flung hand beneath the quilt.

Chapter Sixteen

Shona was in the kitchen, lifting china out of the *preas*. The kettle was boiling. She started guiltily when I came in, as if I'd caught her mid-burglary. "Now," she said, "I'm not gonna go all Women's Voluntary Service on you, but I know how it is when someone dies. I'll make you and Cameron a cup of tea, and some breakfast if you like, and then I'll fuck off and mind my own business."

"No."

She shot me an anxious look, and I clarified, aware I had barked at her. "You don't have to fuck off anywhere. Tea would be nice. But...Cam's not well. I'll sort us out some breakfast when he's feeling better."

"Okay. Poor Cameron. I heard from Archie what happened. Did he take a *teasach*?"

"Yeah, a bad one. How does Archie know?"

"He came back early from that conference on the mainland. He said Sergeant Maguire filled him in. And—this is what I wanted to tell you, Nichol—the coroner's decided there's no need for an autopsy, not if a local police officer who knew you and Harry well would be willing to speak for you. Archie's going to do that, of course. He can't get out here till later today, but he asked me to tell you if I saw you first."

"Okay." I fought to keep my voice steady. "Thanks. That's a relief, about Granda. But I'm not up for company today. If you see Archie again, could you—?"

"Oh, Nichol. Don't shut him out. He's devastated about Harry. He just wants to help you, be your friend."

The flowers she had brought were much too beautiful to lie

neglected. I took a vase from the *preas* and unwrapped them. The scent of the roses enveloped me, citrus and Turkish delight. I smiled, for a second forgetting everything else. "My ma would have liked these."

"Yeah. She loved her flowers, didn't she?" Shona filled the teapot and stared into it as if she wasn't sure of the next stage in the process. "It was terrible, what happened to her and Alistair. I was so sorry. But I never told you. We never went near you, did we? When you came back to the island. Not me or Archie, or any of your friends."

I'd never thought about it. I shrugged. "I didn't exactly rush to your side when Jimmy keeled over."

"Just as well. You might have caught me dancing on his grave or setting fire to his collection of dead moles. I'm serious, though. I don't know—maybe we were too wrapped up in our own stuff, or too young and stupid to know what to do. We want to make it up to you now. Archie does."

I had to keep him away. All my old ideas of right and wrong had gone out the window along with my bedroom-door key. I had only one instinct left. No matter how changed my inner landscape—and it felt as if a hurricane had been through there—no one was going to reach into my home and do any further harm to Cam.

I carried the vase to the sink and ran water into it from the ancient lead pump. "It's not that I'm shutting him out, Sho. I'm grateful to him—to you, for coming out here. But I've got Jen Kenzie and her kid for the next couple of days, so the farm'll be looked after, and—I just need time. Do you understand?"

"Yes. Yes, of course." She brought a tray over to me, balancing it carefully. She did have nice ways, I thought. If I could care for a woman—if I could care at all for anyone else on earth—it would be her, with her unfussy kindness and her wry, straightforward soul. She'd made the tea in mugs but put the milk and sugar in a pretty crackle-glazed jug and bowl I'd forgotten we possessed, and she'd set some biscuits on a plate, as if for an important visitor. "I'll be off, then. I'm glad you've got

Jen and that wee tinker Kenzie, though watch him—that nut didn't fall far from the hazel. And if you run into problems organising anything—the funeral, getting probate sorted—give me a call. I've had some practice lately."

Cam was on the landing, sitting slumped with his back to the wall. I set the tray down and went to him. "What are you doing out of bed?"

"Had to go to the loo. My legs gave out halfway."

He sounded more like his old self. I smiled and tried to sound like mine. "You've not been very well. Halfway there or back?"

"There, unfortunately. Busting for a piss."

There's my nice Larkhall lad again. I couldn't say it. His gentle rough-and-readiness of speech had been so much a part of what I loved in him. "Come on, then. Let's complete your journey."

He groaned as I hoisted him to his feet. "Oh, Nicky. I don't remember much about yesterday, but...I'm so fucking sorry. I flipped out. I left you to deal with everything."

"It's okay. It got dealt with. And I've got plenty of help for the next couple of days, so you can come back to bed after you've had your piss and get properly better."

"But...are you all right? Harry—"

"Not now, Cam." Maybe I'd had a touch of the *teasach* after all. In my dreams, my granddad and Stu Duggan had morphed into one generic, lonely old man and met an endless parade of miserable deaths, by sickness, by water and foul play. I was fine, I told myself. But I didn't want to hear Cam talk about Harry. I pushed open the bathroom door and guided him in. "There. I'll stay if you like, give you a hand."

He turned on me a look of loving admonition. "Och, Nurse Nichol. Where would you put it?"

"Fine. I'll wait outside."

I leaned on the banister. I had briefly considered nursing as a career, oddly enough. My grasp on science was too fragile to make it as a doctor, but I did like looking after people. The least difficult of my adjustments after my ma's death had been turning my hand to laundry and bedlinen, to cooking up breakfasts for Harry and the farmhands. I'd never really minded the brainless slave labour of the sheep feeds, even at my most exhausted—watching the hungry creatures come bleating up to tug at their hay reminded me that something alive was better off for my existence. I'd taken, without realising it, the deepest satisfaction in every stage of Cam's progress from starvation to strong, restored beauty. Alistair had thought me pretty funny, with my need to be always looking after something. He was right. I was. I was also stupid.

The door opened and Cam emerged, clutching the frame for support. Yesterday had undone more than half my good work, laid it to waste. I took his arm. "You look awful."

"You too. Did you get any sleep at all?"

Don't you remember? I was still in my rumpled clothes from yesterday. I'd slept in them, in his arms, in the room where he'd imprisoned us. I didn't answer, helping him back down the corridor. I shook out his pillows, pulled the sweat-damped quilt off the bed and substituted a fresh one. I turned it back and watched while he crawled in, shivering with exhaustion.

"Shona was here," I said. "She made us tea on a tray, biscuits and everything. I'll go fetch it."

He drank his tea in silence, looking at me from time to time over the top of his mug. The biscuits were pink wafers, his favourites, but I couldn't interest him. I knew it was important to keep the liquids going. He really seemed to be on the mend, though I would call Dr. Ferguson again later. I did all the things I would ordinarily have done—steadied the mug when the tremor in his fingers threatened a spill, took it from him when he was done, brushed a stray strand of his fringe out of his eyes.

After a moment he said softly, "Everything's changed,

hasn't it?"

I didn't want to know what he meant. "Yeah. Feels like a different planet with Harry gone."

"I mean you and me. I wouldn't blame you if you thought I could have saved him. I'd understand."

"You've forgotten parts of last night. I tried to tell you. Harry's doctor said he'd had a heart attack before he drove the tractor into the loch."

"God. Yes, I...I think I remember that. There's something else, though." He was watching me fearfully, as if he'd heard the distant rumble of an avalanche and knew there was nowhere to shelter. "What else have I forgotten, Nichol?"

"You told me the real reason you're on the run."

I heard the air leave his lungs. I couldn't look at him, any more than if I'd pitched a brick through a stained-glass window—couldn't look at the fragments and shards. I got up, and carefully put his mug and mine back on the tray.

"Listen," I said. "I don't know much about justice, and...people paying for their crimes. You're as sorry as any man ever was, and me telling the coppers or turning you in isn't going to make you any sorrier. I don't know what to do. All I can think is—stay with me here, and we'll live with it. We'll... I don't know. We'll just try and live with it."

I carried the tray to the door. I *was* a compulsive feeder—even now, in this shell-shocked silence, it was bothering me that he hadn't eaten in so long. "Could you face breakfast?"

"No."

I did look then. He'd spoken quietly, his tone dead flat. His face was expressionless, but at the same time I could read the feelings of a man who might never voluntarily eat again.

"Get some more sleep," I said. "I'll come back and check on you soon. This is still your home, Cam. And...time might make a difference. We'll live with it. I had to know."

I understood now why Harry had wanted to finish the barn roof. I'd had all summer to do it, but for him summer days had been running through his fingers like sand. When I had slogged with grim energy through all my chores—when I'd dismissed Jen and Kenzie home, and checked on Cam for the fourth time and found him asleep, or pretending to be, curled up with his face to the wall—this unfinished business gave me my next handhold, and I seized it angrily. The ladder was there where the old man had left it.

I didn't really know how to patch a roof, not the way Harry did, but I'd watched him often enough, and it couldn't be rocket science. At any rate, banging nails into rafters was a savage kind of relief, and I stayed up there, not breaking rhythm when the skies began to grow dark.

It must have been later than I'd thought. At last I sat back and knelt, trembling, my efforts vibrating through muscles of my arms and shoulders. My left hand was bruised from half a dozen badly aimed strokes, my right beginning to blister. I couldn't feel either. I could smell sulphur, though. Maybe it was the devil, coming to claim my temper for his own. More likely it was Harry, paying me a visit from the place I had no doubt he'd gone, if my ma hadn't managed to catch him en route and bear him off with her to the Summerlands...

No, not sulphur. More like copper or blood. I shifted round and saw the darkness, the premature nightfall, wasn't coming from the west. I was smelling ozone. The blackest summer storm I'd ever seen was piling itself up over Kilbrannan Sound. In a narrow strip beneath the thunderheads, the sky had turned a jaundiced, malevolent gold.

First drops of rain began to hit the slates around me. They were fat as tears, which saved me the bother. I didn't move. I sat, my knees drawn up to my chest, and let the thunder's warning boom roll through my bones.

The thing was that when I'd talked to him—when I'd stood by my bed and told Cam I knew his secret—I'd expected anything but the reaction I'd got. Stupid, because he'd poured it out at the lava-hot pitch of his fever, but my mind since then had erected some rickety defences. If he'd blushed bright red—stammered, denied, crossed his fingers in plain sight and lied to my face, I'd had have taken it. I'd have believed him. He was my Cameron and he was good. Any excuse, any reasons, I'd have granted without question. But all he'd done was sit there, as if a long-expected blow had finally come down. He'd acquiesced.

Christ, couldn't he at least have tried for a redeeming lie? It would have been so easy. *I was off my head, Nichol. I'd had a bad dream.*

I was so fucking furious with him for not making the effort, for hanging himself like this. The thunder roared, and I wanted to scream back at it, but my throat was too dry. When the lightning came, great flashing sheets, I didn't shield my eyes. *Come on, then,* I thought. *Blind me. Strike me bloody dead, up here on this rooftop, the highest point for two hundred yards around. I'm harbouring a killer. I love him more than anything else on God's earth, and at the same time I feel like he reached into my chest and turned my heart to stone.*

A cold wind sprang up, a breath from the storm's dark core. We'd had such a fine spring—too damn fine, with its showers and sweet breezes—and Harry had only secured the roof tarpaulins with stones. The first of them flew aside as the wind snatched the sheet out from under it. I didn't care, but Harry would be so pissed off with me if I let the new rafters get soaked. I grabbed some nails and a handful of rope. Hailstones the size of marbles battered me as I scrambled up to reach the top beam. We were in for it—a proper Arran summer tempest, and God help those at sea. The wind began to scream.

There was something moving on the track that led up to the road. I finished lashing the first tarp down and shielded my eyes against the hail. A human shape, though it was hard to tell in the weird light. The elder trees that lined the track were whipping back and forth, their luminescent blossoms tearing to shreds. Between them, caught briefly in a monstrous lightning flash—yes, a running man, head down, struggling against the storm. My skin crawled. None of Seacliff's ghosts had ever scared me, but this thin figure, caught in desperate flight...

I dropped the hammer I'd been holding. The rope slithered after it and disappeared. The hail was turning to salt-hot lightning rain, slicking the roof in an instant. I fought for grip then gave it up, making my descent in a half-controlled fall, catching at the gutter at the last second for purchase. There was the ladder—too old, too unsteady and slow. I braced myself, aimed for a soft patch of turf, and I jumped.

I wrenched my knee, but it was nothing I couldn't live with. Nothing I couldn't scramble up onto and run, slipping on the hailstones that still lay in the yard. Why the hell did we have so many fences, so many tumbledown alleyways and gates in this labyrinth of a farm? Whatever insane strength had sent me vaulting over obstacles the day before had deserted me now—I just had to climb, gasping for breath, or where it was quicker stop long enough to unhook chains and ropes. The rain drove into my eyes. I clambered over the last five-bar and stumbled out onto the track.

Empty. The next long glare of sheet lightning showed me. The storm was right above me now, the thunder hard on the heels of the flash. Seacliff processed its ghosts quickly, I knew. Al had never been back, but I'd heard my ma singing on the day after her funeral. Upstairs in the gloomy old house where I'd left him, Cam could have found knives, ropes, half a dozen unfinished painkiller prescriptions. He could have found Al's shotgun. His trapped spirit would run forever up this lane, pursued by his sins, manifest as lean black dogs, their coats slicked down by rain, their eyes catching yellow in the storm...

One of them cannoned hard against my legs, knocking me out of the way. I grabbed at the gate for balance. I'd been reading too much Conan Doyle. These Baskerville hounds were nothing more than Gyp, Floss and Vixen. Harry never locked them in at night, and I too had left the top half of their kennel door open, an easy leap if they chose to make it. I shook off my horrified paralysis and ran after them.

Cam had got as far as the roadway gate. The latch on that one required a powerful heft, and he'd run out of strength while he struggled with it. He was on his knees, half hidden by buckler ferns and rushes. This time when the collies found him they didn't crouch or try to herd him. As if pointing him out to me had been their purpose, and beyond that he was up to me, they braided themselves back into their orderly triad and loped away down the track.

Cam hadn't heard them over the roar of the storm. He hadn't heard me. He dragged himself upright as I approached and started to climb the gate. I didn't want to scare him but the wind tore my voice away. "Cameron. Cam!" His useless little Topshop rucksack was over his shoulder, looking as if it contained less than when he'd arrived. I took hold of its strap to restrain him, and he twisted round in fright, losing his hold on the gate, clattering back down. I caught him as best I could. "You stupid sod. What are you doing out here?"

"Let me go."

He began to fight me off. I remembered how he'd dealt with Joe McKenzie and supposed I had his fever to thank for the diminution of his strength now. Still he was fierce and electric in my grasp, the lightning showing me a blank tiger's mask, his eyes wide and filled with anguished darkness.

"How can you want me to stay?" he yelled at me at last, when he'd struggled to a standstill. "You know what I am now. How can you want me?"

I'd had enough. "How can you fucking leave me?" I yelled back. "The old man's barely cold on his slab, and you—you're pissing off back into the night. Are you going to abandon me as well?"

The gale dropped. The change was quite sudden. I'd known it before at the end of a wild island storm, as if some quota of havoc had been reached and there was no call for more. The rain, no longer driven, turned to a drenching vertical torrent. Cam and I stood in the downpour. He was staring at me, water streaming down his face from his sodden hair. He could hear me now without me bellowing at him.

"You'll be ill again," I said more quietly, "if you stay out here. Come back to the house with me."

"Nichol..."

"If you still want to go in the morning, I won't stop you."

"I have to turn myself in."

"I won't stop you. But come home now. Come on." I put an arm around him. After a moment's resistance he gave it up and leaned into me. He could barely walk. I steadied him, drew him close and tight against my strength, and together we set out through the rain.

Chapter Seventeen

The next few days went by me in a grey dream. I was numb, gliding on ice. I welcomed this state of affairs, though it made me stupid, unable to believe in Harry's death even as I spoke to the Lamlash Cooperative about arranging the funeral. He, with his typical dislike of fuss, had left the plainest possible instructions in the most obvious place for me to find them, a brown envelope marked Harold Nichol Seacliff in his dresser drawer, and although it didn't jolt me back to life, I stood for almost half an hour, staring out of his bedroom window. I hadn't known he had a middle name.

The envelope contained his will, a generic one bought from the stationer's but properly witnessed and sealed. It was dated from February of the year before. He must have acted fast after Caitlin and Alistair had died. I wondered how long he'd known about his bad heart. He'd been paying into an insurance plan for long before that, and all I had to do was pick up the phone and tell the funeral home it was time. They already knew, of course. The secretary told me how sorry she was and burst into brief tears before recovering her professionalism. I found it hard to believe that anyone beyond his immediate family would weep over Harry's loss, but maybe I was wrong. And maybe it was just as well, because I was damned if I could cry for him myself.

I went back to work on the farm which was now mine. On the afternoon of the second day after the storm, I looked up from cleaning out one barn and saw Cam busy in the other. He was spectrally pale but back on his feet. I'd asked him to hold off on handing himself over to the authorities until I'd got Harry's funeral out of the way. I wouldn't keep him against his will, I'd told him, but I could only deal with one slice of hell at a time.

He'd agreed, and having settled that, had taken a place in the background, unobtrusively helping me out. He'd plugged in my laptop and recovered my last assignment, a pride-and-joy work I'd have let fall back into binary dust if left to myself, and emailed my tutor in Edinburgh for me when I couldn't think what to say. He'd opened bills and made sure they were paid. He'd taken up all the tasks around the fields and barns that had over the months become his. We ate together, sharing the information we needed to about livestock and business. We slept, when either of us could sleep at all, on opposite sides of the corridor in the great empty house.

There was the most amazing turnout for Harry's service. Cam had put a notice into the *Arran Herald*, but still I hadn't expected a quarter of the number of cars and bikes to be drawn up outside Lamlash Free Church on the wet Tuesday morning exactly a week after his death. There was even a pony and cart.

The tiny car park was overflowing, the minister out in the road, frowning and trying to direct the traffic as it came in. He was a true grim-souled hellfire preacher, but I supposed Harry had trusted him to do things right, and he didn't scruple to complain to me that the biggest funeral his church had seen for years should be for the man who'd never darkened its doorway since he'd come to have his grandsons cursorily sluiced down in its font, and my heathen mother had argued even that much of a bestowal of grace, hadn't she? I was grateful for his grumbling. His hand on my elbow was much kinder than his voice as he steered me to my proper place in the front pew. I didn't need to move again, or look at the cortege when it arrived.

I had the pew to myself. I hadn't even seen Cam that morning. He couldn't come here, of course, not with the eyes of half the Brodick, Whiting Bay and Lamlash communities to stare at him. Nevertheless my heart lurched when another backside thumped down next to mine on the polished Victorian oak.

"I know I'm not family, but can I sit by you?"

God, it was Archie. His nose was as red as his hair, and he was clutching a vast white handkerchief, which had already seen some use. I was touched that he was wearing full dress uniform. For the first time that morning I thought about my own clothes and glanced down at myself, relieved to see that the shirt and trousers I'd grabbed out of the wardrobe were respectable, my jacket a dark enough grey to be called black.

"Course you can," I said, but I might as well have told him to fuck off, and I altered my tone and tried again. "I'd be grateful. Thanks."

"Oh, Nicky. What a shock it was. What an awful loss. Have you been all right?"

"Aye." I had to divert his sympathy. He was ready to sweep me up into his arms. Behind us the little church had gradually packed till it was heaving at its seams. I didn't know what had become of his fears for his reputation, but I was sure it would never recover from the imminent display. "It was nice of you to put on your best gear. Harry would've liked that."

"Well, I'm allowed, for funerals and..." His voice broke, and he leaned forward, burying his face in the handkerchief. "How can he be gone? He was—part of this place, part of the island. Look how all these people have come to say goodbye to him."

Absently I patted his serge-clad shoulder, and he blew his nose. That got us through to the beginning of the service, and all I had to do was listen politely to that. The minister and I had widely differing views about the afterlife, or at least he *had* a view—a bleak one—whilst I felt I might have to wait and see. I wasn't too bothered how soon I found out. I was hungry, bone-cold, tired.

And that was just the beginning. I had to stand around and say goodbye to all the good souls discreetly thinning themselves out before the interment. I really hadn't thought this through at all—about who should be asked to the graveside, or maybe invited for tea and corned-beef sandwiches back at the house.

Minister MhicRuari was having to beckon to Harry's closer friends, Shona and the postman and the cronies from the pub. Archie was still glued to my side. Before I knew what was going on, a group of a dozen of us was gathering under the birches by a fresh-dug hole in the earth.

I let Archie prop me. I didn't have much choice, and he was doing a subtle job of it, disgracing neither of us. No, I hadn't thought about the details. I'd kept my eyes on the embroidered kneeler at my feet in the church, considering the lilies of the field depicted there, and never once looked at the coffin now planted squarely before me in the rain. What I couldn't get away from was the fact of its being a box containing my grandfather's body. Nausea swept me. Archie's arm was round my waist beneath my jacket, holding tight. The minister began the burial rite, and I closed my eyes.

There wouldn't be a funeral gathering at Seacliff Farm today. I wished I'd anticipated the need for one. I would have liked to be a good grandson and do honour to Harry's name, but it hadn't occurred, and serve me right for not consulting Shona like she'd told me to. I had no doubt that Cam would have made and set out the sandwiches if he'd known such a thing was required. But when the final amens had been said—when the people I supposed these days were called graveyard technicians were moving in, their mechanical digger inadequately concealed behind a cypress—I just turned and walked away. It was all I could do. Shona's warm fingertips brushed my wrist as I went past her, but she didn't try to follow.

Archie wasn't so discreet. His big policeman's feet crunched after me on the gravel, and before I could reach the Toyota he dodged in front of me, forcing me to a halt.

"Let me go home, Archie."

"Why? What's there? Your fine lad Cameron?"

I couldn't believe this. For a moment I was just outraged.

Then a thin blade of fear went through me. There was a challenge in Archie's eyes I'd never seen before. "Among other things. What business is it of yours?"

"He should have been here with you today."

"He's not well yet. You know what happened."

"Bollocks, Nicky. I saw him lifting a five-stone tup into a trailer yesterday afternoon. He should have been here. What's he worth, if he won't stand by your side on days like today?"

I tried to step round him. "That's my problem, not yours. Let me go."

"No. Not until you tell me what's going on with you right now. You look sick with the whole bloody world."

"My grandfather died."

"I know. And my heart's aching for you, love. But it's more than that. Why did you not shed a tear for him all the way through that service?"

Sharp replies rose in my throat. *I'm no' so big a sap as yourself*, perhaps, or *tears are for girls and spilled milk*. But the angrier I got, the tighter I would lock myself into this confrontation, which had to end before the crackling black misery inside me found its way to the surface.

I shrugged, took a pacifying backward step. "Pink eyes don't suit my complexion and hair as well as they do yours, Constable."

It almost worked. He flashed me a glance of horror that I'd throw out such a gag at such a time. Then he helplessly smiled. "Oh, you're an evil sod, aren't you? God, I've missed that stupid sense of humour. Come home with me."

"Archie..."

"Come on." He reached out and captured my hand. To my astonishment—the car park was scattered with people emerging from the churchyard, Minister MhicRuari amongst them—he tried to lift it to his mouth. "I love you. I'll take care of you."

"Archie, do *not* hit on me at my grandfather's funeral."

He dropped my hand. No one could go white quite the way

he did. The furies snarling round in me enjoyed their moment. Then the bastards died, leaving me alone with my words— unable to stand Archie, myself, or any aspect of this bloody incomprehensible morning any longer. I shouldered past him. The Toyota's rusty lock didn't turn, and I thumped my fist into her, leaving a dent. Pain shot up my arm. I took the key out, tried again. This time it worked, and I hauled myself into the cab. Gear, ignition, handbrake off. One good check for hapless pedestrians in front of me, and another up the lane for oncoming traffic, unlike that long-lost Spanish coach driver who'd gone down with his vessel. I batted my rearview aside so I wouldn't have to see in it the crash site I'd left behind, and I tore out onto the road.

The kitchen was quiet, full of rain shadows. It took me a moment to discern Cameron among them. His colours had altered over the last week, his brightness dimmed. Another of my mother's stories drifted through my head.

There was a man who found on the beach a scale from a mermaid's tail and thought his fortunes secured, for it was made of sapphires, amethysts and gold. And so it stayed until he took it to the fair and tried to sell it, when all he had in his pouch was a quaint-looking scallop shell. It was like the seal bride, you see, Nichol—we can't hang on to them, not even one little part, unless they want to stay.

Had she been trying all my life to prepare me to face loss? I went in quietly, closing the door behind me. Cam had lit the Aga, and the room was warm, a contrast to the chilly graveyard damp that seemed to have entered my bones.

He had a book open in front of him. When I came closer, I saw it was the volume of mac Mhaighstir poetry. He closed it carefully and looked up at me. "I'm trying to think of a way of asking you how it went."

I nodded, acknowledging the difficulty. "Not bad. I forgot I was meant to ask everyone back here for tea, and I had a row with my ex in front of the minister, but otherwise it passed off with dignity. Are you trying to learn a bit of Gaelic?"

"Just a couple of lines so I could remember them. The ones about the birch tree over the cairn. But I still can't pronounce them."

"*Bidh am beithe deagh-bholtrach, urail, dosrach nan càrn.*"

He listened attentively then said the lines back to me, his accent more west Glasgow than West Isles, but accurate and good. I could have taught him, given time. There were so many things we could have shown one another. I went to lean on the rail of the Aga with my back to him so I wouldn't have to look at what was coming next.

"I'm going to catch the two o'clock bus. There's a ferry around three, isn't there?"

"Quarter past. That's right."

"I'll hand myself to the police at Ardrossan. I can't do it here, not with Archie." His voice scraped. "I'm so sorry, Nic. I have to go."

I knew. He'd told me. I'd asked him to wait until after the funeral, and he'd done that. He was doing the right thing, the only thing he could. In a way it was a pity, because his arrest would have been a spectacular bust for Archie—an unsolved murder, worth a lifetime of stolen golf carts and giving directions to tourists on Brodick high street.

I crouched in front of the Aga. I opened its main oven door and looked inside, where the coals were heaped nicely, emitting a strong steady glow. Only a fool would interfere with a settled fire like that, and I closed the door again. I couldn't seem to get up, though. My lungs had emptied and didn't want to refill. I remembered the trackway at Skull Rock, the spasm of delayed grieving that had caught up with me there. Was I in for it again? I didn't think I could cope. Worse than gastroenteritis, those dry hard cramps. Mortifying, too.

I clutched the Aga rail. I swallowed, tried to choke down whatever the obstruction was in my throat. I couldn't see properly. Oh, great—a stroke, just at this moment in my life when you'd think nothing could get worse. The muscles of my face were contorting. I swiped a hand across my eyes, and it came away soaked. I had to breathe. My throat opened suddenly, and I sucked air in a huge racking sob.

"Oh, my God. Nic!"

I was as startled as he was. I dropped to my knees, attempted to twist away and hide. But the spasm and the sound came again. It was louder this time, painful as rusted metal grinding inside a failing machine. I didn't know what to do with myself, how to recoil from something inside me, and my effort threw me clumsily against the stove door.

Strong arms hauled me back. The only touch I wanted in the world, the only embrace I could bear, locked round me tight. "Are you all right? Are you burned?"

No. Drowning. That was what it felt like. I couldn't tell him. He was pulling my jacket off my shoulder, unfastening my shirt. I buried my face in his sweater. The dreadful sobbing—a year's worth, three deaths' worth, and worse than any of that the certainty that I was losing him—didn't sound so bad from there, didn't hurt me so much. He sat beside me on the rug and wrapped his arms around me tight. His kisses descended on my skull. His voice, shocked and loving, brushed my ear, a formless litany of comfort, sweet names and promises I'd have given my life to believe. Grief wiped me out like a wave over footprints in sand.

It was late. Too late for buses or ferries—a rainy dusk was falling, embers whispering in the stove. Cam and I sat in the nimbus of its warmth, our limbs entangled, our clothes in a heap around us. I didn't know which one of us had started that. I'd cried myself hollow and raw, and the exhausted peace ensuing had felt wrong wrapped up in fabric. I'd have peeled away a layer of skin if I could. Cam had helped me strip—hadn't resisted while I returned the favour. I'd wanted to see him, needed to. Every inch. And here he was before me, beautiful in the twilight. Yet again I tried to match his form, his delicate power, with my preconception of a killer, and I couldn't make it fit.

He was looking straight into my eyes. "My sins don't show on the outside," he whispered. "Not yet. I'm sure they will."

"Mine too," I told him. He opened his mouth, and I brushed a finger over his lips. "Hush. I've got one too now—a sin of my own."

"What did you do, love—leave a gate open? Let the sheep onto the road?"

"No. My sin's that I don't care about yours. Or... Oh, I do. How could I not? But I want to bear it with you. I want to help you hide it. I want to hide with you, here or any place you want to run."

"Nicky, it's wrong."

"I know. Isn't that the point of a sin?"

He kissed me. I couldn't tell if I was tasting his tears or my own. We lay down together, chaste as brothers. He leaned over me, stroking my hair, looking at me as if he wanted to burn my image into his memory.

"Don't," I said. I drew his head down to my shoulder, and after a moment's resistance he surrendered. "You don't have to remember me. I'll be here."

"How? How can we do this?"

"I don't know." I curled around his back. The world would have to go through me to get to him. "I just know I love you. Please give it a chance, Cam. Please stay."

Chapter Eighteen

Seacliff could be a fortress, an island within an island. It had served as one before. A passing group of archaeology students had once noted its position and asked Harry for permission to come and look round. They'd told me the green irregular mounds that bordered the road were probably the remains of Neolithic ramparts, guarding the northern and eastern approaches. The headland cliffs took care of the other two sides. It was very defensible. The only real access was the track, and every day I thought about hanging a sign off the main gate, maybe one of the lurid ones—savage dogs, killer bulls—I'd seen landowners put out to try and keep tourists off their fields despite our proud Highland lack of trespass laws.

I didn't. I didn't need to cut us off physically, and I didn't want Cam to feel trapped. The postman still came rumbling down the rutted lane. When I couldn't put off my grocery run to Brodick any longer, I went without fuss, and beyond a brief hug made no comment on the fact that Cam was still there when I got back. I even tried to contact Archie. Our last encounter echoed in my head, and I felt bad about him, but he didn't return my calls. I couldn't worry about him or anything else for long. The fortress Cam and I were building between us took up all my attention. No need for padlocks on the gates. When we looked at one another, we banished the world and all its pain, raised insurmountable walls to shield one another. We made love with a tight-bound intensity that was part of our castle in the air. Nothing—not even our own dark thoughts—could get to us then. We locked doors behind us, closed curtains, held and bit and bruised each other's bodies for hours at a stretch. We were safe.

After a fortnight or so, it started to feel like a kind of normality. We began to rescue the bits of our lives that had gone overboard, as arts and learning always did in time of war. I picked up my books again, restarted my assignments. One afternoon—it was hot, the sunny scents of St. John's wort drifting over to me from the banks of golden flower heads—I went out to the main storage barn, and I heard for the first time since Harry's death the sounds of hammering from Cam's workshop.

I was glad of it. Such a sign of returning life, that vigorous clatter. I wondered what was getting knocked into shape, what sheet of metal was on the receiving end of his energies. The rhythm made my flesh resound, recalling the wild hard fuck he'd thrown into me at dawn that morning. We'd barely been awake, but that was a great time to do it, before memory or thought could kick in. I'd almost died of the sweetness of my coming, crushed and convulsing in our shared bed, sobbing out my pleasure to the pillow so I wouldn't wake the ghosts.

I pulled my attention back to the task at hand. I'd come in here to fix the barn window. Bad rainstorms were forecast for next week, and soon I'd be harvesting hay into the loft. I'd had some glass cut in Brodick, and I'd found a tub of putty in one of the outhouses, fresh enough to smell evocatively of linseed when I opened it. The afternoon was very warm. I sometimes wished my ma had shared a bit with me about the things she believed, the ceremonies she'd observed throughout the year, but she'd said living on an island where one religion was ready to foist its ideas on me was quite enough. I knew the St. John's wort had something to do with it, and the seeds on the undersides of the fronds of fern. If you rubbed those on your eyes, you would see the world the way you wanted it to be. I rolled up my sleeves and began to measure out the lengths of wood I'd need to make the new frames.

My back was to the door. As usual, getting the numbers right on anything was soaking up all my attention. I was aware of my cat watching me solemnly from a nest of sacking on the bench nearby, but only as a rolling wave of sound, a rich purr that blended itself with the sunshine and the ongoing clatter from the studio. The odd symphony soothed me. I let my mind drift. Ten millimetres made a centimetre, and a twelve-centimetre pane would need five millimetres left clear each side for framing, so... *Oh, come on, Nichol—it's decimal, a system invented so people like you could at least count it off on your fingers...*

The purring stopped. I glanced up. My sleek cat had turned into a spike-furred demon. Her ears were laid flat to her head. She was on her feet, back arched, little jewel of a face contorted into a terrible hiss. I swung round to see what had caused this transformation, and so was just in time to avoid being shot in the back by a total stranger.

He looked ordinary. I'd have passed him in the street. The only strange thing about him was the pistol he was pointing at me, and I knew fuck all about handguns, but I was fairly sure the cylinder round its muzzle was a heavy-duty silencer. I was still half in my other world, of dreams and attempts at mathematics—my first reaction was a sharp sense of annoyance, at myself as much as this random thug. I knew I should have blocked the track.

I said, calmly enough, "Can I *help* you?"

He took me in. "Och, I do beg your pardon," he responded pleasantly, his accent a genial Glasgow burr. "I'm not here for you, though that would have been a hard way for you to find out. You bear a strong resemblance from the rear."

I was catching up, or I thought I was. Maybe I looked more like this man's image of Cam than Cam did himself these days. I knew I would be scared in a minute. He hadn't lowered the gun, and his eyes were cold.

"You're Bren McGarva."

He grinned. Only when it was out did I realise how fucking stupid I'd been. I could have bluffed this out, whatever the hell it was. If he was here on the off chance, if he was working his way round the south Arran farms, I could have feigned never to have heard of or seen Cam. But only someone who knew him would know that name.

"It's all right," my gunman said, almost soothingly, as if reading my thoughts. "I wasn't in any doubt. I'm not McGarva, though. You don't send a shark after tadpoles like Cameron Vaughn."

Vaughn. That was a nice name. That fit him, I thought, and I was glad he was Cameron still. "He's not here," I tried. "He was for a while, but he was in some kind of trouble. I sent him away."

"Oh, right. Yes, you look like the type who'd banish a poor runaway." He paused, attending to the music of creation still pouring from the studio, enough to wake the dead. "God, is that him in your workshop? Is the wee punk still making his piles of rubbish? He did like to think he'd amount to something more than Bren's errand boy one day. He did like to think he could escape."

I thought fast. We were facing one another in the same barn where I'd pointed my own gun at Cam on the night when he took shelter, in more or less the same positions, and it probably served me right. I'd told him a lie then, and Cam had believed me. "I don't know what you're on about. That's one of my brothers at work in the shed, and he'll have the bloody hide off you when he sees what you're doing." I decided to go the whole hog. "There's three of them. They all carry rifles."

Maybe I'd lost the knack. He just looked amused. "You *had* a brother," he said. "A mother, Caitlin, and a grandfather, Harold, all recently deceased. So I know all about you, you see, and I know that's Cam Vaughn crashing away in your barn, because he's been here since February, when you fired a farmhand to make room for him."

Kenzie. A chill stole down my nape. Kenzie, who had disappeared from the island like a guilty dream. I could have wished Harry back again, to help me rue that day's work if for no other reason.

"Wrong farm," I said stubbornly. "That's Nichol Seacliff you want. He lives up the road."

My visitor jerked the gun at me. "Enough. Go and fetch Cam, Nichol Seacliff. Nice and quiet, mind, or I'll go and fetch him myself."

I could hear an engine. Only someone who lived here in the world's-edge silence would notice it, especially under the racket Cam was making in the shed. To this guy's traffic-deadened ears it would mean nothing. I didn't know what it might mean to me, but I went for one last stall. "May I tell him who's visiting?"

"Well, I have'nae brought my business cards with me, but if you tell him it's his old pal Baird from Easterhouse, that ought to bring him fast enough."

Tyres crunched on gravel. Baird heard that all right. A moment later we were staring at each other as a car door banged and the main yard gate squealed wide.

"Who the hell is that?"

I held his gaze steadily. "It's hard for me to tell from here."

"Then go and look. Get rid of them, fast. I'll be listening. One word out of place and I'll put a bullet in your spine."

I went out, hands in my pockets, as casual as anyone could wish. My acting skills weren't great, but if I stuffed it up and Baird shot me, at least the sound might give Cam some warning. I was prepared for the postman, a delivery, at worst maybe a spot check from the veterinary inspector.

What I got was Archie Drummond, parking up his great unmissable police truck right in the middle of my yard. He didn't see me. He appeared to be deeply involved in a quarrel with his passenger, who, when she pushed open her door and climbed down, turned out to be Shona Clyde.

She stamped round the front of the vehicle and intercepted Archie as he got out. "Seriously," she said, clearly in continuation of an ongoing argument, "think twice about this, Archie. You're not gonna do any good here by—"

"Good afternoon," I greeted them, and they both wheeled to face me. "Everything all right?"

Shona recovered first. "Oh. You're there, Nichol. Yes, everything's grand. You've been a bit scarce around town, that's all, and we just thought we'd drop by and see you."

"That's nice. I tell you what, though—could you come another time? I'm a bit busy, and—"

"Oh, for fuck's sake." That was Archie, frowning in disgust. "Busy doing what? Your precious bloody farm boy?"

"*Archie,*" Shona snapped. "You promised to sort this out nicely."

"I know. But I'm so bloody sick of his infatuation with this lad, Sho! I've got to tell him."

"Tell me what?" I asked because it would have looked odd if I hadn't. I hoped the answer was short. The postie or some poor random delivery guy would have been bad enough, but somehow I'd ended up with the three people I cared most about within ten yards of me, all in range of Baird's gun. "Come on, Archie. I really haven't got time to talk."

"Fine. Then shut your mouth and listen. Joe Kenzie's living in Glasgow now. He phoned me the other week and said he had some information. Your Cameron's face—his and a couple of others—is plastered all over the Easterhouse estate on wanted posters. They're after him in connection with a fucking gangland murder. An old man, Nichol, knocked off for nothing more than his telly and his wristwatch! So—"

"Joe Kenzie's a crackhead."

"I know. He was selling me this story, not giving it away. You think I'd dump this on you without checking? But it's true. Your bonny student's from Larkhall, not a Dumfries college. He's nothing more than a lying wee hood."

Shona grabbed his arm. "Button it," she growled. "Archie, you sod. I know you have to tell him, but not like this. You said you'd be kind."

God, how was I going to get rid of them? "It's all right,

Shona." The clanging from the shed had stopped. That meant Cam was at the welding stage. That in turn meant that any minute now he'd need fresh air, a break from the heat, and he'd be out here too. "I know about Cam."

Archie's mouth dropped open. "What?"

"I know who he is, what he did. He told me."

"Then...what in the name of Christ are you doing keeping him here? You used to know right from wrong, Nicky Seacliff. You might have started shagging me before they lowered the age of consent, but other than that you were the primmest, most upright bloody—"

A gun jabbed hard into my back. I jolted in shock but bit back a cry. I lifted my hands, for all the good that would do. Shona and Archie were recoiling, staring past me at Baird, who had obviously had enough of our island soap opera. "Fuck's sake," he snarled. "You little bastard—how the de'il did you manage to call the police?"

I closed my eyes. "I didn't," I said dryly. "They just have the most amazing bloody timing. Archie, is it your fault this guy's here?"

"What? No! Who is he?" I could see him trying to morph back from jealous ex into police officer. He wasn't doing a very good job, but at least he was stepping in front of Shona, shepherding her behind his back. "Now, Nicky, you're a hostage. Just keep calm. Don't antagonise..."

"Baird," I supplied for him tiredly. I didn't feel like introductions. "His name is Baird. Bren McGarva sent him."

"Bren... Oh, shit."

"Means something to you, does it?"

"Yes. Kenzie told me about him. But I didn't... I wanted to see you first. I just made some enquiries."

Baird gave a short grunt of amusement. "You twitched Bren's web, copper. He's got threads of that running all the way to the top of the Strathclyde police. That's all it took."

"Oh, my God, Nichol. I'm sorry."

"Don't bloody worry about me," I snapped. "It's Cam he's after," I tried to glance round and winced as the gun muzzle drove deep into my ribs. "Listen, Baird—there's no need for these two to be here, is there? Especially the woman. Let her go. She won't say anything."

"Aye, she looks all ready to go back home to her knitting, doesn't she?"

I bit back a sigh. Shona, having recovered from her initial fright, had emerged from behind Archie's shoulder and was standing with her arms crossed, looking thunderbolts at Baird.

"What is she doing here anyway?" I asked. "What did you have to bring her with you for—to nursemaid you in case I lost my temper?"

Archie flushed bright red. "What business is that of yours? We've been...going out, if you have to know. Is that a problem for you?"

She turned on him. "We have *no'* been going out, Archie Drummond! You've been *asking* me to go out, and I've been telling you not to use me as a stand-in while you get Nichol out of your system!" She glanced back at me, brow furrowing. I could see her measuring the differences between us. "Which, now I come to think about it, is a bloody worrying thing for you to want to do. Nichol, I made him bring me with him. He was swearing all colours about Cam, and I thought I could make him keep a civil tongue in his head."

"Shut up, all of you." Baird clearly couldn't believe what he was hearing. Probably he hadn't factored brawling islanders into his plans that morning. "Is there *no* man on this island that's not fucking bent? You—Nicky, or whatever your nancy boys call you—go and fetch Vaughn now, or..."

But there was no need. Across the yard, the workshop door was opening. Cam emerged into the sunlight. He was unfastening his gauntlets, reaching for the strap of his welder's mask. His T-shirt was sticking to him, his arms streaked with carbon and rust. "You all right, Nic? I thought I heard voices."

There was a moment—a space between two heartbeats

when I would have chucked Shona's life and Archie's away with my own, sacrificed anything to give him a warning shout. Then it was too late. He pulled the mask free and looked up.

The mask clattered to the cobbles, echoing weirdly in the silence. He stood frozen for a second. He hadn't bothered dyeing his hair again, as if he knew that he and all of us were in the hands of fate. His dark roots were showing. They suited him somehow, like the soot marks and the sweat. He was so damn lovely. Even the sun and the breeze seemed to think so, caressing him, lighting him up.

"Baird," I said hoarsely. "What do I have to do to make you leave him alone?"

He was up close to me. I felt him shrug. "Sorry," he replied, and almost sounded like he meant it. "McGarva wants him silenced. He's the last loose end."

"He hasn't talked till now. Why would he start?"

"Aye, we've all been wondering what's been holding his tongue. Quite the conscience on him, little Cam had. A bit of a liability to Bren, but he was useful." He raised his voice. "Weren't you, laddie? You come on over here now, nice and slow. You're looking good, by the way. Nothing like a few months of fresh air and clean living, eh?"

Cam crossed the yard. His hands were raised like mine, just far enough to show cooperation, no plans for sudden moves. His face was calm, his eyes empty. "Baird," he said, coming to a halt a couple of yards away. "Here I am. Let Nichol go."

"Cam, no. Stay away from him."

Baird gave me a pat with his free hand. "Don't be daft, now. Cam's doing the right thing." The pat became a shove, and I stumbled as he pushed me aside. He strode over to Cam, who stood like a statue while he took possession, grabbing one shoulder, shoving the gun into his back. "That's better. Time to go. All McGarva wanted was a nice neat execution if I found you on your own, but your mates here have complicated things. I'd have to shoot this copper if I killed you here, and the girl, and your bonny boyfriend, and that would leave Bren far more cleaning up to do than you're worth, son. So just you come with me."

"Don't," I rasped. "Cam, don't let him take you away."

The empty gaze fastened on me. It kindled and filled, and I saw there enough love to last me a lifetime. "I have to. I deserve this."

"You don't. All right, you killed someone. But throwing away your own life won't fix it. I told you, we'll live with it. I'll help you, whatever it takes..."

I fell silent. Cam was looking at me in a mix of disbelief and absolute horror. Baird for some reason had broken into a broad grin. We stood there in the sun and the wind, and then he began to laugh. "What—you think this little penny-counter killed Stu Duggan?"

"Not on his own, he didn't! He had McGarva to help him, and some other lads, and..." I shut up, Baird's words sinking in. "Cam?" I said uncertainly. "You... You told me. After Harry died, and you had the fever, you told me."

Baird put his head back and roared. "What?" he choked out when he could. "The accountant? McGarva's wee bed-warmer? Och, he was there that night. So was I. Bren and his lads kicked Duggan in, and this one—your killer—stood in the corner and watched. Pissed yourself, didn't you, killer Vaughn? Right down your jeans, like a poor babby." He wiped his eyes, gave Cam's hair a ruffle that almost looked like affection. "Jesus, what did you tell your boyfriend that for? We had to stop the car for him, Nicky, five minutes after we left. He couldn't stop puking. And when Bren let him out, the little fucker ran for it. That's your cold-blooded murderer. Vanished like a fart in a high wind."

"Nichol. You thought I'd..."

"You told me." They seemed like the only three words left to me. I tried again, but then even they wouldn't come.

"I dreamed about him. About Stu Duggan, every night. I saw it in my head—how they went for him and knocked him down, and I just stood there. I could have helped him and I didn't."

"You just witnessed it."

"Just? I might as well have killed him. I dreamed about him every night, until..."

"Until you thought you had. And then when you were ill—"

"I *told* you that?" Cam put an unsteady hand out towards me, his brow wrinkling in disbelief. "I told you I'd murdered poor Duggan myself?"

"Yes."

"And you... You kept me here. Oh, God. You loved me anyway."

He tore away from Baird. I stepped forward and grabbed him, squeezing my eyes shut in anticipation of a shot. I swung him round to shield him. If Baird fired now, it would probably go through us both, but I couldn't care, couldn't let him go. He hung on to me, pressing frantic kisses to the side of my face. Blindly I returned them.

Before I could work out why Baird was letting us have this moment it was over. Maybe it had just been his pleasure to snatch Cam back out of my arms. It felt like he'd ripped out my liver—I cried out helplessly at the pain of it.

Baird locked a chokehold round Cam's neck, lifted the gun to his temple. "All right, lover boy. Back the fuck off. Aye, you two and all, or I *will* shoot the little bastard right here in front of you." He started to retreat, dragging Cam with him. "Car's just in the lane. Handy, that, a downhill track. I just cruised in on my handbrake, easy all the way. Make it easy for me now, Cameron."

"Cam, don't fight him."

I whipped round. Archie was at my elbow, one hand extended placatingly towards Baird. "Don't fight," he said again. "Do as he says."

"Shut up," I croaked. "What the fuck are you doing? He's gonna take him off and kill him."

"He'll do it here if we freak him out any more. Nicky, step back. I'm trained for this."

"You've done a bloody brilliant job so far."

"No. I've fucked it all up, I know that. Let me help now. Listen, Mr. Baird—you're not going to get far, and right now it's just assault, not murder. It's best you stop this now."

Baird didn't look freaked out. If anything he seemed to be enjoying himself. "Or what? Will you come chasing after me in your wee toytown truck?"

"Not if you let Cam go. I will if I have to."

"What about if I do this to it?" He lifted the gun. Both he and the silencer were efficient—the muzzle spat twice, and the police Rover sagged, its front tyres hissing. "I'd put one in the tank," he went on, "but we don't want to be noisy. Oh, and I tell you what—you look the responsible type. Will you still chase me if you've got a casualty to tend?" He swung the pistol in my direction, and then he grinned, whipped back and aimed at Shona.

Archie moved in a blur. I'd known he could shift—Christ, all those times he'd heard a rustle in the marram grass and thought we'd been busted, hissing at me to pull my pants up and run, legging it off down the dunes like a bloody gazelle. He dived in front of Shona. The gun popped again, and he jerked, crashing down onto the barnyard cobbles.

Cam cried out, a yell of inarticulate horror. "Stop! I'm coming with you, all right? I'll come. Don't hurt them anymore."

Baird looked down at Archie, prone and motionless at Shona's feet. "Ah well, copper," he said agreeably. "Have it your own way."

I began to follow him and Cam towards the gate. Cam no longer needed to be dragged, but Baird was keeping him steadily at gunpoint. In the gateway, Cam turned to me. He gave me a look of raw pleading. "No. No more. I've got to go."

"I'll find you. Wherever he takes you, I'll..."

"I love you. Look after Archie."

He was gone. From beyond the hedgerows I heard doors slamming, the roar of an engine. A blue Ford Mondeo bumped past the gateway in reverse. There was a gap in the fence a few yards up where you could three-point turn if you were careful. I couldn't see. The gap was just round the curve of the track. I heard how neatly Baird did it, the revving and the economic mesh of clutch to gears. I turned and ran back into the yard.

Archie was sitting up, holding his upper arm, or trying to. Shona had him propped against one knee and was shoving her bundled-up shirt into the shoulder of his jacket. She had on a vest underneath, but I knew the lack of it wouldn't have stopped her. "Keep still, you daft bastard," she ordered him as I stumbled to a halt beside them.

"Christ, Archie. Are you all right?"

"He's fine. It's just a nick, a flesh wound."

Archie jerked his head up. He was colourless apart from a smear of blood on his face. "I'm not sodding fine," he said. "He shot me. I've been shot."

I crouched in front of him. I was almost sick with relief to hear him complaining, but I needed him. "Archie, you're a copper. Help."

He stared at me. Then he seemed to take my point. He nodded curtly. "Okay. Sho, help me up."

"You shouldn't be moving."

"You just told me I was fine. Nichol, grab my other arm. Get me to the Rover."

"He shot your Rover too," Shona reminded him as we hoisted him to his feet.

"Yeah. I only need the radio."

Once he was up, he made it to the truck on his own. I stood, arms wrapped tight round myself, a shroud of unreality settling round me. I heard static then a short exchange of what seemed to me mostly numbers, alphas and tangos and foxtrots. Shona came up and put her arm around my waist, and I only realised then that I had been swaying.

Archie emerged. "Right," he said. "That's every car and officer alerted, shoreside and the mainland. They're relaying descriptions to the ferry staff. Unfortunately the force on this side is pretty much me, though they'll send the chopper from Ardrossan as soon as they can. I need to get on the road."

"Aye." Shona gave me a quick squeeze and went to check he hadn't bled through the makeshift bandage. She glanced assessingly across the yard. "I wonder why Baird didn't shoot Nichol's Toyota too."

"Probably," Archie responded, distractedly dragging his stab vest and portable radio out of the Rover, "because it looks like a big pile of rusting shit. Does it still run, Nicky?"

It took me a second to organise speech. "Yes. Yeah, of course."

"Then go get me the keys."

"They're in the ignition."

"God. There really is no point to law enforcement on this bloody island, is there? Right, I'm off."

I grabbed his sleeve, though gently. He was shaking finely, and pale as a cod. "You can't drive."

"Okay. Chauffeur me, but if we find him, you stop out of the way and let me do the police bit. Shona, get into the house and lock yourself up in case he comes back here. I'll have one of the girls at the station drive over and pick you up as soon as—"

"Oh, no." Shona stepped between us, her eyes flashing. "This doesn't turn into some kind of boys'-own outing now. Nichol drives like a pussy, and..." She fell silent. She pushed her fringe out of her eyes. "Archie. Did you just stop a bullet for me?"

"Aye. What about it? What else would I do?"

I left them staring at each other. I went and got into the Toyota, started her up and brought her lumbering over the yard to within ten inches of them. When that didn't break their confrontation, I leaned my elbow on the horn. Archie jumped as if he'd been shot again. Shona ducked her head, and they both ran to climb aboard.

Only a trace in the road chippings, a memory of fading engine sound, gave me a direction at the top of the track.

There was no other junction for three miles. Unless Baird had taken the Mondeo off-road across the heather, we'd find him. The moors lay wide and bare. There was no place to hide a car and drag a person off to murder them. We were only a couple of minutes behind. I nodded at each of these assurances from Archie and Shona, who seemed to be taking turns to keep me sane. I valued it, but it made no real difference. My foot was down, my eyes fixed on the next turn, the next crest of the road. I was choiceless as an arrow in flight.

Shona added, "And he's more gob than action, I reckon. He must've pulled his shot to miss me from that distance."

I almost felt sorry for Archie, but he had been distracted by finding a mobile signal, and was now demanding a roadblock— or someone's old caravan, or a pair of tractors, or whatever could be spared—at the Crow Farm turn-off.

"He doesn't know the island, Nic," he said, hanging up. "He'd have headed for Brodick otherwise, tried to hijack a boat. This way he's got nowhere to run. Hoi, easy on the bend! You're gonna flip us."

I only had the truck's solid weight to thank for making the curve. Shona had been right—normally I did drive like a pussy around here, mindful of stray sheep and tourists. I should stop and make her and Archie get out. The only life I was allowed to risk like this was my own. I should hand the wheel over. I was an aching mess of raw loss and need from my guts to my fingertips, but I had to calm the fuck down. I started to brake. Maybe if I didn't tell them why, just veered over and pushed them both out...

No need. I crested the next hilltop, clear air under all tyres, and slewed to a grinding broadside halt. Twenty yards down the road, wheels still spinning, the Mondeo lay on its roof in a ditch.

Chapter Nineteen

Black rage threatened my vision. Shona grabbed my shoulder as if to hold me in one piece, but a moment later I saw Cam. He was blood-streaked and bruised, scrambling away from the overturned car. Baird was heaving himself out of the driver's-side window. Cam gained a rise in the ground. He fell to his knees in the heather. He was clutching Baird's pistol in one hand, and he took a shaky aim. "Stay where you are, you bastard!"

I half fell out of the Toyota. Archie struggled out on his side. "All right, Cameron," he shouted. "That's grand, okay? You did it. But leave it there. I'll deal with him now."

Cam thrust out his free hand towards us. "Stay back." He jerked the gun at Baird, who was on his backside in the road now, dazedly shaking his head. "You were right. I never could kill a man. But I could shoot a cockroach like you, no bother at all."

"Aye, if you...knew where the safety catch was." Baird brushed shards of glass out of his hair. He looked at Cam, and the wreck of the Mondeo, in astonishment. "You mad wee fucker. You took us off the road!"

"Better that than go another inch with you. How do I work this gun?"

Baird broke into raucous laughter. Ignoring him, I slipped past Shona's restraining hand and splashed through the ditch towards Cam. "Can't expect him to answer that," I said. "Not while you've got it pointed at him."

"Don't come near me." Cam lurched upright. He almost fell over—desperately steadied himself. "I want to kill him. It isn't bloody fair."

"What isn't, sweetheart?"

"I tried so hard to get out. I learned stuff, tried to get good at things. Every shitty council estate we lived in, I did my night schools, my classes."

"You are good at things."

"But wherever I turned—if I tried to get a decent job, a nine-to-five, there'd always be somebody like him in the way. Gang lords like McGarva, loan sharks threatening to call in their debts. Letting me work for them to pay some of it off, dig myself in deeper. I didn't know how to get past them."

Baird was still laughing. "It's hardly Bren's fault if your sorry face got passed all round Glasgow on wanted posters, is it?"

"No. It was my fault. Nicky, I just couldn't see a way out."

"You should be grateful for the job opportunities." Baird chuckled. "Promotion, too—off the shop floor and into his bed. Not bad for a miserable wee nobody."

I tried to gesture Baird to silence. "Shut up. Are you trying to kill yourself?"

"Well, like I say, I'd be really shit scared if he could get the safety off that gun."

I was close enough to Cam now to touch him. I could see the trembling rigidity of every muscle, the tears beginning to carve white channels through the blood on his face. His thumb was probing blindly near the weapon's catch. He'd find it any second. "Cam, ignore him. Put the gun down and come home with me."

He turned to me in anguish. "That's all I wanted. A home with you. I didn't know until I saw it."

"Well, it's waiting there, just down the road. I'm waiting."

"No. I was spoiled for you before I ever met you." He swung back to face Baird. The gun clicked at last. "Spoiled by men like him."

I hadn't seen Archie make his quiet way uphill to stand

beside us, and I jumped when he spoke. "Och, Cameron." He took hold of Cam's trembling wrist, drew it down. "You're not *spoiled*," he said gently. "And Nicky's no saint, as you'll find out the longer you live with him. Don't you go and dirty your hands now."

He took the gun from Cam, calmly as if it had been a cup of tea. Cam surrendered it—partly in astonishment, I thought, at the kindness in his eyes. Out in the road, Baird immediately showed signs of struggling to his feet. The kindness vanished. "Right, you trigger-happy mainlander thug, you! See if you come round my beat, shooting at my girlfriend." He strode off in Baird's direction, Shona running to meet him from the other side. I wasn't sure which of the two of them was making Baird blanch in fear. "And I *do* know how to work the safety catch on this. Isn't that right, Sho?"

"Aye, that's right. He went on a course, Mr. Baird. In Glasgow. I am no' his girlfriend, though."

Cam laughed. It was brief and soft, a sound I hadn't thought to hear again. He turned to me, his face lit by its old smile, the one that had ended an endless island winter for me. "You came after me."

"Yes. Always. My God, what did you do to the car?"

"Grabbed the wheel."

"You could have died, you nutcase."

"Better that than let him take me away."

There was glass in his hair too. Carefully, shielding his eyes, I brushed it clear. I lifted his chin and tried to see where the blood was coming from. I was being calm and sensible. It wasn't the time to grab him, crush his ribs to dust with the relief of finding him. "You're hurt. Is it just these cuts, or..."

"Nicky." He ran a hand down the side of my face. He pushed back my fringe, stared at me as if seeing me for the first time, or seeing a new world. His eyes were alight with wonder. "Even when you thought I'd murdered Stu Duggan..."

"Hush." I forced down a sob so hard I almost choked on it. "All over now. I love you."

He folded into my arms. I buried my face in his hair, and I listened to the sounds of midsummer on my island. Gorse pods were crackling in the sun. When the wind shifted, I could hear the voice of the sea, woven through always with birdsong and mermaids. Cam's fractured breathing, his soft repeats of my name, the one thread that gave meaning to the rest, turned it all to music. I held him, careful of his ribs but tight, tight, and I closed my eyes.

Other sounds—a weird percussion, felt at first rather than heard, high in the air to the east. Then, more homely, the crunch of big feet through heather, a cautious approach. I didn't want anyone near us, not yet, and I raised my head and glared at Archie over Cam's shoulder. "Give us a few minutes."

"Er... Yeah." He shifted awkwardly, adjusting the bundled cloth beneath his jacket sleeve. "Thing is, that's the police chopper on its way out from Ardrossan. They'll be landing in a minute, and..."

Cameron stirred in my arms. I felt the beginning of his attempt to move away from me, and I restrained him, pulling him back close. "Okay. What about it?"

"I've arrested Baird on suspicion of the murder of Stu Duggan. He's handcuffed to the door of your Toyota, the one that isn't rusted through. But I also have to..."

"What?"

Cam took hold of my shoulders and eased me back. "He's trying to say he has to arrest me too."

"He's saying no such thing."

"I didn't kill Duggan, but I stood and watched it happen. Then I didn't tell anybody. I've got to pay."

"You couldn't have done anything. Couldn't have stopped them."

"Still." He didn't let go of me. His grip became bruising, and he leaned his brow against mine, closing his eyes. "It makes me an accessory. Doesn't it, Archie?"

"That's for the courts to decide. All I know is...I'm so bloody sorry."

He released my arms. I tried to grab him back then to interpose myself between him and Archie. "Don't you dare. Not either of you. Christ, I just got you back!"

"Nicky, love. You'd make Satan feel better about himself. But this has been burning into me all the time, eating me alive. I *want* to pay."

Chapter Twenty

The last day of July, and all the doors and windows were open to the vast late-evening heat. It lay lazy in the corridors of Seacliff Farm, penetrating to the coldest and most ancient of its bones. I sat on the bed in my ma's room, watching the white curtains drift. I'd opened it up just half an hour before. She didn't sing or show herself to me anymore, so it was up to me to trust the impulses that came from the essence of her living inside me, in my heart and the spirals of my DNA. I'd expected cobwebs, the inevitable smell of disuse. I'd expected a locked door. Harry had sealed the place up like a tomb, or he'd told me he had, but the lustrous bronze handle had turned as soon as I touched it, as if someone inside had been waiting.

The room was fresh, cool as water. The surfaces of her walnut dressing table and desk gave back the light just as they always had. She'd tolerated every kind of dirt in the farmhouse below, but this had been her sanctuary. There in their niches or on shelves at the cardinal points of the room were her creatures, little things she'd let me play with when I was a kid but took gently back from me and replaced afterwards, time-blackened carvings in oak. Clockwise from the north—a bull, a small stout man with wings she'd told me was an angel but looked way too happy and mischievous for that, a lion, a coiled dragon she'd called Griffin. I was grown up now so I hadn't touched them. I'd sat on the bed, looked out through the window I hadn't opened, and watched the curtains drift. Maybe Harry had come in here and tidied up until he died. It didn't seem the kind of thing he would do.

As if the thought had been enough to summon him, I

smelled bitter smoke. I sighed, closing my eyes. It wasn't Reynolds, not his favourite, the one Cam had kept him supplied with once he knew the old sod's preference. It was his rancid Black Ox. The kitchen still stank of it at a certain hour each night. For every ten times I switched the immersion heater on, five times I'd come back and find it switched off. The radio and the kettle too. I heard stamping footsteps upstairs. Doors banged when there was no one but me in the house.

It was becoming a nuisance, quite apart from the whole effect of making me think I was insane. I sat up straight on the bed. I didn't open my eyes. "Harry," I said. "Harry Nichol Seacliff."

The silence in the corridor became attentive. I took a deep breath and let it go. "Right. Listen to me. I loved you with my whole heart, old man, and it's your own fault I couldn't tell you that while you were still alive. I love your farm too, and when I have a son—or a daughter—I'll pass it on to them, with your name and all Caitlin's stories. I want to stay. But if you haunt this place, I'll pack my bags and go, and I'll leave it to you and the wind."

I sat still for a long time. Then, when the strange heavy quiet had dispersed, and summer air and jackdaws' roosting calls were filling the room once more, I got up, still with the prickling sense that I was being watched. I looked once more round Caitlin's room, then I gently closed the door.

Harry wasn't in the corridor, but there were his dogs, sitting in a triangle without a centre point. I'd done my best to care for them, but they were thin and lonely. Vixen, as was customary, curled her lip at me and snarled. There was no point in talking to them.

Well, not in English, anyway. "*Coin mhath,*" I said. "*Ag éisteachd.*" *Good dogs. Listen to me.* "Your master's gone, and I'm sorry. But you know what time of year it is. I've got shearing coming up, and then the beasts to put in folds as nights draw longer. I need dogs, good dogs that can herd sheep for me."

I shut up. *The beasts to put in folds as nights draw longer?*

Clearly the last two centuries had never happened for the Gaelic-speaking parts of my brain. Anyway, the dogs were gazing up at me in total incomprehension. *"Tha mi duilich. Na biodh cùram ort." Sorry. Never mind. It doesn't matter.*

I set off down the stairs. When I heard the padding feet behind me, I knew a moment's atavistic fear. Then Floss shoved her wet nose into my palm, and Gyp jostled his way to my side. Vixen, who would always be the tougher nut to crack, took a wild leap over him and shot ahead, but stopped and sat down waiting by the door.

I ruffled her ears as I went past. The yard was hot and very quiet. It had been such a long afternoon, and I'd waited as patiently as I could. I'd walked by Cam's side every step of the long, long month just gone, but there were places I couldn't go, and one of those was the arena where he stood and faced himself. A price had been asked of him, but it hadn't been the one he'd expected. I'd often wondered if a medieval flogging or the sacrifice of a limb would have better scoured out the guilt from his heart. As it was, he'd been given bail and a suspended twelve-month sentence on condition that he testified against Bren McGarva, Baird and the rest of his gang.

Even desperate to set things right and do justice by Stu Duggan, a grass-up on that scale had run against Cam's good west-Glasgow grain. He'd told me last night—the night before the trial, in our grim Travelodge room near the district courthouse—that he'd rather have done the time, if he could have borne to be parted from me. But he'd stood in the witness box for just over an hour this morning and told the truth—so help him God, though he'd looked at me the whole time, not at the Bible on the stand, and not at Bren McGarva, whose stony-faced leer had never altered from the start to the finish of his ordeal. After that—it had seemed so strange, the drop into the ordinary, like common daylight after the opera—I'd been allowed to hail us a taxi, take him with me back to the hotel, pack our bags and catch the ferry home.

The crossing had been smooth, but neither of us had felt

like tackling the overpriced sandwiches. We'd sat in what Calmac called the viewing lounge, which suggested 1920s grandeur and consisted, rather worryingly on a huge, tourist-packed ship, of cracked benches and broken curtain rails, and when at last I'd picked up the Toyota and driven us back to Seacliff, he'd asked for the first time to be alone.

I stood in the yard, watching the swallows weave quick shadows over the cobbles and walls. I'd known he was okay because the rhythmic song of hammer to metal had rung out from time to time through the afternoon heat, and I'd stayed within earshot. But the last two hours had been silent, and waiting had been hard.

I'd been watching the workshop door, so I jumped when the gate creaked and he emerged from the paddock behind the barn. He looked exhausted but gave me such a sweet smile that my heart contracted and bumped out of beat. The collies glanced at me expectantly. Well, it was worth a try, and Cam looked as if he needed bringing home. I tried a particular whistle. "Go on, *coin mhath*. Fetch Cameron."

They were superb herding dogs. Not even the leeriest sheep could have minded their light, quick arrival, their subtle placing of themselves, one to the side, one behind, one leading more by suggestion than force. Cam was laughing by the time they'd delivered him up to me, a rich, resentful, despite-himself sound I hadn't thought to hear again. "Nichol Seacliff, don't you ever dare get your dogs to round me up again." He glanced at them. Floss and Gyp, job done, had sat down with dignity, but Vixen was dancing for attention, tail waving. Cautiously Cam scratched her skull. "Hello, then, bonny girl. What have you done to them anyway?"

"We had a talk. Are you okay?"

"Yes. I've been working. I had to finish welding outside—it wasn't going to fit through the workshop door in one piece."

"Can I see?"

"Yeah, sure. Come on."

I followed him back through the gate. On the way, I tried

another experimental whistle, and the dogs to my astonishment turned as one and trotted off towards their barn. I'd take them out a good feed later and try them with penning the animals we had in the south pasture for tomorrow's shearing round. I couldn't imagine the magic would last, but...

I stopped dead, catching my breath. Between the barn and the drystone wall, in a sheltered spot where he had liked to stop and contemplate his kingdom between tasks, there was Harry. If I moved, changed my angle, he would be gone. No ghost this time—only shapes in metal, six or seven of them, angled indescribably to catch his shape and form. Around him, helixing upward in bright reflective strips of aluminium we'd scavenged from the Brodick dump, were his dogs. You would only see it if you came in through this gate, and only the family ever used it. You would have to be a Seacliff.

My throat was knotted painfully. I put out a hand and sought Cam's. He caught it and came to stand by me, wrapping an arm round my waist. "Can you see?"

"Yes. God, yes. How the hell did you do that?"

"I started it before he died. Then I didn't dare finish it. I didn't know what he'd think."

"He'd have bloody loved it. He..." I paused, imagining his reactions, and I started to laugh. "He'd have been unbearable. In the pub with his mates—*yon lad made a statue of me. Beat that if you can, with your portrait-painting grandson, Angus Brodie.*"

It took Cam a good few seconds to find a smile, and it was full of sorrow when it came. I wasn't much better off. My eyes were stinging, vision blurring. I took him in my arms when he turned to me, and we clung together.

"I wish he'd seen it, then."

"Oh, you know this place. Probably he can."

"Nicky, I feel like I didn't pay for anything. It was hell—in the courtroom there, saying all that. But I didn't pay anything, not really. I didn't make anything right."

I stroked his hair—beautiful crow's-feather Celtic hair now, since his pretrial visit to the Lamlash barber's, where the last of his disguises had been swept up and cast to the wind. "I don't think it works like that," I said roughly. "Paying, I mean. How can we? You took McGarva and Baird off the streets for the next old man. Maybe that's as good as it gets."

"Shit. I wish it had been better."

"Maybe it will be. We just live our lives, good ones. Pay that way."

He leaned into me and sobbed. "Nic, I love you. You saved my fucking soul."

He was hot and vibrant in my arms. He smelled of his afternoon's work. This time when grief burned up into passion there was, thank God, no one and nothing to hinder it, no fear to make us run for cover and closed doors. Arms tight round one another's waists, we stumbled as far as the sunny gap between the barns where we'd set out the first bales to dry. I went down hard, dragging him on top of me. He ripped into my shirt, and I groaned in pleasure as the sunlight hit my skin. We lived half the year in winter darkness here but, God, when summer came, for its brief spell of days, it was perfect.

I got hold of his T-shirt, and together we wrestled him out of that, held ourselves apart for long enough to deal with zips and buttons. That would have to do. He sucked at my left nipple till the right one was hard as a pebble for want of attention, then shifted over, making me arch my back and shout. He thudded down beside me on the hay and I fastened a good solid grip on his arse. "Come on, sweetheart. Give it here."

His breath exploded against my neck. "Oh, God. This is going to be...unceremonious."

"Yeah. And short." I dragged him hard against me, and he thrust harder still, ramming his rigid shaft against mine. I cried out again at the relief of it, the hot sacred comfort. We'd shared a bed each night of this endless month and barely touched—not like this, though we'd slept with limbs entwined, shipwrecked sailors clinging to one spar. He grabbed my backside with a strength now more than equal to my own. He sought my mouth.

The press of his tongue, deeper with each struggling thrust of our hips, tore a howl out of me that spent itself in soundless vibration halfway down his throat, and I came, whole body convulsing in the savage joy of release. I held tight to our kiss, our cock-to-cock clench. He was there too. He shot against my belly, long spasms racking him, chasing themselves in a tangle with mine to stillness and shuddering conclusion.

He was exhausted. He could barely lift his head—I wedged my shoulder beneath it and caught his fall. "All right. I've got you." His hand drifted up to my face, caressing. I grasped it, turned to kiss the palm. Already he was casting off from shore, one corner of his mouth curling up in a shattered half-smile. His fingers laced into mine, and their grip stayed tight even when the rest of him was warm limp deadweight in my arms.

I woke suddenly, heart jolting. Over the last month I'd learned to sleep lightly. Cam had put most of his enemies out of the frame with his own actions, but Bren McGarva's grasp had been large, and I wouldn't normally have let myself pass out so completely in the open air.

Still, Glaswegian hit men didn't tend to announce themselves with cheerful beeps of their car horn. Cam planted a hand on my chest and pushed himself halfway upright. "Is that someone up by the gate?"

I yawned. Initial fears dismissed, I wanted to drop back into postcoital languor. "I dunno. Ignore them. They'll go away."

"Oh, that's just what they're not allowed to do." He made a grab for his T-shirt, gave me a brisk pat on the belly. "Come on, gorgeous. It might be custom."

I followed him up the track, picking hayseeds out of my hair. Cam and I had taken to putting the odd piece of his work by the roadside, as Harry had suggested, and it hadn't turned out at all to be a bad idea, although after one near miss we'd had to move them back from the curve and into the gateway. I should have predicted that the jump-out effect of the sculptures' imagery would be more startling still from a moving car. Now we displayed them at the beginning of a long straight stretch of road, so as to keep potential buyers well clear of oncoming traffic.

The beeping came again, more impatient than cheerful now. I tucked in my shirt and tried to look businesslike. I was acting as Cam's informal agent in these sales, mostly because his astonishment whenever one happened made his customers doubt their own taste. A sporty BMW was purring in the gateway now, its owner watching us over the top of her sunglasses. An enterprising luxury car rental firm had opened up in Brodick, allowing visitors to tool around in vintage Porsches and suchlike for the day if they wished, but this lady looked like the car was hers.

"Finally," she called out as we jogged up to the gate, and I was relieved to hear an accent less imposing than her haircut and vehicle. Birmingham, maybe, and not unfriendly. "Don't you two like the thought of making sales?"

Cam reddened and started to apologise. I laid a hand on the small of his back, which was our signal for him to shut up. "No, we like it a lot," I said, returning her smile. "We were just busy. Can we help you?"

"You can tell me if I saw a full-blown naked mermaid leap out at me from that tower of abstract bits of scrap. Not that it's not a nice thing in its own right," she added to Cam, as if concerned for his feelings. They always knew which of us was the artist. "But there's something else to it, isn't there?"

"Well—aye, there is."

I stepped back. Once he got talking about the work, he was generally fine. I leaned against the gate while he politely asked the lady out of her car and walked with her back and forth along a few yards of the roadside. We got some good reactions. She was trying hard to look less impressed than she was, but the wobble of her high heels at the crucial viewing angles gave her away.

"Very fine," she said eventually. "Intriguing. What's your

best price?"

Cam cast a pleading glance at me. I'd tried to get him to cost out his labour hours, to value his products as more than the sum of their parts, but when it came to his own work, my hard-nosed underworld money man was hopeless.

"We could do three hundred," I said boldly.

Cam's mouth dropped open, and I tried to indicate to him subtly that he should shut it again. We'd sold a couple of pieces for over a hundred pounds now, and this one was much larger—his best yet, apart from his incredible memorial to Harry. I didn't think it was such a wild reach.

Maybe I'd been wrong. Our visitor had planted her hands on her hips and was gazing at me in disapproval. I didn't want to lose Cam the sale. "Or," I began philosophically, "if you were thinking of paying in cash, I'm sure—"

She flicked out an index finger at me. It was very businesslike. Down in the Midlands she probably had staff who fell silent at that gesture just as promptly as I had done. "Don't you dare offer me a discount."

"Er... Don't you want one?"

"Here's the first thing nobody tells young entrepreneurs setting up on their own, especially creatives. Punters value your work according to the price you put on it, not their own artistic insights, because nine out of ten of 'em don't have any. The tenth, like myself, won't mind stumping up the cash."

I tried to work this out. "Then..."

"Yes, I'll give you your three hundred pounds for this piece, Mr..."

"Seacliff. Nichol Seacliff."

"And the sculptor?"

"Cameron Seacliff." I'd thought Cameron Vaughn had a great ring for an artist, but his eyes had filled with such pain when I suggested it that I'd thrust the subject aside, kissing my apologies onto his eyelids and mouth.

She shot a glance between the two of us. "Hm. You don't

look like brothers. I'm assuming you're acting as this young man's agent, Nichol, or his manager. If I catch you underselling his talent and potential again, I'll tell my spotter not to bother with the photo shoot or the article in my gallery's next magazine. As for paying cash—my God, do you think your customers are drug dealers? Get yourself a credit-card facility sorted out. And a website. PayPal." She reached into the glove box and pulled out an expensive-looking wallet. "Right. My assistant will be by tomorrow to collect, so have it wrapped up and ready. And make some arrangements for delivery, shipping. You can't expect people to cart off things like this in the backseat of their cars."

Cam and I watched the BMW roar away. When she had vanished into summer dust, we turned back to the gate and started off together for the house. I bumped my shoulder gently against his. "Sorry I undersold your talent and potential, love."

"Don't worry about it." He pulled the wad of crisp twenties from his pocket and looked at it wonderingly. "She was nice for a drug dealer, wasn't she? Right—here's the tax, the bill contribution and a wee bit for the savings jar. Remember to put it all down in the accounts, and I'll prepare an invoice for the assistant."

"Thanks," I said. I was intrigued. This was the first time he hadn't handed me the whole amount. I liked the idea of him out on a spree, not that Brodick high street offered much scope. "Going to treat yourself, then?"

"In a way. I've never seen the Southern Pyrenees. Or the Northern ones, if I'm honest with you. The medieval tower has a balcony, so I'll sit up there and flirt with the Basque gardener while you're off discovering his linguistic roots."

"Did I let you sleep in the sun for too long, you poor...?" I stopped dead in the middle of the lane, remembering a rainy evening in March when I had been asked what I wanted. "What have you done?"

He put his hands on my shoulders. "Now, Nic, don't make a fuss. Archie said you would. It's only a fortnight, okay? I reserved it a long time ago, back when you started paying me, and this..." He released me long enough to pat one pocket. "This'll take care of the balance."

"But you can't—"

"I can. I checked with the courts. I can travel abroad, as long as it's within the EU. In a way, I know I should live on bread and water in the barn for twelve months, but this is for you, so it doesn't feel so bad."

"I don't mean that." My heart was racing. In a moment I would have to find the words to turn him down, but for now I was just swept away by the gesture. No one had tried anything like it for me in my life. He wanted to take me on holiday. "I can't let you spend that much money on me. And I can't leave the farm. And...what has Archie got to do with this?"

"I had to tell him so I could arrange with him and Shona to look after the place."

"You and Archie have been...chatting?"

"Yeah, a few times. He's no' such a pain in the rear now he's not a copper anymore."

I stared at him. It was true that Archie now had time on his hands. Promoted to sergeant as he had wished, even commended for bravery, he had quietly resigned, as if all this time he had been trying to prove a point to himself. When asked, he said he hadn't counted on being shot at in between rescuing golf carts, but I wasn't so sure.

"That's good," I said unsteadily. "I want you to be friends. Er... Do you get the impression I get there, with...?"

"With him and Shona? That he's pretty much moved in? Yeah, I do."

"I mean, she's still saying she's not his girlfriend."

"He says he's not her latest farmhand. But whatever. He bet me fifty quid I wouldn't get you to go. That should cover the airport taxes."

"Cam..." I wasn't even sure which part I was protesting now. "No."

"Why not? I've won my bet, haven't I?"

I stared at him. A wave of surrender was breaking in me. It wasn't just the holiday, though suddenly I could see the tower, the melting heat, the handsome Basque gardener turning away in disappointment as I came home early with my notes and my recordings. It was him—Cameron, the whole unforeseeable fact of him. Brave, fierce, faulty, every day setting out to further my interests, to put me first. Shocked into what might be a lifetime of nightmares by watching a man die, but ready to kill for me. Loving me.

I took his face between my hands. "Yes," I whispered. "Yes, you won your bet, you beautiful violet-eyed bloody demon, you. And when we come back..." I kissed him then turned him gently round so we could look down over the gorse-patched moorland, across the cliffs and out to the indigo sea. "When winter comes, and all this is wiped out in sideways rain the way it was when you first got here..."

"We'll run it. We'll get through it."

"I don't know if it's a forever deal, a sheep farm in the middle of nowhere. But I want to try, for Harry's sake. And I love it all when you're here. It's like you made it new for me. You—you *are* my forever deal." There it was again, that dangerous, beautiful word. In Gaelic, wilder and lovelier still. "*A-chaoidh.*"

"Yes, forever, Nic. *A-chaoidh.*"

About the Author

Harper Fox is the author of six critically acclaimed M/M novels, including Samhain's *Driftwood* and *The Salisbury Key*, and the bestselling *Nine Lights Over Edinburgh* and *Last Line*. Her novels and novellas are powerfully sensual, with a dynamic of strongly developed characters finding love and a forever future—after the appropriate degree of turmoil. She loves to try and show the romance implicit in everyday life, but she writes a sharp action scene too.

To find out more about Harper and see updates on her current writing projects, please visit www.harperfox.net.

Can love repair a shattered life in time to save the world?

The Salisbury Key
© 2011 Harper Fox

Daniel Logan is on a lonely quest to find out what drove his lover, a wealthy, respected archaeologist, to take his own life. The answer—the elusive "key" for which Jason was desperately searching—lies somewhere on a dangerous and deadly section of Salisbury Plain.

The only way to gain access, though, is to allow an army explosives expert to help him navigate the bomb-riddled military zone. A man he met once more than three years ago, who is even more serious and enigmatic than before.

Lieutenant Rayne has better things to do than risk his life protecting a scientist on an apparent suicide mission. Like get back to Iraq and prove he will never again miss another roadside bomb. Yet as he helps Dan uncover the truth, an attraction neither man is in the mood for springs up against their will. And stirs up the nervous attention of powerfully placed people—military and academic alike.

First in conflict, then in passion, Rayne and Dan are drawn together in a relationship as rocky and complicated as the ancient land they search. Where every step leads them closer to a terrible legacy written in death...

Warning: Contains bombs, archaeology and explicit M/M sex, not necessarily in that order.

Available now in ebook and print from Samhain Publishing.

www.samhainpublishing.com

Green for the planet.
Great for your wallet.

It's all about the story...

Romance

HORROR

www.samhainpublishing.com